REVENGE GROWS HARSH

Scree charged from the tavern, but Beauty was already there. He grabbed the Griffin's extended wings from behind, at the base, and twisting down with all his force, broke the animal's shoulders. Scree hissed loudly in pain and surprise.

Josh and Beauty immediately dragged the crippled beast around the corner and into a lightless alley. Beauty held it down, squirming. When the Griffin got its first good look at Joshua, it spat. " 'Uman stink," it cawed.

"Keep talking," whispered Josh, coming close, his knife out. "The right words may ease your suffering." He stared at the gnashing creature through the memory of his family's gored remains. He raised his blade and tickled the Griffin's throat. "Keep talking," he repeated solemnly.

Also by James Kahn
Published by Ballantine Books:

TIME'S DARK LAUGHTER

World Enough, and Time

JAMES KAHN

A Del Rey Book

BALLANTINE BOOKS • NEW YORK

A Del Rey Book
Published by Ballantine Books

Library of Congress Catalog Card Number: 80-66559

ISBN 0-345-32700-4

Manufactured in the United States of America

First Edition: November 1980
Second Printing: November 1985

Cover art by Heather Taylor

Illustrations by Jill Alden Littlewood

Contents

Maps   vi, vii, viii

Prologue   1

Chapter 1, In Which The Story Begins   5

Chapter 2, In Which It Is Seen That Time Is A River Which May Briefly Stop, Yet Then Moves On   19

Chapter 3, In Which It Is Seen That Life Is A River Of Pain   31

Chapter 4, In Which The Company Doubles And Finds A Mascot   50

Chapter 5, In Which The Travelers Learn Of A New Animal In The South   65

Chapter 6, In Which The Hunt Heats Up   78

Chapter 7, On The Origin Of Species   100

Chapter 8, In Which The Company Falls Prey   116

Chapter 9, The Trial   134

Chapter 10, The Terrarium   161

Chapter 11, In Which The Travelers Lose Some Time   179

Chapter 12, On The Waterfront   200

Chapter 13, In Which The Travelers Reach The City Of Light   234

Chapter 14, The City With No Name   257

Chapter 15, In Which The Hunt For The Lost Children Concludes   281

Chapter 16, The New Animal   311

Epilogue   334

SOUTHERN CALIFORNIA

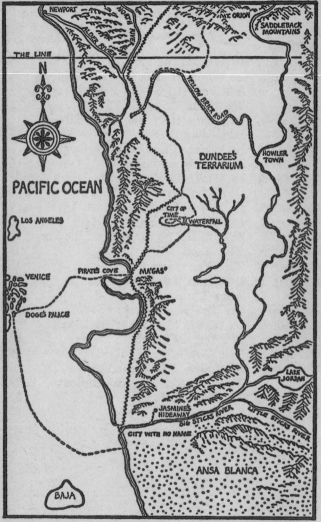

NORTHERN CALIFORNIA

CAPTIVES' ROUTE   SEARCH PARTY

THE CITY WITH NO NAME

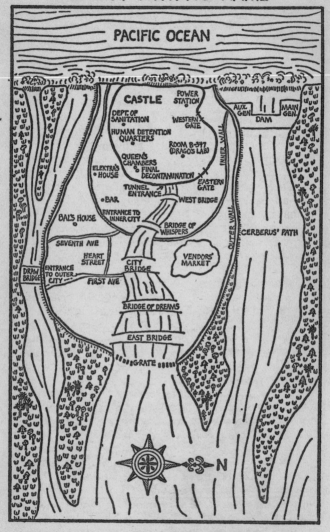

Prologue

A pure, low, demented cry tore the fabric of the night. It was a blind, inhuman sound, terrible and brief.

The six people in the large log cabin looked up simultaneously; at each other, at the window, at the door. Their pulses jumped, pupils dilated, hairs stood erect—all suddenly adrenaline-heavy, atavistic.

"What in God's name was that?" said Mother.

Father stood up and checked the latch on the front door, made sure it was secure. "Wolf, most likely," he muttered. He peered out the window into the night. "Don't see nothin'."

"I'm afraid, Mommy." The little boy looked up from the floor where he'd been playing. A menagerie of tiny carved wooden animals surrounded him.

His mother looked relieved to have her own thoughts pulled back to their quotidian domain. "Now there's nothing to be afraid of, Ollie. Just an old coyote." Then, with a hint of loving sternness: "Now put away your toys and get ready for bed."

This seemed to break the tension that had formed, like thin ice, over the room. Ollie gathered up his little wood carvings and went into the other room to get undressed. Father walked from the window over to the fireplace full of glowing coals and peat. He warmed his hands, then unhooked the kettle that was hanging there and poured himself a cup of hot water. "Anybody want some tea?" he asked.

Mother shook her head No. Dicey didn't answer. Dicey was fifteen years old, a child bride. Joshua, her love, had been gone hunting for two days now. It might have been two centuries. Every noise, every change of wind, signaled his danger in her heart. This animal sound riveted her face to the door, and masked all other sounds, including the sound of conversation.

Old Uncle Jack, Dicey's father, rose slowly from his rocker, walked three steps across the room, picked the heavy rifle out of the corner where it leaned, and examined it. Rusting old single-action; sometimes it fired and sometimes it didn't. He checked the load, fiddled with the action. "Mebbe go wolf-huntin' in the morning," he mumbled. Wolves were familiar dangers, almost old friends. Uncle Jack spit into the fireplace, and the spittle cracked and jumped.

Even Grandma finally lowered her eyes from the window, went back to her needlework. She was a suspicious, unyielding old lady, many hardships old. She lowered her eyes, now, but never her guard. The lines of age that furrowed her face were both price paid and prize won.

"Help your cousin get ready for bed, Dicey." Mother spoke quietly, trying to give the girl something to do besides brood over dark fantasies.

Dicey went into the other room to help Ollie wash up. She found him sitting on the end of the bed, staring out the back window into the impenetrable blackness.

"What do you see?" she asked him.

"Think Josh is okay?" he whispered without looking up.

"Of course he is. Why wouldn't he be?" she snapped. She was angry with the young boy for voicing her own fear. What if the Gods heard?

"He promised he'd read to me when he came home."

Dicey softened. It wasn't Ollie's fault her beloved was late. "I'll read to you," she stroked the back of the youngster's head once. "Get in your jams real fast and come back into the parlor and I'll read to you until bedtime. I'll read *The Magic Pencil*." That was his favorite story. In no time he was scaring up his bedclothes.

So the cabin gradually resumed its rhythm. The reading, the sewing, the tinkering. Dicey murmured softly to her young cousin, who was nodding off to sleep before the dwindling embers. An ancient oil painting of sailors and nets hung over the fireplace. On the mantel was an old family sword, from the War; some clay figurines; a chipped vase full of dried flowers. A bowl of fruit occupied the center of the table. Colorful crocheted rugs patched over the floor; Grandma's quilt lay on a bed. The fading fire, gray smoke drifting up the flue. The harmony. The—

Once more, the unholy moan outside, much closer now. Not like a wolf. Like a nightmare.

They all looked up again, six heads in unison, as if on the same string, a string of fear. This time no one looked away from the door. Jack stood up and started toward the rifle. "Father . . ." began Dicey. And then it happened.

The entire door burst into the room, torn from hinges and lock, and three creatures thundered in without pause, screeching and bellowing. The first was a Griffin—body of a lion, head and wings of a huge eagle. It screamed insanely. It half-flew, half-pounced on Jack immediately—before he could even raise his gun—and gored his belly open with its razor talons, and screamed again in chilling triumph. Griffins hated even the smell of Humans.

On the heels of the Griffin came a creature so deformed and depraved it had never had, nor ever would, a name. Its scaly face had one eye, misplaced, and no nose, and a mouth that could not contain the fat tongue that hung like a piece of meat down the chin, and drained foul-smelling matter. Its sex was out. It hated all living things.

While the Griffin was killing Jack, this other Thing crushed the father's head with a single blow. It was about to abuse the hysterical mother, when suddenly the third creature entered, and snapped his fingers. The Thing turned briefly, snarled, stopped what it was about to do, and merely killed the mother. Then it grabbed up the two children, Dicey and Ollie, in its powerful arms, and carried them off into the night. The Griffin quickly tore out the heart of the old grandmother, shrieked, and flew off.

The third creature stood, still, in the doorway, surveying the carnage. Three dead, one disemboweled and dying, two abducted. He smiled. He was tall; handsome, in a thin, dark way. His hair was black, and evil white fangs protruded down over his lower lip. Two great, spoked, brown-black leathern wings completely enfolded his spindly body. He was a Vampire.

He walked over to the body of the dead woman, knelt, and sank his teeth into her neck. He finished quickly. When he was done, he licked his lips, licked her neck once more, licked his lips one last time, and walked out of the cabin.

When he'd walked five or six feet, and was clear of the portico, he opened his huge webbed wings and flew.

CHAPTER 1

In Which The Story Begins

IT was a clear, bright day. The sky showed brilliant, cloudless blue all the way to the horizon in the west, and though the air was still brisk, intimations of spring were everywhere: a V of migrating ducks appeared overhead, the arrow of their formation pointing, like a collective thought, to their destination; the creek that laced over Cachagua Pass was now a stream; fruit trees were suggesting buds.

At the edge of the orchard, two starlings fought over a seed, then hopped quickly up into a high branch as two people approached. Joshua and Rose walked slowly into the clearing.

Joshua was a good-looking young man of twenty-seven summers. Strong, weathered features were set off by placid, blue-green eyes; a gently curving nose came down to a firm, straight mouth. He had the body of an outdoorsman, all lean and no fat; yet there was something soft about it as well, or tender. His whole manner and being, in fact, suggested opposites, hence complexity, consequently depth. Too, he was a quiet man.

His dark hair hung down to his shoulders in soft curls, though frequently—especially when he hunted —he wore it in a ponytail, tied with a length of thong. His chest was bare, his pants were soft, worn leather. He wore high rawhide mountain boots. On his beautiful embroidered belt hung two knives, throwing knives; and stuck in the top of his left boot was a third, for infighting.

And finally, nested into the top of Joshua's right boot was a quill pen: he was not only a hunter, but a Scribe.

5

Rose, the woman he walked with, was his friend and the wife of his best friend. She carried her simple, southern good looks naturally, without burden or taunt. Her grace seemed to come from the earth; and now that the earth was coming alive, Rose, too, was blooming.

Her long black hair fell to her hips over her lincoln green shift. Tied decoratively into her locks were two beautiful feathers, wing feathers from matched falcons she'd had as a child. She'd set the birds free when she realized it was better to be falcon than falconer; she kept the feathers, still, as reminders of this truth.

Joshua had slept in their barn the previous night, on his way home from a two-day, moderately successful hunting trip.

"I'll leave you the rabbit, I'll take the squirrel," he told her as they stood at the end of the orchard. A squirrel and a rabbit is what constituted good hunting at that time: the woods and fields were played out, overstalked. Most of the game had moved north in recent years, and Josh found himself having to trek farther and farther to find anything at all.

Rose knew it was a hardship to spare the meager game; but they were friends, and gifts could not be easily refused. So in return she offered to read his eyes: she was a seer, and for some a healer as well.

She sat him on a large rock at the end of the grove and had him fix his vision on a point down the hill, had him stare past all the rolling grassland, the twisting brook and bushy briar, to fixate on a craggy stone formation a hundred yards away, to keep his eyes from moving. She stared intensely at his pale-blue left iris.

"When was the last time I read you?" she asked as she studied the pigment in his eye.

"Maybe a year ago," Joshua shrugged.

"That's too long. You've got a lot of changes here; there's a lot that wasn't here last time."

He pursed his lips. A bird of some kind flew past his field of vision, but he forced himself not to look, even though it might have been an omen.

Rose said, "You've lost something lately, something

important. But you'll find it again, there." She brought her face closer to his a moment, then backed off again. "What have you lost?" she asked.

"Nothing I can think of," he tightened his brow.

She ignored his response and continued. "I see a long hunt coming up. . . ." She frowned. "You will almost die, and then . . ." She stared deeply now, past his iris, through his lens, into the dark of his eye. "And then . . . and then . . . you *will* die." Her face knotted; her vision swam in his thick future. "You will die by water," she went on, "you will drown. But then, I cannot see how, but clearly, there—you will live again!" She sat up straight. He looked at her questioningly. She shook her head: "I cannot see deeper."

The leaves whispered secrets in the trees as a cool wind swelled briefly, then dwindled. Joshua didn't disbelieve a word of what Rose told him; he'd never known her to be wrong for him. It was a strange reading, though, strange and upsetting, not like her usual readings, and Joshua couldn't interpret the meanings.

"What should I do?" he asked.

She looked perplexed. "Let me give you some herbs I've got in the cellar. They have healing properties that might be of some use on a long hunt. Take them when you tire."

He nodded acceptance. He admired her knowledge. He himself could read and write, of course, and there were some who regarded that as powerful magic. Black magic, even. But Rose's medicine was pure and good, and as powerful as any Josh had ever known.

The day was beginning to heat up, and a fat blue-bottle fly buzzed over and sat on the nose of Joshua's dead squirrel. He brushed the insect away, then looked at Rose again.

"Take the squirrel, too," he told her. He wanted her to have something more than the one puny rabbit for her little family.

"You needn't, Josh," Rose answered sincerely. "We still got plenty fruit stored."

He shrugged, as if to say it was okay, he wanted to give it to them. She smiled, as if to say okay, they'd be happy to take it. He reached up into a low branch, examined a small, hard bud.

"You anxious to see Dicey again?" she asked him. Dicey was his young lover, his dear cousin, his new bride.

He smiled, knowing Rose had lain alone herself for the past ten nights. "Where is that husband of yours?" he chided her.

She laughed in return. "Should be back anytime now. Seed sellers' convention in Port Fresno was over yesterday morning." She refused to be the subject of the tease, though. "Betcha miss Dicey," she pursued the matter with a sly, yet somehow ingenuous wink.

Joshua nodded drily, admitting he did. "Don't miss her daddy, though, for sure," he went on. "I could see a lot less of old Uncle Jack and might never miss him."

"Tz, tz," scolded Rose, "and you call yourself a family man." She spanked his bottom playfully. He bent his head in mock chastisement.

She walked a few steps into the orchard, picked a small nut off the ground, and tried to crack it on a tree. It wouldn't crack. Josh tried to take it from her, but she hid it behind her back and giggled. He just watched her and shook his head: so often when she wasn't a wise woman, she was a young girl.

They walked along a peaceful, clear path between two straight rows of young pear trees. The sun filtered through the thin leaves and landed in fuzzy patches on the ground, where it mottled last year's dead flowers, broken twigs, cicada shells, and clover. All the world at that moment was serene.

Two wild ponies pranced in the distance, too far away to be heard, just running for fun. They disappeared over the farthest hill, whose loamy slope, on the nether side, met the sea.

"Looks like they're in love," said Rose. Then both were quiet again, as their thoughts drifted contentedly over their own loves—Rose's awaited, Joshua's awaiting.

Rose headed out of the orchard again, drawing her buck knife out of her belt as she walked, to pry open the nut she was still holding.

Joshua followed. The starlings in the upper branches decided they weren't ever going to make it back to the seed they were after, so they flew away. Rose broke open her nut and gave half the meat to Joshua. They chewed meditatively, feeling very close.

"Love," mused Josh, echoing her last word.

"Love's the gravity of the soul," she smiled.

"You mean no matter how high it flies it always comes down?" he teased, intentionally misunderstanding. "Or do you mean it pulls apples from the tree of life and knocks you on the head till you see stars?"

She threw a flower at him in feigned annoyance. "I mean it pulls spirits together."

"Ahh," he bowed. "Like heavenly bodies."

A blush filled her cheek. She had been Joshua's lover before—and even during—the Race War. The time held many warm memories for them both, but by tacit agreement they never discussed it. Not since Rose had married.

She took his hand, now; squeezed it. "You're dear to me, you know. Both of you. I sometimes feel as if we're three circling planets in search of a sun. . . ."

He shook his head, smiling. "You talk like an old book."

"And you like a loose-leaf with pages missing," she laughed, pushing him away. They momentarily held each other with their eyes; then released their hold. In the silence that followed, many things were left unsaid. Josh knew he would love her always—as a sister, a confidante; and as one who shared his closeness to his other best friend, her husband. Rose, in turn, blessed her fortune, to love and be loved by two such as they. The world seemed a glorious place this day.

"I'd better be going soon," Joshua finally spoke, softly, checking the sun. "Mother gets peevish if I'm gone too long."

Suddenly from down the road behind the trees came the sound of hoofbeats. They both heard the gallop at the same time. Rose's face lit up warmly, like summer fire. "That'll be him comin' home now," she grinned with unconcealed relief, and ran off down the path that led to the main road. Josh, too, smiled happily, for he recognized the familiar pace of his old friend's approach. They would share a homecoming toast.

Joshua stepped out of the grove, walked along its neat edge to the road, and watched Rose running down to meet her returning love. "Beauty," she called to him, "Beauty!"

He approached her at a canter, fifty yards from Joshua. By the time they reached each other, she was panting gaily. He stopped, leaned down, and they embraced passionately for a long few seconds. "Beauty," she whispered. He brought his mouth down on hers, and their tongues exchanged a soft, wet caress.

"I've missed you," he told her when she finally let go. She put her hand up and stroked his short, golden beard, his smooth throat; and finally brought her fingers gently down the curly yellow hairs of his broad sun-browned chest. She missed his body next to hers.

"Climb up," he said more loudly, "Josh is standing out there all alone, he looks like a lost puppy."

She giggled, hiked up her dress, jumped up on his back; and he set off for Josh at a gallop. She loved riding him this way, bareback, her arms wrapped around his chest from behind, her fingertips rubbing his wind-hardened nipples, her knees pressed firmly about his flexing foreshoulders, her heels nuzzling his flanks, her face buried in his long, golden mane.

Joshua watched the two ride toward him—Rose straddling his good friend's back—and he raised his hand in greeting, in affection, in admiration: Beauty was, had always been, the most graceful Centaur Joshua knew.

The three reclined on the grass in the smile of the noon sun, sipping apple wine. Rose lay with her head on Beauty's side; his tail flicked away the occasional fly. They were talking and joking.

"I'll bet you've completely forgotten how to shoot," scolded Joshua.

Beauty smiled. "I haven't drawn a bow since . . ."

"Give up this farm," Joshua shook his head, "you weren't meant to be a farmer."

Rose kicked lazily at Joshua. "You leave my Beauty alone, he's a good farmer—"

"And a rich one, now," Beauty laughed. "I sold every seed in Port Fresno."

"—and strong as a Horse," Rose continued her thought, patting Beauty's haunch with just the slightest trace of innuendo. Beauty brushed her face with a snap of his tail.

"Stronger by half than the puny animals you call Horses," he snorted. "It is said that when the noble race of Centauri migrated to this continent from our own, long Before the Ice, the local Centaurs of this land were so shamed by comparison that they all donned dog-masks and were forever after known as Horses."

Josh and Rose laughed. Beauty's pride in his ancestry was well known to them—it was said by many that his great-great-great grandmother had been a leader in the heroic trek over the land bridge which had connected the continents Before the Ice. Sometimes pride in his heritage puffed the Centaur up a bit too much, though, and then he became a target for his friends' gentle jesting.

"The first Centaur. Now I'd always heard," smirked Joshua, "that Horses were here first, that one day a Horse met a strumpet on the road—"

"Enough," said Beauty balefully, "I *know* this joke."

"—and the strumpet said, 'I've a grand treasure between my legs if you've the Horse-sense to find it.'" Josh continued, chuckling. Rose's eyes twinkled.

"Enough, I say," warned Beauty.

"So up her love-nest the Horse thrusts his head and when he's up to the neck, what happens but he gets stuck—"

"Enough!" Beauty boiled. Josh and Rose did nothing to hide their merriment. Above all, Beauty was a proper gentleman.

"Sometimes," he continued, greatly put-upon, "you can be the most tasteless boor. I suppose you're only Human, though, so I must make allowances."

He couldn't long stay angry with those he loved, though, soon relenting to their apologies and prods.

And so, well into the cradle of the afternoon they sat, warmed by the sun and the company.

The yard was perched on the high slope of a gentle hill, and in the intermediate distance they gazed on the gray Pacific. Far, far away, near the almost invisible horizon, a small, triangular white sail could be seen.

"A boat alone," mused Josh. "Pirate?"

Beauty shook his head. "Too close in for a pirate ship. Probably the Port Fresno mail run." He finished his wine.

"What's the word in Port Fresno?" Joshua asked. "Anything about the War? Any new Kings or Popes to worry about?" His tone was light, but he saw a shadow cross Beauty's face.

"Nothing on the War," the Horse-man said, "but there is something." He paused, gave Rose a sideways glance. "Bands of savages, pillaging and killing, all up and down the coast." He paused again. "Vampires have been seen."

Rose made a disgusted, loathing sound in her throat. Joshua tilted his head. "Hard to believe," he said. "Never heard of Vampires coming this far north."

Beauty shrugged. "That was the rumor."

There was a long moment's silence. The sun somehow looked lower in the sky now, the sky itself less joyous.

Josh rose. "Well, I'd best be gone, the day's not waiting." The thought of Vampires north of the Line was a chilling one; bleak news for the Human race. Was there no end to troubles on this earth? Josh wondered.

Rose stood and kissed him on the cheek, and then Beauty stood, too. Beauty said, "I will go with you."

"That better be a joke." Rose warned.

Beauty raised his hands in apology. "I have to go give Moor his seed money. I should have dropped it off on the way in, but I could not stand the thought of keeping you waiting," he placated.

She looked skeptical.

"It is a two-hour trot," he protested, "I will be back

before the day is cool." And then, as her frown softened to a pout, he continued, "Cool enough to warm you up, woman." He bent down, kissed her quickly, and grabbed a handful of her bottom. He was rarely so demonstrative in public; but then, Joshua was hardly public.

Rose pulled her fingernails lightly down Beauty's chest, down his belly, and then scratched the sensitive area where man-belly became steed-chest. His shoulders tensed. "You beast," she growled, and bit his lip. He flared his nostrils, reared up on his hind legs and pawed the air.

"Begone and hurry back," she shouted, and slapped his rump. He took off down the road. Joshua jumped up on his back at a dead run, and the two disappeared over the hill as Rose watched, shaking her head, smiling.

Joshua's cabin was less than half the distance to Moor's farm from Beauty's, but a little out of the way. It wasn't until they'd traveled almost an hour that Beauty slowed to an easy clip, and then stopped altogether.

"What is it?" asked Joshua. He jumped down to the ground and stretched his legs. He knew the Centaur well enough to know when something was on his mind.

Beauty pawed the earth. "There was something else in Port Fresno," he said. "I did not want to upset Rose too much." He knew he would never understand Humans completely; but of one thing he was certain: they could assimilate only small amounts of information at one time, they could not intuit the large sweeps of meaning that constituted the real world; they had no sense of the essence of wholes, though their understanding of parts was admittedly great. So Beauty was never quite sure what had to be spoken, and what was implicit even to the Human mind.

Joshua's eyes narrowed. "What?"

Beauty threw his head back and forth, waving his mane. "It is only Humans who are being attacked."

Joshua met the Horse-man's eyes with his own. "Race War again?"

Beauty looked puzzled. "Could be. They are kidnaping young ones, though. Pirates, maybe. Slave trade."

They were both silent, digesting the information, thinking of all the hard times they'd seen and were yet to see. "Anyway," Beauty went on, "after this errand, I am restringing my bow and staying close to home." Then he nodded at the forest ahead of them. "These woods are dark, Joshua. Keep your people in the house after sunfall."

Joshua looked down at the ground and nodded. Beauty backed off a few steps and raised his right arm. "Until soon, friend."

"Until soon," returned Josh. Beauty turned and ran off in the direction of Moor's farm, while Joshua headed into the wood.

Josh knew something was amiss as soon as he neared the cabin; not a sound, not a movement. No Ollie playing, no Mother singing. He dropped to one knee and listened. Only a mockingbird, mocking.

Joshua put down the last squirrel he'd been carrying and slipped a knife out of his belt. He waited. Still nothing. He ran silently through the trees around to the front of the house, to try to get a look in through the west windows.

What he saw was that there was no door. And when he looked past the doorway into the main room, his insides twisted tight.

He ran into the house, knife in hand, and looked around desperately. Dead, all dead. He sucked in his breath audibly, trying to take in the scene. Mother, Father, Grandma, Jack. All horribly mutilated, irrevocably dead. He knelt by his mother's side, his eyes filled with tears. He held her hand. Cold, stiff.

There was a noise in the corner, and Joshua swiveled with knife out, all his fury and grief concentrated instantaneously in the steel blade. But it was Jack moving, not quite lifeless yet. Josh ran over to the old man and held his head up.

"Uncle Jack, what happened?" He wanted to say

more, but his voice wouldn't work, his throat was constricted, and dry as his eyes were wet.

Jack looked up at him. "Joshua, is it you, boy? I'm dyin' boy. Glory help me."

Joshua shook him gently. "Jack, who did this?"

Jack focused a little. "Two monsters and a bloodsucker, boy. I tried, I tried . . ."

"What about Dicey and Ollie?" whimpered Josh. "What about Dicey?" he begged.

"Carried 'em off," whispered the old man. "I'm dead, boy."

"What did they look like?" persisted Joshua. His despair was already forging grief into hate.

Jack's voice hardly moved air. Joshua had to lower his ear to the man's mouth. "One was a lion-hawk. One was a bloodsucker. And one foul thing no man should ever give name to and I thank Glory I'm dyin' so I'll never have to remember its face." He closed his eyes, then, and died.

Joshua ran through the cabin, looking for something, anything. He wanted to run, to fight; he felt, for a moment, as if he were going crazy. He picked up a chair and smashed it repeatedly against the floor; he kicked the wall twice, as hard as he could. Then he remembered what he'd said to Rose about not missing Uncle Jack, and he sat down on the rug and cried and cried and cried.

When he finished burying them, he sat down at the table in the main room and stared into the cold fireplace. He felt hollow, but somehow clean; purposeful. His life to this minute was over: his life from now on had commenced.

He pulled the quill from his boot and dipped it in the tin of ink he'd just mixed from ashes, dried blood, and water. On the thin, hand-pressed paper before him, he slowly, methodically wrote:

Here lies the family Green. Old woman Esther, sons Jack and Bob, and Bob's wife Ellen. All were Humans. Murdered viciously and without provocation by a Griffin, a Vampire, and an Accident, as

*sworn by dead Jack. Jack's daughter, Dicey, and
Bob's son, Ollie, abducted by same. Surviving son
Joshua, hunter and Scribe, hereby sets this record
and claims Venge-right, on this 14th day of March,
After the Ice 121.*

*Joshua Green,
Human & Scribe*

He slipped the quill back into his boot. Next, he rolled
the parchment into a tight cylinder and fitted it into a
thin, stainless steel tube, which he sealed at both ends.
He had a whole box of these tubes—Scribe-tubes—
stored under the bed. He took two more empties and
strapped one to each leg. Finally, he wrote an identical statement on a smaller paper, and secreted that
one in his belt.

He went outside again and began digging one last
hole, among the four graves he'd just laid. The day
was dimming, and he was tired. He suddenly felt an
oppressive need for sleep coming over him. Soon he
would rest from his ordeal.

When his hole was two feet deep, he dropped in the
paper-filled tube, and began to cover it over. He had
to stop momentarily, though, as another wave passed
over him, a pressing, physical need for sleep, almost
nauseatingly intense. He closed his eyes. The absence
of visual input relieved his dizziness somewhat; but
almost immediately this sense of sleep-pressure was
replaced by a discrete pinpoint of light, deep inside
his internal field of vision. It seemed far away, this
tiny bright spot, but somehow it seemed to be tugging
at him, exerting some ambiguous, gentle pull, like a
cool draft sucking softly down a well, like static electricity, like the ambivalent gravity of a first kiss, like
long-awaited sleep, like . . .

He opened his eyes. The sun was almost down.
He quickly finished filling in his hole, and then marked
the place with a wood marker bearing the standard
symbol of the Scribe, which he carved into the wood.
Only then did he notice the black smoke rising, ten

miles to the north. He stared at it dumbly for a few moments, then whispered the dreadful realization: "Beauty's farm . . ."

Grimly, he started running.

Joshua was a hunter, and that meant it was not rare for him to run two or three hours without pause; so he reached Beauty's farm easily in less than an hour. He needn't have hurried.

The farmhouse itself was razed, smoldering in its own charcoal now. Beauty stood staring, weeping mutely into the rubble, as if looking for some sign in the smoke. He was at once majestic and beaten.

Josh walked over to the Centaur, his own anger and sorrow fed anew by those of his friend. There was shared grief now, a new bond between them. And shared hatred—strongest bond, perhaps, of all. They were patriots, now, compatriots, in the land of loss.

He told Beauty his story, what he'd found at home. Beauty told Joshua he'd returned to the farm an hour earlier and found—this. Rose was gone; no trace of Human remains in the ashes. The one thing Beauty had found, near the house, was Rose's knife, sticky with blood.

"But it wasn't Human blood—I know that smell well," said the Horse-man. "It was . . . vile blood." He squinted back his tears, his venom.

Joshua nodded. "Jack said one of the creatures was —what sounded to me like—an Accident." They couldn't look at each other.

Beauty held up Rose's bloody knife. "A wounded Accident, now." He threw the knife into the dirt.

Some feet away, beneath a broken board, Josh saw a feather. Feather of falcon. He picked it up, and they both stared at it with burning eyes: it was all that remained of Rose.

"I'll take it for my quill," said Josh. "It will give us power to find her, if I use it to write with." He cut the tip into a quill point with his knife, and stuck the newly fashioned pen into his boot, replacing his old one with it.

Beauty did not believe in the power of Scribery as

did Josh; but he knew that from this time on, whatever resources they could tap, whatever powers they
could individually draw upon, they would need.

They looked at each other a moment, and the moment was theirs. They held hands, on that spot,
through the night.

In the morning Joshua set the record, marked it
with his sign; and the two young hunters made a plan.

CHAPTER 2

In Which It Is Seen That Time Is A River Which May Briefly Stop, Yet Then Moves On

THE hills of Monterey formed a promontory on the tip of a crooked finger of land that pointed southwest into the blue Pacific. The base of the peninsula curved gently back to a coastline that ran east, and then smoothly south all the way to Port Fresno. From Fresno the coast turned east again, and then south once more down to Newport, near what once had been the Mexican border. Of course, since the last war there were no more borders; only frontiers.

Beauty's farm lay in the southern meadows of a depopulated area that extended north to the Ice Country. The Ice Country itself was uninhabitable: a vast, frigid zone, the penumbra of a glacier that sat snugly on the top third of the world like a white electrocution cap. The glacier moved ten miles south every year now, extending the boundaries of the Ice Country with almost imperial resolution. Monterey had grown accustomed to seeing the invader's frosty designs as late as June.

South of Beauty's farm were scattered ranches, settlers, trading posts. Population density increased farther south, until there were actually cities now and then—usually walled, self-sustaining centers where people and other animals gathered for companionship, for commerce, for protection.

Beauty's farm was ideally situated. Cool and sparse enough most months of the year to be uninteresting to adventurers and soldiers; warmed enough by the Pacific currents to make fruit-growing easy. Beauty hadn't ever considered leaving before—once he'd settled down there with Rose—and neither had Joshua.

So it was with considerable regret that they folded

up their lives and slid them like wedding suits, into the bottom drawers of their memory. But they were hunters now, and a successful hunter can afford only one thought: the prey.

They set off in the morning, as first light trembled. Beauty carried only his bow, and a quiver; Joshua had his knives and his falcon-feather pen.

There was no trace of the Vampire or the Griffin, save a green wing feather from the latter—they'd obviously made their escape by air. But the wounded Accident left a fairly easy trail—of blood, smells, footprints, and sign—which Beauty and Josh tracked east from the farm for many miles, into a woodsy marshland.

There the trail turned south.

Tracking became a little more difficult through the marshy scrub, but Josh had a good eye, and Beauty an equine sense of smell. So they kept up a steady pace all morning; silent, side by side, senses alert. When their shadows were short they paused by the rim of a pond, to rest and to eat.

"He is paralleling the coast," said Beauty, flaring his nostrils into the wind. "Still south."

Josh lay on his belly and sipped from the pool. "He's slowing, though."

Beauty nodded, shook his mane back and forth, pawed the ground.

Joshua stood up. "Be still, Beauty. Thoughtful rest is the hunter's friend."

Beauty snorted. "Spoken like a Scribe." He stood at the edge of the cool water and watched his reflection dance in the ripples that still ran from the spot where Joshua's thirsty lips had touched. Beauty scorned the Human religion of Scribery. It elevated unreal, meaningless scratches to something they were not, turned them into powerful tokens. It promoted false patience, false hope, false priority. Beauty shrugged: it was but one more Human enterprise that remained cryptic to him.

Josh put his hand on his friend's back. "We'll find our people."

Beauty turned his head, and his lips thinned in half-smile. "It is good to hunt with you again." He gave all his words equal weight, and his meaning was many-layered, alluding to much that had passed between them. First, it referred to the fact that he was born to the hunt, had always hunted, had missed the hunt these past few years on his farm. It referred also to ten years earlier, when he and Josh had hunted together all the time, when they together supported an extended family of friends and relatives on their game. It referred to the great Race War that had pitted Humans against all the other species, had divided Beauty and Joshua; had even forced them to hunt each other. Until Beauty was wounded by a Human prince, and Joshua hid him in the woods and nursed him back to health, with Rose's help.

When the War ended, national boundaries were gone, and Kings and Popes went on waging their own personal wars here and there for land and power; but Beauty put down his bow and swore to be farmer the rest of his days, and give part of his crop always to what was left of Joshua's family.

So now he meant to tell Josh that it was good to hunt again, good to hunt with *Josh* again, good to hunt *with* Josh again, good to *hunt* with Josh again.

Josh understood and said so with his face.

A nearby orange tree provided the two hunters with a meal of the sugar-heavy fruit.

"Where do you think he'll go to ground?" Joshua mused when lunch was over.

"There is a Forest of Accidents some hundred miles east and south," said Beauty, "but I doubt the thing can last that far. Best just to stalk and corner." He paused. "I only hope we catch it before it dies, so we can question it."

Joshua nodded. "We need more information if we're ever going to trace the others."

"If it is slave trade this concerns. I know two places to nose about. One is a brothel, half a day from here. The Accident may head there, in any event."

Joshua smiled grimly. "I remember. We went there once, fifteen years ago."

"It is not so nice a place now, I am told." They

shared a brief, painful thought: their loved ones, sold in chains, to pirates or worse.

"And the other place?" Josh asked.

"A pirate camp, on the coast south of Newport. I have friends there, as well, who may help."

"Pirates?"

"Now, yes. Once they fought with King Jarl's Elite Guard." Jarl was the Bear-King, and his Elite Guard Service—the JEGS—had won many battles against the Humans in the Race War.

Joshua remembered them well. "But then if this isn't slave trade, if this is war again . . ."

Beauty left the question unanswered. It lay between them for a moment, then blew away like the ashes of yesterday's fire. "We are brothers in deep ways now. They cannot make us hunt each other again."

Joshua felt the truth of this. "Rose read my eyes yesterday," he said.

"What did she see?" Beauty asked quickly. He didn't always believe in Rose's predictions, but they held special import now, if only as tokens of his beloved.

"She told me I lost something." They looked at each other with sad hindsight. "She said there'd be a long hunt, though, and that I'd find it again." He put the force of promise in his voice.

"What else?" Beauty insisted, buoyed by the vision.

Joshua chuckled. "The rest needed translation, and we didn't have time. She said I was going to drown— but that I'd live again."

Beauty laughed too. "Better not tell that to the Pope's men. They would drown you for blasphemy, and if you lived again they would drown you doubly for double blasphemy and insolence."

They both laughed long and heartily, the more so for the relief that they could still laugh at all.

They were about to set off again, when Beauty twitched his ears to the side and said, "What was that?"

"I didn't hear anything," said Josh.

"Shh."

They both listened. The wind, a cricket, the leaves. And then, a subtle sound, almost not a sound at all, barely a disturbance in the air.

They crept silently toward the noise, through tall grass and shallow puddles. It grew indistinctly louder, and seemed to be coming from behind a large rock formation. It made the sound a hand makes passing through spiderwebs.

Beauty stood clear of the rocks and strung an arrow. Josh took out his blade and sidled around through increasingly muddy wash to the far side of the stones. Knife in hand, he crouched a moment behind the largest piece of granite, then leapt over it blindly to the other side.

He was ankle-deep in mud. Before him was a pool, five yards across—a tar pit, covered with a quarter inch of water. And at the edge of the pit, just beginning to sink, was a brightly colored butterfly, its four-foot wings beating wildly to try to pull itself into flight, out of the tar.

Josh smiled sympathetically. He reached out, grabbed the terrified creature by its dark furry body, and lifted it gently out of the mire. It shivered violently.

He carried it back to where Beauty was standing, bow drawn. "Just a Flutterby. Trying to drink the water off a tar pit," Joshua explained. The animal was quivering now, its delicate red-and-gold wings straight up in frightened attention. Josh carried it back to the pond and began to wash the tar off the large insect's belly with sand and lemon juice from a nearby tree's fallen fruits. Beauty put up his bow and walked over.

"Poor thing," the Centaur shook his head. "They are beautiful, but not, I think, the smartest of creatures."

"Lovable, though." Josh finished washing the Flutterby's body clean, then placed it on some dry grass in the sun. "There you go, big girl, you'll dry off soon enough."

It sat there timidly. Its ebony body was glistening wet; its flower-thin wings rose and fell slowly, tentatively, with each respiration. Its heart continued to palpitate so quickly that the sides of its dark slender body seemed almost to vibrate. It looked at Joshua, and its scared, warm face smiled.

"It will be safe here," said Beauty. "It will fly within the hour." He looked at the sun. "We should be gone."

Josh grunted agreement.

They started off, but didn't get fifty paces before Josh stopped. "Wait a minute. Be right back." He ran over to the pond, broke open an orange, and laid several juicy slices on the ground in front of the Flutterby. Shyly, the animal lowered its eyes.

Josh ran back to where Beauty was waiting. "Let's go," he said, and they continued south at a trot.

Not only the contour of the western coastline, but the terrain itself had undergone considerable alteration following the quakes of Fire and Rain, and then once more after the Great Quake, the Change, which seemed to mark the beginning, some six score years earlier, of the steady southward creeping, from the Pole, of the Big Ice.

A temperate band of hills and wood extended from Monterey down to past Port Fresno, but there the land quickly became subtropical. Newport, in fact, was carved out of and surrounded by rain forest, and no one civilized had ever been much south of that since no one knew when.

The marshland over which Josh and Beauty were trekking was itself highly variable in character. Areas of bogs, fens, and marshes were interspersed throughout, sometimes in great density; on the other hand, great spans of grassy plain extended sometimes for miles. It was hilly in places, rocky elsewhere, and there were even scattered acres of trees.

It made tracking difficult. The wounded creature had gone over stony flats that held not a print, through foul mire that absorbed all smell. Josh and Beauty kept on the trail, but they had to slow down. At one point they even missed a turning, and had to backtrack a mile before they picked up the true scent.

The sun was still high when they came to the shore

of the Venus River. The Venus was a long water that ran from inside Mount Venus in the east, all the way to the sea. It was fairly calm where it cut through the marshlands, but a hundred yards wide, and too deep to tell how deep.

They were both good swimmers, but Josh was hesitant, water-shy, remembering Rose's vision. Beauty admonished him, though, and assured him Rose had been speaking in metaphors. They stood at the muddy edge for a few minutes, watching the slow, implacable current move, like time, toward them and then past them. Leaves bobbed on the surface, and rotting logs and dragonfly wings. A flower floated by, and as it came even with them it paused, on an eddy or undercurrent, and for a moment the whole world was still for Joshua. The moment passed.

Josh and Beauty exchanged a glance, jumped in at the same time, and raced to the other side. On the other side, there was no trail.

"Most likely let the current take him downstream," said Joshua. "We'll do best to walk west along the bank, pick him up where he came out."

"So it would want us to think." The Man-stallion tightened his eyes and shook himself dry. "But a strong Accident can swim upstream. And its home-forest is yet east of here."

"The brothel's west," suggested Josh. They both thought in silence for a time, considered alternatives. "We could split up," Josh added. He didn't want to: Beauty was all he had left.

Beauty placed this thought precisely, between his temples, behind his eyes, and examined it from all sides. "No," he said.

Josh quietly approved. Then: "We'll walk east, upstream for a mile or two, and if we don't pick up the trail, we'll turn back and follow the river west. He couldn't have swum upstream more than two miles."

In a measured voice, Beauty replied: "Yes." This was the Human way, to try to cover all the possibilities. Such an approach had its merits, Beauty conceded to himself, when Horse-sense failed.

It was a standing joke between them, Beauty's economy of words. Quiet Josh was positively garrulous next to his equine companion, and frequently teased the Centaur about his dour, parsimonious speech. Beauty, in his turn, would accuse Josh of logorrhea, of being a Scribe just to scribble, of meaningless chatter. And so it went.

Josh looked at his friend now, after the two monosyllabic retorts, and said, "Tell you what, stamp your foot once for Yes, twice for No. Okay?" It was his great joy in life to tease his golden friend.

Beauty looked down his nose distantly at Josh, raised his right front hoof, and tapped the young man backward into the river. Joshua splashed and spluttered momentarily, then pulled himself out.

"Like that?" beamed the Centaur angelically.

With a gleeful whoop, Joshua jumped on top of Beauty's back, leaned his full weight to one side, his hands in the Horse-man's mane, and wrestled the Centaur to the ground. They rolled around the mud, horseplaying for a full minute before Josh looked up to realize they were completely surrounded by a party of hostile creatures

He stood up slowly, hands away from his knives. Beauty jumped up in a single motion, then stood perfectly still, waiting.

There were five of them, all with weapons drawn, forming a semicircle around Josh and Beauty at the riverside. Silent savages.

One was a big fellow, hair covering most of his face. He aimed a crossbow directly at Joshua's middle. Beside him stood a gaunt, toothless woman holding a zip gun—these primitive firearms exploded as often as not, but one never knew. Next to her was a muscular man with no arms and the head of a large black bird, and at his side a gorilla smiled, opening and closing its fists. And finally, the one who seemed to be the leader: a tall naked woman with a saber in her hand and a black cloth hood over her head, her brilliant green eyes staring out through the two holes cut in the cloth. On her right shoulder was branded an upright trident.

For a full minute nobody moved. It was an animal

thing. Each was sniffing the air, reading the wind. Josh felt a droplet of sweat congeal under his arm and creep down his side, precipitating out of the hot afternoon sun, the tension in the air. Finally the woman in the hood spoke, in a low willful monotone.

"Are you believers?" she said.

Josh tightened. The question identified the interlopers as BASS—Born Again 'Seidon Soldiers—and although they looked pretty scruffy, they were known to be among the best infighters. Furthermore, they considered themselves highly moral, and Joshua knew this meant they were labile and dangerous.

"Our journey is a moral one," Josh spoke to the hooded woman.

"We are tied to no King," explained Beauty.

"Nor the Pope," added Josh. BASS were under the command of the Doge of Venice, and though the Doge was aligned with the Pope, there were factional hostilities. The BASS worshiped Poseidon or Neptune, God of the Sea. Their religion prophesied that someday the sea would reclaim the land, and then Neptune would rule the whole watery world.

"Are you believers?" repeated the hood-woman.

"Our mission is Venge-right," tried Josh. "Vampires have killed our people."

"Perhaps they had right," said the hooded woman. The Bird-man made a raucous noise in his throat, like the sound of a ratchet being turned, and then was silent again.

Josh noted Beauty's hind legs flex slightly, ready to spring. "They had no right," growled Beauty. The hairs on his mane stood semierect.

"Nonbelievers lie for their own ends," said the hooded woman. Her eyes were on Beauty; her hand tensed on her saber.

"Our journey is moral," repeated Joshua. He felt the situation was deteriorating quickly; something had to be done. His fight was not with these people. He wanted only to show them that neither was their fight with him. So he decided to gamble. "Our power comes from the water," he intoned.

He saw them all stiffen. Beauty looked at him skeptically, questioningly. Josh knew these people had a complex, mystical, baptismal relationship with the sea, and he suspected they would react strongly to his statement. He was right; the atmosphere was suddenly electric.

"Water is sacred . . ." warned the hooded woman. The Gorilla stopped smiling. The Bird-man opened his beak wide, almost as if he were silently screaming.

"The water gives us our power," Josh pronounced. "I can make fire from water."

The man with the hirsute face violently shook his head back and forth. Beauty looked ready to leap.

Josh walked away from the bank with slow, deliberate movements. He gathered up a handful of dried grass and bark, then brought it back down to the river and set it on the shore. The crossbow and the zip gun followed him like afterthoughts.

He picked a long blade of green grass and tied a little loop in it, too small to let a berry pass through. Then he dipped the entire blade of grass in the river, and when he pulled it out, there was a bead of water jiggling and balanced delicately in the loop. The others watched these mysterious manipulations in fascination.

Holding one end of the blade, he positioned the loop about six inches over his pile of dry grass, the hot postmeridian sun glaring through the refractive bead of water. He moved the liquid lens up and down a few inches until the focal point fell directly into the center of the kindling, and then he simply sat, motionless.

They all watched him. The ritual had obviously impressed them, as did all water-rituals. Beauty held his breath. No one spoke.

In a few minutes smoke began to rise from under the tiny glare of the water-filled, grass-loop. Joshua blew lightly on it. The smoke disappeared, then floated up heavier, and then the grass erupted in soft yellow flame.

The creatures backed off; except for the hooded woman. She stood, unmoving.

"Your power is from the water," she said finally.

She made a sign to the others, and they all ran off into the forest that lined the south side of the river.

Beauty was amazed. "Where did you learn that?" he demanded.

"In a book," shrugged Josh.

"Scribes," Beauty shook his head tolerantly. "You are lucky you were not hanged for a sorcerer."

"Words make the strongest magic sometimes."

"Silence is stronger," said the Centaur.

"I'm talking about written words."

"Then why did you not just scribble something in the sand for the BASS to read? Or show them a book?" Beauty did not share his friend's feelings about the power of the written word.

"I didn't have a book here. Besides, BASS don't trust people who read or write." He spoke with the tolerant condescension of one who knows himself to be right, but appreciates the ignorance of others.

Beauty became suddenly thoughtful. "They are far north for BASS."

"Raiding party, maybe," agreed Joshua.

Just then there was a soft humming noise behind them. They turned quickly. Sitting on the bank was the Flutterby, its red-and-gold wings moving slowly up and down, a hopeful expectant smile on its black little face.

"She followed us!" exclaimed Josh.

"Go back, little one," Beauty spoke calmly to the timid creature. The face remained upturned at Josh.

"You can't come with us," explained Josh. "We're hunters." The frequency of the soft humming rose as the little heart beat faster.

"She cannot keep up," concluded Beauty. "Come."

Josh and Beauty turned and started trotting east upriver, looking for signs of their prey. The Flutterby's face fell, but she lifted herself airward and floated patiently, high above her new friends.

There was no trace of the Accident upstream, so the hunters returned west. They found evidence of the wounded creature's exodus, around sundown, and followed the trail out of the river, into the woods, and finally across clear, open fields.

It was near midnight when they saw the red light in the distance, the creature's foul footprints leading directly toward it. They looked at each other and started walking in the same direction.

It was the old brothel they were approaching, and the creature was there.

CHAPTER 3

In Which It Is Seen That Life
Is A River Of Pain

TORCHES filled the cave with grimy light. Close to ninety Humans cowered at one end, herded into the corner by a dozen Accidents, as the vile creatures exchanged harsh mutterings in their guttural language. At the other end of the cave a flock of Vampires mingled. Many slept among a cluster of empty tumbrils. Some were talking, some seemed to be making plans. Two were feeding off the white dying body of a man named Moor.

The smoke from the torches twisted, like so many wraiths, to the ceiling, where it hid in the recesses, breathlessly still. The Accidents chose a few of their group to stand guard, while the rest went to sleep in whatever stagnant pools they could find. Accidents loved to repose in the thin slime of moldy caverns. It was near midnight.

Though it was near midnight, none of the Humans slept.

"What will they do with us?" Dicey asked Rose for the twentieth time. They huddled near the center of the confined area, surrounded by the terrified faces of their fellow prisoners. "Are we going to die?" she pressed, begging for reassurance.

Rose stroked her young friend tenderly. "They won't kill us, child; don't fret. If they were going to, they'd have done by now." She almost believed this herself. In any event, her words eased Dicey's mind. Each time Rose spoke like this, the young girl's face became visibly soothed. Ollie wasn't so fortunate. He'd remained mute and staring ever since the ordeal at the cabin. He sat in Rose's lap now like a too-real doll.

"If I only had something to write with," Dicey went on whispering, "I know I could get us out of here."

Rose nodded patiently. Though she could read somewhat, she didn't belong to the religion of Scribery, she had no real faith in the magic of writing. Still, she would do nothing now to quell Dicey's hope.

Dicey went on, "If Josh were here he could write some powerful lines. He can turn Word into Sword. He could read them all to sleep and we could walk out of here."

Rose smiled. "I don't think Accidents care much for reading, sweetheart."

Dicey looked thoughtful. "Why are they doing this to us?"

"Hard to know. But Accidents hate Humans, and that's just the truth. Don't know about these Vampires and the others. My mother used to talk about Vampires, back south. Hateful creatures. The Accidents *look* horrible, I know, but I just pity them. The Vampires, though . . ." She spit.

"How come Accidents hate us so much?" Dicey wondered, passing her gaze over the varied countenances of the loathsome beasts.

"Accidents used to be Humans, child. Long time ago, before there were Scribes, when Centaurs lived on their own continent, and Vampires never flew north of the Line. Used to be Human, but they drank a potion they thought would make them Gods, and that's what they turned into. Now they hate the Humans who are left for not taking the potion."

"That's not what it said in the book—"

"Books don't know everything, child—"

"Don't call me child," Dicey pouted. "And books do, too, know everything. And the book I read said there were no such things as Accidents, they were just figments of imagination that we invented to punish ourselves for—"

"Dicey, these Accidents are real. These are not imagined. Their smell alone ought to be enough to gag you." That was the trouble with Scribery, as far as Rose was concerned—much of it was fairy tale, and so did not distinguish between history and metaphor.

The young girl was silent. Two monstrous fiends near the wall squabbled over the remnants of an old man they were eating. Dicey looked like she might become hysterical. Rose turned her around by the shoulders.

"Let me read your eyes," she told the girl, to keep her occupied. She stared intensely into Dicey's left eye. It was dark, opaque. Like an endless night.

"What do you see?" asked Dicey.

"Happiness and long life," lied Rose. She could see nothing.

The moon was a yellow ripe fruit hanging low in the sky, ready to burst. In the near distance the serene Pacific could be heard sighing. The wind slept. Josh and Beauty advanced on the brothel with exaggerated slowness, prolonging the last anticipatory moments to savor that mixture of fear and cunning that is the hunter's lust.

The brothel was a grand old wooden house, three stories high, with gables, extra wings, and garden cottages. A large plate-glass window faced out on the open field that fronted the building, and in the window burned three fat candles in clear red plastic jars. Candles could be seen flickering everywhere in the front room, making wild and changing forms out of the shadowy figures who moved within.

Out back was an enormous barn; and a windmill, which normally generated some electricity for lights, refrigerator, games. But there was no storage battery, so there was only electricity when there was wind, and tonight the wind was resting. A quiet night.

Josh climbed the five rickety stairs to the front door and knocked. Beauty waited behind, at the foot of the steps. The plan was to enter as patrons, do some discreet sniffing around; and take the wounded Accident alive, if possible—it had to lead the hunters to its accomplices, and to the orphan Humans.

There were footfalls inside, and the door was opened. The old madam stood there in an evening gown, all four hundred pounds of her. Her face was painted in primary colors, and she wore a peacock-feather wig. Two big bouncers stood beside her and behind.

The old madam looked at Josh, glanced briefly at Beauty behind him, then fixed her stare on the young Human. "Come on in, Trouble, we been waitin' for ya." Then, again to Josh, without looking at Beauty; "There's stables out back for his kind."

Beauty's nostrils flared, and he skittered back a few steps. Josh turned to him. "Forget it," he said quietly. Then, louder: "The stable might be just the place you want." He looked back and winked broadly at the madam. The madam smiled; she didn't like horses, but she didn't want trouble.

Beauty didn't take insults lightly, but he understood Joshua's double meaning, and knew he was right; the creature was as likely in the stable as anywhere else. Besides, it would give him a chance to look over the grounds. He reared up once and cantered around the side of the house. Josh went in the front door.

It looked even bigger on the inside than it did out front. A great room with a high-beamed ceiling spread off to the right, lit by a crystal chandelier, sparkling with candles. A player piano bobbed on madly in the corner. Off to the left a carpeted stair-

case curled upstairs, and beside it, in a side room with
the door ajar, a group of six noisily played cards.

Joshua entered the main room. The madam said,
"You find somethin' ya like, Trouble, an' we'll discuss it," and then wandered off, leaving Josh on his
own.

The room was filled with buyers and sellers of
every description, trysting quietly in the dark and fluid
candlelight. In one corner a pale, gaunt man spoke
in low tones to a female Vampire; she was naked,
though her brown wings loosely encircled her; and
as the man spoke, he slipped his hand down under
the smooth, thin wing-skin and fondled the slope of
her heavy breast. She threw back her head, let out
a throaty chuckle, and a long white tooth glinted at
the corner of her mouth.

A Satyr lounged on the couch, goat-legs up on a
table, a smile on his face, a young woman in his lap
and another at his side. Their moist eyes were glazed,
and their hands urgent in his fur; it was not immediately apparent whether the Satyr was buying or selling.

Shadows danced in the stairwell.

Near the dark side of the room two Hermaphrodites
explored each other's darker sides.

Something like a Troll exposed his hump to someone
with bulbous lips and a vacant stare; a black Cat
lapped distractedly at the inner thigh of a frail, hair-
less woman wearing a black half-mask; a man whispered something in a woman's ear.

Josh scanned the group, but saw no sign of any
Accidents. Where would it be? He thought of everything he'd ever read about them, but there had never
been mention of Accidents going to brothels. The black
Cat looked up, and her strange eyes met Joshua's for a
long moment; then she jumped down from her couch
and disappeared. As Josh was about to try another
room, a pretty girl walked up to him. She was no more
than four feet tall, wearing a gauzy half-slip and a
thin half-smile that was at once shy and hungry.

"Looking for me?" she said. Her voice tinkled like
fine crystal breaking in a muffled room.

Josh began to shake his head, but stopped and decided to take a chance. "What's your name?" he asked.

"Meli," she smiled. "Will you dance with me?"

He smiled back. "So you're a Dryad," he nodded. Her name was a giveaway. "What's a wood nymph like you doing in a . . ."

Her face lit up like autumn fire. "I *knew* you were a hunter," she exclaimed. "You know the woods, I could feel it." She danced around him once, then pressed her diminutive body up to his. "Take me up to room 17," she whispered gaily.

Madam walked up. "You found somethin' that suits ya, Trouble?"

Josh dug into his belt and extracted one of the five gold pieces cached in the lining. The madam examined the coin in the candlelight, then tasted it. "This'll buy you a *lotta* trouble, boy," she said, laughed uproariously, and swatted him on the bottom. He swatted her bottom right back, and she laughed even louder. Then Josh took Meli's hand, and they went upstairs.

Beauty trotted once around the buildings, but saw nothing of interest. Two small cabins, a watering hole, a medium-sized garden, a few goats and sheep. All very innocent.

He hoped he could catch the Accident alone, without Josh. He could make the beast talk quickly, and he could kill it quickly. Humans hesitated too often in these matters, they had too many motives, too many second thoughts. And Scribes were the worst of the lot.

Beauty was glad to be a Centaur. Centaurs had the gift of balance—physically, spiritually, intellectually. They defined grace on the earth both in demeanor and being: their graceful behavior was well known, and their spirit was forever poised toward the patch of sky in the constellation Equus, where God was known to live. But most important for Beauty—was that Centaurs had a history.

An ancient, royal history. It extended back thousands of years, to the birth of animals, to the earliest days after the continents congealed. A history of heroes, myths, principles, and—naturally—balance. It was a heritage weighted with responsibility. He wore the mantle proudly.

Not like some of the other animals you saw crawling around. Animals you might see once and never see again. One-of-a-kind creatures, without a past or future, the dregs and the flotsam. Like the Accidents.

The thought of the wretched beast brought Beauty's senses back to the moment, to his resolve. He put his nose to the air. The wind was beginning to respire, but not really enough yet to catch the blades of the windmill behind the barn. He walked up to the stables and opened the door.

Inside he was greeted sourly by an old man who took his piece of silver and told the Centaur he could have the use of any stall for an hour. Beauty thanked him curtly and started to look the place over.

It was a big L-shaped structure with rough-hewn cubicles all along the walls. Paper and straw littered the dirt floor, and candles were set out every five feet or so. Three open windows near the ceiling provided the only ventilation, and allowed some thick waxy moonlight to pour in.

Beauty walked a few steps and opened the door to the first stall. A pretty bay mare stood inside, her big brown eyes fearful. Beauty smiled and backed off. In the next stall a heavyset woman lay on her back in the hay, her teeth yellow, her dress open.

Next was an Equiman girl—head and torso of a woman on the upright hind legs and tail of a horse, she was the sterile cross between a Centaur and a Human. Beauty's child with Rose would have looked like this, and Beauty stared into the girl's eyes from the depths of his own lost future. She clopped her hoof in the dirt, and tossed her hair, and half-laughed, half-whinnied, and made a kissing expression with her lips and rubbed her breasts and slapped her Horsebottom. Beauty withdrew.

Centaurs lolled in the next two stalls, aged and mangy, and then there was a roan stallion mounting a gray female Centaur, and then some empty stalls, a young boy, an old woman, a couple of ponies. No trace of the Accident.

He went back into the stall with the young Equiman girl and closed the door.

"Hi-i-i-i," she whinnied, smoothing the hair under his flanks.

He bent down and nuzzled her neck. "I just want some information," he whispered.

Josh closed the door to number 17, walked to the bed and sat down, while Meli danced over the floor like a leaf in a crosswind.

"You always this happy?" Josh asked. He'd never heard of a Dryad living anywhere outside the woods.

She flittered up to him and sat, feather-light, on his knee. "This is *my* room," she confided; then jumped down to the floor and did a pirouette.

"But why aren't you out in the forest with—"

She leapt up, pushed him back flat on the bed, and straddled his chest. "This is my bed," she said quietly. He began to answer, but she placed two fingers on his lips. "My tree," she said. "They cut down my tree to make the bed." Joshua looked at her open face and nodded softly. Every nymph was said to have a tree that was her own, about which she had special feeling, of which she had special knowledge, with which she had special communion. Some said a Dryad withered when her tree died.

He ran his hand along the hard ash bed frame. She got off his chest and lay beside him. "Hunters understand the trees," she said distantly, hugged him, stroked his chest.

"And you understand losing something dear," he responded. He needed to enlist her aid, and saw this immediately as a way of securing her empathy. She brought her head up, nibbled the side of his chest. He felt vaguely sleepy. "I've lost something," he continued, "something close to me, like your tree."

"How awful," she declared somberly.

"It was stolen, too. Taken from me in the night." He forced himself not to think directly of Dicey; it was far too painful, and he needed to keep cool. Meli was responding, though, to Joshua's repressed feelings; and to her own, clearly felt: tears filled her eyes.

"What was it?" she asked timidly, afraid to hear his answer, trying to erase the image of her tree being cut.

"My lover," he whispered. "My bride." He held his mouth firmly closed.

"How awful," she repeated. She smoothed the wrinkles from his brow with her fingertips. "Who stole her? Do you know the man?"

Mercifully, he forced his thoughts again on to his revenge, off his pain. "The thing that did it is here," he replied. "Hiding. Meli, you must help me find him."

She was frightened, suddenly, and uncertain. A dozen fears assaulted her at once, all meeting at her lost tree, her lost life. "But what if she's dead?" she cried.

Josh refused to entertain this thought—they hadn't kidnaped Dicey just to kill her. "No," he said categorically. "Besides . . . we're Scribes."

Meli looked partially relieved, partially confused. "I met a Scribe once," she nodded. Then: "What's a Scribe?"

"We read and write," he began. "We believe in the power of the written word. We learn things in books. We believe the Word is God. Words tell us everything. If we learn something important, we set it down in writing, and then it lives forever, and other Scribes can read it in a thousand years and know it the same as we do." He paused. "That's why Dicey won't die. Because her name is written. Even if her body is destroyed, I can lay down her life in scripture, and she'll live as long as the words, and every time her words are read by another Scribe, she'll feel joyful."

"That's beautiful," said Meli. The wind outside rose a bit, rattled the window. The lights in the room went on dimly for a moment, as the windmill outside began to generate some electricity; but then the wind subsided, and the lights flickered out. The candles on the table continued to glow warmly.

The sleepiness Josh had felt earlier returned. He forced himself not to yawn. Meli sat up, put her slight hand on his breast. "Will you do something for me?" her voice quivered. "Will you write the name of my tree?"

Josh was moved. He got up, walked over to the table and sat down. He picked a piece of bramble out of his boot, held it to the candle flame until it started to burn, and then dropped it into a little cup he found on the windowsill. When the bramble had burned itself out in the cup, Joshua stuck his thumb down onto it and crushed it into soot. His flesh was pricked in the process, and two or three drops of blood fell into the cup. Finally, he spit into the mixture of blood and charcoal dust. Meli watched the whole thing with mixed wonder and doubt.

Josh tore a piece of dirty white sheet off the bed and laid it flat on the table. He took his quill out of his boot, dipped it into the makeshift inkwell, and wrote in careful block letters on the small cloth: MELIAE. Then he handed it to her.

She stared at it lovingly, turning it this way and that, holding it up to the light, smelling it, touching it. It made her so happy, Josh tore off another piece of sheet, and wrote on it in flowing script: *Meli*. He handed this second scrap to her, and said, "This is *your* name."

She held it gingerly, lest it break. The wind whipped up the lights once more, then let them down slowly. Muffled laughter floated up from the downstairs. Meli pressed the two cloths gently together, then looked back at Josh. "I'll help you find your tree," she said. "What do the thieves look like?"

Back to the hunt. Josh felt his muscles tauten once more. "One is an Accident," he said, "and he's wounded. I know he's here somewhere. He was with a Griffin and a Vampire earlier, but they split up. He might be meeting them, though, here or somewhere else."

She scrunched up her face. "I haven't seen any Accidents tonight."

Josh found himself suddenly profoundly sleepy. He had trouble keeping his eyes open, and sat down on the bed.

Meli went on. "But there *was* a Vampire and a Griffin here before, and just waiting around, too, they didn't want to dance or anything . . ."

The press of sleep became overpowering, and Josh closed his eyes. He felt vertiginous. Meli's voice was getting farther and farther away.

". . . but they said they couldn't wait long, so madam sent them down to room . . ."

Everything faded into blackness, without sound, without direction, without substance. And at the end of the blackness, an intensely bright, infinitely distant spot of light. Distant, but somehow palpable, like the memory of perfume. The light exerted light-pressure, only it was a negative pressure, a kind of subtle suction, teasing Joshua through the endlessly unfolding black ether. . . .

Beauty reached into his quiver, pulled two silver coins out of the pouch, and handed them to the Equiman whore. She took the money and tied it into a loop in her tail.

"Now tell me where the Accident is," said Beauty.

She put her finger to her lips and motioned him in closer. He leaned his head down to hers, put his ear to her mouth. With an unexpectedly swift stroke, she brought a two-foot plank down on the side of his head. He heard rather than felt the blow. Then in the space of a moment after the sound of the *whok*, he felt surprise, anger, dizziness, and fear. He turned and stumbled out the door of the stall.

She followed him, yelling. "Dirty bounty killer, filthy scummy parasite," she screamed, whacking him about the loins.

He stumbled and got up. Animals were coming out of their stalls to watch. Beauty felt a rivulet of warm, thick blood begin to flow down the side of his face. He saw the old man approaching out of the corner of his eye, and he reared up to defend himself. The old man walked right past him, though, grabbed the raging Equiman by the wrist, and knocked her unconscious with one gentle, reluctant punch.

Beauty quieted down. The old man came up to him. "Sorry about that, mister. She goes kinda crazy, sometimes. Her old man was killed by bounty hunt-

ers. You better go." He handed the Centaur his money
back.

Beauty trotted out of the barn and sat in the grass
about a hundred yards away. His head was beginning
to hurt, but the fresh air cleared his mind.

It was a good lesson. He was a hunter not a detec-
tive. Houses, walls, cities were not for him. Besides
which, he'd been too trusting in the stable, too un-
wary.

Too long away from the hunt.

He lay back and let the cool rising breeze dry the
blood on his head. Time to sit and wait and watch.
He could do more with his eyes and ears in an open
field than in any barn or brothel.

He let his senses accommodate to the night, and
set a vigil.

Josh opened his eyes. No more sleep hunger, no
burning hypnotic light. He lay on his back in the
room's half-darkness, and for a moment couldn't remember where he was. He turned and almost rolled
over on Meli, lying quietly beside him. At his movement she jumped, then sat up straight, then hugged
him happily.

"Oh, you're alive," she breathed, "I was so scared
you—"

"What happened?" Josh raised himself up on an
elbow. "What are you—"

"You just went down, I thought you were dead, I
got so scared, I didn't know what, you didn't move,
I was afraid to tell anyone, and then you didn't wake
up and—"

"Wait, wait," he sat up. He looked down. He was
naked. He looked at her questioningly.

"Well, you weren't waking up," she explained,
"and I shook you and talked to you but I didn't call
Madam because she'd get mad, especially if she found
out you wrote my name, but you still didn't wake up,
so I took off my clothes and . . . well, pretended like
I was your lover and you just found me. Only I found
you. Only you still didn't wake up." Her expression
was one of self-satisfied guilt.

Josh was confused and annoyed by whatever had happened. He got up, quickly pulling on his clothes. This was the second time he'd suddenly fallen asleep like that—without warning, without choice. It disturbed him both because he felt out of control, and because it left him so vulnerable. He stared cautiously at Meli, fearful of all the treacheries she might have inflicted upon him during his failing consciousness.

She looked hurt. "I'm sorry if—"

"No, no, everything's fine. Just—" he squeezed his temples, as if to press away his evil suspicions—"you were telling me something before, about a Griffin and a Vampire . . ."

She nodded. "They were waiting for their friend. They were mean."

"Where did they go, Meli?" he asked.

"Madam told them to wait in room 21, down the hall. She said she'd let them know. They made a mess in the front room, they made someone leave, and everyone got angry at them, so Madam made them wait upstairs."

Josh checked his knives. The wind was blowing constantly now; not hard, but enough so that the filaments in the light bulbs in the small room glowed a deep orange-red.

"Show me where," he said secretively. He knew nymphs loved to reveal secrets.

Her face flushed and her eyes blazed with the fire of complicity, and she took his hand and let him out the door.

They stood noiselessly in the hallway, listening for sounds of danger. The coal-red electric wires along the corridor grew brighter and dimmer as the wind rose and fell outside. They started quietly down toward room 21.

There was suddenly a jumble of noises downstairs—loud voices, footsteps, doors. Meli looked at Josh—"I'll go see," she said, and ran down before he could stop her. He walked on alone, to room 21.

He put his ear to the door. Silence. He bent down and put his eye to the keyhole. Dull, electric-red flicker. He took a knife in each hand and began to turn the doorknob.

When he felt the latch click, he pushed the door open and lunged in on his haunches. Tense silence in a darkening room. The lamp on the table dimmed from blood-red to complete extinction, and only two small candles by the bed continued to shed light. Josh turned slowly, searching every shadow. When his stare fell on the bed, a shadow moved.

Josh raised his knife. The shadow stood up and walked to the edge of the bed: it was the black Cat he'd seen downstairs earlier. The Cat shook her head slowly back and forth at Joshua, then raised her paw and pointed to the open window, where the wind was billowing the curtains.

Josh gaped uncomprehendingly at the small animal. It whined. He walked up to it and scratched the top of its head, between the ears, and it lifted its head higher into the pressure of his fingers. There was a noise behind him and he swiveled, but it was only Meli standing at the door.

"Don't mind her," said Meli, indicating the Cat. "That's only Isis. She's kind of odd."

"So-o-o-o?" purred Isis. It was halfword, half meow.

"Nobody else here," said Josh to Meli. "What was going on downstairs?"

"Just a bunch of King Jarl's soldiers, come to have some fun." Jarl, the Bear-King, had soldiers posted all through the areas south of Monterey—a "peace-keeping force" that had moved in following the Race War, and never left.

"Yarrrrrl," said Isis, licking her paw.

Josh said to Meli, "Are you sure they were in this room?"

Meli nodded vigorously. Isis jumped down to the floor, padded across the room, and leapt up on the windowsill. "Soouuuuth," she meowed. Outside, the wind began racing.

Josh stared across the darkness, first at the strange little Cat, then at Meli. "What did they look like?" he asked.

Meli thought a minute. "The Vampire was tall, even for a Vampire. He had long long black hair, down to here, and his eyes were dark and scary. Griffins I don't know, they all look alike to me but this one was big and I think he had a broken beak."

The last candle flared and guttered, and then the room was dark. The wind wrapped the house.

Joshua's pupils opened wide in the darkness. "I'm going to look around," he said, and walked back into the corridor. Meli went with him.

They looked into rooms through secret windows Meli knew of. They saw things Josh had never even heard of before—things that stirred him, unsettled him. Passionate animals in compelling patterns of embrace, terrible scratchings, furtive moans. He wished he had time to write down everything he saw.

They tried hidden doors. Isolated candles lit their immediate surroundings. Forms and shapes moved out of corners and along walls in the darkened chambers, as the wind outside steadily rose.

Joshua stared through the long dark hall, out the window into the rising wind. He thought: dark hall, rising wind. Dark. Wind.

Joshua stopped. "Something's wrong with the windmill," he said.

Meli looked at him blankly.

"The windmill," he repeated. "It was making electricity when the wind was coming up, and now the wind is stronger but the lights are all off. Don't you see?" He turned away. "Something's wrong in the windmill."

His pulse snapped up with the realization, and its implications. The prey was being run to ground.

"I'm going out," he told her. "You stay here." She looked at him quizzically, baffled. He hugged her briefly. "I'll be back," he said, and left.

Beauty stood motionlessly on the lee side of a slope that gave a good view of the whole panorama—house, barn, cottages, gardens. The smell of the creature was still in the air, but with the wind blowing so hard now, and shifting direction so much, the odor was impossible to localize. The ochre moon gave good light, though: Beauty would see what there was to see.

His head stopped hurting, and was even numbed, now, by the chilly wind. He had his bow out, an arrow loosely strung.

His beacon eyes searched the complex slowly, methodically. Main house, lantern-lit, mostly quiet, occasional laughter bubbling over on a flight of wind. Stables, quiet. Cows and sheep, asleep. Windmill, quiet and still. Cabins, dark.

Windmill. Why was the windmill quiet and still when the wind was so angry and wild?

There was a movement by the back of the big house, and Beauty watched carefully as the lone figure ran a few dozen paces, stopped, and looked around. The figure stood frozen there for perhaps a minute, then began running—straight at Beauty. The Centaur raised his bow.

At a hundred paces he could see clearly it was Josh, so he lowered his weapon and waited. A few seconds later they stood facing each other. Josh was panting lightly. "The windmill," he said. Beauty nodded.

They approached the old wooden tower from the east, walking in the shadow it cast by the low-hanging moon. Its top rocked slightly in the wind. One of the big propeller blades was broken and flapping; but still, in all that current, the fan did not turn.

They found the door around the other side, half open in the glare of the moon. Beauty readied an arrow; Josh unsheathed his steel. They entered in a crouch.

It was dark inside. Moonglow filtered through broken slats and rat holes in the walls, throwing distorted images around the circular room. Most of the floor was taken up by a large ancient generator that ran lines out to the main house, and up to the blades at the top of the mill. A long wooden ladder leaned against the wall, all the way up to a trapdoor that allowed the drive shaft to exit down.

The Accident was there, dangling by the neck from the severed drive chain that connected the big fan blades up top to the turbine generator on the floor. He was dying. Josh climbed up the ladder and cut him free, and the horrible creature tumbled to the floor.

They knelt by his broken body.

"Uluglu domo," said the Accident. His belly was torn open, the mark of a Griffin.

"What's he saying?" asked Josh. "Do you know their language?"

Beauty nodded. "Domo dulo," he said to the Accident. "Odo glutamo nol?"

The ugly creature opened his eye for the first time, and looked at his stalkers. "Ologlu Bal," he said, coughing blood. "Bal ongamo, nu ayrie gludemos, oglo du, Bal naglor nopar dos. Gluanda Bal seco, ologlu tas ululu. Endera Gor mororo gul endamo eglor."

Beauty nodded. "Nglimo tu? Nagena gli asta log nak to."

"Glumpata no glas enti borama, noglu esta tas Bal o Scree tudama glu. Tudama gluanda, Gor es to narag."

"Ednatu?" pursued Beauty.

"Glisanda nef. Riaglo tor ologlu mindamo. Orogra tomo orogra mu. Ti do gorogla mel donu."

Beauty shook his head. "Gluana no tomo, ululu gorono Gor."

"Nef nef, gliamo," said the beast. "Ologlu Bal enta gashto boro, ologlu lev Scree, es piram glu. Gogolasma. Engelli tor. Glidon gliamo, mirelli aj su gol." With that he grimaced and died.

"What did he say?" asked Josh.

"He said he was betrayed by his friends, a long-haired Vampire named Bal, and a Griffin with a broken mouth, named Scree. They were supposed to meet him here, and they killed him."

"Does he know where they went?" Joshua no longer had any thoughts, good or bad, for the Accident. His mind now focused entirely on Bal and Scree.

"They went south. Scree lives in Ma'gas' at the edge of the rain forest. It is the pirate city. Bal lives even south of that. They have Humans with them, tied in a cart, but only Bal knew where they were being taken. This one did only what Bal said to do. He hopes now we kill them both, Bal and Scree. He said his name was Gor and he was glad to die, for life is a river of pain."

They were silent a few moments. There was a sound behind them, and they turned. Isis, the Cat, stood in the doorway. She tipped her head behind her, indicating the big house, and said, "Yarrrl."

Josh went to the door and looked. Four lanterns swung and bobbed toward him, midway between the mill and the house. "Jarl's men," said Joshua. "We'd better move."

They slipped out the door as inconspicuously as possible, but the moon snagged them. Voices amid the lanterns began shouting: "There *is* somebody in the windmill!" "Saboteurs! Get them!" "You there! Halt!"

Josh jumped on Beauty's back. "Run over the hill in the open, then circle around back to the house."

"I think the time has come to leave," suggested the Centaur.

"I have to see if Meli wants to come with us. She may be in trouble."

Isis slipped into the night. Beauty galloped over the hill, the soldiers' shouts and snarls getting more distant with every stride. He made a wide circle in the shadow of some trees, doubled back to the house, and stood, tense and alert, under Meli's window. Josh got a foothold in some ivy and began slowly to scale the dark side of the brothel.

He was almost to Meli's window, when the sounds of renewed commotion could be heard at the windmill. The voices barely carried over the raucous wind. "Murder!" "A dead Accident—" "The Centaur did it!" "He was—" "—someone with him—" "—get after them—"

Josh felt the ledge to Meli's window, and with one final pull, hoisted himself up. Through the glass he saw her. She sat, naked, in the lap of an oriental Vampire. With one hand she reached up behind her, stroking his pale cheek; with the other, she reached down between her legs and stroked his insistence. His right hand reached around to her chest, rolled her tightening nipple between his thumb and long-nailed forefinger. Her head was tilted to the side, her eyes half-closed

His teeth were buried deep in her neck, and cherry-black blood trickled down to her shoulder. She gasped.

Josh tapped on the glass. Meli looked up, saw his face, an apparition at the window. Slowly she brought her first finger up to her lips: Shhh. Imperceptibly, she shook her head. Her face was mischief and resignation together, and invited Joshua's complicity. Their eyes met. Their eyes spoke. Joshua backed down the side of the house.

As he hopped on Beauty's back, Jarl's soldiers were raising the posse in the front room. Whoops, oaths, and growls could be heard. Madam said, "I knew that boy was Trouble."

Beauty galloped off in the opposite direction from the way the soldiers had first seen him leave, and he didn't stop running or changing course for quite a while. They weren't just hunters, now; they were hunted.

CHAPTER 4

In Which The Company Doubles
And Finds A Mascot

THEY ran for two hours straight; first south, then east, then south, then west. They made it to the seaside as the moon dipped under the horizon, and ran north through the salty surf for an hour before finding a place where a tumble of rocks and slate spilled into the ocean from the cliffs above. Up this stony spine they climbed, leaving no trail. They continued walking east again, sticking to creek beds and game paths for still another hour; and didn't rest finally until they found a cave with a back door at the edge of a small wood, just as the false dawn opened her eyes. They slept until late morning.

The evening cool burned off slowly, even at the wood's border. When Josh awoke, he found himself nestled along Beauty's furry belly, curled against the cold. He stood and rubbed himself all over, shaking off sleep; and then stood still, cocking his head, listening for anything the forest might be able to tell him.

The forest said much. The wind in the treetops was from the west, strong, bad for tracking. A woodpecker rapped out a lunchtime tune. A chorus of crickets entertained themselves: they were audience-shy, and could be depended on to stop their performance if anyone showed up for the show. The lighting was all dappled greens and browns, and Joshua never tired of it.

He took out some paper from one of his Scribetubes and assiduously covered it with small script from his quill, recording the events that had led them to this point. He tried to set the record in this way at least once a day, though he knew the Word was forgiving of occasional lapses. When the writing was done, Joshua rolled up the paper and returned it to the Scribe-tube he'd secured inside his boot. "The Word is great, the Word is One," he spoke softly to himself.

Beauty arose, shook all over, and managed to provoke a jay into squawking at him for a full minute. When the blue mad Bird finally flew off in ornery, self-righteous satisfaction, Josh looked over to Beauty and said, "Well?"

Beauty stretched. "Well, we need not worry about Jarl's toads. If they pick up our trail at all, it will not be for days. We will be out of this land."

"That's only half a well," smiled Joshua. "We're on a pretty cold trail ourselves."

"We know they headed south," said the Centaur.

"South is a big place."

"We could head direct for Ma'gas', where the Griffin lives."

"We don't know they're going there. And I'd rather catch up before they got that far."

Beauty agreed. "I think we will do best to follow a loose trail between the brothel they left in the night and the Forest of Accidents."

Josh looked doubtful. "That's more east than south. Why that way?"

A brown Rabbit ran up, sniffed at some clover, began to chew. Beauty stretched his hind legs, one at a time.

"Griffins dislike walking, and Vampires hate work of any kind. These two have a cart full of Humans to drag along now that their muscular friend is dead. They will be wanting help."

Josh nodded. "And another Accident is their best bet." Beauty rubbed his rump against the bark of a crusty old oak. "I can see them bickering while they walk. 'You pull, you old bat.' 'No, *you* pull, you miserable Bird, it's *my* turn to fly.' "

Josh laughed. "We could get ahead of them and volunteer to pull the wagon."

"We already pulled Jarl's hounds off their scent."

"Say, maybe they could find other things for us to do. Draw their water . . . plant their crops . . ."

"Slit their throats . . ." suggested Beauty.

"Slit their throats," chimed Josh.

"Surrrrrrre," came a voice behind them. They spun around, Beauty rearing, Josh crouching low. Sitting serenely in a puddle of sunlight, feet tucked under her, eyes half closed, was Isis, the black Cat from the brothel.

"Isis," said Josh. Isis smiled.

"Who is that?" demanded Beauty suspiciously.

"The Cat in the house last night. Remember? She warned us about Jarl's men, in the windmill."

"Well, why is she here?"

Isis opened her strange eyes wide. "Noooo. Howwww?" she purred.

"Yes, and how, indeed?" the Centaur continued.

"She must have picked up our scent," said Josh. "We're not really all that far from the brothel, after the big circle we made."

"Surrrrre," smiled Isis. She stood up, padded over to Josh, leaned her back against his leg, and purred. Beauty shook his head. "Dumb animals just seem to love you."

Whereupon Isis arched her back, fluffed up to twice her size in fur, and hissed viciously at the Centaur. Beauty raised his eyebrows. Isis quieted down a bit, looked sulky, and growled, "We'rrrrrre nooooo foo-ooooolllll."

"Got a bit of Human blood in her, I'll wager," Beauty laughed. Then, more seriously: "I do not like how easily she found us, though. Or how silently she crept."

"Why did you come?" Josh asked the little creature.

Isis looked down, then up. "We'rrre yourrrr girrrrl," she pouted. She flopped over on her back, played wildly with Joshua's bootstring for a few seconds, then rolled onto her side, resting her paw lightly on his toe.

The two hunters laughed. Josh stooped down and scratched the Cat's belly furiously. She had a delicious spasm around his hand, brought her hind legs up and kicked wildly at his arm, bit him on the back of the wrist, jumped away, then stood calmly preening herself as if nothing had happened.

Beauty pawed the ground. "Your following is faithful, Joshua. But we must go."

Isis stopped her preening. "Nooooooo," she mooned.

"We've got to go, Fur-face," explained Josh. "We're after the Vampire whose room you were in last night."

Isis opened her eyes wide, then nodded knowingly. "Ohhhhh," she purred.

Beauty pricked up his ears. Josh said, "Why, you know something about them? You know where they went?"

The Cat nodded discreetly. "Knowwww wherrrrrrre."

"We are not taking a Cat on a hunt," warned Beauty.

"But she may know something," Josh considered. "And she already helped us at the brothel, and she found us here, so she's obviously got a good nose. Besides, she's sneaky. I think that may come in handy."

Beauty looked skeptical. "It will be dangerous, little Cat. Are you ready for that?"

"Surrrre," she swaggered, strutting over the leafy dirt between them.

"It would be easier for you back at the brothel," added Josh.

She raised her eyebrows, turned her head to the side, and spoke, as if to the rock that lay in the path, "We'rrrrre borrrrred."

"And you know which way the Vampire is headed?" pressed the Centaur.

She shrugged a Yes, as if being asked to repeat herself didn't deserve further comment.

"Then let's go," smiled Josh.

Isis grinned and leapt up on Joshua's chest. Involuntarily his hands came up and held her there. She looked up, hissed in a low, sultry voice, "Kissss," and licked his lower lip once. Then she leapt down, ran ten yards into the forest, stopped, turned around, looked at them and drew open her eyes, her pupils dilated with dark excitement. Josh and Beauty stared into the subtle strangeness of her black Cat face, and realized at

the same moment that staring back at them were
black round pupils in blue round irises balanced between curving eyelids with black eyelashes; eyes that
were not Cat-eyes; but were Human.

The corners of her mouth pulled back, and she
hissed: "Yesssss." Then she turned and ran, Cat-fast
into the forest, and Josh and Beauty ran after her.

"You there, what are you doing?" the Vampire
demanded. He had long black hair, and his name was
Bal.

Dicey shook her head bleakly. She was too frightened to speak. Bal strode over to where she sat, pulled
her roughly off the floor of the cave. No one else
moved. Rose stood still as earth a few feet away, holding a rock behind her: it was in her mind to bash the
Vampire's head in if it looked like he was going to
hurt Dicey.

Bal looked at the ground where the young girl had
been sitting. He saw she'd found a piece of chalk,
and had been writing a sentence over and over on the
stone. He read aloud: "WORDS SAVE US. WE ARE FREE."
He laughed, tore the chalk from Dicey's trembling
hand and inserted his own block letters in the top
line of her writing, so it now read: WORDS ENSLAVE
US. WE SCARED. FREEDOM IS AN ILLUSION. He laughed
again, turned on his heel, and walked back among the
milling Vampires.

Rose moved close to Dicey. "It's okay, it's over
now," Rose whispered; but Dicey couldn't stop shaking, couldn't tear her eyes off the markings on the
floor, the way Bal had twisted her words.

Bal was shouting orders to the assembled creatures
now. A Griffin stood at the Vampire's side, sharpening
his broken beak on a stone. "All right," Bal called,
"time to move out. Get the prisoners moving, seven in
a cart. Be quick about it there, Ice take you. We split
up at South-marsh and rendezvous at the other side of
the Forest. Step lively, there, you bloat. Here, Uli,
give that Accident a hand."

Harshly, the Accidents and Vampires began herd-
ing the Humans into the covered tumbrils. Some of

the Vampires exchanged words in the high-frequency beeps they used only when under stress, or very excited. These sounds were inaudible to most other creatures, but not insensible: they caused fear and distraction. Even a sluggish Accident would step lively to get out of range of the signals.

The dispersal continued. Rose held on tightly to Dicey and Ollie, to keep them together in the confusion.

Dicey couldn't stop shivering.

The woods were lovely, dark and brief. The three hunters left them quickly, and continued mostly east, if a bit north.

The area was hilly, covered with a thick brown-purple heather that scratched their legs but had a wonderful spring smell. An exaltation of larks passed at one point, flying west to east. A good omen. Vernal flowers tested the air, and the breeze was a gentle laughter. All in all, a good day for journeying.

And nobody loved an adventure better than Isis. She was positively exhilarated. She'd race ahead through brier and short grass, outdistancing the other two by a hundred yards. Then something would catch her eye, some movement or vapor, and she'd hunker down and stare intensely at the occult perception, and then her back legs would start to rev up; and then she'd pounce—have it out with the bramble or grasshopper or molecule she'd focused on—and then Josh and Beauty would catch up, and Isis would run ahead.

Occasionally they passed a totem, or a fetish—a pile of bones, a mask of feathers—constructed by some local shaman to ward off passing evil. These affected Isis in strange ways. Some she would approach cautiously, on tiptoe, and sniff all around for minutes; some she ignored entirely; one she hissed at, attacked, and ran away from; one she pranced up to as if she'd been expecting it, and unceremoniously urinated on it. Josh and Beauty treated them all with equal disinterest—the only significance to them of such signs lay in their state of disrepair, which re-

flected how long it had been since interested locals
had been around.

They crossed a great plain, next, where craters
pocked the land. Many battles in many wars had been
fought in this area between the sea and the Forest of
Accidents. These large holes that they passed were
scores of years old, for they were smooth and variably
shallow, and filled with soft yellow grass.

At the end of the plain they came to a rise, which
they climbed easily. It was topped by a plateau—
absolutely flat, hard, and gray—upon which they
stood and rested a minute. The plateau was shaped
like a huge table, perhaps fifty feet wide and extending one hundred fifty feet long, where it crumbled into
dirt at each end. It afforded a grand view of the plains
they'd just left and the valleys beyond.

At one end of the long table of rock was a small
square hut of rusted steel, chipped paint, broken glass.
They walked up to it and stared inside. Empty. Beside it was a mound of sun-bleached bones. Atop the
door of the hut was a series of strange white markings
on a faded green board. The travelers stared at the
marks a few moments. Then Beauty turned to Josh
and said, "Scribery." Josh nodded. Beauty went on:
"What is its meaning?"

Josh stared a moment longer, then answered. "It
says 'Toll booth.' "

Beauty furrowed his brow and tilted his head. "But
what is the meaning?" he repeated.

Joshua pursed his lips. "I think it means this was a road once."

Beauty snorted. "It seems a lot of effort was expended to go a short way."

Josh nodded. Suddenly Isis said, "Morrrre," and pointed down the hill. Josh and Beauty followed the direction of her paw, and saw, in the valley, three or four hundred yards distant, two tiny figures pulling a cart. In an instant Beauty was running at a full lope, and Josh not far behind.

When they were a hundred yards short, they saw the two creatures look up, shout, break away from the cart, and begin running. Beauty galloped down and headed them off, his bow taut. Joshua covered the creatures' retreat. Everyone stopped.

It was not the Vampire and the Griffin. It was an Elf and a Rool, and they quivered with fear. Joshua walked over to the cart they'd been pulling, and looked inside: dishes, flowers, a rocking chair, colored fabrics. He walked back as the Elf was saying, in a voice that cracked, "Are you going to kill us?" The Rool was tall and thin, covered in soft amber fur; he wouldn't open his eyes.

Beauty lowered his bow. Josh relaxed. "No, we won't kill you," he said.

"How are you called?" asked Beauty.

The Elf seemed to relax a little. He was only two feet tall, but wore high-heeled boots to try to look larger. "I am Fofkin," he said. "This is my friend, Rool." Rool kept his eyes closed. Rools were all named Rool, because nobody could tell them apart—not even other Rools, it was said.

"You gave us a wicked scare," Fofkin went on. "Our people are taken by demons, our home is sacked. We run all day and mourn all night."

"Rooooool," cooed Rool, like a wounded dove. His eyes stayed closed.

"We beg your pardon," Beauty bowed sincerely. "We have lost our own, and seek them now."

"What manner of creatures did this to you?" asked Josh. "Was it a Vampire and a Griffin?"

Fofkin jumped a foot in the air and sat in the grass.

"A Vampire, yes. He was in charge. But no Griffin. Three others. A big Lizard, a Sphinx, and a Faceless One." He shuddered. "The Sphinx used to live right up there, in that little shack up on the flats. Used to eat anybody who wandered by, but he never bothered anyone down in the valley before. Must've been the Vampire put him up to it. Poor Mary."

The Rool curled up into a big ball of fur and rolled over next to Fofkin. The little Elf petted him tenderly.

"Your people," said Beauty. "Are they also Elves and Rools?"

Fofkin shook his head. "Humans, every one. Kidnaped. Every one drug off and stuck in a big closed cart and pulled away. Poor Mary." A tear filled his eye and dawdled down his cheek.

"Rool," came the muffled sound from inside the ball of fur.

"Which way were they headed?" Josh asked softly.

"South," said the Elf.

Isis strolled up, sat down, and began licking her belly. Joshua looked down at her. "You still know where you're taking us?" he demanded.

"Surrre."

There was a faint humming above them, and Josh looked up to see the red-and-gold Flutterby hovering excitedly over their heads. Isis leapt straight up, six feet in the air from a sitting position, took a swipe with her paw, and almost bagged the Flutterby with one blow. As she landed on her feet in a crouch, Josh swatted her backside with the flat of his hand. "You leave that Flutterby alone," he scolded. Isis looked unconvinced, half ready to spring again. The Flutterby gained altitude.

Beauty laughed. "Dissent among your minions," he chortled, and Joshua gave him a dirty look. The Flutterby settled on Josh's shoulder.

"Looks like it's made up its mind to follow us," Josh fretted. "I guess we'll have to call it something." The Flutterby smiled demurely and hummed.

"How about Humbelly?" suggested Beauty. Isis kept a dour eye fixed on the gentle bug.

"Humbelly it is," agreed Josh, and tossed the creature back into the air, where it fluttered giddily all around.

They bid good journey to Fofkin and Rool, wished them well, and set off once more east, in the direction Isis led them. Humbelly bobbed playfully over Joshua's head, and then over Isis'. Isis swatted and jumped at the dancing wings, but to no avail, until she finally just purred "Whorrrre" under her breath, and ignored the silly creature entirely.

Once, around midafternoon, they saw a battle in a dale off to the northeast—fifty-odd creatures fighting, hand to hand on a bloody field. It looked like some of Jarl's Guard against an unknown faction. Josh was tempted to stop, to see what was what; but Beauty just shook his head and kept walking: whatever it was, it wasn't for them.

In the early evening they came upon the tracks. Wheel tracks, from a heavy cart, mingled with the foot and claw prints of the animals they wanted. Isis almost touched her nose to one of the prints, sniffing intently at its meaning. Finally she lifted her eyes to Joshua's, and nodded her head. "Herrrrre," she said.

They followed the trail due east for several miles. At the edge of a pine grove, the tracks were joined by those of another cart, and other animals. Here they all turned southeast for a while, until they were met by still a third set of wheels, and five more animals.

The terrain was becoming rocky now, and it was increasingly difficult to distinguish whose prints were whose. In addition, some tracks would disappear, where an animal had flown away; some walked off; some joined up. It was a confusing melee. At the north rim of a quarry still almost a mile from the Forest of Accidents, the three wagons split in three different directions; and despite intensive sniffing and study by Isis, Josh, and Beauty, it was impossible to tell which set of tracks belonged to the cart carrying Rose and Dicey.

After much debate, they decided to follow the trail going east for a ways, at least until they could decipher more about the animals in that group. They hadn't gone more than a half-mile, though, past some ancient broken tombstones, when they saw her.

Lying, still and pale behind a furze bush, was a figure. They approached slowly and stared. It was the nude figure of a young woman. Smooth, red-haired, vulnerable, beautiful. Lifeless. Josh walked up to her and felt for a pulse.

"Nothing. Cold as earth," he said. Isis smelled the woman's foot and backed off.

Joshua looked at the motionless face. She couldn't have been more than twenty, yet there was something about the face that bespoke age; reason; depth. It was more than the distance and darkness that color the mask of death, it was more than the lure of amnesiac sleep; it was subtler, it was . . .

She opened her eyes. "Help me," she whispered.

Isis laid her ears back, Beauty shuffled in the dust. Josh picked the woman's head up off the ground, and as his fingers cupped the back of her scalp, he felt a slow trickle of oily liquid oozing out a small nozzle that was almost flush with the skin.

"You're not Human," he muttered in surprise.

"I'm Neuroman," she whispered. "Help me."

"How?" he asked.

"The quarry back there," she gasped. "At the bottom of the north slope, under a slab of white granite with a red vein in the shape of a J. You know what a J is?"

Joshua hesitated, then nodded. "I can read," he said. In some places, people were burned for being able to read.

"There's a container there." She faltered, closed her eyes. "Bring it to me."

Josh got up and ran back to the quarry, slid down the north grade, and easily found the J-veined rock. Under it was a steel pint can. Stenciled on the can in blue and gold paint was the word HEMOLUBE. And then in small black letters underneath it: *Grade AA, U.S.P.*

Josh stuck the can in his belt and scrambled back up. He sprinted over to the supine figure. Isis sat on her haunches, watching. Beauty was kneeling down, feeling the woman's forehead. "Cold and dry," he said. Humbelly sat in the grass at a distance, wings moving slowly up and down.

Josh pulled out the can. The woman seemed to be aware of his return, and opened her eyes. She said in a low voice: "Roll me over. Fill me up."

Josh rolled her on her belly, parted her hair. On the very back of her head, a small valve was open, the size of a fingernail. There was a slightly smaller spigot on the can. Josh punctured this with the point of his knife and carefully poured the viscous red fluid from the can into the hole in the back of the head of the prone figure. When the can was empty, Josh closed the head-valve with a snap.

The figure lay still for sixty seconds, during which period Josh once again had the odd physical sensation that time had stopped, or at least slowed down considerably. Suddenly the woman turned over and sat upright.

"I'm alive," she said, simply.

Joshua took a step back. "Who are you?" he said.

"My name is Jasmine." Pause. "I owe you my life."

"You don't owe me anything. I do what I do."

She had a feeling, and smiled.

Beauty interrupted softly. "Who did this to you?"

She shivered. "A beautiful, long-haired Vampire, and a Griffin."

Beauty stiffened in tense satisfaction.

"Whyyyyy?" whined Isis.

"They thought I was Human," said Jasmine sadly. "The others were. They left me for dead when they found out I wasn't."

"What others?" Josh stepped forward.

"Six others, in a carriage, tied together. All Humans." She stopped. "Were they your people?"

"Most likely," Josh breathed, eyes ahead.

"Well, then," said Jasmine, standing up, "we must find them."

The sun dipped its last light under the crest of the nearest hills, putting everything in a somber cast: the first intimations of the evening chill. In the quiet of the moment, Isis suddenly half stood, cocked her ears, jerked her head to the left, and froze. The others looked in the same direction, but saw nothing. Suddenly the black Cat sped off to the top of a long rise of rocks to the west. In a few seconds she raced back to where the others stood.

"Yarrrrl," she growled.

Josh ran silently with Isis to a niche in the rock pile, and peered over it across the western plain.

Walking slowly toward them, a quarter-mile distant, were ten of Jarl's soldiers on their trail. Five appeared to be Bears, two were Ursumen; the other three Joshua couldn't discern. He ran back to the others.

"JEGS," he panted. "Too many to fight. We'll have to run."

"I dislike this running *from*," Beauty said distinctly.

Jasmine looked from face to face; finally at Beauty. "When I was young, two hundred fifty years ago, there was a truth well known. It was said that for every thing, there is a season. Your fight, I think, isn't with these soldiers."

Josh and Beauty looked back toward the rise, where Jarl's Elite Guard would be tracking in a few minutes; and then ahead, at the Forest of Accidents looming in the near east.

Jasmine spoke again. "I know a place to wait and think. A sanctuary, a friend's hideaway. In the Forest."

She held their faces in hers. They looked at each other. She turned and began to run toward the Forest. "Come on, then," she called quietly over her shoulder. They all followed her at a trot, and by the time they reached the edge of the wood a few minutes later, night had fallen flat.

The Forest. A blackness filled the air, deeper than any thought, a blackness without form. Shapes could be imagined in the night, differentiated from the night only by subtle, textural variations—here, a glossier black; there, more flat; there, a thickening in the blackness: wet rocks in a stream, a cluster of young trees, an animal.

Occasionally through the matte of clouds that was the sky, a fleck of starlight escaped; but was caught immediately in the web of vines and branches that canopied the forest. No light this night.

And it was cold. As the heart of a fish. As the color of snow in shadow.

And quiet, still. No sound rattled the leaves, clicked the stones. No rodent skittered, no tail slapped, no thing moved; except once, perhaps, the flapping of a great bird could be heard high above the fringe of the farthest trees—but this noise, if it even existed, was quickly absorbed by the faint stale wind, and carried into the depths of the wood.

So. Black, cold, quiet, still. A sense of breath lost or held, of a momentary pause in the flow of things, of . . .

A pure, low demented cry tore the fabric of this weave. It was a blind, inhuman sound, terrible and brief.

The five animals stopped; listened; held their breaths. This wood concealed Accidents.

"It's not far," whispered Jasmine. Beauty held an arrow drawn.

They tiptoed across a game path, into a thicket. The night and the smell of moist earth surrounded them, like different kinds of overgrowth. Another noise, in another direction, made them all turn their heads at once. Something rustled. There was a click.

A blast of light flooded to the left. Josh involuntarily brought his arm up to shield his face. Beauty raised his bow. It looked like a shaft of light breaking, *de novo,* out of the substance of the night; and then like a door of light opening in the face of rock Josh now saw standing straight as a wall a few feet into the undergrowth. And then he realized it *was* a door being opened in the rock there, and a light shining out from inside the rock. And now a figure stood in the doorway, silhouetted by the lamps in the room beyond. Jasmine walked up to the dark figure in the rock.

"Is Lon here?" she asked in a hush.

"Whom shall I say is calling?" said the form in the doorway. He ushered the five fugitives in quickly, and closed the door behind them. Outside, no trace of door remained. Only a large boulder, one side flat and mossy, half buried in the jungle-thick forest.

CHAPTER 5

In Which The Travelers Learn
Of A New Animal In The South

INSIDE, a small room had been hollowed out of the center of the rock, so its walls and floor were of stone; with a stairway descending immediately into the earth. As soon as the hunters entered, they were led by the doorman down two long flights of these turning stone steps. So steep was the descent that Beauty almost fell twice, and had to keep balancing himself with his hands on the walls.

Finally they reached level ground. A spacious tunnel led them, wormlike, many paces to a great gothic archway, which opened upon a wood-paneled room, thirty by fifty feet long, fifteen feet high, decked with rough-hewn cedar. Paintings lined the walls, illuminated by golden candelabra. Velvet overstuffed chairs proliferated; oriental carpets, crystal chandeliers.

"Wowww," meowed Isis.

The doorman left. Suddenly in walked a singularly handsome man with short, straight hair; deep sensitive eyes; skin of reddish hue; long, powerful fingers, and the secure smile of a civilized patron, his mouth parenthetically punctuated by a gently curving fang at each corner. He was a Vampire.

He spread his wings when he saw Jasmine, and his smile widened. As she ran up to him with her arms out, he encircled her, warmly touching his lips to her neck.

"Lon," she murmured.

"Jasmine," he replied. He pronounced her name "Yahzmeen." His voice was deep as the grotto.

"Whoa," cautioned Isis. Josh and Beauty were tense, confused, ready to bolt. Josh cursed himself for falling into such an easy trap, and wondered if he could kill a Vampire at close range. Beauty measured the distance to the door, the distance to the creature. He would not make the first move. Treachery must always lose strength when it must declare itself. Humbelly fluttered around the room, mindlessly upset.

Jasmine finally broke her embrace with the Vampire and turned back to the others. "This is my friend, Lon," she said. "We're safe here. Lon, these are my friends . . . but I don't know your names," she realized in midsentence.

"Josh, Beauty, Isis, and Humbelly," said Joshua, indicating with his hand. His voice was thick with coiled energy.

Lon bowed from the waist, so low that his forehead almost touched the floor. "It is my deepest honor to welcome the friends of my friend," he intoned. Draping his body were sheer silks of deep orange and chocolate brown, which flowed like flames through the ether when he moved. He rose from the bow to his full height, with the words, "Please accept my hospitality."

Neither Beauty nor Isis moved. Josh bobbed his head, tentative, uncertain. "Thanks," he said.

Lon smiled beneficently. "Come, we shall eat." He put his robed arm around Jasmine's shoulder and escorted her out the door, talking continuously of old times, new times. The others looked at each other, shrugged, and followed.

They went down twisting passages, some lit, some dark; through a large natural cave, dripping with stalactites; past an underground spring, cool and still; along another carpeted room, filled with antique musical instruments of every variety—clavichords, pianos, French horns, oboes, dulcimers; and finally into the dining room.

It was enormous. Jeweled sculptures held court over one end of the room, their intentions made shadowy by the glow of ancient lamps. Gilt objects adorned every surface, some powerfully magical, some merely exquisite. Scattered around the floor were scented animal skins: sheep, tiger, bear. Against one entire wall an enormous fireplace crackled brightly with burning cedar. A long, low central table of two-inch oak, which looked like it could easily accommodate a banquet, sat stoutly on the floor, surrounded by dozens of pillows, large and small, multicolored in soft exotic fabrics.

"Please, sit," said Lon with an expansive sweep. He reclined on a pillow at the head of the table; Jasmine sat cross-legged on his right. The others sat comfortably on the floor around the table, propping themselves against the luxury of the down cushions. Humbelly, settling near the fireplace, immediately fell asleep.

A man surreptitiously ran in, whispered something into the Vampire's ear, received a long, whispered reply, then ran out again. Lon said something to Jasmine; she laughed. He turned, finally, to the others, an apologetic grimace on his face. "First, we shall drink," he said.

He picked a small glass bell off the table and jingled it softly. Instantly a beautiful, pale young boy came silently into the room, naked but for his jewelry, carrying a tray of liqueurs. He padded around the table, stopping to offer each guest a glass, placing a small bowl in front of Isis, coming finally to the Vampire host, who took the remaining glass and raised it. "A toast," said Lon. The young boy scurried from the room.

Lon went on. "Jasmine has just been telling me you saved her life. For this act you may consider me your most loyal servant." He bowed his head half an inch. "So, a toast. May servant and master find each other worthy." He drank from his glass. The others raised their goblets in the amber half-light, like torchbearers at a secret ceremony. Isis sniffed her bowl.

They were relaxing somewhat, but still uncertain. Joshua's hand was never far from his knife. He was about to speak some of his thoughts, when Lon raised a staying hand. "Please," said the Vampire. "I can see you are suspicious, and uncertain of my intent; but I assure you, I am sincere. Jasmine has told me what little she knows of your plight, but we can discuss this further after the meal. In the meantime, since you are apparently being pursued by Jarl's Guard, let me tell you what I have done." Josh and Beauty watched their host closely. He smiled and went on.

"My spies tell me the JEGS were hard on your sign, inside the forest, still half a mile from the entrance of my cave. I have dispatched two of my fastest Humans, my prize palomino, and my cleverest Cat to continue your trail where you left it, flee north, and lead Jarl's soldiers a merry chase through the forest. For a week, or until Jarl's hired assassins are eaten by Accidents, whichever comes first." He laughed heartily. "No, don't protest. My people love a good chase, and in any case, they've been idle too long." He drank again. Jasmine leaned over and kissed him on the cheek.

Josh closed his eyes. Beneath the fog of suspicion that filled him, a feeling glowed viscerally. It wasn't rational, but it was real—like the sudden intuition of cool rain welling at the pit of a hot summer day. In a single motion, Josh raised his eyelids with his glass. "To our host," he said, and drank. Isis nodded, lapped from her bowl. Even Beauty relaxed.

"Then let the meal begin," answered Lon, ringing his little glass bell.

Two boys and two girls entered, bearing appetizers on trays of silver—wine-soaked fruits, spiced morsels of fish, breaded game hearts, sweetmeats, and pickled lizard tails.

The servants wore nothing, or shifts of rare silk. One brought Jasmine a linen caftan to wear. It was only after the beautiful Neuroman had put it on, when she was suddenly no longer naked, that Joshua was aware of her sexuality, of something like ungrounded electricity, or like a hot spring pressing to explode through her cool exterior. Beauty noticed it too; but ever the gentleman, he looked away.

Another round of drinks.

The next course was soups: robin's-egg soup, dove-liver soup, honey-grass soup. Every dish was a creation, visual as well as gustatory; every creation a masterpiece. Joshua sucked up the new sensations like a baked sponge in water.

Next began the music. The chamber quartet, too, dressed in oranges and browns, the colors of the house. Instrumentation consisted of a flute, a harp, a lyre, a cello. The lyric strains seemed to haunt the room, subtle as memory, recurrent as the waves of a hidden lagoon. Josh had the peculiar sense, suddenly, that all this had happened before—that he'd been here, in this scene: these ornate decorations, this melodious hall, that pillow—the way it leaned, the fragrance of these oiled servants: thought he'd been here; but, of course, he hadn't.

More wine. The main courses appeared: stuffed geese, fried squid; sautéed fetal cow meat, tender enough to dissolve on the tongue; succulent rarebit, candied oysters, lamb tartare. The music changed to something lighter, the table conversation wandered gaily from bass to treble; the evening warmed. Presently, the dancing began.

Seven delectable young veiled men and women danced, as if possessed, among the sculptures at the far end of the room. Lon mentioned proudly that they were his favorite concubines. He called one, named Lissa. She ran over to him, rubbed his back, sat beside him, shared his meal for a while as he fondled her. Another—a young boy named Peter—seemed jealous of the attentions Lissa was getting; so he came over to Lon's other side, trying to press his favors on the Vampire. Lon grew distant, though, and dismissed them both back to the dance. Josh watched the two concubines return to the rest of the harem: as they passed, he saw their necks were bruised black and blue along the jugular tracks.

Desserts. Pies, custards, fruits, cheeses. Brandies. Coffees. Smokes. A ferret-faced man came out and did sleight-of-hand tricks for a short time, then left. The fire simmered, the music calmed. Humbelly woke up, fluttered around the room a few times, sipped some mulled fruit wine from a dish, fell back asleep. The night had become mellow.

Puffing on a long-stemmed pipe, Lon settled back.

Layers of smoke laced the room like thick, sleepy air. Previously exuberant figures began to curl in the corners. "And now," said Lon, "the troubles."

Josh told him their story. Lon listened, keenly interested, nodding from time to time. When Josh was done, Lon contemplated his fingernails a few moments, then spoke. "Well. Jarl's soldiers are no longer to be a problem for you, I trust. As for the other . . . I know this Sire Bal. He is Sangnoir. Bad blood." Vampires always called other Vampires "Sire," even when there was little love between them. Lon showed his distaste now by pulling his lips back over his teeth, baring his fangs briefly in the ritual grin of aggression.

"It is not just Bal, though," said Beauty. "Rumors are alive in the land. Humans are being kidnaped. Vampires are being named."

"And I'm not so sure we're rid of the JEGS that easily," added Joshua. "They found us over a trail I'd have had trouble following myself."

Lon nodded gravely. "Perhaps. As for the rumors you mention—they are more than rumors. Something is happening." He paused a moment, staring into his glowing pipe, then went on. "There is a new animal, in the south. So my people tell me. No one knows much about the creature, whether it be fish, fowl, or fiend. But some things are certain." He relit his pipe, which had gone out. The others studied him attentively. He continued. "This animal is directing these abductions. Sires have been enlisted to organize the raiding parties, and the Humans who are taken alive are all taken to the new animal's den, somewhere near the Big Sticks River. What happens to them there is unknown. The Sires who participate in this genocide are rewarded—they are allowed to keep their pick of the Humans, to fatten their harems." He lowered his eyes in shame. "It is loathsome, of course. But what is one to do."

"And what of the other creatures?" interjected Jasmine. "The Griffins and all."

"They are all in the pay of the Sires, though I suspect the money and gifts flow north from the new animal. In any case, these creatures all have reason to hate Humans. Accidents, most of all. I think that is why this Forest has become the main rendezvous point in the north."

"Why do Accidents hate us so much?" Josh wondered, hurt and angry.

Lon raised his eyebrows, as if he'd been asked a simple question by a child, then suddenly realized he didn't know the answer. Jasmine said, "Humans created Accidents, Joshua. That's why." Josh remained unclear. Jasmine added: "It's a long story. I'll tell you another time."

Lon went ahead. "It may be as simple as slave trade on a large scale: all the marauding groups meet at the southeast of the Forest; the hostages are pooled and taken, *en masse*, to one of the pirate cities by a few of the leaders; the rest of the raiders remain up here for continued abductions and general terrorism."

"Do you know what route they follow south?" asked Beauty.

Lon shook his head. "No, though I have some suspicions. This Sire Bal, I'm certain, is one of the captains. He will be making the journey south with the captives, I can almost guarantee. And I know the trails he is likely to follow. We used to hunt the Rain Forest together. Many years ago."

"The Terrarium?" questioned Jasmine.

Lon nodded. "You know the area well, Jasmine." She squinted her eyes. He went on. "From the North Saddlebacks down to the pirates' cove."

Jasmine looked hard into the unblazing fireplace, at an image only she could see. "That was a long time ago," her voice echoed from far away.

"As I said, many years," repeated Lon. "And I ran there with Bal-Sire even before I knew you."

She looked at him meaningfully, then turned to Josh. "Yes, I know the area," she said.

"It is difficult terrain to navigate," commented Beauty. "It would be preferable to catch them before they get that far. We should leave now."

Lon laughed. "Only a fool would attempt my Forest at night." Beauty stiffened. Lon caught himself. "My intention was not to imply you a fool, sir. I merely fear for your safety. This wood is black at night, and it is common to underestimate the savvy of these Accidents. A common, fatal mistake. They are cunning, these *pauvres bêtes*. Ugly brutes, but clever. And they know their woods. Best to stay here tonight, I think, and sally out in the morning."

"He's right," said Josh. Beauty nodded reluctantly.

"We can leave at first light," added Jasmine.

Beauty frowned. "You have been kind to lead us here," he said to Jasmine. Then, to Lon: "And you, to shelter us." Finally, to the floor: "But I hunt alone. This tracking party is getting far out of hand. We might as well hire a trumpeter to announce us. Please, do not think me ungrateful, but this is a thing for two of us, not an army."

Josh found himself silently agreeing with the Centaur. Isis hissed softly. Lon puffed meditatively on his pipe. Jasmine waited a moment, until she was certain Beauty had nothing further to say, then answered him. "You're letting Venge-right cloud your judgment, both of you. Three times over. First, you have no idea how many creatures will be escorting the hostages—it may *be* an army. I suspect you'll need as many allies as you can find. Second, I'm your equal or better in a fight any day of the week, and Lon can vouch for that. What's more, I'll bet that little Cat there can hold her own or more." Isis growled approval. Josh liked the Neuroman's spunk, at least. Lon smiled. Jasmine stood up. "Third, I'm the only one among you who knows Dundee's Terrarium well enough to track and second-guess Bal, if he gets that far." She pointed at Beauty, scolding. "That's why you should want me to go," she repeated, "but by Neptune's Middle Fin, that's not why I'm going. I'm going because this boy saved my life, and I always repay my debts, and I always define the terms." She picked a glass of wine off the table and downed it hard.

"Her words have merit," said Josh.

"Words," scowled Beauty. Then, resigned, to the Neuroman woman: "I cannot stop you. Still, I do not like it."

"You mistrust words?" Jasmine asked him, her manner softer now.

"Words are a sorry attempt to describe what is."

"Words can approximate the truth," she replied.

"You cannot convince me with words of something I know to be false by experience or feeling."

"Words are their own truth," asserted Joshua. Normally this was a topic he and Beauty avoided discussing; but they were all a little heady from the liquor and the moment: sentiments were bubbling up like steam in a simmering kettle.

"Words just reflect the truths of their times and their places," said Jasmine, warming to the subject. "For example . . ." She paced before the fireplace, a bright burgundy wine in her hand. "For example. When I was still young, in the late years of the twentieth century, people rarely used verbs anymore, except in the present tense. The past was so depressing, and the future so frightening, that only the Now had any power to instruct or inspire. Not that it was all that instructive *or* inspirational, frankly, but you see, we had no truck with pasts or futures, so it became chic to discard all grammars but the present indicative. So we said, 'I eat,' and that had to do, since nobody cared if you *had* eaten, or were *going* to eat. The words were just reflections, though. Of the way things were. Does that make sense?"

Beauty's expression looked as much like a wall as an expression could. "I hope you do not talk so much when you hunt," he said.

Jasmine paused, smiled. "That reminds me of a story," she began. "I was walking with a Captain of Clones, some hundred and fifty years ago, stalking a renegade Hedon in the jungle south of the Line. Well, I just talked and talked about this and that, and after a while, the Hedon jumped out of the trees at us, swinging his machete. I got him, though, dropped him at the Captain's feet.

"Well, the Clone Captain was a little peeved, just like you. 'You always talk so much when you hunt?' he said. I just smiled, though. If I hadn't been making so much noise, that Hedon never would have found us, and we might not have caught him. So you see, it's all a question of definition—whether you think of yourself as hunter or hunted, and how you make use of that. And that gets us back to words again, doesn't it?"

Beauty stared at her as if she'd come from another planet. He had never wanted a hunting partner less. She'd been kind and helpful, true—but so much chatter turned his stomach. It made him positively disharmonious, tilted his equanimity. Once more, he measured his words: "I hope you do not talk so much when you hunt."

There was a second of silence, punctuated by an eruption of laughter so loud that the Flutterby woke up. Lon raised his glass. "To the hunt," he said.

"To the hunt!" they all toasted, and a cheer went up. Soon, everyone was talking at once, and even Beauty relented to the mood. Toasts were answered with vows, the music resumed, the dancers whirled in every corner. Humbelly fluttered until she fell asleep again. Even Isis got up on her hind legs to do a rowdy jig.

Josh was so sated, he was moved to sing a song, which he seldom did in the company of strangers. So he bade the musicians follow him as he sang out, in a lovely, clear voice:

> "The hunter, he did cross the plain,
> and then he ventured home again,
> the merry merry feast will soon begin,
> among the leaves so green-o."

At which point Beauty joined in with his gravelly baritone, in various harmony:

> "Well it's hey down down,
> ho down down,
> hey down ho down derry derry down,
> among the leaves so green-o."

Followed by more cheers, more music. More drink, talk, play. Stories, gloriously told, of battles heroically fought, of journeys unconditionally traveled, of mortal trials tried.

Until finally, some time later, Lon stood and said he would be going to sleep. He showed the guests to their sleeping quarters—a lush, private room for each—telling them it would be his honor if each of them would take to bed a chosen favorite from the harem. Josh and Beauty politely refused; Lon intimated that he understood, though Josh suspected the Vampire felt hurt, if not insulted by the rebuff. Jasmine selected the beautiful young servant boy with all the jewelry, picked him up easily in her arms; carried him off into her bedroom.

Lon had a special surprise for Isis: a champion Persian with long violet fur. The two cats eyed each other, sidled up next to each other. "Mnnnnnn," said Isis, as the Persian followed her hotly up a dark corridor into a seldom-used section of the cave.

Humbelly woke up long enough to flutter a bit nearer the glowing coals; and finally, the whole household was asleep.

At sunrise they convened in the library: walls engorged with books, ceiling to floor; Josh had never seen such. He stared in profound wonder at the stacks of antique volumes, folio editions, gold-leaf bindings. "You can read," he whispered to Lon as if it were a shared secret. Lon only laughed.

Josh considered carefully, then with great ceremony asked Lon if it would be possible for him to leave his scriptures—including those he'd written the previous night, before falling asleep—leave them with Lon, for safekeeping, here in the company of all these other books. "They could share thoughts with each other when no one else was reading them," Josh added.

Lon was touched. He accepted Joshua's treasure with high moment, saying he would be honored to harbor the writings with his own coveted texts. Gently, he placed Joshua's records on the shelf; when the manuscripts were finally nestled, he took Josh by the arm and said, "There is something I would show you."

He led Josh to a hidden door, then through it to a

hidden room. Once inside, Joshua momentarily had to
hold his breath: all manner of surpassing things were
here.

"My museum," said Lon.

Josh walked from shelf to shelf, intuitively and completely silent. Strange artifacts sat in delicate display,
mysterious machines from another time. Colored glass
beakers, some connected by elaborate coils, filled one
whole wall. A small collection of crumbling, ancient
books was propped on the end cubicle. Josh read the
titles: all contained the word *Alchemy*.

Another section of the room was devoted to various
dried herbs, animal parts, and raw gemstones. Timidly
Josh walked up and down aisles of curious devices.
All were labeled: Slide Projector, Television, Film
Projector, Audio Cassettes, Video Cassettes, Holographic Laser Projector, Tape Recorder, Lava-Lite,
Cloud Chamber, Van de Graaf Generator, Jacob's
Ladder, Crystal Ball, Alpha Wave Stimulator, Cardiac Pacemaker, Self-Contained Underwater Breathing Apparatus, Electroencephalograph, Radio, Mi-
crowave Oven, Nutty Putty, Operator-Gene Ligase
Control-Pak, Refractive Index Distortion Panel, Hyperbaric Gestation Modulator, Magic Wand, Geiger
Counter, Bubble Gum, Magic Eight Ball, Hypno-Lite;
the shelves were endless, the articles on them potent
with silence.

"The magic of times past lives here; antiques of
sorcery from every age," Lon spoke from the doorway. "And though museum it is, every item here is in
working order—oh, the moving parts must be hand-
turned, now; electricity is such a rare luxury—but the
magic contained in these potions and contraptions is
still strong. You can feel it when you walk in the
room."

Indeed, Josh had been aware of this power from
the moment he'd stepped in. He felt as if he were still
holding his breath.

"I've never shown this room to anyone before," Lon
went on. "It is my special gift to you. In this way we
share the magic, as our books share thoughts with
each other."

Josh was overwhelmed with the magnanimity of the gift, the magnificence of the room. He said, simply, "I'd like to see it again, someday."

Lon smiled. "So you shall," he said, and led Josh back into the library.

When all at last assembled, fond adieus were bid, along with stern admonitions.

"Go east first," said Lon. "That is safest. Don't turn south until Mirror Lake. From there you must rely on your hunter's sense only."

"We'll be fine, Lon," answered Jasmine. "You also take care."

The noble Vampire took a burnished brass-handled épée off the wall and handed it to his old friend. "This blade has tasted the blood of many foes. May it never hunger in your hands."

She took the épée from its scabbard, lovingly examined it, replaced it in its sheath, strapped it to her waist. "I'll use it well on this hunt, dear friend." They hugged long and silently.

To the others, each, he gave a tiny gold locket, shaped like a blood-drop. Josh strapped his to his belt; Beauty tied his in his mane; Isis wore hers tightly at the neck. "These you must keep with you always," said Lon solemnly. "If ever you need my help, send this locket back, and I will come. Or show it to my friends wherever they be, and they will aid you." He hugged them all briefly. "Enough," he said. His eyes were moist.

Finally he escorted them to another hidden entrance, deep in the golden morning of the forest, where they emerged through a bark-peeling door in the trunk of a massive eucalyptus tree. The Vampire watched them disappear quietly among the green shadows. "Go in good blood," he said, and returned to his cave.

CHAPTER 6

In Which The Hunt Heats Up

THEY walked in silence as the wood thinned and then thickened again, while morning doves sang of love in the leaves. Every degree the sun rose through the trees, it burned off another minute, another dewdrop. Squirrels chattered, frogs belched. The forest was manifest.

The travelers walked single file along a narrow game path that meandered east toward Mirror Lake. Beauty led the way, Jasmine behind him. Josh brought up the rear. Isis darted back and forth between Josh and Jasmine, stopping suddenly, getting tangled in one's legs, then running slyly back to the other. Humbelly, who found six thousand distractions in the spring-born flowers, was rarely seen—though not rarely enough for Isis, who took a flamboyant swing at the Flutterby whenever the opportunity presented itself.

Joshua had time to study Jasmine's backside at length. Smooth, perfectly defined muscles contoured her legs, from her feet—which were bare—up to her mid-thighs. Across her back was thrown a mid-length cape, mottled green and brown, over which her orange-red hair streaked like lava from her head.

She piqued Joshua's curiosity. She implied a great deal merely with her body—the way she carried herself, with a cool physical presence that intimated there were things about her which could not be seen, or perhaps even known. Then, of course, there were the myths about Neuromans; the legends: they were immortal, some said; devils, others would swear; they had powers, secrets, resources.

Josh had never, to his knowledge, met one before. He certainly hadn't expected anything like Jasmine.

After an hour walking in her footsteps, after much internal debate, after titillation finally outstretched intimidation, Josh walked up closer to her and said, "Are you really two hundred fifty years old?"

She turned her head briefly over her shoulder, smiled, then kept walking, maintaining Beauty's steady pace. "Nearer three hundred," she said. "Born in nineteen hundred and eighty-six A.D., a year of great changes, great change. Know what happened that year?"

Josh shook his head. "Don't know much but tall tales and campfire stories about anything before the Coming of the Ice."

"The Coming of Ice, now wasn't *that* a time. Right after the Great Quake, summer of 2191," she reminisced. "Some people predicted that, you know, but then people were predicting lots of things that never happened, so who knows. Anyway, 1986 was the big nuclear power plant disaster back east, killed over a million people. I don't remember it personally, of course, I was just born then, but people talked about it with tears in their eyes long into the next generation. Some antinuclear terrorists just took control of the facility at Oceanspring and threatened to blow it up. So the government sent in its antiterrorist force, and the place blew up anyway. Million people died. Neptune's Middle Fin, if that wasn't the end of nuclear plants, no doubt about it."

Beauty threw half a glance behind him: he thought he'd made it perfectly clear he did not approve of conversation while hunting. In addition, his sense of propriety was at least mildly upset by the epithet Jasmine had used—a vaguely derogatory, crudely sexual allusion to a mythical part of Neptune's anatomy. Not that he believed in Neptune; but neither did he believe in impropriety. The others didn't notice his glare, though, so he simply picked up his stride. The path was becoming overgrown with vines and mulch, as if it were less frequently trod in this area; but the Centaur forged on.

"What's a nuclear plant?" asked Joshua. He'd heard the word, he thought, but wasn't sure. Somehow, he had the impression a nuclear plant had no leaves and no roots and was shaped like a poison mushroom.

"Ever hear of uranium?" Jasmine asked as they stumbled over a clatter of dead branches.

"Geranium?" answered Josh. A wild flower, then; not at all like a mushroom.

"Never mind," laughed Jasmine. "It's just as well. If no one ever finds out about nuclear energy again, it's probably just as well. Kind of sad, though, to think of all the history that's been lost." Jasmine had spent the last fifty years of her life alone, more or less—in endless exploration of this adventurous new world—consciously alone, wonderfully alone. She'd had enough of people during her first two hundred fifty years to last her many lifetimes.

But lately, just lately, she'd begun to get lonely. So it was with considerable zest and feeling that she'd decided to string along with Josh and Beauty. She liked them, she felt she could talk to them of all the things that mattered—felt, in fact, now that she'd begun, absolutely compelled to talk, for whatever cathartic reasons.

But now as she started to ramble, she was overcome with a certain melancholy. It was a sense of loss, more than anything—of all the things she'd known in her life that would never again be; things no one would ever again know, that she could never fully explain, however much she wanted to, however much they wanted to hear.

She went on to Josh, "There's so much you can't understand—how different it was . . . before. You have this muddy notion. From fragments of old books that still exist; from legends made of half-truths that squeezed through all the apocalyptic changes of the twenty-second century; from the fantasies and lies of wandering storytellers who heard it from others who never lived through it, who never even knew anyone who lived through it. Fragments is all you have. Very few of us are left anymore who knew it then as it really was."

Josh heard the remorse in her voice. What an odd creature she was—all clever and sad and mysterious.

And how much she seemed to know. He could learn from her, he was certain. He felt about her almost the way he felt when coming across an old book—expectant, ravenous for the knowledge he would gain, wonderfully scared at the naïveté he would lose. And here she was before him, a living book. He wondered if all books shared the sadness he felt in Jasmine.

He gingerly put his question forth—to tap her font and to console her in her isolation: "Tell me . . . about these nuclear plants."

Yes, she liked these people. She could see even Beauty was listening intently to her, though he of course maintained his silence, to set a good example. "Nuclear plants," she continued, "were a way to make energy using a powerful poison. And it was a good way to make energy, but the poison was too strong for us to contain. It exploded all over us, it leaked out of the waste cans it was stored in, it made everyone paranoid and power-mad." She paused a moment. "In fact, I thought I wanted to talk about it, but now I've started, I'd rather talk about something else."

She talked about her hometown in 1986: the boy she loved when she was eleven; the way the air felt just before a tornado; the way the jasmine smelled in her bedroom as it bloomed on summer evenings. That was why she'd taken the name she'd kept all these years, because of that perfumed memory. She talked herself out just short of a burbling swamp directly in their path. Beauty veered right to avoid the decay. Jasmine held back a breath—she sensed left was a better direction.

Before she could voice her hesitation, though, three creatures leapt out of the brush, smelling of death. Accidents. One had horrible rows of teeth; one had an insect sort of tube for a mouth; one had no face at all, just a thick fleshy head, blind and neckless. Foul, angry creatures.

Jasmine had her sword out in an instant, and before Beauty even turned, the Neuroman had decapitated the first grizzly Accident with a single sweep of her blade.

Isis sprang high at the second attacker, sinking her

claws deep into the thing's eyes. It screamed and reeled backward, bringing its huge hands up to its face. The little Cat clung to the Accident's shoulder, though, gashing at its neck with tooth and claw, until she struck jugular; and jumped to the ground.

Josh was caught a mighty blow on the back by the Faceless One, and fell forward into the heavy brush. The creature quickly closed for the kill, but Josh turned and thrust his knife into the eyeless meaty head: the Accident fell hard and still beside him.

Beauty reared up to bring his hooves swiftly down on the screaming creature already mortally wounded by Isis; and in a moment, stove in its brain.

In thirty seconds it was all over.

Josh picked himself up painfully. A large bruise was already starting to flower across the lower half of his back. Jasmine wiped the putrid blood from her blade over some dry grass, then carefully resheathed it. Isis, puffed up to twice her size, slowly let her fur down, still suspicious of movement in the dead Accidents.

Beauty snorted. "We had best leave quickly. Even Accidents have friends in this wood."

Josh pulled his knife out of the eyeless creature's head, cleaned the steel with dirt and moss. He felt good. He was another Accident closer to Dicey.

Beauty felt bad that he'd not even had time to string arrow, so he took some of his anger out on Jasmine. "Perhaps if we made less noise . . ." he glowered.

She bowed a token bow, a gesture to his pride. He prided himself on his honesty as well, though; so added, with only a little less force: "Still, you were quick. And fought well." With which he turned setting a brisk canter down the path.

Silently, the others followed.

The little compartment was dark and cramped and ripe with the sweaty smell of fear. It rocked slowly, over bumps, up, down, to the side. Rose could see shafts of daylight filter through cracks in the wooden walls of the covered cart: the light shifted over the shadowed forms of the six others who were tied up around her: souls in Hell.

Outside she could hear the bantering growls of her sentries as they walked alongside the cart. She had their voices memorized, so she could identify them if she ever . . . the thought never went further.

She guessed it was late morning now, by the color of the slivers of light that crossed her eyes. Late morning and a light wind. Nearby, the sound of—

There was a bump, a dip; a crash, as the entire cart tipped to a forty-five-degree angle and lay still. Rose sat pressed against the grainy wall; she waited without moving. Suddenly the back door was thrown open, and a cascade of light filled the little cell. A figure stood in the obscure beyond. "Everybody out," it said. The seven bound hostages piled out of the cart, then stood, squinting, on the grass.

Rose viewed the situation, her hands tied behind her. The cart they were being carried in had broken a wheel—it now lay at a dead tilt in the ditch. Irreparable.

The seven prisoners huddled together—Rose, Dicey, Ollie, and four others whom Rose had never seen before their mutual internment. Their hands were all bound behind them. Surrounding them were eight guards: three Vampires, four Accidents, a Griffin. The guards were discussing their dilemma in low tones. Dicey and Rose came closer together and whispered.

"What'll they do now?" asked Dicey. Her voice quavered through her stoic façade. Ollie still looked to be in shock, huddled into himself, unspeaking, autistic.

"Don't know," answered Rose. "They'll have to walk us wherever they're taking us, I suppose."

"Josh will be sure to find us, now," Dicey concluded. "We'll be leaving sign all over the ground."

Rose nodded. "Sign and scent," she specified, and spat on the grassy dirt beside her. Dicey smiled, twisted around. Her hands still bound behind her, she delicately maneuvered her fingers to pull from Rose's head a long, dark hair, letting it drop to the ground.

One of the Vampires looked over. "What's going on

there?" he demanded. Rose and Dicey were silent. The Vampire strode over in three large steps, grabbed the young girl by the shoulder, pulled her back to his cohorts. She screamed as he put his teeth into her neck and sucked her ruby blood.

She ceased her cry and froze in terror, while he took his pleasure. Rose stood, horrified, for a few moments, then ran at the fiend. The other prisoners stared blankly, dumbly on. One of the other Vampires struck the onrushing Rose a dispassionate backhand to the face: she fell, unconscious before she hit the ground. The creatures all laughed.

The Vampire abusing Dicey pulled his mouth from her neck, licked his lips. Blood oozed from the marks he'd left in her. She whimpered. The Vampire passed her to his friend beside him, and said, "For you, Bal-Sire. Primed and siphoned." They all laughed again, as the Vampire called Bal forced Dicey to him, clamping his mouth on her bleeding neck.

She closed her eyes, went limp in his grip. He finished drinking quickly, though, only to shake her awake rudely. Into her stark, staring face he spoke, cool, cruel, articulate:

> "A sudden blow: the great wings beating still
> Above the staggering girl, her thighs caressed
> By the dark webs, her nape caught in his bill
> He holds her helpless breast . . ."

Dicey's eyes returned Bal's gaze in mad, stupefied horror, her blood drying at the corners of his mouth. He abruptly passed her on to the third Vampire, who slurped disgustingly at her open wound.

The first Vampire grabbed her wrist, now, bit it, and began lapping at the flow. Bal stopped him quickly, though, saying, "Enough, Sire Uli. A dead Human is of little use to anyone." One of the Accidents who was listening turned to the one beside him and said, "Uman dugro. Oglo dor." All the Accidents laughed.

Bal smiled. "The Accidents have their own feelings about Human life," he said. Uli let go the bleeding wrist of the now swooning girl; the other Vampire extracted his teeth from her neck. She fainted. Uli dragged her back to the cluster of shuddering Humans and dropped her in a heap. A few yards away, Rose began groggily to awaken.

The Vampire resumed discussion. The Accidents stood together a short distance away, conversing with each other as softly as their ugly language permitted. The Griffin perched on a rock by himself, preening his feathers with a broken beak.

Josh peered over a shelf of rock at the motionless lake. No animal stood at the shore to drink; no fish stirred the surface. This water was dead.

Josh turned back to his companions. "No one there. Let's head south."

The others agreed. "Animals never use this lake anymore," said Jasmine. "It's all salt and peat."

They dog-legged south, the four of them. Somehow Humbelly got left behind at a floral distraction. Each of the others noticed her absence at some point, but each thought, with reason, it was probably for the best; so no one said a word.

After an hour of steady jogging, they came to a span of rolling meadow. First a long, furze-covered dip, then a slow, bushy ascent, where a muddy game-path climbed the rise, veering right.

There'd been fire in this part of the forest, years before; so all the trees were young. The evidence of old fire reminded Beauty of his farmhouse aflame, causing him to walk more quietly. Everyone seemed to pick up on this feeling, as if echoes of the roaring blaze pervaded the air. Jasmine watched every step, lest she crush some fragile recollection. The thin shadows cast by the saplings crisscrossed the ground like bones. Even Isis trod quietly.

Joshua stepped softly in any case: the pain in his flank, where the Accident had struck him, was beginning to nag, like an unwanted guest. Every pace was accompanied by a small hammer in his back, tap, tap, tap. He made no mention of his pain, though, for he was still young, and foolishly thought stoicism was the stuff with which the wise tempered their bravery.

It was over this charred ground that Beauty first noted the creature circling high above them. Jasmine followed his gaze. "It's been keeping pace with us about three miles," she said.

"You have good eyes," he commented.

Josh looked up, squinting. "What is it?" he asked.

"Too high to tell," Jasmine replied.

"Best to keep moving," Beauty murmured, never missing a step.

Isis hissed once and scampered ahead, crouching in every available shadow, then darting on.

Unconsciously, they moved faster: flying animals were dangerous. Even if this one wasn't a Vampire on the prowl, it had to be regarded as life-threatening until proven otherwise. And it was always unnerving to be watched. Beauty strung an arrow; Jasmine and Josh bared their blades.

They passed under a wild-grape arbor, and when they emerged, the shape in the sky was gone. Not one of them breathed easier.

A bamboo grove spread before them, like a green rustling sea, filling all directions. And since there was no way to estimate the extent of its perimeter, into its depths they plunged. Within a matter of yards, they were completely surrounded by the ten-foot stalks.

Headway was difficult The grove thinned and thickened. Jasmine led the way, so she could chop with her épée as necessary. The constant *sshhhhssshh-hsshh* of the wind in the bamboo made tracking even harder, for now auditory as well as visual cues were lost. They tried to aim due south.

For many minutes they pressed this way, when suddenly a large-winged shadow passed directly over the leafy tops above their heads and thundered into the brush beyond them. They stopped short, breathing only with the wind. Up, ahead, a furious rustling drew near. Then it ceased.

Beauty, Josh, and Jasmine separated, their weapons drawn, and circled the recently active silence. Isis remained behind, to coordinate the attack.

Silently, Jasmine crept around behind the interloper.

She felt edgy, but somehow tranquil at the same time: she'd been in this moment a hundred times before and she moved with liquid purpose. Poised, confident, she waited for the signal to attack.

Josh had somewhat more difficulty. His back was hurting worse; he wasn't certain where the beast had come to rest; he wasn't certain what the beast even was. He was anxious; but determined.

Beauty viewed the situation with the most equanimity as he made his way through the brush around the right flank: Beauty was, at base, a hunter; and this was a hunt. Beauty felt in balance.

Isis waited a full minute for the others to get positioned. Then, at what she sensed to be the right moment, she let out a signal screech, and the others descended from three directions on their quarry. They pounced into what proved to be a small clearing in the grove. In the center of the clearing was a wounded roan Pegasus.

The winged horse tried to rear back when the three armed hunters approached; but her hind foot was badly damaged, so she stumbled to the ground, her big nostrils flaring, wings flapping wildly, terror in her eye. Beauty laid his bow on the ground in front of her, to show her he meant no harm. The others sheathed their weapons.

Beauty knelt down beside the frightened creature, stroked her head evenly, calmed her fevered stare. "So this is our sinister flying stalker," he said to his companions, his own relief mingled with the winghorse's anguish.

Josh saw that one great feathered wing was caught between two bamboos. He freed the wing and folded it gently back against the Pegasus' dark, sweating body. Isis entered the clearing now; suspiciously, she hung back. Jasmine, meanwhile, examined the animal's wounded hind leg.

"This isn't just broken," she said, wrinkling her brow. She brought her nose up to the raw skin over the fetlock. "This foot's been burned."

Josh walked over to Isis, scratched her between the ears. The Cat closed her eyes, concentrating on nothing but the fingers.

Beauty nuzzled the still-terrified Pegasus, then softly whinnied into her ear. "What's the matter, girl? You step in a fire?"

At that moment another shadow passed over the clearing: a long shadow, lasting many seconds. The Pegasus shrieked and tried to stand, knocking Beauty back, kicking Jasmine's chest. Josh looked up to see the barbed tip of a green scaly tail float quickly through his field of vision and out of sight. Isis hissed.

In less than a second a huge stench filled the grove, accompanied by the baritone sigh of gas escaping out a tunnel under pressure. With a strength and speed they could not have imagined, Jasmine leapt into the thickest bamboo, dragging Josh and half pulling Beauty with her, as she screamed the single word "Dragon!" In the next moment the entire clearing erupted with a muted *wamp,* in flame.

The bamboo shielded them from much of the heat; but even so, Josh got singed, and Beauty lost some tail. They looked back into the clearing: the ground and closest trees were scorched black and bare; the dead Pegasus was all aflame, its burning feathers sending charcoal smoke to the sky.

"We haven't much time," Jasmine breathed rapidly. "It'll fire this grove until we're all cooked. Beauty, where's your bow?"

The Centaur felt at his back, but it wasn't around. He looked back into the clearing. "There," he said. They all looked. The bow lay on the charred ground, burning beside the pyre of the winged horse.

Suddenly the shadow passed again, closer this time, and immediately a section of trees went up in flame across the other side of the clearing. Josh twisted to get a look at the beast, but it hurt his back so much—from the blow the Accident had given him—he cried out in pain and fell to the ground.

Jasmine yelled, "Come on, then," to Beauty, over the roar of the burning trees, and ran into the clearing. Without a second's thought, he followed: she'd taken command of the situation, and he trusted her. She pulled out her épée and began chopping at the base of a sapling whose topmost branches were blazing furiously. "Dragons aren't that hard to kill," she panted, "but we've got to do this fast, we might not get another chance."

"I . . . I have no experience Dragon-fighting," he confessed. "I was always taught to leave them be, and . . ."

"Okay, here," she finished chopping and handed him the base of the burning stalk. It looked like a torch with a fifteen-foot handle. He took it from her as she climbed on his back. "Joshua," she yelled, "crawl through the tall grass toward the burning area. Quick." She directed Beauty into the section adjacent to the area of flaming bamboo. "It'll fire the area opposite to the one it just fired," she whispered. "Fortunately, they have pretty stereotyped behavior." Just as she spoke the grove opposite them burst into smoking conflagration. "Shades of napalm," she muttered.

Now only the last and west edge of the clearing remained safe. "Move to the center of the eastern edge," she whispered. Beauty moved silently through the thicket and almost stepped on Josh.

"Watch out!" Josh yelled under his breath.

"Quiet," Jasmine said. Then, to Beauty: "Now. It'll fire the area across from us next, and then it should fly directly over us. As soon as you see that explosion, I'm going to stand on your shoulders, you hand me the torch, and then hold on to my legs so I don't fall off you. Got it?"

Before he could answer, the distant grasses glowered into flame, and Jasmine jumped up onto his shoulders. He handed her the burning bamboo, gripped her calves tightly so she wouldn't fall.

Jasmine thrust herself up until she stood straight on the Centaur's shoulders, wobbling slightly, the long torch in her hands, the highest leaves of the bamboo grove scraping her chest. She looked up in time to see the Dragon swooping past her, perhaps ten feet above her head: a thirty-foot winged lizard, green, foul-smelling, evil, its eyes on stalks, its mouth dripping flame. It wasn't looking down, but back; so it didn't see her. Its pale, scaled underbelly glided sleekly over Jasmine's face, and when two-thirds of its length had passed her by, she rammed the burning bamboo stick up the beast's cloaca. The creature instantly exploded; the shock wave blew Jasmine to the ground.

The three of them lay there for a moment, surrounded by dying fires in a dying wind. Then without a word, they stood and walked back to where the Dragon had fallen.

It was as ugly in death as life. Its belly was blown wide open, from breastbone to tail, its putrescent entrails spilled on the ground. A webbed spine rose like a sail from its back, between two great spiky leather wings. Its stalked eyes lay askew in the dirt, its black mouth was open.

"Wretched miscreant," Jasmine glowered, shaking her head. Then louder: "Stupid brutes, and slow. Their bowels are ballooned up with methane—they fart constantly. Then when they want to breathe fire they just belch while they gnash their teeth—their teeth spark when they hit lots of elemental magnesium in them, I think. In fact, we should take some with us for flints." She bent down, picked up a rock, and smashed in the Dragon's dentition. Then she picked up the black, broken tooth fragments and handed two each to Josh and Beauty.

Josh was impressed. He prided himself on his hunting abilities, but he'd rarely seen anyone as cool under fire as Jasmine had been. He put the flints carefully in his pocket—more to be kept as a reminder of this event than as a means for starting some future campfire.

Beauty, too, was beginning to have mixed feelings about the Neuroman. She'd fought well twice, now. If only she didn't talk so much.

Only Jasmine failed to feel very triumphant: there was little satisfaction for her in killing large dumb animals who were merely searching for food. No challenge and little justice. She satisfied herself only in the knowledge that there was little loss here—Dragons were simply not very worthwhile.

With a sudden thought, Josh looked up. "Isis," he said. Then he called, "Isis?"

Momentarily the little Cat appeared, the sorriest of expressions on her face. Half of her backside fur was burned away, leaving pink, naked skin. She grimaced as the others burst out laughing. She briefly assessed the situation, walked over to the dead reptile, and perfunctorily urinated on its face.

As they made ready to leave, Beauty said, "Your knife, Joshua." He took the blade from his friend and neatly sliced open the lizard's thoracic cavity. Next, he located a long, strong rib—still intact from the explosion in the Dragon's belly—and carefully cut it out of the rib cage. He stripped the fat and muscle from the bone, notched both ends, and finally laid the six-foot rib in the dirt. The others watched patiently.

Next, the Centaur filleted open the inner aspect of the beast's back legs, and with careful dissection exposed the length of the sinewy flexor tendon that ran from the hip past the knee—the hamstring. He cut the tendon at both ends, then tightly secured each end to one of the notched tips of the rib he'd prepared, stretching the tendon taut across the arc of the bone. Now he was finished, and he slung his strong new bow over his shoulder. "Let us not dally," he spoke evenly, and resumed a steady southward march, as if nothing had happened.

The others smiled comfortably and followed. They all felt in good company.

On the far side of the bamboo wood the terrain became hilly, covered with scrub. The aging sun cast long shadows. It was turning into a long day. Josh felt tired.

It was a world of struggle through which the companions made their way. The signs of this were bright at every turn: in broken, half-buried skeletons; in suspicious, hidden eyes that stared at the passing party from bushes and caves; in the totems that stood cockeyed at random intervals, staking territory, warding evil; in empty shelters, crumbled with age. Struggle and change.

At the edge of a slow rise with an eastern face,

in a shallow stone gully, they found the crippled cart. Footprints were everywhere. The smells of fur and dander settled over the grass like a film of new snow. Josh kneeled, picking up a long strand of Human hair from a low branch. Hard sign.

"It can't be long now," said Josh, his eyes focused in the direction the mass of footprints headed.

Isis, sniffing the ground, suddenly hissed. Beauty ran over, knelt, rubbed the caky dirt between his fingers. "Blood," he said. He smelled it himself. "Human." He paused. "Dicey's, I think."

The hairs on Joshua's neck stood upright in ancient response. He began trotting south, close on the wake of the disaster.

Nightfall. The four stalkers perched on a cliff ledge. Below them, in the distance, spread along the furrows of a dying creek, lay the Accident camp. Perhaps fifty Vampires and other creatures mingled with their shadows among the fires and tents of the bivouac, while clumps of Humans could be seen tied together in the outlying darkness. It was far enough away that faces could not be seen.

"Too many to storm," whispered Josh. "We need a plan."

"I say we wait here until they move out," proposed Jasmine. "We can strike them easier on the trail."

"No," answered Beauty, "we may lose them. We have them now."

"We have nothing," Jasmine shook her head. "We have dust in our mouths."

Beauty scowled. Josh waved them both quiet. "We need a plan. I'll slip down there and check it out. Maybe I can even cut them loose, we can just all sneak away." He generally tried not to exhibit such bravado; but the twisting pain in his lower back was growing almost too loud to ignore, and made Josh bold with fear, reckless with urgency.

Beauty shook his head. "It is too dangerous. You would get caught. Besides. I want that Vampire's neck in my hands."

"Not until Dicey is safe," cautioned Joshua.

Isis, whose head had been turning from one to the other as each spoke, walked up to Josh. "We're your girl," she said. Her eyes penetrated his.

He knitted his brow at first, then realized what the little Cat was saying. "No," he said, scratching her between the ears, "it's too dangerous, Fur-face."

Jasmine's expression illuminated. "No, she's right, she's the one to slip down into the camp. She'll be able to sneak in easier than any of us. She can tell the others we're here, without being seen. She may even be able to bite their bonds loose. If not, she can scout the area, come back here, and tell us the lay. I say she goes."

Beauty had to agree. "I think the Neuroman may be right this time, Joshua. I think . . ."

Josh was shaking his head saying, "She can't go, and that's all there is to it, and she can't go because . . ." But as he looked around to where Isis had been sitting, he saw he'd been talking to the wind. Isis was gone.

She crouched under a thicket, her ears forward, her nostrils flared, her pupils dilated by darkness and excitement. In the near distance, three Accidents sat around a dwindling campfire, playing some kind of game with carved bones. Isis suppressed an impulse to mark this perimeter with a few drops of her urine and leave the creatures to their own bad company.

Two Vampires walked over, stood very near her hiding spot as they spoke to each other of easy conquests over powerful foes. She could see their feet from her bush, smell their smell. She remained crouching, motionless as earth, breathless as stone. The Vampires moved on. Isis respired.

She skittered silently through some high grass to the back of a tent at the edge of the firelight. Inside the tent, voices mixed.

"—a company of Jarl's Guard in the forest . . . tortured two of the Accident—"

"—damn their eyes, what do they want with our lot? Double the sentries, then—"

"—or if we stay here any longer—"

"—must cross the Big Stick by the end of—"

"—only the Queen—"

Isis couldn't make out much of the conversation, but the smells were strictly Vampire, strong and pungent. She tiptoed around the side of the tent, waited in the dancing shadow. A breeze came up from the direction of the creek bed, then died; but now there was a new smell. A Human smell. The bloody-dirt smell she'd found earlier in the day by the broken-down cart.

She sidled along a fallen tree crawling with termites; padded up the creek's ravine; stopped short as a rat ran across her path, bold as brass; walked more slowly, approaching camp noises: clattering pans, laughter, growls. She could see now that the tents formed a large loose circle, with bonfires scattered about. Empty carts were parked at the mouth of what seemed to be a canyon of sorts. Groups of ten or twelve Humans were tied at the ankles to each other, in the areas outlying the heat from the fires. An Accident guarded each group, but most of the guards were drinking, talking with friends, dozing: it was a fearful collection of animals, and none of them much thought anybody would be foolish enough to attack them here.

Isis followed the blood-smell she remembered from the afternoon. It led her up the gully to a cluster of prisoners, most of whom were asleep. The Accident who guarded them was nodding off against a rock. All the myriad frightening odors vibrated in the cool night air.

Isis gingerly approached the young sleeping girl with the strong blood-smell. This was the one. She had bruises and punctures all over her neck and wrist. Isis put out her paw, touched the girl's arm. No response. She put out her claws and pressed them firmly against the girl's pale skin. The girl moaned and turned, arousing the older female Human who slept beside her. The older one opened her eyes, looked straight at Isis, made to speak. Isis raised her paw to her mouth and said: "Shhh."

The older girl sat up, startled. Isis whispered,

"We're here." The older Human began to speak again, obviously confused, but Isis raised her paw, walked three steps to Rose's ankle, and began to gnaw at her ropes.

Josh kept his gaze fixed on the Vampire encampment, but could see no unusual movement. He couldn't decide whether this was good or bad. Beauty stood near a young birch, cutting arrows. Jasmine sat, eyes closed, in full lotus position, apparently asleep.

Joshua was uncomfortable. Not just from the emotional tension—the infinitely distant nearness of Dicey and Rose; but physically discomfited as well. He turned. He sat. He couldn't find a good position. He took out quill and paper and tried to set the record, but couldn't find the words. His back, heavy with the ugly mark left by the Accident, was steadily throbbing. He stood up, felt his forehead break into a sweat. He walked several steps back from the cliff face, opened his pants to pass water against a tree.

It wasn't water he passed. It was blood.

Then the cold sweat broke over him again, like a thick winter wave. Then he passed out.

When he awoke he was lying on his back on good old ground, Jasmine's face hovering above him to the right, Beauty's to the left. "What happened?" he said.

"You're losing blood," warned Jasmine. "Lie still."

"But what—"

"Your kidney was damaged—torn, probably—during the fight today," Jasmine spoke very slowly. "It may heal, if you can lie very still. For two or three days."

"Three days!" Josh rasped. Beauty remained silent, stern. "Ridiculous," Josh began to laugh, but the pain in his back stabbed him with brutal disregard.

"I was once a doctor," Jasmine continued. "Listen to me." She brought her face close, forcing Josh to look at it. "It's not a bad laceration, or you'd have bled to death by now. Still, if it doesn't heal, you'll continue to lose blood, and you will die. It's that simple."

Josh looked to Beauty for support, but Beauty was

clearly worried. Josh looked back to Jasmine. "But the Vampires . . ." he said. He couldn't help flinching from the flank pain the force of his words provoked.

Beauty nodded slowly, as if to himself. "Perhaps it *would* be best to wait until they break camp," he spoke the words deliberately, each a dart pinning Josh to the ground. "We can choose our terrain, to our advantage. Perhaps the Neuroman *was* . . . right." He had difficulty with the last word, but his conviction over Joshua's safety was strong. Josh, pressed low under the heart and weight of it, could not move.

They carried him delicately down to a large cavern Jasmine had discovered in the cliff wall, approachable only by a steep narrow path, protected from view by a gorsey overhang. In addition to the natural camouflage, they covered the entrance over with palm branches and fern, so when they finally gathered together inside, no one could glimpse them from any angle; nor could they see out.

Jasmine regaled them with stories of past adventures, partly to take the edge off Beauty's obvious impatience at the delay, partly to ease Josh to sleep, take his mind off his injury.

"We used to hunt Dragon all the time," she began. "Big old fart-bags. Used to be a price on their skins, for you know, fashion clothes. But it was a sport, too. We'd see how close we could get; it was the greatest feat if we could touch them before we killed them. There was a time when there were arenas for Dragon-fights—like bullfights, just you and the Dragon, and sometimes your picadors. Oh, it was grand theater, I can tell you. The matador, in a little asbestos suit, and then the Dragon, overfed to give him gas, and then starved to make him mean. Wasn't much of a fight, of course, even so—they were never the brightest animals. Oh, the dance the matador would do around the beast, though—so much ritual and romance. Pretty much wiped out the Dragon population, I'm afraid—that's why you hardly see them anymore. Not much loss, though, far as I'm concerned—they were always creatures who were much more wonderful in myth than in reality. Some things are just like that, I guess—

brilliant fantasies but they just don't translate well into the real world. Wouldn't surprise me if most fantasies ended up that way, in fact." She stopped talking to look over at Joshua: his eyes were closed. Jasmine smiled and returned to the perch on the cliff ledge above them, to take the first watch. Beauty and Josh, in the cave below, settled into a deep brooding silence, until at last Joshua fell completely into a deep, brooding sleep.

Isis was almost through Rose's ropes, when the Accident sneezed and woke up. Isis froze. The Accident's waking yellow eyes fell directly on the small, still Cat. "Glombo tog," spat the Accident. Cat-meat was a rare delicacy.

Isis didn't wait for further conversation; she scatted through the underbrush into the night.

"Tog lumpu! Oglondo tog!" bellowed the Accident, loping groggily after Isis.

Bal emerged from his tent. "What's the beast babbling?" he muttered with annoyance.

Uli, by his side, said, "Something about a Cat, Bal-Sire. Too much pepper-wine, the lout."

Isis tore back up the creek bed, scattering last year's leaves behind her. The Accident lumbered along in her trail, then stopped when she was obviously out of reach. "Tog debluk," he stormed. Angrily, he turned, to see who among his prisoners was responsible for this unsatisfactory interlude.

Isis dashed over the ridge, into a dispersion of ferns. She crouched, waiting. Ears up, tail puffed. No one came. Slowly, her fur came down, her claws retracted. Through the fronds that hid her, she could see, a hundred yards down, the campfires jump higher—stirred up and refueled by the bristling, aroused guards, the nervous lieutenants. Shadows jumped frightfully. Isis smiled, licked her paw, drew it over her ear, down her head. It was difficult being such a clever Cat in a world of such dull wit. Tedious is what it was, tedious beyond understanding. She felt thoroughly unappreciated—by the Accident, who didn't know how fast she could really run; by the Vampires, who didn't even

know she existed; by the prisoners, who hadn't known
what she was doing; by the crowd at the brothel, who
couldn't comprehend her art; by Beauty, who didn't
ken her cleverness; by everyone and everything who
didn't bother to notice exactly how terrific she was—
unappreciated by the world. Except for Josh. He understood her. He loved her. For him, she would do
all.

There was a scream, up the creek bed. Human, female. Shadows converged on the place where Isis had
left the prisoners. At the sound, at the movement, her
fur stood erect over her entire body. Her nostrils widened, her ears twitched. She took three quick steps out
of the fern cover; stopped, sniffed; and darted silently
back toward the enemy camp.

Josh was awakened by the sound of Jasmine sliding
furtively into the cave. She replaced the propped
branch she'd dislodged, to leave no trace of her entrance.

"What are—" began Beauty.

Jasmine brought her finger to her lips. "Shh," she
said. "Jarl's Elite Guard, again." She pointed to the
ceiling of the cave. "Above us now."

The three were totally silent for five full minutes.
Finally Beauty said, "I hear nothing."

Jasmine breathed easier. "Neither do I. That means
they can't hear us, either."

"What happened?" Josh whispered.

"I was watching over the cliff at the Vampire
camp. Nothing much doing. So I walked back about
fifty yards to get some water at the spring we passed,
when who do I see but that same damned bunch of
JEGS that was sniffing up our trail back at Lon's.
Fewer of them now, and scragglier. Meaner, too."

"Coming this way?"

"Coming, hell. I ran back to the little half-path we
found trailing down into this hole. Rigged up a loose
pile of rocks and gravel all along the area, so if anyone should start to wander down in this direction it
would kick off a slide and dump the stuff all over our
doorstep. Give us about a minute's notice. Anyway,

just as I finished, I peeked back over the cliff edge one more time, and there was the whole bunch, marching right up to our lookout perch. That's where they are now, thirty feet straight above us, just drooling over the perfect view they've got of the Vampires and Accidents."

"Maybe it will take their minds off us, for a change," suggested Beauty.

"I wish I could hear them," mumbled Josh.

"Thirty feet of rock is pretty good muffler," Jasmine said. "And all that foliage, and the overhang. Soundproof, at least." She let her eyes drift upward, then around to the three walls of the cave. "I just wish this place had a back door."

CHAPTER 7

On The Origin Of Species

BEAUTY laid arrow on string as he sat down facing the cave entrance. Josh dipped his quill pen in a puddle of bloody muddy urine, extracted some paper from the Scribe-tube still strapped to his leg, and began to write.

Jasmine laughed, not unkindly. "Lord, what fools these mortals be," she said.

Beauty looked annoyed. Joshua put down his pen. "Meaning what?" he replied.

She shrugged. "Meaning you're suddenly so somber. The Centaur there looks like he's ready to make his last stand, you're writing your final fare-thee-wells. Suddenly everyone's getting so *meaning*ful." She looked exasperated.

"What would you have us do?" demanded the Horse-man defensively.

"Nothing, absolutely nothing. Nothing *to* do. We're here, they're there, we've just got to sit tight. No use getting morbid about it. If they start to come our way, we'll hear them. *Then* we can get significant. Until then, I'd just as soon tell stories to pass the time."

"Stories?"

"Yeah, know any good ones?" she smiled. "Stories about mortality are my favorite. They're entertaining *and* instructive. Anybody know the story of the appointment in Samara?"

"It seems to me," Beauty spoke slowly, "that stories about death can hold little entertainment value for those as close to its gates as we."

"On the contrary, Brother Beauty," Jasmine twinkled. "Distance breeds disinterest, and humor is the mother of truth. If you can joke or spin a tale about the jaws of your darkest fear, you might just end up learning something about teeth."

"Easy words for an immortal," said the Centaur. It was not simply his own circling death on his mind; it was Rose's as well, and Joshua's.

"Is that what you believe?" Jasmine's eyebrows went up.

"Some say so."

"If words were only as powerful as the Scribes would like to think . . ." she began. Josh tensed. Jasmine stopped, then went on. "No, I can die—you saved my life, truly, yesterday. Though if I wait for natural causes, whatever they are, it'll be a thousand years, most likely. . . ."

"With so many years ahead of you," intruded Beauty, "why are you not more worried about being killed early by the JEGS? You should be *more* concerned than we—you have more to lose."

Jasmine sat against the cool stone wall. "I find proximity to my fears instructive. Besides, I'm not so sure long life is as valuable as I once thought."

"How is it that Neuromans live so long?" posed Joshua. He lifted to his mouth the water-skin Jasmine had brought back from the spring.

"How is it," mused Jasmine. "How, indeed. Well. A story not so entertaining as the Fast Thermonuclear War Story, nor so instructive; but a story to pass the time, nonetheless." She scooted along the floor until she sat between the others, at the end of the cavern farthest from the covered doorway.

"Neuromans were once Human," she began. "No, it's true, you needn't look so alarmed. When I was young, the world was a different place. It was ruled by Humans, for one thing, there were billions of them. They raised children, and armies, and buildings that scraped the sky, and general hell, and drove gas-burning wagons on huge rock-hard roads that ran thousands of miles, through mountains and under rivers. Lived in giant cities, millions of people crammed in together. Horrible places, but exciting. People were suffocating in the stench of their own machines. People were killing each other because they couldn't think of anything better to do. Some people hated the color of the epidermis of other people, and some hated certain body parts, and some hated thoughts, and others didn't think at all. Lots of talk about God, and sex was on everyone's mind, one way or other. Nearly everybody could read and write. There were so many lights burning at night, the Milky Way could never be seen. Some people flew all the way up to the moon, just to sit on it. Doctors were pulling the hearts out of some Humans, and putting them into others. Scientists were photographing atoms, bottling electromagnetism, sculpting genetic material, squinting at the edge of the universe. Hypnotism, scientology, guru gearloose transcendental biofeedback. Civilization was going mad." She sat back, closed her eyes, saw it all again. "It was a hot time to be a Human being." She smiled knowingly. "*I* was born Human."

Josh was quickly spellbound by this intriguing picture of the strange land of his forefathers. Magnetism, mountain-tall buildings. And everyone could read. Most of it was new to Josh—few reliable stories ever filtered down anymore, good histories of what it was like Before the Ice. It fascinated him to think of early Humans—not so dissimilar from himself—living so differently.

Even Beauty could not help being drawn into the tale, could not help warming to the weaver. "You, a Human," he whispered in a combination of frank disbelief and total acceptance. "And what of Centaurs? What did they do while Humans reigned?"

"Oh, Centaurs didn't exist here," Jasmine assured him. "Many animals didn't. Not until much later. But that's another story." She ignored Beauty's incredulity to continue her narrative. "In any case, I was born in 1986, like I said earlier, the year the nuclear plant at Oceanspring had a meltdown and wiped out a big chunk of New England. Not to mention the radiation sickness, the burns, the birth defects. Makes me gag just to think of it. No use you two knowing any more about nuclear energy than that. It was a kind of power people thought they could put in a box and use however they wanted to: take it out and shoot it, or turn on a light, or take an X ray—no, don't ask me what that is—but what happened was, they couldn't close the box. That's what they found out in 1986, the year I was born.

"Born down in L.A. before it was an island. Now *that* was a town. Convertibles, movie queens, Disneyland—you don't know what I'm talking about, do you? Oh well, never mind. Ashes to ashes, we used to say. Well. Things hobbled along for some years after the Oceanspring disaster, probably would have for a lot longer, but there was another disaster, much bigger. Of international proportions. Ever hear of oil?"

Josh and Beauty looked at each other, then back at Jasmine. "You mean like whale oil?" asked Josh.

"Oil that gushes black out of the ground, that makes gasoline, that burns. Fuel oil."

They shook their heads. Jasmine sighed, then laughed. "It's hard to know where to begin this story." They looked at her expectantly. Joshua had quite forgotten the pain in his back. Jasmine went on. "Oil was a natural substance, pumped out of wells in the ground. It was processed and burned, and the energy it gave off lit the lights of the world, powered transportation, heated the chilly, cooled the hot, oil did it all. Only sometimes it would spill out of the ships that carried it and cover the sea with thick, black slime. That was called an oil slick, and Humans hated it.

"At the same time, there were special scientists called genetic engineers. They—Lord, how am I ever going to—okay, they were . . . well, the sort of magicians of their time. Only the magic was young, and they were all sorcerer's apprentices. Anyway, they found out that every creature is made of millions of tiny organisms called cells that are too small even to be seen. And at the center of each cell is an even smaller chamber called a nucleus, and inside of each nucleus are bands of stringy material called chromosomes. And making up the chromosomes, like beads on a chain, are millions of little messages, called genes. And these genes are the messages that tell each creature what it is, how big it is, what shape it is, what it likes to eat, what it thinks about. And these sci-

entists discovered the code that the gene messages
were written in. So the scientists could go into the
cells, and write whatever messages they wanted to.
So that's what they did—they found a bacteria, which
is a certain kind of cell, and they rewrote part of the
message inside the cells—that's called genetic engi-
neering—and when the geneticists had written exactly
what they wanted, then the bacterial cells that they'd
written in were able to eat oil. Not only that, they
loved to eat oil. So the people turned the bacteria
loose on the oil slicks, and the bacteria ate all the oil
off the surface of the water."

Josh was riveted. Here was a true story, of wizards
who performed magic, formidable sorcery—by writing. By seizing and harnessing the ineffable, occult
power of the written word. Thus it shall be written;
thus it shall be done. He'd heard stories of a time when
everyone could read, but he'd always discredited them
as apocryphal. Reading and writing, he believed, was
an ancient art limited to a privileged few. This, at
least, was what his parents and friends had always
led him to believe. Furthermore, though he could
perform feats that seemed magical to others, he knew
that anyone could learn the same tricks—if they could
read. But now here was a story about prehistoric
Scribes who performed true magic with their religion.
Or perhaps it wouldn't seem so, Josh thought, if he
could only understand their scripture. He made a
mental note to study ancient languages.

Beauty respected all magic, if it was real, but he
didn't know whether to believe this or not. It sounded
a lot like Scribery, about which he was deeply skeptical. He'd heard various stories over the years about
what the world was like Before the Ice. Each story
was more fantastic than the last: tales of animals who
couldn't talk, of invisible kingdoms, of ships that flew
to the moon. Somehow, though, the way Jasmine was
speaking—it was as if she'd actually seen the things
she was describing. Again, Beauty began to view the
Neuroman in a somewhat different light.

Jasmine saw she had her audience, and continued.
"So one day there was an oil spill. The G.E.'s—that's

the genetic engineers—spread their special germs all over the oil, and that was the disaster. The bacteria spread. Not just happy with one little oil slick. Spread on the water and started infecting oil-tankers, off-shore drilling sites, pipelines. Pretty soon there was an epidemic, and then a pandemic, and before you knew it, before anybody could find a good antibiotic, most all the oil and gas in the world were gone. The lights went out.

"That's how I remember my twenty-first birthday, candlelight and warm beer—the refrigerators went out, too. Well, power came back slowly, over the next ten years. Windmill generators were perfected, solar collectors, ocean-current turbines, storage batteries, geothermal units, fecal-methane converters, alcohol burners. By the time I finished medical school, the country was cooking again. That was the setting when I got into things—a couple of technological calamities lowered the pace, but they created a new interest in ingenious alternatives.

"Sail ships thrived again, and neighborhoods. And horses. Everyone needed a horse again to get around. But there just weren't enough at first, not for everyone, and horse farms couldn't turn them out fast enough. That's when cloning was really perfected— the G.E.'s were given a task and they rose to it. Learned how to clone a horse in a laboratory to a full-size colt in thirty-five days. Well, you can imagine the assembly line. In two years everyone had a horse."

"What's a Clone?" asked Josh.

"Oh, dear. Well, cloning is a way of writing the proper code word into the gene-message in a single cell of some creature, so that the cell multiplies and grows into an exact replica of the original creature. This became very important later—oh, when I was about thirty. That's when it became apparent that since the Oceanspring disaster, with all that ambient radiation, there were a lot of people who either couldn't have babies, or could only have defective ones. A lot of people. So they said, well, if you can clone horses, you can clone people. Here they'd been screwed out of progeny by technology, and now they wanted to settle out of court. They wanted something of themselves to live on, like all creatures do. They wanted a piece of immortality. And suddenly now they were told: *No children.* I tell you, they were furious. They started having themselves cloned dextro and levo. Of course, the government tried to regulate it, two to a family and so on, but the rich kept making more and more, probably saw it as a way of producing cheap labor, and then the poor wanted clone subsidies, and then there were pirate operations, quasilegal clone agencies, and—well, you know."

They did not exactly know; but they got the flavor. Humans, making copies of themselves over and over. "Remarkable," Beauty said quietly. Somewhere far far away, an animal howled, soft and searing as the memory of a scream. The three comrades looked up momentarily at the hidden entrance, then at each other. Josh laughed to find himself—at least temporarily— less interested in events outside the cave than those inside Jasmine's brain. Beauty answered with a comprehending smile.

"Anyway," Jasmine went on, "the reproductive system wasn't the only one beginning to fail in people then. All that radiation was starting to take its toll, thirty years down the line. People were getting bowel cancers, lung cancers, leukemias, aplastic anemias. People were dying. Other animals, too, the radiation affected everyone. Something had to be done.

"That's when the subject of Neuromans came up.

"See, every organ system was being induced to carcinogenic transformation by the long-term residual radiation, except the central nervous system. The good old brain and company." She tapped her skull with forefinger. "So someone thought, well, why don't we just replace everything else with artificial parts, just transplant the brain and nerves into a completely prosthetic, unbreakable, unaging body.

"Well, I tell you, I heard that idea when I was thirty, and I spent the next ten years of my life, along with a lot of other people from a conglomerate of fields, working on the problem. Artificial hearts were easy—nuclear-powered Teflon hearts had been successfully transplanted into lower animals many times. Lungs were no big problem, the concept of membrane oxygenators had only to be miniaturized. Arms, legs, aluminum bones, modular circuitry; all conceptually and technologically rather simple.

"Blood. Now there was a problem. How to create an artificial, long-lasting, oxygen-carrying fluid that . . . but you're not interested in that kind of detail. Suffice it to say the problems were all solved. Time, it was felt, was crucial, so animal trials were abbreviated. Clinical experiments began with Humans. Dying Humans, of course. Volunteers, naturally. People with nothing to lose. The key, it turned out, was the community of genetic scholars, once more. They engineered another cell—a fungus, actually, a cousin to mucor mycosis—to virulently eat living Human tissue, all Human tissue except nervous tissue and supportive cells. A large inoculation of mucor could disintegrate a body in under a day."

"But who would volunteer for such torture? Is it not wiser to die young, with dignity, than to suffer such mutilation?" asked Beauty sincerely. "To be eaten alive by fungus?"

Jasmine smiled. "*I* volunteered. And I think, perhaps, you're right. Still, I don't know if I ever *had* enough dignity to match the three hundred years I've been given so far. In any case, I had malignant lymphoma, I had one year to live, so I volunteered. At least, I took one step forward, and all my associates took one step back. There hadn't been any complete successes to that point, and experimental subjects were really still out on a limb. Anyway, I did it.

"They put me to sleep, lowered my metabolism with drugs, and near froze me until I was peeking through Death's cold keyhole. Then they lowered me into a hyperbaric tank of the newly invented blood solution, injected me with mucor and painted me with it as well. My body was a culture medium inside and out. In a day, I was nothing but a tuberous brain trailing the stalk and fine-branching filaments of my entire nervous system.

"Then the reconstruction began. Direct osmosis of

oxygen and glucose in the specially prepared bathing solution kept my brain and its cables alive, while round-the-clock operating teams microsurgically connected nerve to wire, nerve to transducer, wire to sensor. The basic life-saving operation took a week—connecting the heart, the lungs, and so on. The refinements—musculature, plastic skin, oral feeding apparatus, voice—took over a year. But I walked out of there a new woman. One of the early successful Neuromans.

"Of course, there were some difficulties, some things to get used to. My sense of touch was inadequate, sometimes numb, sometimes painful. I couldn't taste at all, though that hardly mattered, since all I could eat were simple sugars. My balance was miserable. Subsequent operations changed all that, naturally—we all benefited from refinements over the years, and many of my initial inadequacies were rectified. My diet was expanded, my senses made more sensitive. My eyes, for instance, became much more sophisticated than Human eyes—though I must say, the images were strange, and took some getting used to. My skin was much tougher. My heart was powered by a plutonium cell and would be pumping long after my brain was dead. And my brain, if it came to that, was perfused by a solution containing a congener of BHT, a preservative which was discovered way back in the 1960s to prolong the life of nerve cells: my brain would live to be a thousand, if the animal studies were accurate.

"So there I was, wobbling like an infant. The first generation of a new race. Of course, I couldn't have children. Couldn't even be cloned, you can't clone nerve cells. But there I was, there I was."

She closed her eyes, to better see the old tinted picture of who she had been. Beauty stared at her in mute admiration: her bravery, her cowardice, her agony. She opened her eyes. "Pity I can't cry anymore," she said. "Not a very useful function, I suppose, if you're not Human."

Josh reached out and touched her hand, tenderly. It startled her out of reverie. "Naturally," she said. "Naturally, it made a lot of people want the operation.

Other centers began performing the surgery, but it was expensive and time-consuming, and even though it was refined over the years—much more sophisticated, more elegant models than I were made—it was finally abandoned. I think a couple thousand Neuromans were constructed eventually. I don't know how many are left. Anyhow, that's why Neuromans live so long."

The air was silent for a time. Outside, faint forest noises crept around the cave mouth, but didn't come in. A spider soundlessly scurried up the wall, saw this was not the right time, scurried back down into his crack.

Josh said, "So when we found you . . ."

"I was bleeding to death. Ordinarily I don't need a refill of Hemolube but once every fifty, sixty years, unless my valve gets opened like that. I've got about five hundred cans buried away up and down the coast, though, in case I ever get caught short. It's not made anymore, of course."

During the retelling of the story, Beauty had felt a certain gnawing, an undefinable malaise, unrelated to the story itself. He couldn't grab hold of it, but it grew, or maybe just pressed; then every time he was about to get an inkling of it, it shifted. Now in the silence of the aftermath, he found it. "And from what isolated continent did Centaurs migrate here, that they were not yet involved in these grand designs?"

Jasmine looked at Beauty with the soft, sad eyes of a reluctant parent about to tell her child where babies *really* come from. "It was a time," she began, "of decadence. In its truest sense. Society was in decay. Events had occurred that made the Human race aware, fundamentally, of the proximity, the imminence of death. Radiation sickness was random and irrevocable. It was manifestly not possible to buy long life by being moral, or sensible, or productive, or even rich. Yet at the same time, some people, also by a seeming random combination of circumstances, were undergoing operations which, if successful—eighty percent died on the operating table, by the way— promised virtual immortality. Chance and circumstance and the moment were the legs of the tripod upon which society was balanced. Wasn't that a time," she mused a moment, then went on.

"The situation made it opportune for people to gamble and play, with death and life. Self-destruction, after all, is the best form of self-control, when control over your own life is not an alternative. So that was the way society went for a while. Suicide, violent crime, drug addiction soared. Creative suicide, especially—people paid huge sums of money to have their deaths orchestrated. National parks were set aside for war games—where people could go to kill each other, and not be a danger to people who wanted their decadence softcore. Opium dens and sex parlors multiplied. Funerary art became *the* high art form. Everyone dabbled in death, in life, and in fantasy.

"The science of any age is always a manifestation of the fantasies of the age, and our science was no different. Genetic engineers were the executors of our social subconscious. Spurred on by successes in cloning, by their role in creating the Neuromans, they began truly to unlock the secrets of the genetic code.

"They knew the alphabet of the genetic messages and by the middle of the twenty-first century of our calendar, they had mapped the order and meaning of every letter. Once it was discovered which genes said what, it was not difficult, using established methods, to splice genes from one animal with genes from another, and thereby create—a new animal."

Beauty's eyes opened wide at the implication that teetered precariously above his head.

"For example," Jasmine continued in a somewhat slower voice, "it was possible to splice the genes coding for the head and torso of a Human with those coding for the torso and legs of a horse, in such a way that the resultant creature, after full embryonic development . . . was a Centaur."

"No!" Beauty thundered, standing, suddenly, to his full height. There was anger in his eye, mixed with fear and grief. He looked like a child who'd just been told he was adopted. "It is not possible," he whispered harshly. "I have heard stories of the migration of Centaurs—stories of Before the Ice, how there were five great continents; how this was the Human continent, which they destroyed with neglect; how Centaurs fled here when their own land was destroyed by Vampires in the Hundred Days' War, how . . ."

Jasmine stopped him with a raised hand. "No, Beauty. Those are myths of your origin. Every species creates legends of its own beginnings, and those tales of continents and migrations are your myths. This history of mine: this is truth."

He looked at her in despair, his gaze a plea. She pressed the point. "Many of the creatures now in existence are results of these early experiments in genetic mapping and recombination. Cats with partly Human brains, like Isis, for instance. Such crosses were popular among the rich—as pets, curiosities, status symbols. It was the natural extension of the ultimate decadence—making fantasies real as reality decayed into mire.

"After a short time, it wasn't even all that expensive to commission mythological creatures—Sphinxes and Centaurs and whatnot. The middle class began acquiring them. Even zoos began buying examples. Then, of course, it became chic among the rich to outdo themselves, to get kinky. Vampires, naturally, were favorites—Human bodies, vampire-bat metabolism, specially engineered regulatory genes to control wing size. And of course, Humans raised them, trained them, nurtured them. So they became, truly, an expression of our dreams, fantasies, nightmares, and wishes. New, never-before-thought-of combinations, were conceived, their genes rewritten. Governments, naturally, grew their own secret stable, bred for their own secret purposes. Dabbling with life, myth, and death. It was the national sport.

"Of course, there were accidents." She paused at the mention, to let Josh and Beauty conjure up all the grotesque possibilities. But they knew only too well the results of these tamperings, the errors that still populated the forest. The small cave somehow became darker, and more chill. Unconsciously the three drew closer together. Jasmine spoke softer now.

"Not only in the early experiments, but even later,

in small underground labs. Horrible miscreants. Mistakes. Fortunately, many of these were sterile; but not all. And not all were destroyed at birth, either, as they should have been. They are still relatively few in number; but they are despised by everyone, including themselves." She turned to Joshua. "And you wonder why they hate Humans so much."

Beauty still looked stunned. To cover, somewhat, the bareness of his emotion, Jasmine continued in a subdued patter. "Most descendants of engineered creatures, naturally, have strong ambivalences about Humans—love and hate for their creators; submission and rebellion—even if they no longer understand the origin of these feelings. It's normal to feel these things, Beauty. But to understand these emotions, to know them openly, is to control them, to stop them from controlling you."

"It makes us no different, you and I," said Josh to his old friend. He tried to hold the Centaur close with the strength of his loving gaze.

"The Centauri is an ancient and noble race," Beauty insisted quietly to the wall.

"Noble, without question," Jasmine pursued. "And nobler still, to be so in its infancy. Centaurs have evolved a great racial visage for themselves in two short centuries. The Human race, in five thousand times as long, has all but extinguished itself. And as far as that goes, neither race can lay much claim to age, I think, with ants and termites still building kingdoms beneath the earth."

"I dislike this talk of race," snapped Josh. "Every animal is its own animal. Beauty, can you think differently of me now, after all we've shared?" he demanded.

Beauty looked to Josh, then dropped his head. "You are no different, old friend. *I* am different. So *we* are different."

"You're no different to me, old Horse. Unless you start acting different."

"I act as it pleases me to act," the Centaur said with a haughtiness Josh had never seen. "Besides, this Neuroman's story is obviously a child's tale."

"It's not, Beauty," Jasmine spoke quietly. "You know I speak truth. Think. I'm the only one you've ever heard speak who was actually there."

"But this is nonsense," he railed. "Tricks with words, again. More fool Scriberies . . ."

"Hold your tongue, Beauty," Josh cautioned. "There's no need to—"

But Beauty was losing his balance. "No need to nothing! You probably put her up to this—you try to convince me with words again."

"I try to convince you of nothing," Jasmine said evenly. "I tell you merely what is. I know you can feel the truth of what I say."

"How easy for you with heart of steel and wire to speak of feeling," the Centaur spoke bitterly.

Now it was Joshua's turn for anger. "Why you sullen, self-pitying gelding, your mother must have been a jackass." Beauty's mane stood on end. Josh continued. "Here you've just found out you're of a brave new species, you could be inheriting the earth, and here you are—"

"Do not think you can humiliate me, Human, just because you—"

"*Human!*" Joshua's voice rose. "So *that's* where your noble race stands. You humiliate your*self* with your infantile racism. You can't even—"

"I can't even—"

"Stop!" shouted Jasmine, and the confrontation halted instantly. There followed a bleak, shamed silence. Jasmine let the empty soundlessness press them a bit closer together again, press them back into shape; then spoke, barely audibly. "I think you've just found out what the Race War was all about. *Really* all about." She searched their faces with her own, but they hid behind mirrored eyes. She put one hand on Joshua's head, one on Beauty's back. "Strong feelings divide us. But the same feelings bind us. Please, both of you. We're a family."

Beauty turned away, faced the west wall. Josh lay back, staring at the ceiling. Jasmine sighed. "I didn't mean for my story to break us," she said. "It's a common ancestor we share, a Human ancestor. We're simply evolving differently. My evolution is leading to a dead end, nowhere else. Who knows where yours will lead? I thought you were strong enough for this, both of you, I thought . . . well, what's the difference what I thought. You two get some sleep, you need it. I'll take the first watch, my eyes are better than yours at night anyway." She turned away.

Jasmine knew Beauty believed her—there was no other reason for him to have become so upset, to have been thrown into such disequilibrium. She was not sorry, though. Shocks such as these were the only good test of character and mettle—and she wanted to be certain she was in the company of strong souls before she went any further with them into whatever dark regions this quest led.

She heard Josh and Beauty talking quietly to each other, now, in a recessed corner of the cave—sounds of apology and regret mingled with pride.

"Forgive me," she heard the Centaur mumble, "I did not mean—"

"No, no, it shook me up, too," Josh was whispering. "She was—"

"—it *has* to—"

"—by tomorrow if we—"

"I must consider the implications of—"

Something about the energy between these two—their strength of purpose, their confused idealism—made Jasmine glad she'd come along. They gave her something she'd been missing for many years: a reason. Quietly, she left them to their own.

She walked to the mouth of the cave, sat on her haunches, peered through the foliate cover into the daring night. Fog was beginning to roll in over the short hills like stray thoughts; wispy at first, quickly disappearing. By the time it was thick enough to fill the stony basins and creep over the heather knolls, the moon slipped under the horizon, and the darkness was complete. A chill pervaded the air that would have clung fast to any Human skin, but Neuromans were immune to such vagaries of weather. Jasmine registered the temperature fall, but felt no discomfort. It was an hour before she even thought to look back at her friends, to gauge their distress; Josh and Beauty lay peacefully in the corner, curled together to share warmth; asleep.

An hour before first light, in the whisper of the false dawn, a tumble of rocks crashed down around the cave entrance. The three sprang alert: Josh drew knife, Beauty arrow, Jasmine sword, as they stood in readiness facing the ragged portal. They waited.

Thirty seconds. Beauty felt snared, but yet withal content at the opportunity, finally, to fight. Josh hoped only that he would not die before he avenged his love. Jasmine steadied her reflexes, studied her fear.

One minute. There was a scratching at the outermost stones; some of the camouflaging leaves fell apart. Beauty bent his bow as two palm fronds fell into the cave. A long moment; a crash; and in ran a small raccoon, the black rings around its eyes making it look like nothing so much as a cartoon ghost. It stopped, looked the three hunters over, turned and walked out again.

The tension broke somewhat, but nobody relaxed. Jasmine stepped gingerly forward and peered through the greenery. "No one else out there," she muttered. The others remained silent. Jasmine motioned them to be still, then slipped outside into the misty dim morning.

CHAPTER 8

In Which The Company Falls Prey

FOR five minutes, not a sound; not a whisper. Jasmine finally re-entered the cave with saber sheathed, looking perplexed. "Gone," she said. "All gone."

"The JEGS?" asked Beauty.

"JEGS, Vampires, Accidents, Humans. All left town."

They went up to have a look around; even Josh, who walked as if on thin ice over black water. The lookout perch above ground was vacant, now, a patchwork of prints that led finally down the bluff. Inexorably, south.

And far below, the Vampire camp was evacuated. A couple of empty wagons could be seen, left behind like old shoes.

"They won't be waiting for us," said Josh. "Let's get moving."

"You're still in no shape . . ." began Jasmine.

"My water's almost clear this morning. And my back hurts much less," he replied. "In any case, I'm going." He looked resolute.

Beauty was somewhat in conflict, though he was clearly anxious to be off in pursuit. He looked at Jasmine tentatively. "Perhaps if he rode me . . ." he questioned.

Jasmine didn't think she could restrain them any further, so she shrugged affirmatively.

Beauty held out his arm, Josh pulled himself up on the Centaur's back; and without further ado, they set off at a walk.

The prints merged, presently: Vampires, Accidents, Humans in loose formation; JEGS in pursuit. Josh was relieved to be behind Jarl's tenacious soldiers for once.

The hunters walked in silence for some hours, an easy quiet, concentrating on the trail. They felt much closer to each other following the previous night's recriminations. Private demons aired, they could focus with clarity, now, on the thing they shared, the thing that unified them—the pursuit of the enemy.

Since Josh was riding, he took the opportunity to set the record in wobbly script, marking the past day's events down on paper. For ink, he used spit and the natural dye from crushed blueflower petals. For support, he used Beauty's back. "The Word is great, the Word is One," he whispered quietly when he was finished, replacing the folded paper neatly back in its tube.

The sun never came out of the clouds all morning, keeping the air cool and expectant. Violent weather was foreshadowed. Beside a shallow, racing brook, a dead weasel lay on the cold dirt, its eyes still open, seeming to watch. Very likely an omen.

Joshua grew meditative to the gentle rhythm of the Centaur's pace. His thoughts wandered everywhere. He mused on Jasmine's funny speech patterns—the strange accumulation of verbal mannerisms she'd acquired over three centuries of discourse. He wondered about Isis' beginnings, what she thought about, what she'd encountered in the Vampire encampment. He wished Beauty silent strength in weathering Jasmine's revelations. He tried to visualize what Dicey was doing at that very moment. He saw the clouds change from animals to trees to mysteriously unknowable shapes. He smelled the wind. He lost himself in trivial sensations; spilled random thoughts into space.

Toward noon, the barometer fell discernibly. The clouds took on a bleak and fitful mood. In the south, now, the ragged peaks of the Saddleback Mountains rose darkly out of the horizon, like the unmoving spine of an unsleeping reptile. The wind changed direction, yet again. All nature seemed intent: there was little inconsequential movement.

As the tracks of the quarry veered somewhat east, the hidden sun passed its cryptic meridian. Each

hunter marked the moment with an internal clock, a
hunter's sense. Over plain and moor, they followed the
winding trail with singular absorption; in thought,
though, each followed an independent track.

Jasmine mused repeatedly on the existence of the
new animal in the south to which Lon had referred.
What manner of creature could it be? To her knowledge, no new animals had been created, discovered,
or evolved in almost two hundred years. At least since
the total collapse of the old technocracy, Before the
Ice. So what was the nature of the beast? A thinking
animal, clearly. Certainly malevolent. But what? Invented Before the Ice, perhaps, and dormant until
now; programmed, perhaps, to awaken a century
later, after the Ice Change. Or maybe just a recent
mutation. Or maybe there wasn't a new animal at
all—maybe this was just an obfuscating rumor, a
smoke screen to disguise simple Vampire expan-
sionism, Accident terrorism, carnal anarchy, slave
trade. Or was it something entirely other?

Joshua thought about Venge-right. Under the old
laws, personal vengeance sought against those who'd
perpetrated violent, personal, unprovoked crimes was
allowed, even expected. Josh felt entitled, legally and
morally, to his revenge. Even though there were, of
course, no laws anymore. None, at least, that everyone
adhered to, or considered just. Joshua had read law
books, and was uncertain at this point whether
Venge-right had meaning any longer; or whether it
now had the same force and ethic behind it as the
act of the creatures who'd murdered and abducted
his family: the force of will. He thought this; and then
he thought that perhaps Beauty was right after all. It
was bad to read too much.

Certainly most other animals felt this way—reading
was evil, tainted. It set Scribes apart. It excluded them
from the animal communtiy at large, and consequently
bound the Scribes together all the more closely. It
gave Scribes the feeling that they were somehow
better and worse than all other creatures. And this
made them aloof.

Since his earliest days, Josh had registered this

sense of being an outsider—that somehow he was simultaneously feared, envied, and despised for his birthright. It made him wonder now—as he so often had before—about the origin of Scribery. Early religious tracts dated it to six thousand years Before the Ice—when the Word was made manifest to the first Human. All other words had been made from that first Word, from permutations and combinations of the original letters. Then in the First Age of Darkness, the first Word had become lost, and it had been the quest of all scholars since that time to find it again. There were allusions to it in subsequent, derivative texts, references to the original documents—footnotes to the Word. But most books had been destroyed in the holocaust Before the Ice—so the Word was not likely ever to be found; nor the true beginnings of the religion. It was something he would ask Jasmine about. She might be able to shed some light.

The day inched along; they continued walking. Beauty noted a natural dip in the landscape that marked the end of the territories overseen by Jarl— the beginning of the Doge's domain. Of course no one could lay true claim to any lands since the Race War, but different powers had different areas of strength and influence, and the JEGS' authority waned in the southern provinces.

Beauty liked Jarl, certainly better than he liked the Doge; and so was somewhat uneasy now. He'd fought with Jarl's infantry in the War, fought proudly. Jarl believed in animal virtues, not Human aesthetics. Jarl had no morals, but he knew what was right. And war or no war, he fought for his knowledge.

As did Beauty. The Centaur realized something finally: it was proper to fight for what was correct in the moment; this was an animal virtue. Not to dwell on what once *was* right, or even on what once *was*. Those were Human foibles, Scriptic illusions. So it truly made no difference what the origin of his race was. Nothing mattered, in fact, before his immediate memory. This thought cheered him. Ancestry was a Human conceit—Beauty could find his strength in the animal ways.

He cocked his head in the wind. It would rain soon. Bad for tracking. Beauty stifled the urge to pick up his pace, lest he injure Joshua. He felt his friend's hands holding loosely to his mane, and kept a steady walk.

The Old one in the sky cleared his throat, and the three comrades tilted their heads at the rumble of thunder.

In spite of the menace of the gathering sky, Josh felt himself getting sleepy.

In less than an hour, they were inside the Forest of Tears. Planted years before as a tribute to some person or idea now unknown, the forest had flourished, spread. Weeping willows, mostly, now so thick it was impossible to do anything but weave through them. So thick the sky was invisible. So thick nothing else grew besides the occasional onion, the silent moss, the quivering fern.

Josh slipped down off Beauty's back soon after they entered. His bruised flank still hurt, but no more did he have the deep, visceral pain that had choked his movement the day before. He was a fast mender, a trait that had saved him not a few times in the past.

The light in the wood was eerie, foreboding: dark, violet prestorm rays filtered through the heavy leaf-green cover into the cool, earth-colored air: dream-light. Josh took out his knife and carved a short message into a fat willow trunk, marking the date, the person, the intention.

Beauty shook his head. "Scribbles," he muttered, not even bothering to make the sarcastic hand gesture he frequently did just to annoy Joshua. "You might want to leave them a map of where we are going as well," he added pointedly.

"No one following us now," answered Josh. He would have said more, but stopped to anticipate a yawn.

"It wouldn't hurt to rest here a few minutes anyway," Jasmine commented. "We haven't stopped all day."

"Fine," jibed Beauty. "Maybe he can write a book."

Josh finished his mark, then turned to Jasmine. "There was really a time when everyone could read and write?" he asked in wonder.

"All Humans," she nodded. "But then, years before the Coming of Ice, people got so angry at all the destruction caused by the intellectuals, there was a huge backlash. Books were burned, universities bombed. Got so nobody trusted anybody who could read. By the time the Ice came, everything was so fragmented and chaotic already—well, that was just the last straw. People even blamed the *Ice* on books."

"Books have always been blamed for what's wrong in the world," Josh nodded. "The power of words has always been feared."

Jasmine shook her head. "Words are neither more nor less powerful than those who write them, Joshua."

"But the closer we get to the First Word . . ." he began.

"No such word will ever be found," she declared.

"But it will be deduced," he assured her, "extrapolated backward from all the words that—"

"No, Joshua, words have none of the magic powers that your priests ascribe to them. There are no words anyone could write that could make the Ice come or go, make the Accidents disappear. . . ."

"But it was words in secret codes that made the Accidents appear in the first place—so you said."

"Not the words; only the force the words described. And it was those forces against which all the other creatures rebelled—though they didn't exactly understand the forces, so they—like you—chose to think it was the words themselves. That's when reading was outlawed. And that's when Scribery emerged."

"When?" Josh asked tentatively. He wasn't sure he wanted an answer.

"Oh, maybe fifty years Before the Ice. After the Clone Wars. I'll tell you about those some other time. But during the Clone Wars, all the Humans left on earth—except the children—were killed by the other species. Every adult Human. The children were spared because the animals—well, because animals don't fear children, I suppose. Reading and writing, were banned, then—as a Human scourge. But that didn't last long. The children began to grow up, and sure enough, found some books their parents had hidden. Some of them could read, and you know what a child does if something is not allowed. So a secret society formed around young Humans who could read. They taught others and the cult grew."

Somewhere outside, lightning whipped the sky, muted as if seen through closed eyes down in the forest. A moment later, though, thunder shook the ground, and a moment after that, the hypnotic patter of heavy rain could be heard scratching the forest roof. Jasmine continued.

"Some Humans, of course, believed what their animal friends told them—that Scribery was evil. For others, though, the Word was strong. They didn't know much history—only random facts from fragments of old books—but what they didn't know, they made up. From half-remembered stories, from daydreams and nightmares, from hopes and fears. The same way Humans have always made things up. That was the inception of Scribery as a religion—a mythological belief system created by rebellious orphans."

To Jasmine's surprise, Josh only smiled. "Your story isn't directed at *all* to the power of words, then. Only to the science of reading and writing as you knew it—*before* the ascent of Scribery. For all you know, the concepts gleaned by the first Scribes, a hundred and fifty years ago—children, though they may have been—were far more advanced than any of the writings of your age on which they were based." When speaking of Scribery, Josh often talked like a book. "Scribes may have discovered many more powers to words than you ever knew. For all you know the magic of the latter-day Scribes *may* have caused the Coming of Ice." Again, he smiled. "If our religion is indeed so young, the more power to it. But I suspect its seeds are much older, and its secrets just more tightly kept during earlier centuries."

Jasmine's eyes twinkled at her young friend's combined acceptance of her history and adherence to his own beliefs. "Joshua, hunter and Scribe, I bow to your faith in the magic of the Word. I only pray you not to let it cloud your judgment in matters of greater moment than debating the Coming of Ice."

Beauty raised his eyebrows, remotely interested. "Pray, what *did* cause the Coming of Ice?" It was obvious he'd always subscribed to the Book theory, without ever really having given it much thought.

Jasmine smiled. "Don't know, exactly. Started with the Great Quake, you know, that was the big one that dropped so much of the continental shelf. But that's not to say the quake *caused* the Ice. It's just an Ice Age, that's all, it's just something that happens every few hundred thousand years. Glaciers, they used to be called. The ice will keep coming down farther south for a while, then it'll all go back up to the pole where it belongs."

A few raindrops finally managed to wind through the mat of leaves that ceilinged the forest. They dropped, one by one on the yellow-mulch ground, plop, plop, as if the trees were actually crying.

Josh sat down, unexpectedly tired.

"You need to rest longer, Joshua?" asked Jasmine, her tone one of concern.

"No, no, I'll be fine. . . ."

Beauty was impatient to go, partly to resume the hunt, partly to be free of these woods, whose confines frightened him unreasonably.

"Come, you can sleep on my back, little pony," he said affectionately, covering his own ill feelings.

Josh bridled at the implied affront to his stamina. "I'm fine now, I can walk myself, my fine furry . . ." he began, standing up. But as soon as he stood, he sat down again, hard.

Jasmine and Beauty ran over to him. "What is it, Josh, are you all right?"

"Fine, I'm fine . . ." he said, or at least he thought he said. In fact, he hadn't said anything at all, he was unconscious to the world. And to Josh, for the third time, a strange thing happened. He slipped, under a crushing pressure of sleep, into an embryonic blackness, where a dark wind pulled him toward a now unmistakably growing pulse of primally intense light, through the countless measure of the void.

"Don't go," whispered Dicey. Fear contorted her face.

"I'm here, I'm not going anywhere," Rose reassured. She'd just turned to pick a potato off the ground for supper. In her arms she continued rocking Ollie, resting now, still mute from the ordeal.

"Just don't leave me alone," Dicey reiterated more softly.

Not that either of them could go anywhere. They were still tied at the ankles, surrounded by the thirty-four other Human hostages huddling against the cold rain. Ten yards away, under the shelter of a large, acutely angled cement slab—a crumbled wall from a crumbled era—stood the escort guard: Bal, Uli, Scree, three Accidents, and a female Vampire named Ena. Vampires didn't like being so physically close to Accidents, because of the odor, and just because; but even more than that, Vampires detested rain, and since this was the only shelter within eyeshot, they swallowed their hubris to wait out the storm.

Ten yards away, the Humans sat; soaking, shivering under the downpour. Five already had died on the forced march—from sickness, fatigue, hunger, blood loss. Those who died were given to the Accidents. Those left were of hardier stock. But the trek wasn't over.

Dicey pulled closer to Rose, for warmth and comfort. The young girl's neck was black and blue, her skin ashen, red. Rose extended her arms, brought the girl in, held both children tightly, sharing body heat. She took a bite of the wet, raw potato and passed it to Dicey. The young girl looked at it bleakly and began to cry. Rose stroked her dripping hair.

"There, there," murmured Rose, "this won't last forever. We'll get wherever it is they're taking us, and we'll be warm and dry and fed and rested, and Joshua will find us. And my Beauty."

Dicey bit into the hard sustenance and chewed without conviction. "If I knew a strong enough word, it would free us," she said. "Josh would know how to write it."

"They'll come armed with more than words, when they come," Rose said in monotone. She didn't think much of the power of words against the likes of Vampires and Accidents.

"They won't need more, if they have the right words. Some words can make walls fall down, and some can burn flesh and some can make boats fly and some can make ten thousand people follow you. Just by reading the written word. Some people, you know, think you have to *find* powerful words, that have already been written. But Josh thinks—*I* think— you can *calculate* what a powerful word must have been, just by knowing all the words that came from it. If you were smart enough, you could even come to the First Word that way." Her face fell, then, into a jumble of lost directions. "If I only knew the right words." She began printing ancient powerful words in the dirt: *Abbacadabba. Omen Sesame. A-OK. Heil Hitler.*

Rose stopped chewing the mouthful of potato she'd been working on, put her mouth down on Ollie's thin, blue lips, and force-fed him the spit-and-starch mulch. The little boy hardly stirred; but managed to keep down most of the pap. Rose turned back to Dicey. "If there is such a word, Joshua will write it," she assured the frail girl.

"I'm afraid, though," Dicey admitted. "The one they call Bal—he can read."

Rose smiled sympathetically. "Joshua can read better, I have no doubt. Now. Turn this way, let me try to read your eyes again." She was as disturbed by her inability to see into Dicey's eyes as by anything else. But she never lost hope. Her will was strong and she would live. Help was everywhere. Josh and Beauty would come. The water from the sky gave her strength. And wasn't there even a funny little Cat in the night who'd almost gnawed through her bonds? No, nothing was lost: this was but part of the world.

Across the muddy flat, Bal stared at the sky. "Bloodless rain," he swore.

Ena, the woman Vampire, sharpened her nails on the rock behind them. "I'm bored," she whined.

Bal looked at her blankly, then exposed his neck in her direction. A small Vampire joke.

Uli looked at Bal. "I like not this waiting, Sire Bal. Jarl's troops are not standing still, I warrant."

"Ice take Jarl's troops," hissed Bal. "We're no longer in their lands, they've no reason to follow further. Besides, the rain will stop soon." Bal hated rain more than most. The Griffin, Scree, suddenly flapped its wings, left the wind-break, and made a few low passes over the cowering Humans, just to frighten them for his own entertainment. Ena laughed. One of the Humans, a shirtless, muscular man, broke from the pack and started running, desperately. He was on a ten-foot tether, though, which caught him short. He fell hard on his face, and lay where he fell. He was cut above the eye. The blood streaked over his forehead as the rain poured down upon him.

Ena saw the blood.

Her nostrils flared, her nipples hardened, her wings spread. With a single swoop she was on him: on the ground, over him, atop him, straddling him, her huge leather wings covering them both like a slick brown umbrella.

Everyone watched—the Humans, in horror; the Accidents greedily anticipating the remains, if the victim died. Uli salivated. "I could use a little of that," he said under his breath.

Bal barked out, "What did I tell you about killing the goods!"

Ena pulled in her wings, pulled her mouth off the man's neck; sated. He was alive, but unconscious. The Accidents grumbled. The man's neck kept oozing blood slowly into the mire. Ena continued to lay on top of him, rubbing her bare breasts and hips into his back and buttocks, lapping at his throat, growling, puffing her wings, fondling his mud-slippery chest.

"No manners whatsoever," muttered Uli, licking his lips.

Bal did not like to see resentment in his ranks. "Go

on, take some nourishment for yourself, Sire Uli. We'll be here yet another hour. Not too much, mind."

Uli prided himself on his restraint, though, especially when he could demonstrate this trait to his superiors. "In a bit, perhaps," he said, yawning.

Bal had no one to impress, however; and his blood was up.

He snapped his fingers once.

Dicey's head shot up like a marionette on a string. She let out a small gasp. Her eyes were glazed, scared, red.

"What is it?" asked Rose, alarmed. "What's the matter?"

"He w-wants me," she stammered. Her teeth were chattering.

"How do you know?" Rose demanded. Three times, now, the beast had had the young bride.

"He called. He's waiting now." She looked achingly at Rose. "Help me," she whispered.

Rose stared deeply into her young friend's eyes. As before, she could read nothing. Black as wells into the earth. She held Dicey fast. "I'll keep you here. They'll have to tear you from me."

Dicey embraced Rose for a few moments, then pushed herself away. She stood up, her face a complex mixture of resignation, loathing; Rose could not tell what else those eyes had seen, would see.

"Well," Dicey spoke, almost calmly, "at least it gets me in out of the rain. . . ."

"Dicey . . ." Rose held out her hand.

Dicey turned away. "And maybe he'll read to me again. . . ."

Isis sat hunched over on the soft side of a shallow grade. The rain drenched her motionless body, matting the black fur, running in gushes and rivulets down her flanks, her head, into her eyes. She looked like the scrawniest, saddest cat ever invented. She watched.

Through the foggy shower she observed the distant creatures: a large group huddled in the rain; a smaller group protected by a sloping rock face.

She'd been following them half the night and most

of the day. Far enough to be invisible to them; close enough for her to see. When they stopped to eat, she stopped to eat. When they stopped in the rain, she got soaked, chilled.

She wasn't thinking of the water, though; her eyes never blinked. She watched. The storm, she knew, would wash away all trail, all scent; and she alone would be able to follow. And only if she watched.

She'd watched since the moment of the Human scream. She'd run back into the camp to find that the Accident who'd been chasing her had returned to tear one of the Humans in half. Not the girl-Human with the blood-smell, and not her friend. But another Human in the same group. There was a great hubbub after that, yelling and scurrying and murmuring and dithering and various other strange behaviors common to larger animals. Then they split into several groups, and all broke camp—right then, in the middle of the night. But who could understand Vampires? Who would even want to?

They'd all separated, then, and Isis had followed this group, the one with the girl-Human she'd tried to free. Three Vampires, three Accidents, a Griffin, and many Humans. All day she'd stalked them. They would never spot her, of course, she was too stealthy for that. The question was how to snatch the ones she wanted without getting caught. She narrowed her eyes into slits, and imagined herself carrying the coveted Humans in her teeth all the way back to her beloved Joshua, to drop them at his feet: a present. How he would love her then! *Then* she would be appreciated. He would scratch the special spot between her ears until she could no longer stand; and then she would fall, helpless, against his foot, and her eyes would close, and . . .

She opened her eyes. She must keep them open now. To watch.

Josh opened his eyes. Above him Jasmine's face loomed, her fingers touching the pulse in his wrist.

"What happened?" he said.

Beauty's face came into view. "You passed out

again. We have been pushing you too hard." The
Centaur looked deeply worried. "We can rest here a
while. The devils will not escape us. You lost more
blood than we thought."

Joshua shook his head. "No. No. This was different. This wasn't like blacking out from the bleeding.
This was . . . different."

Beauty assumed Josh was minimizing so he could
continue the hunt. "No," he shook his head knowingly, "we will stay. . . ."

"No, I'm telling you. This is something else. It's . . .
it's happened before."

Beauty shook his head; but Jasmine, whose brows
had been knitted in perplexity, suddenly pricked
her ears. "Wait, Beauty, let him speak. There *was*
something strange in this. If it had just been hem-
orrhage, his pulse would have been rapid. But his
pulse—I've been feeling it the whole time since he
went down, and it's . . . undecipherable. First it was
slow—deadly slow, down to twenty beats a minute.
Then suddenly up to two hundred. Strong, then weak.
Regular, then irregular. Now it's completely normal,
sixty a minute and strong."

Josh sat up. Beauty looked doubly concerned now.
"It's these spells," began Joshua. "I've been getting
them for a week or so. I feel sleepy, like I've been
drugged. Then it all goes black, except for this bright
light. This light . . . like a magnet. Then I wake up."
He looked to Jasmine for an answer.

She examined him briefly but completely. "Headaches?" she asked him. "Odd smells? Nausea? Dizziness? Double vision?"

He shook his head No to everything.

"I'm not certain," she said, stroking her cheek.
Then her mood lightening, she helped him to his feet.
"We'll just have to wait and see."

Beauty didn't like it, and said so. Outside, the thunder echoed his sentiments.

"Nothing else *to* do," Jasmine shrugged. She really
wished he could understand that stance. He only
grumbled. She said no more, though her thoughts were
darkly speculative. These spells of which Josh spoke

had the distinct flavor of an organic brain syndrome of some variety. Epilepsy seemed a likely candidate. Tumor, possibly. Narcolepsy could not be ruled out. In any case, she reminded herself—as she'd just pointed out to Beauty—there was nothing to be done but wait and see. Sometimes, unfortunately, that was the hardest thing to do.

So off they went. The trail was easy to follow, though the farther into the wood they went, the darker it got. Bear tracks split off at various points, which Beauty found disconcerting. He rose up from studying one set of prints closely, and hit his head on a low-hanging bough. It reopened the gash he'd sustained at the brothel, and a trickle of blood flowed slowly down his face.

Jasmine ran up to him quickly. She grabbed a handful of spiderweb from the crotch of a nearby tree, and smoothed the tangle over his wound. It immediately stopped bleeding.

"It didn't look like you hit yourself that hard," she commented.

"Oh," he brushed it all aside with a hand motion.

Joshua chuckled. "Happened two days ago. Hit with a two-by-four by an Equiman whore."

Beauty scowled. Jasmine smiled. "Oh, I see," she said with a knowing wink.

Beauty looked embarrassed. But this pain reached Jasmine as quickly as his physical pain had, and she hastened to touch him again, her hand on his hand, her eye on his eye. "I'm sorry," she said quietly, "that was mean of me."

His hand responded to her pressure for the briefest moment; then he shied, coughed, turned away. She looked off, after him; then down at the ground to avoid looking in at her own feeling.

The hunt resumed.

The patter of rain on the treetops continued to accompany their journey through the dim, tinted ghost-light of the forest. Low-dangling willow branches brushed their faces every few steps, as the woods became even thicker. Josh had the uneasy feeling they were being watched.

Jasmine's special eyes were of little advantage in dense terrain where there was an obstacle every few paces; but Beauty's sense of smell was keen as ever—and something was bothering it now. He didn't know what it was. Still, something was making him skittish, and they all respected such notions. They walked slower.

The forest cleared somewhat, and in the clearing was a totem. A ring of snake skulls, each biting the back of the one before it.

"Ouroboros," said Jasmine.

"What's that" asked Josh.

Beauty didn't like it. He shuffled backward, looking left and right.

"The serpent who swallows his tail," muttered Jasmine. "Ending, beginning."

"What?" Josh pressed.

There was a noise, off in the thick. All around them the willows swayed on undercurrents.

"Let's leave this place," Jasmine said quietly.

They advanced on the trail they'd been following. The rain without seemed to be abating some. The air in the forest responded by clearing a bit; though it remained gravid, impending. The hunters closed ranks. They drew weapons. They walked stealthily, senses alert to movement, sound, intuition.

Joshua felt watched.

Once again, the forest thinned, then opened. They found themselves on a grassy knoll. Ahead of them stood a virtual wall of willows, trunk to trunk with barely space for a stone between them. Josh turned to Beauty. "Turn back . . ." he started to say. Too late.

Four Bears, an Ursuman, and a Human—if he could be so called—closed in from the trees. JEGS. The Human went at once for Jasmine with a wicked spiked staff, thinking to kill the woman quickly. She engaged him with her blade, though, backing directly to a large tree, so no one could sneak behind her.

Joshua threw his first knife into the heart of the closest Bear. The animal wailed, and died instantly. Another soldier caught the young hunter four claws across the chest, but Josh backed him off with a serious arm wound. Bears were too proud to fight with weapons.

Beauty disabled one immediately, coming down on the animal's shoulder with the full weight of his hooves, while simultaneously stringing an arrow. He was about to loose the arrow into the chest of another charging Bear, when he looked into the animal's face —and stopped. The Bear stopped as well, and the two creatures faced each other in silence.

Jasmine, meanwhile, had run the churlish Human through, and was now hand to hand with the Ursuman. Josh was similarly engaged with another Bear who'd appeared. Suddenly two ropes landed around Beauty's neck, pulling him to the ground. The Bear he'd been facing screamed a tremendous growl to the sky. Josh received a blow to the back of the head with a huge paw. Jasmine killed the Ursuman, but he fell on her sword, leaving her weaponless. And suddenly it was all over.

Jasmine surrendered quietly to two brown Bears who flanked her, to the center of the clearing. Josh was out cold. Beauty slowly stood, the ropes hanging loosely around his neck—two grizzly Humans holding the ends—and faced the great Bear whose visage had initially stayed his attack.

"D'Ursu Magna," said Beauty, with moment.

"Beauté Centauri," growled the Bear.

They each took a step forward and hugged a great Bear-hug. Jasmine and the others looked on with a combination of shock and curiosity.

Beauty spoke. "I should have known only you could have followed such a trail as the one we left. You look well, ugly one."

"And I should have known your devious sign the minute I saw it . . ." nodded the Bear. Then, with pained regret: ". . . and abandoned the hunt."

They stood without speaking a moment, then D'Ursu Magna said, "Come I must take you to camp. You are our prisoners, now, there's nothing else to be done. Please, old friend, don't bolt. The Judge will decide your case. . . ."

"The Judge is here?" asked Beauty in surprise.

"Not a mile from this spot. Listen, Beauté Centauri, I will be your counsel. Whatever was your reason for being here . . . please: join us now. I can guarantee it is the only plea that will have the Judge's ear."

Beauty took the ropes from his neck. Joshua was revived, Jasmine helped him up. And so the prisoners were escorted from the battlefield by half a dozen brave soldiers and true, whose brothers lay dead but for singing them into Heaven.

The group made slow headway through the thickening willows, into dark and clinging undergrowth, twisting shadows. At last they emerged into a great space, where the willows arched at a stately fifty feet, and the dome of the forest looked like a verdant cathedral.

Fires blazed here, spraying light, roasting fowl. Scores of creatures played games, shot the long bow, wrestled, drank ale. All manner of animals resided herein. The caravan of guards and prisoners entered the great forest hall and stopped. The Bear-soldiers dispersed to their own with tales of battle and tales of woe. Music laced the leaves.

D'Ursu Magna took Beauty, Jasmine, and Joshua across the clearing to its opposite end. They passed jugglers, dancers, swordsmen, and the like until finally they stood warmed by the light of three campfires. And there before them, sitting in a living throne carved out of the most massive, aged weeping willow in the forest, was the two-ton, jewel-encrusted, black-furred figure of Jarl: the Bear-King.

CHAPTER 9

The Trial

SITTING, Jarl measured ten feet from footpad to crown; standing at full menace, he was near eighteen. Around his neck hung raw gems—rubies, emeralds —glittering as the earth they came from, precious fruits of the rock.

He had a certain natural majesty. His snout was ebony, his teeth pearl. His eyes radiated their own deep light. And buried in the brown-black fur of his ankle was a thick gold chain: memento from his days as a Human captive, a touring circus bear—he wore it always, to remember.

He sat impassively in his willow-tree throne as D'Ursu Magna brought the prisoners forward. Only his eyes moved, alive with the sparks of the campfires that surrounded him.

D'Ursu Magna spoke. "Your Wisdom, we have the prisoners—Beauté Centauri and two companions. They gave fight, but stopped when they saw who we were. Prisoners, bare your necks to Jarl, King, Brother, and Judge."

Baring the nape of the neck was the ritual animal way of conceding defeat or paying homage. The three comrades did it now, with equal parts of prudent wile, honor, and fear.

Jarl sat forward slightly, his eyes the color of sapphires. "Centaur, I know you," he said.

Beauty raised his head pridefully. "I fought with you in the War, your Honor."

"And fought well, your Wisdom," added D'Ursu Magna.

Jarl's eyes flashed brighter than the flame at D'Ursu, then back at Beauty. "So, Centaur, you have a champion in our ranks. How come you to know each other?"

"D'Ursu Magna was my lieutenant on half a hundred noble campaigns," said Beauty, looking hard on his old friend.

"Is this true, D'Ursu?" Jarl turned his curious features on the Bear Chieftain. "You were this Centaur's lieutenant in my army during the Strife?"

"In forty-four battles I was his lieutenant," answered D'Ursu Magna, looking straight at Jarl. Then, staring into the trees, he continued, "Once, he was mine."

Joshua quite unexpectedly felt a pang of jealousy—for what reason, he could not say—but submerged it for the more important matters of the moment.

"Soooo," growled Jarl, nose in the air, "how come these proud veterans to be here? How are they charged?"

D'Ursu cleared his throat, pawed the ground. "Charged with killing an Accident, your Wisdom. Without Justice." He spoke softly.

Jarl's eyes became stern like the glowing coal. "This is a serious charge, Brothers. To kill an animal, except in defense, or except for food, is the gravest crime, an act without Justice. And even an Accident is an animal. Not less so nor more than Bear, Centaur, or Human." In the background the noises of two hundred-odd animals could be heard: wrestling, telling stories, laughing, growling, gaming, purring, and preening. Jarl paused to listen a moment, eyes closed, then went on: "How do you plead?"

Josh spoke up. "We didn't kill him—I'm not saying we wouldn't have if we'd found him alive. His traveling mates did it, though—a Vampire and a Griffin— and we've been on their trail ever since."

Jarl leaned forward once more. "You, Human, how are you called?" He licked his paw reflectively.

"My name is Joshua. I'm a hunter and a Scribe."

"And a fighter by the claw marks on your chest," smiled the Bear-King. "But can you prove what you say, Joshua Hunter?"

"He speaks truth, on my word," Beauty said solemnly.

"Beauté Centauri has never lied," came in D'Ursu Magna. "He—"

"Hold," cautioned Jarl to his ursine chieftain. "You will have the opportunity, D'Ursu Magna. I will first hear out the accused."

D'Ursu looked chastised and was quiet. Jarl returned his gaze to Joshua. "The proof," he prodded.

"There's no proof but telling," Josh spoke straightforwardly. "The three creatures killed my family, and kidnaped my brother, my bride, and Beauty's wife. We set out in Venge-right and to recapture our own." Here he produced a scroll from his Scribe-tube and handed it to Jarl. It was the copy of the letter of intent he'd buried in his yard the day he'd found his family murdered. It stated the circumstances of the hunt and it was dated.

Jarl cast an inconsequential glance at the paper, but did not take it. "We do not read here," he growled.

Josh put the document back and continued. "We caught up with the assassins at the brothel. I spent time with a wood nymph named Meli who was with me until I tracked the Accident to the mill out back, and when Beauty and I got there, the Accident was dying —killed by his accomplices, he said. Your soldiers saw us there and mistook us for the killers. That's what happened, and if you're as great a Judge as they say, you'll need no further proof." He folded his arms across his chest.

D'Ursu looked aghast. Jarl smiled; then didn't smile: "Revenge is not an animal virtue," he intoned. There was a resounding pause.

Joshua tensed. If the axis around which these arguments revolved shifted from the specifics of a dead Accident to the ethics of Venge-right . . .

For the first time, Jasmine spoke. "If, as you say, King Jarl, Humans—like Accidents, Centaurs, and Bears—are animals, we must accept it as natural and evident that Human values are animal values; and hence Venge-right, a well-known Human virtue, must be an animal virtue as well. Which is not to say, of course, an animal mandate."

Jarl turned his great head toward the beautiful Neuroman, addressing her with studied reserve. "You have not an animal smell, Sister. What is your part in this matter?"

She told him.

He listened intently, nodding. When she was finished, he said, "It is unusual, in my experience, for an Immortalist to risk so much on so insignificant an adventure."

She seemed to bristle. "No more unusual than for a Great Bear to be lost so far south," she said with some sarcasm, referring to Jarl's apparent violation of the Doge's territories. D'Ursu Magna's whiskers twitched violently at her remark. "Besides," Jasmine went on, "no adventure is insignificant when undertaken in the company of friends."

Jarl laughed, a deep, booming chortle. "Well spoken, Immortalist. No fight alongside comrades is without merit. Nor am I lost."

"Then the Doge no longer controls these lands?" she pressed.

D'Ursu Magna spat, but said nothing. Jarl's look became serious, smoldering as a damp woodfire. "The Doge never controlled anything but his own piscivorous bowels. No animal does. It is Human arrogance to dream otherwise. Every animal controls itself and no other. Such is the nature of the beast. It is our renaissance to realize this."

D'Ursu Magna snarled an emphatic *Amen.* Jasmine stroked her chin, as Josh and Beauty followed the exchange closely. "Then," began Jasmine, "your intention is to move farther south still."

"My intention is to move where I will, when I will, as the notion moves me. If there are others who wish to join me on my excursions, that is their prerogative and my honor. If any be shackled to the Doge, I will liberate them. If any try to stop my free and animal movement—I will give them something to remember the rest of their short lives."

"Then your intention *is* to move south—against the Doge himself?"

"I have been camped in this wood for some time. I like it well here, at present."

"But when your army grows—then you will move south?" she pushed.

D'Ursu became angry. "The Judge will do the interrogating at this tree!" he growled.

Jarl smiled. "As the spirit moves me. I may indeed move south."

Jasmine backed off a bit to change directions. "I only ask, your Animal Honor, because, as you may be aware . . . there is a new animal in the south, whose intent seems to be focused on controlling other animals. . . ."

"Of little concern . . ." Jarl gestured.

"But you just said . . ."

"Of little concern since, according to my information, only Humans are being coerced in this new animal's attacks. And since this so-called new animal is certainly Human itself—since only Humans have ever evidenced such abnormal behavior—and since it is of little consequence to me what Humans do to each other, as long as their insanities and injustices do not spill over to harm other animals . . ." He let his sentence trail off, his conclusions obvious.

Beauty looked long on the Bear-King. "You can understand, though, your Honor, our need to catch these animals who have stolen our people. To save what is left of our families." He spoke with the slow urgency that comes upon someone who must make another understand.

Jarl reflected, his eyes embers. When he spoke again, his gaze encompassed the group. "Hear me well. Of this murder I absolve you. You had purely the odor of truth about you as you spoke of it—I smelled no fear, nor yet deceit. On this other matter: I pray you—abandon your vendetta. Venge-right is a Human conceit and of no earthly value to right-thinking animals. Join instead with my merry band.

We wander freely and without smallness of soul, and will do so until our contagion has spread through every forest and hill."

His tone was sincere, his message heartfelt. D'Ursu Magna caught Beauty's troubled stare with a look of intrigue. Josh was shaking his head solemnly. Jasmine forced the issue. "And if we do not wish to join you in your crusade? If we seek our own grail?"

Jarl, the Bear-King made an expansive sweep with his great paw. "Feel free to rest here in my camp as if it were your own. D'Ursu Magna will make it his passion to see to your comfort. Stay as long as you like until you decide—to join with me in the animal ways, or to choose the Human path—the arrogance of racial destiny, the self-destructiveness of greed, self-righteousness, and rationalization. I will ask you tomorrow morning for your decision. I would ask now, but . . ."—singling out Joshua for a pointed stare—"I know it takes longer for Humans to decide what is right than for most other animals."

With which he waved them all away, closed his eyes, and settled immediately into a state of brief but resplendent hibernation.

D'Ursu Magna ushered his charges back toward the center of the giant clearing. Here an enormous fire blazed, sending smoke and light up, finally through a hole cut out of the branches in the forest ceiling, seventy feet above them. Through this distant window stars could be seen sparkling in the black velvet sky. It was a clear night.

Josh looked around carefully for the first time. There was activity everywhere. Wrestling bouts between Bears occupied one center of attention, surrounded by a ring of noisy animals, jeering or cheering on their favorites. An archery contest was underway along the far alley. Humans and Ursumen were battling with sword-sticks against the tree-line, laughing and landing blows. Everywhere games.

"Neptune's Middle Fin," Jasmine exclaimed under her breath.

"I wish you would not use that expression," mut-

tered Beauty. Jasmine's stature had grown in his es-
teem since she'd spoken so forthrightly to Jarl—so it
bothered him even more now to hear her use such
crass language.

"It offends you?" she asked in surprise.

"It is common. And you are not common."

His criticism flattered her, in a left-handed way,
and she made a mental note to try to hold her ec-
lectic, polycultural vocabulary in check. She smiled to
herself as D'Ursu began to show them around.

Near the great central fire, the biggest crowd seemed
to be assembled. Jasmine, Beauty, Josh, and D'Ursu
ambled through the jostling animals until they stood
at the edge of the event: a large, torchlit space; a
dramatic performance was underway.

Animals of every variety filled the stage. In the center stood a Giraffe—stately, still, its neck completely
wreathed in willow boughs, its flanks draped with
bark. Beside it, two Tigers quietly caterwauled to the
sky. Seven huge Frogs sat one atop the other like a
breathing totem pole, the topmost Frog holding a twig
somberly in its toothless mouth. Three Snakes twisted
braidlike up a motionless Bear's upraised arm. Flying
Monkeys, trailing spiderwebs, that sparkled in the
campfire, flew unhurried circles over the assembled
players. In the foreground, everyone's attention seemed
directed to three animals engaged in impassioned conversation—a four-foot Chameleon, a large old Tortoise, and a Unicorn.

"What is it, what's going on?" Josh whispered to
Beauty.

"*Shoshoroo,*" Beauty said solemnly, his gaze immediately fixed to center stage.

D'Ursu Magna sidled up to Josh and spoke in low tones. "It is the great animal opera. It tells the story of the greatest of all our legends—the legend of Shoshoroo, the eldest tree of the Forest."

Jasmine nodded. "I've heard of it, of course—but I've never seen the play itself."

"Outsiders rarely do," D'Ursu agreed. "You are quite fortunate."

Beauty was mesmerized by the scenario unfolding before them—he'd not seen a performance in many years, and it was clearly evoking many memories in him.

"What is the story?" Josh whispered to D'Ursu. In the clearing, the Unicorn sat with the Tortoise, facing the Chameleon who danced a slow writhing dance to the strains of the wailing Tigers.

D'Ursu spoke quietly. "It is the story of Shoshoroo, the aged tree who takes his name from the sound the wind sings in his hair. He calls all the animals in the world to him, and when they are all assembled, he speaks only his name—Shoshoroo, Shoshoroo. The language of trees has long been a mystery, but Shoshoroo's meaning is revealed to them: the time has come for them all to turn into trees, until the world is one great Forest without animals. There is resistance at first, many animals are reluctant and self-satisfied. They don't wish to change. There are songs of protest, songs of question. Shoshoroo answers them all, though, and gradually the rightness of his vision becomes evident. The first act ends with his famous song:

> The Forest endures
> Uru Shoshoroo
> Talks to the stars

Shoshoroo
Her roots hold the world
Together in quiet arms,
The wind in her hair,
Shoshoroo."

D'Ursu stopped speaking for a moment, obviously moved by his own rendition of the verse. In the clearing, the Chameleon was changing colors as he danced: wood-brown, flame-orange, leaf-green, night-sky-black. A Satyr played melancholy sounds on reedy pipes, while the Unicorn sang. Beauty, watching mutely, nodded; his eyes filled with tears.

D'Ursu continued his narration in a growly whisper. "In the second act, each animal speaks to the question of why it will be good to die—speaks of the final ecstasy, the fear and wonder, of changing into something greater than yourself. Of your entire species dying, to make such a change; of the entire world, extinguished but for the Forest.

"We are in the final act now. All but three animals have made the tree-change. They make their final farewells before submitting to the passion of the Oneness. Animals from the audience have been joining the players on stage all along, as they have been so moved, to become part of the Forest, and may continue to do so as you watch. The Chameleon, there, has just restated his belief that life is change, the change to death part of that; the waiting Forest will be for him endlessly changing, and endlessly the same. Here, he is changing now."

The great Lizard leapt high on the Giraffe's back and sat there without moving, the color of willow bark. Several animals among the spectators moved into the growing ranks of players in the clearing. Some held branches, some were costumed in leaf-robes; some merely stood, steady as oak. The Tortoise walked three times around the Unicorn, making a series of gravelly clickings with his beak, finally stopping and pulling completely into his shell.

Josh and Jasmine stared on in rapt fascination. Beauty wept openly. He thought of the last time he'd seen the opera performed—after the battle of Babar-Dün, the bloodiest battle of the Race War, the carnage of which had chilled everyone's lust for war—all of his fallen comrades had been buried in shallow earth at the feet of the trees of that forest, their souls had gone into the trees, they had become part of the legend; and those animals left behind had performed the opera in their honor. Beauty had played the part of the Unicorn, the last animal to change.

The Unicorn on stage now walked slowly among the tree-still animals, and sang in a silvery tongue that Josh had difficulty understanding:

> "Tortoise tell me life too short
> to learn the things that must be learn:
> Quick as light in water-night
> or the whisper of the fern:
> only death is long enough
> to teach the sky's design,
> the colors of Shoshoroo,
> the soft perfumes of time.
>
> "But no Shoshoroo
> no Shoshoroo
> no Shoshoroo
>
> "Ohhhh
> Too much we learn in this dark life;
> its knowledge keeps us reined;
> and but in death, Shoshoroo,
> is innocence regained
>
> "Innocence regained, Shoshoroo
> innocence regained,
> I'm coming like the wind, Shoshoroo
> blowing through my mane
> Shoshoroo is my name, Shosho,
> Shoshoroo is my name
> Shoshorooooooooooo
> Shoshorooooooooooo"

At these final lines, the whole chorus of animals joined in—Cats and Birds and Gazelles and all—over and over, chanting "Shoshorooooo, Shoshoroooo," until it really did sound even to Josh like the wailing wind blowing up the caves and forests of the depths of his soul.

The opera was over, the animals dispersed. D'Ursu put his large paw on Beauty's back and spoke to Jasmine. "He cries, now, like a Human. It was not always so."

"Be quiet, ugly Bear," Beauty said with love, regaining his composure. "These friends want none of your blabber."

"Perhaps," D'Ursu persisted. "Even so, I would tell you all that Beauté Centauri saved my life too many times for this poor Bear to count. And the last time it was on account of this play—he dressed all up in the branches of a great bush, and so doing, edged close enough one night, without being taken for the horse's ass he was, to snatch me from the enemy camp and blow like Shoshoroo into the forest's night." Whereupon he laughed with a mighty roar, embarrassing Beauty greatly.

Josh nodded, impressed anew with his old friend. "I read of such a trick once—a man named Macbeth . . ."

D'Ursu Magna slapped Beauty's rump. "Next you'll be telling me *you* can read," he laughed even louder.

Beauty only smiled indulgently at the lieutenant. "Foolish Bear," he muttered.

Joshua's ear was suddenly attracted to a darker corner of the glen, where a joyously sad conclave of animals were singing their dead warriors into Heaven. A low, growling drone held unbroken against the melancholy counterpoint of pizzicato yelps and wails, while the simple refrain was chanted over and over, rising and falling:

"Animal change, animal fly
Animal forest, animal sky."

The four friends watched the ceremony briefly, then walked on in silence, each treading the water of his or her own thoughts.

Jasmine felt honored to have seen the performance. She hoped only to live to keep the memory. It was as D'Ursu had said, not a play for outsiders; though Jasmine preferred not to dwell upon the implications of that statement, she couldn't stop herself. And the more she considered it, the more uneasy it made her.

Josh was a bit overwhelmed—by Jarl, by the opera, by the camp itself, as they strolled through it now. Wolves rolled playfully with Rools; Elves, Satyrs, Centaurs, and Nymphs talked, ate, pondered. Firelight danced over sleeping cubs. Joshua had never seen so many different animals living together in such content. Oddly, it gave him a deep ache in his belly's marrow. D'Ursu Magna saw Joshua's feeling clearly, though, with the eyes of an animal at peace.

"Joshua Hunter," said D'Ursu. "Captain of my captain," he went on, including Beauty in his plea: "Your family is gone; give it up. Join ours. Your people have been reclaimed to the earth or the sky. Let them go, and your Human morals with them. Live the animal life with us, on this very spot; in this very moment."

Josh and Beauty exchanged a long searching look. The peace of this encampment seemed somehow a long way from the perils and demands of the hunt. It was Jasmine, finally, who spoke. "I can't help but be unsettled by Jarl's racism."

D'Ursu was incensed. "Racism! Animals of every race live in Jarl's light. We brush backs like the leaves on the willow tree, and Jarl our trunk."

"But Humans—" Jasmine began.

"Humans live here too—"

"But Humans are Jarl's niggers. If they behave the way he wants them to behave, he allows them rein— 'Animals *should* be this way. Humans *shouldn't* do that.' Well, I won't be a party to any causes or movements that dictate the behavior of others. I long ago gave up the word *should*." Whereupon she stalked off, followed, after a moment's hesitation, by Joshua.

Beauty and D'Ursu were left, sitting, alone at the fireside, heads down.

"She has reason," Beauty said at last.

"She is clever," answered D'Ursu.

Beauty was saddened by the distance he perceived to have grown between himself and D'Ursu. He still felt great love and affection for the old Bear; but they had taken different paths when the War ended. Beauty watched his friend now as if from afar. He wished he could make D'Ursu understand his feelings —his love for Joshua, his new appreciation of some of the Human virtues, his pride in his farm—but he didn't know where to begin.

"I must go in the morning, D'Ursu Magna. If it were your kindred they had abducted, you would do likewise."

The Bear Chieftain shook his head. "If creatures attacked us, I would fight for my family. Gone is gone, though. Here and now is the animal way."

Beauty touched the longing for Rose in his chest, the memory of her smell, the anticipation of her future smiles; his hatred of the creatures who took her, his craving to hunt them, to cause them the same pains they'd caused him. He also thought of Jasmine's story, of the beginnings of modern species: bits of animal in every Human; and Human in every animal. "It is not my way, though, D'Ursu Magna. Not my way." With sad clarity, as he spoke, he realized who he wasn't; then he wondered if he would ever discover who he was.

D'Ursu rocked on his haunches. "He will not let you leave on a vendetta, old friend."

"What will he do?"

"Kill you, most likely. For food."

Beauty nodded, paused. "You like it here?"

The old Bear smiled, a million-dollar smile with three missing teeth. "I like it fine. It is not the old days, but I like it fine."

So they settled back and tacitly agreed to ignore the chasm of years and traded glorious tales of the last great war to end all wars, when they'd fought together for justice and each other.

Joshua and Jasmine meanwhile had joined the perimeter of the wrestling matches, becoming quickly wrapped up in a contest between a small Gorilla and a large Ursuman. Dozens of animals stood about, shouting encouragement or advice, laughing, barking. Jasmine whispered to Josh: "The Ape has it—he's not even winded yet."

Josh stuck out his lip. "The other one's bigger, though. Sheer bulk."

Jasmine yelled something at the Gorilla, turned to a Satyr standing beside her, and said, "You people ever do any betting on these bouts?"

The Satyr looked shocked, then supercilious. "That's so *Human*," he sneered. Jasmine started to turn away, but the Satyr grabbed her shoulder, and lowering his voice, said, "However. I'll take five to three on Clubfoot. That's the Bear."

Jasmine won on the next fall, which left Clubfoot dazed and snarling in the dirt. The Satyr, whose name was Granpan, took Jasmine back to his campsite to pay off. Josh went along for lack of anything better to do, though his dark thoughts were not on the wagers, but jumped uneasily from Jarl's offers and demands to Dicey, Ollie, and Rose, to Venge-right, to escape, to Beauty and D'Ursu, to the dwindling of the Human race, to the new animal, to books, to Vampires; to food: ultimately he realized he was hungry.

Granpan's friends sat around a small fire peripheral to the main body of activity in the camp. Three Nymphs, an Elf, a Rool, and a Hobbit. Introductions were made. The Nymphs were Willow, Sugarpine, and Palm; the Elf was Siskin; the Rool, Rool; and the Hobbit, Windo. No one was over four feet tall.

When they found out Joshua was hungry, the Dryads pulled him down to the hearth, where they insisted that he share their raisin cakes, gorp, and root salad. Siskin threw some more onion-stuffed-potatoes onto the coals. Granpan paid Jasmine's bet with a packet of gold dust, while Windo sat meditatively puffing on his long pipe, wiggling his brown furry rabbitish feet toastily near the blaze. Rool sat curled at the Hobbit's side, rooling quietly. Jasmine accepted an offer of Granpan's locally famous grog.

"Will ye be stayin with's then?" asked Siskin, eyes a-twinkle.

"No," smiled Jasmine, sipping. "Just tonight, I think. We don't want to tax your hospitality."

"It would be fairer if you stayed long enough for me to win back my gold," joked Granpan.

"Thee are pretty," Sugarpine told Joshua, her face glowing warmly from the fire. "Why so glum, hunter?"

"Some grog will do wonders for him," Granpan chided.

"All who weep be not glum," advised Willow.

"I—I'm sorry if . . ." Josh began. He'd been feeling increasingly edgy about the situation they were in; now he felt worse for being so unreceptive to this show of genuine hospitality.

"He's not meaning to be rude," Jasmine apologized for him. Then, more pointed: "He's yet to learn to do nothing when nothing is to be done." Josh looked at her. She indicated the wood's edge with a tilt of her head. "With sentries every five yards, we could hardly leave tonight in any case."

Granpan laughed. "They're to keep invaders out, not to keep friends in."

"Ah," said Jasmine; but Josh nodded imperceptibly at her. The animals at large, it seemed, were not aware of the special position of the new prisoners/guests.

"Well, then," Granpan roared, "there's nothin' to be done but pass the cup and tickle." At which he fell backward joyfully, accidentally spilling his cup on Rool.

"Rool," said Rool, and licked himself clean.

"Sorry, old boy," Granpan excused.

Joshua did have a little drink, and it did loosen him up a little. "It's a happy clan you live with here, Granpan. I envy you."

"Thee make it happier still," Sugarpine cooed, nuzzling Joshua's shoulder. He put his arm around her, succumbing to the pull of her spirit.

"And you, Windo, so quiet," prodded Jasmine. "Happy with your lot?" She had a great affection for these short, pointy-eared, rabbit-footed creations. They'd been genetically engineered for the children of the rich in the middle decadence of the twenty-second century—even mass-produced for a time, they were in such popular demand, such a coveted myth. But they did not do well, either in the culture that bred them, or in subsequent, harder times. They were a race that needed more nurturing than the world could supply, Jasmine suspected. In any case, they were becoming extinct.

The Hobbit's glazed pupils scarcely moved as he took his pipe from his mouth. "I have a lot to be happy, which is more than a lot of my lot can say. But lot it is, so happy am I by a lot."

Jasmine looked quizzically at Windo, then over at Granpan. The Satyr just laughed uproariously. "It's that stuff he smokes," he dipped his head at the Hobbit, and winked at Jasmine.

"Did you ever think of setting out on your own?" Jasmine asked the strange little creature.

Granpan wagged his head knowingly. "They don't do well out there," indicating the lands beyond.

"No," agreed Jasmine, "they're too gentle by half." She turned her head to Josh before continuing. "By the early 2100s Hobbits were running around everywhere. Every children's zoo had a village of them, every connoisseur of myth had one. Then the Germ Wars of 2116 erupted, killed most Humans and related species that weren't resistant. Thinned out the Hobbits considerably. Then the Nuclear War on July 4th and 5th, 2117. Razed most of the big cities that were still standing after all the looting and burning that had gone on during the Germ Wars. It was like the final suicidal spasm of that whole decaying culture. Lot of things died then, and Hobbits were just one more expression of that dying dream. They've sort of perked along ever since then, losing a few more each year. Competition was just too fierce, I guess. It's hard to keep a gentle dream alive, with so many nightmares crowding around." Jasmine realized she'd been rambling on more to herself than anyone else. She stopped and looked up.

To her surprise, she found everyone listening to her. The animals loved mysterious tales from passing strangers, she recalled, though——they gave her neither more nor less credence than they gave any wandering minstrel: to the animals, all the stories were true, and all the stories wonderful. She smiled wryly at the audience: only Windo ignored her narrative, lost deep in his own reverie. "He must miss his kin," Jasmine looked softly at the distant little creature.

"His soul be sad," nodded Willow, "for his people are fading like the leaves in winter."

"We're his people, now, ye know," protested Siskin. He drew on Windo's pipe, then passed it back.

"We're all each other's people," proclaimed Palm, suddenly standing and dancing a Belonging dance. Granpan picked up his flute and accompanied the Nymph's entrancing jig. Neither Sugarpine nor Willow could stay down long once the music started; soon all three Dryads were pirouetting gaily with their shadows in the magic light of the blossoming night-fire.

Siskin got up to dance next, and even Windo tapped his foot in time to Granpan's pipes. Others gathered round, and leapt about like the very flames; and lutes were strummed and songs were sung, and even Jasmine, tone-deaf-and-dumb, clapped a bonnie beat.

Between the flow of the grog and the flow of the music, Joshua needed no prodding. When the others paused to catch their breaths, he sang out:

> "The Hunter is a cheerful sight,
>   His hearth is warm, his fire bright,
>   His songs they fill the winter night,
>   Among the leaves so green-o"

At which immediately he was joined in chorus:

> "So it's hey down-down, ho down-down,
>   Hey down ho down derry derry down,
>   Among the leaves so green-o."

And on and on until, eventually, everyone tired of singing, and settled down to some serious storytelling. Jasmine was a great success at this, regaling her listeners with Aesop's fables until the cows came home.

Granpan made it halfway through the story of the fox and the lion when he started feeling chilly. The fire was dwindling to coals. Palm began cuddling up to him, and before he knew it, they were making their own loving heat under the cover of cool night and warm voices.

Sugarpine found Josh again before too long. He was heavy with wine, light with music, deep with kinship, staring at the residual raindrops that hung on the tips of the willow leaves and sparkled like ripe tears in the firelight. As she snuggled into his weakly protesting arms, he felt the pressures of his trek dissolve into the temporary past and future. All he knew for the frozen moment: her chest on his chest, the wind on his back, starlight through the trees; and the calming sussuration of soft-spoken background conversations like waves on the shore.

Sunrise.

Jarl strolled among his minions, growling jokes, biting ears. When he came to the breakfast coals where Joshua, Beauty, and Jasmine sat quietly talking, he stopped, smiled, sat. "My animals like you," he nodded at them. "I hope you will stay with us."

Beauty, with even force: "We will not, sir."

The Bear-King lost his smile. "Then, sadly I must . . ."

"You must convene a court, your Honor. We claim the right to trial by pack."

This was an ancient prerogative. If an animal so offended the social order that other animals began to turn on it, it could claim a tribal judgment rather than fight or flee. These judgments were binding and immediate. If the judgment was death, flight was no longer an option. This was before the time of Animal-Kings, though, when packs ran wild, and chaos burned across the land, in the years after the Ice. It was the way animals policed themselves and purged themselves. When the Kings came, there was no more need for pack-trial: the Kings were the Judges, they made the Law; or rather, the Law flowed through the Kings.

Still, trial was an ancient prerogative. And Beauty

had spoken loudly enough so that many animals heard him. Heads turned. A silence fell.

Jarl thought a few moments, staring at the ground. Finally he looked up. "And as it is your right, so you shall have it."

The jury, selected by Jarl, sat semicircle either side of his throne, facing the accused. They numbered eight: Granpan, Willow, Windo; Three-claw, an old Bear; Droo, the Owl; Gray, the She-Wolf; Louise, an Ursuman warrior; and Rool, a Rool. They sat somberly, four on a side, poised like the King's judicial claws. The rest of the animals stood crowded around, listening, watching.

Jarl began the proceedings. "This gathering is called not because your King would have it so, but because it is mete." He paused for effect. The animals were quiet. "The accused have been asked to share our den, but have refused that they may revenge, in violation of Natural Animal Law. Furthermore, in their pursuit toward this end, animals have died. Accused, what say you?"

Josh stepped forward. He addressed the jury. "My name is Joshua, Human, and Hunter, and Scribe . . ." He told their story completely once more. The animals listened attentively.

When Joshua finished, Beauty said only, "I have nothing to add. Our mission is private, of no concern to you. We wish only to be on our way, to reclaim our people."

The jurists turned, then, toward Jasmine. She spoke briefly. "I'd just like to emphasize a few things. First, the idea of revenge should be irrelevant to your considerations. Whether we three feel vengeful or not is a matter for our hearts, not your verdict. The issue here is plain: animals attacked my friends' families and killed without Justice. We have hunted these animals since then to save what family is left.

"Second, I joined in this hunt because this Human saved my life, though he didn't have to. It's important for you to know this—his spirit is good.

"And last, we have killed no animal without Justice.

Only to defend ourselves, only when forced. Such is our story."

There was a pause while the jurors rustled, whispered, scratched. Finally Jarl spoke. "I will waive my own opening statement on behalf of the Forest. Witnesses-For the accused, come forward and speak."

A long silence filled the glen, as animals looked up and back to see who would speak for the three who would fly in the face of Jarl's wishes. Nobody moved. Only the leaves whispered urgently to each other, passing their opinions like an excited gallery. Just as Jarl was about to speak again, D'Ursu Magna stepped forward. "Animals, I speak for Beauté Centaur." There was a hush. D'Ursu Magna was a Chieftain, and greatly respected. All animals gave him ear. "Some great time ago," he went on—animals had only vague understanding of past or future beyond a span of days—"there was a great War. I fought with honor as did many of you, under our wise King Jarl, alongside countless brave animals, against the Humans who had for so long enslaved us, caged and humiliated us, experimented on us, bred us for their pleasures and our misery. In this noble War, my captain was Beauté Centauri.

"A braver warrior did not exist, nor a truer animal. Many times when I was wounded, he saved my life at his own peril—once, on the Plains of Babar-Dün."

Many animals murmured here. Even creatures with the shortest of memories, who didn't exactly remember the battle, still kept its feeling with them. D'Ursu continued: "Neither did Beauté Centauri ever break trust with animal, though he were sorely tested. In the second year of the War he trusted me to lower him by rope into the pit of the Mosian Firecaves, that he could retrieve a casket of gems hidden there, that we might use the stones to barter with the Humans for hostages. The fires taunted him all around, but he never flinched, saying only for me to lower him a little lower, for the jewels were not far." There was silence, now, a collective shudder: the image of fire out of control, of an animal swinging in a pit of flame, terrified the creatures of the forest like no other image. Again, D'Ursu went on.

"He carried small beasts on his back wherever he walked, just to give them rest. Once, we two bore a message of great import from Skorl, the Bear-Prince, to the western packs. Humans caught our sign, but Beauté Centauri ran howling into the north, leading the enemy wide that I might steal away in safety with our command. It even happened that—"

"Enough!" roared Jarl from his throne. "This begins to tire us, D'Ursu Magna. It weighs not on the question at hand."

D'Ursu glowered at his King, but remained silent. The whole glade seemed to hush. Finally, D'Ursu spoke again; more quietly, but very near defiance. "He never spoke falsely, nor killed without Justice. He could have killed me in battle yesterday, but did not—again, to his own risk. If he says his hunt is just, I believe him. He has not the smell of deceit or Humansickness. He wishes to leave. Let him leave."

The animals all began chattering at once. D'Ursu Magna was a powerful voice in the Forest. But there was a more powerful voice. "Silence!" growled Jarl. There was silence. "Next witness," he called.

Beauty stepped forward. "Your Honor, I would like to speak."

"Defendants may not Witness their own acts," the Bear-King reminded.

"It is not myself I Witness," said the Centaur, "it is Joshua. In the same War D'Ursu Magna spoke of, I also was wounded, near death, alone in hostile territory. My life was saved by this Human—my enemy. Under great danger to himself he harbored and nursed me—me, an animal and his sworn enemy—out of his love for me, and the animal virtues. Animals: this is no ordinary Human; this one abides in the Heart of the Forest." Beauty's last line was a reference to an old animal legend with which all were familiar—in which it is said that the Heart of the Forest beats only once every millennium; that to find the Heart, one must see it as it beats; that to see it, one must first know what it looks like, and that to know it, one must abide in its very center at the moment of its beating. It was a special legend, and for Beauty to speak this way evoked a special response from every animal, even those with no love for the Human race.

Jarl waited a considered moment, then called once for any last Witnesses-For, then called twice; and as his jaws opened for the last call, Sugarpine the Nymph stepped before the throne:

"Wisdom," she whispered, "I would speak for the Human."

"Address me not," he growled soft as down. "Your words are for the jury."

She took one step back, to face the whole panel. "Friends," she spoke barely more boldly, "last night he was tender to me."

There was a passage of time waiting for her to continue, but she did not. "Go on, child," Jarl prodded.

"That is all," Sugarpine apologized meekly, then quickly retired back into the animal crowd.

"Very well," Jarl harrumphed. "Final call, Witnesses-For."

There was a small commotion in the middle of the gathering. The commotion worked its way forward quickly until it spewed into the arena a small surprise witness: Fofkin, the Elf.

"Your Renowned Masterfulnesses," squeaked the playful Elf. "I am Fofkin, prince and pauper, cousin to Siskin, your own beloved Elf. I came to your happy camp with me friend, Rool, three nights ago, or four, or maybe six. And I know these travelers." He did a little somersault for emphasis. "Yes I do," he went on. "Bad animals stole off me Mary. A Vampire, an Accident, and a Never-You-Mind. And these kind people stopped us nice as you please and said they were chasing the bad animals and they would get me Mary back if they could, and a fine fare-thee-well. I never kept a strong hope for me stolen darlin', Your Very Highnesses, but these two had a moment to spend a kind word on our Troubles-we-never-asked-for, whilst they were surely boggled and bound with Troubles of their own." He sat down lightly, dropped a single tear to the leafy ground, and added, "I didn't even know they were here until the Trial started, but your Bountiful Skynesses, I hope you'll let them go so they can find me Mary and send her home to me." He did a double somersault, and, with a small commotion, vanished back into the crowd.

Jarl cleared his throat. "Is that all?" his voice rumbled, suggesting that that had better be all. No one answered. "In that case," he continued, "Witnesses-Against."

Three-Claw rose from his place beside Jarl. "He killed my sister," he said, pointing at Joshua. Josh recognized Three-Claw, now, as one of the Bears who'd been singing the dead into Heaven last night.

"It was battle," replied Josh. "It was with Justice."

"Not if your mission was without Justice," Jarl interjected. His impatient voice sobered the very leaves. "It seems to me," he went on as if he'd been asked, "that the crux of this trial rests on the justice of your journey. Character witnesses for and against are neither here nor there. What this body must decide is the question of merit in a quest intimately involved with Venge-right. My position is clear on this matter: it has no merit; it must be stopped. It is part and parcel of the Human drive to control and it has no place in a free animal world."

"May I humbly submit, your Honor, that your years as a Human captive, forced to dance before jeering crowds, have colored your vision." Only Jasmine dared speak this way against the force of Jarl's vision. "Your Honor," she continued, almost tauntingly, "you sound almost vengeful."

Jarl stood to his full height, and it was a frightening figure he cut. Not an animal breathed. "You mock me, Sister," he almost whispered.

"She meant nothing . . ." Beauty began, breaking an oily sweat.

"I meant for Jarl the Wise to see that revenge is relative, like time," Jasmine's voice rose. "Animals know only of the present. Humans, to their grief, stand on the precarious moment as if it were a peak, and from the crumbling precipice view the panorama of the past behind, the future below. It's a dizzying spectacle, your Honor, from a lonely post." Something in the way she spoke caught them all—the jury, the audience, the Judge. Something that made the strangeness of her words familiar. "An animal struggles in the Now—it eats, loves, fights. For a Human, the struggle is as far as can be seen in all directions: a past battle, just there, over in the landscape three weeks down the mountain is as clear—or clearer—in the southern light as the battle raging in the cloud-shrouded moment he's perched on. And there, there's a winding path leading right from that past battle, up over the peak, and down into some future valley. The two events are connected, though, the past and the future, and revenge is one of a thousand paths that connects them."

The image was illuminating to all the curious creatures, but to none more than Josh. "And Scribery is another path," he marveled.

Jasmine nodded. "The religion of Scribery is one of the most ancient Human paths over the mountain. With it, vast expanses of the past were mapped, myriad future courses plotted. It was a road well traveled once, but it got lost in a crossing of too many paths, and now it's just one of a thousand again.

"Religion was always a popular Human way to connect the slopes of history and destiny. So was magic. And genealogy. And astrology, and governments and crusades. And revenge. All caught up with one foot on either side of the mountaintop, connecting the two never-quite-reachable Cities—Before and After.

"And every animal here knows that walk." She turned her gaze on every member of the jury; even on Jarl's towering visage. Beauty felt Jasmine's words drive into his chest like a spear, underscoring his fear and confusion about Human origins of the Centauri. Joshua felt himself clearly—a stark, visual image—standing on the mountaintop viewing the scene: the people, some dead, some yet unborn; the dreams, the memories, the plans—all spread out around him, below him, gentle plains, craggy gullies, steep drops, distant shadows. It made him swoon.

And every animal there did know that rise with the

view into both valleys. It was a short walk for some, stretching only from lunch to dinner with a sheer, black dropoff on either side. But others—Jarl, for one —could remember earlier years, could envision what might yet come.

"I am old, your Highness," Jasmine spoke slowly, putting feeling in her voice. "Older than you, older than this forest, older than the Ice Change. I've seen much, to my joy and grief. Many years before the Coming of Ice there was a great confrontation between Human and animal, called by some the Clone Wars. The animals were sick of the Human-sickness; and the Humans, to rebuild their numbers, made thousands of copies of themselves, called Clones; and the animals, in fury over what the Humans had done over the years, killed them all but the children. It was a vengeful act, Jarl, and all the animals joined in. Such is our heritage. Do not deny it: you can master that part of yourself only by knowing it."

Jarl sat back down slowly into his willow-throne. He felt the Neuroman's words. Perhaps it was only a question of distances, then. Perhaps there *was* something animal in the way of revenge. Or something Human in himself?

"Jurors," said the Bear-King. "Have you any questions of the accused?"

Granpan shook his head No.

Windo puffed his pipe. "It's a pretty sight from way up there, I don't doubt, but down here there's no fallin' off. You can have your stony paths. Only tell me this. When I'm down here hindside to o' your peak, is your next step the one that starts the rockslide on me and mine?"

Jasmine smiled at the winsome Hobbit. "I think maybe your peak is higher than mine to begin with. I could never hurt such a one as you, until the day the rocks fall up."

Willow spoke next, to Joshua. "Have you ever killed a tree?"

"None I didn't have to, to keep the breath of Ice off my back," he told her honestly.

Three-Claw said, "You killed my sister. She should be alive, but for your journey. Where is the Justice?"

"*Should* is a word I gave up long ago," Jasmine answered sadly, "when I realized how little of anything I understood. I don't know, Bear-friend, where is the Justice."

Droo, the Owl, was next, saying, "Droo-roo hoor hoor thooew who who ooo . . ." It was a long, involved question dealing with epistemology, which partly due to dialect, no one else really quite got the gist of.

Rool fell asleep.

Gray, the She-Wolf, lowered her eyelids. "And when you find these animals who stole your pack . . . you will kill them?"

Josh and Beauty nodded firmly.

Gray went on. "And this will satisfy you? This will end your search?" It was clear Gray thought otherwise. Humans, she knew, were never satisfied, and never ended their searches.

It was Beauty who responded. "I cannot answer to those questions. Things have happened to me in recent days that make me wonder if satisfactions will ever be mine. I know neither who I am, nor what is expected of me. Only that I must find my Rose."

Josh nodded. "It's unfinished business. You wouldn't wound a Caribou and then leave him to wander. You'd stalk him and kill him."

"Not if I weren't hungry," said the Wolf.

"There are different kinds of hunger," said Josh.

Louise, the last juror, said simply, "How will you go to find them?"

"South, into the Terrarium," said Jasmine. "We believe they're heading for the new animal."

Jarl came out of his brooding shell. "Go, then. I have learned something of myself today, which I must consider. Good journey and good sleep." Saying which, he closed his darkening eyes and hibernated.

"Well," grumped Granpan, "I suppose I won't be winning any gold back now."

Jasmine laughed as she strapped her épée around

her waist. "When you storm the Doge's palace you'll have all the gold you want."

Good-byes were said, or not, as feelings went. Jasmine assumed the lotus position and meditated for ten minutes, to prepare for the continuation of the hunt. Josh primed his falcon quill, laid out paper on a flat rock, and set the record. Beauty waxed his Dragonrib bow until it glowed like still water in the sunset. Camp activities resumed, animals played and dozed. Soon the trial was but one more poorly remembered festivity to most of the creatures, a pleasant pause in the flow of their lives.

D'Ursu Magna accompanied the hunters out of the glen to the edge of the woods.

"May we meet in the Great Forest," said the Bear.

"I wish you well, D'Ursu Magna," Beauty replied.

Josh and Jasmine bared their necks to the Chieftain; then turned and set off.

By noon the three seekers made the shadow of the Saddleback range.

CHAPTER 10

The Terrarium

THE climb up the north face of Mount Orion was not difficult. It was one of the smaller Saddlebacks, and Jasmine knew all of the passes.

They were quiet on the ascent, each following stray thoughts from here to there. In the cool silence of the afternoon sun, the mountain itself seemed absorbed in reverie. Sometimes the wind would pick up, keening through the canyons like a painful memory; then fall like a dying breath.

The rock was igneous, the foliage sparse. As the air rarefied, the scarps became steeper, more glazed, less traveled. Yet in spite of the glassine surfaces, the climbers reached the summit quickly. A mere thousand feet above sea level, they looked back in the direction from which they'd come at the chiaroscuro of criss-crossing paths that had led them to this point; and then looked ahead, to the south: down four thousand feet into the jungle below sea level that was their future. Dundee's Terrarium.

The Terrarium was ten thousand square miles of rain forest, surrounded on all sides by the Saddleback Mountains; a full half-mile below sea level; simmering over pensive lava beds, pocked by hot springs: a steaming cloistered greenhouse. Every day the mists would burn off the rock beds, rise through the dense mosaic of light and leaf, reach the cooler air at sea level—still a thousand feet below the insulating peaks —then condense and rain down on the jungle, cooling things briefly. Until, an hour later, the steam would begin to rise again, and the process would repeat. All day, all night, an hour of rain, an hour of steam.

It was difficult to see much of the Terrarium itself

from where they stood, because of the patchy cloud cover five to six hundred feet below them. But they felt it, smelled it, a huge gloating pit waiting impassively for its next victims to drop in.

Few who ever walked into Dundee's Terrarium walked out: Jasmine knew this for fact. She'd spent years of her life learning a thousand twisting paths down there, she knew it as well as anyone alive, knew it certainly as well as Bal knew it. She had no doubt about her ability to track the Vampire and his hostages in the Terrarium, for Bal was not her most treacherous adversary—it was the jungle itself, now as always. A thousand twisting paths she'd learned there, yet she'd left, finally, knowing full well she'd barely scratched the jungle's hide.

"I've never been a pantheist," she said as they began their descent, "but this jungle is alive. And sentient."

The climb down was relatively easy. Not too steep for Beauty, and plenty of ground cover to cling to. At six hundred to a thousand feet below the crests, they found themselves completely engulfed in the cloud bank. It was slow going here. Visibility was no more than a foot. Beauty hung on to Jasmine, and Josh to Beauty, so nobody would get lost. For a brief second, Joshua feared they would wander here in these cloying mists forever.

Finally the trio emerged, like ghosts from a dream, below the cloud line, and saw it fully for the first time: the Rain Forest. They paused a moment to regard it, to address it; and then without further ado, took the last long leg of the descent down into the belly of the beast.

They reached the first fringes of undergrowth about an hour before sundown. The temperature and humidity were both approaching a hundred, from two directions. It wasn't raining, which meant it was steaming: wisps rose in sultry spirals from the ferns; water ticked patiently drop by drop from palm frond to rock, where it quickly evaporated once again. The air was palpable.

Jasmine led the way in. She seemed to know just

where she was going; even though no path was evident. Knee deep in feathery fern, then chest deep in bird of paradise, she took them; carefully, around bubbling hot springs, then quickly over a short table of baking slate; and finally under the first tree cover of sagging plantanos, laced through with a wild tangle of crawling vines.

Joshua had a sense of foreboding. This unfamiliar vegetation had all the sinister odor of memories' breath, and Josh wished he were once again running clear on open plain. He silently thanked the Word for crossing his path with Jasmine to lead him through this suffocating murk.

Beauty, too, found himself grateful for Jasmine's presence. She'd proved herself able on more than one occasion, and if she knew these woods, so much the better. He felt somehow more balanced, again, after the episode at Jarl's—or at least, less teetering. He was ready to resume the quest. He thought to himself, "I may not yet know if I be Human or creature, invention or inheritor, but this I know: I am hunter." It felt good now simply to look for sign among all the possible places the world can hide it.

Jasmine alone kept her mind—at least temporarily —free of thought. She concentrated only on her senses; and of these, the predominating was the sense of return.

They made it into the trees as the sun vanished below the mountains; but strangely, almost horribly, the nightfall was not dark—because filling the pools and rocks half submerged in the wet black soil clinging to the lower regions of the moist bark on the trees, was the glowing unreal aura of red phosphorescent algae. It seemed to seep from the earth, this glow, sitting like a motionless red tide, casting an eerie garnet hue in the waking shadows of the steaming night.

For the first time, Joshua was scared. Inaudibly, he sang to himself—an old powerful incantation his mother had taught him many years before: "Ai bee see dee ee ef gee; aitch eye jay kay, el em en oh pee . . ."

Dicey lay her head down in Rose's lap as the rain continued its tepid drizzle.

"I wonder what it feels like to be dry," mused the young girl.

"At least we're warm enough," answered Rose. She stroked the girl's forehead.

The other Humans around them dozed, or picked over the remains of the small lizards they'd been given to eat. On the other side of the clearing two Accidents made low gurgling noises, tearing apart and gnawing on a dead panther. Beside them, the Vampires slept.

At the edge of the enclosure, a small forest pool was alive with raindrops, heavy with the red glow. Rose stared dully into its depths, trying to remember what it was like to be free and happy. She yearned for her Beauty. Behind her, her new friend Nancy sat wet-nursing Ollie, who was still mostly catatonic. Nancy's own baby lay gaunt and sleeping in her other arm.

Somewhere in the jungle a hyena chattered insanely. Nancy shivered, in spite of the heat.

"Want my jacket?" asked Rose. She felt her own needs less urgently when she was helping others. She knew this about herself, and made use of the knowledge as a musician who soothes himself by soothing others with his music.

Nancy smiled wanly, shook her head. She was slowly approaching the edge beyond which help lay.

Dicey distractedly rubbed at the bruises on her neck, her eyes unfocused.

A small bat suddenly flapped into the space, dove at them, bit Mary on the foot. Mary was Nancy's sister, and her husband had been Fofkin the Elf. She swatted at it with her hand. It quickly flapped up into the trees, rested for a moment in the crux of a dead branch, laughed excitedly for a brief second, and flew back into the jungle thick. Rose looked at Mary's foot: it was bleeding. They both glanced anxiously at the Vampires, who still slept, undisturbed. Rose put a handful of leafy mud on the wound; then took off her jacket, put it around Mary's shoulders. Mary sighed and lay back down. She searched for sleep.

Eric, a gangling fair-haired lad, crawled over. "Will someone lie with me?" he asked plaintively. "I need to lie with someone."

There was a tired, empty silence. Mary regarded him and held out her arms. He smiled limply, lay down beside her. They held each other, motionless, belly to belly, cheek to cheek, she looking over his shoulder, he over hers; into darkness.

Nearby, a bird screamed.

The Accidents finished their meal and went to sleep.

As the quiet rain stopped, the ground began to steam, like red death.

"Here," said Rose, passing garlic cloves to Mary, Nancy, Dicey, Eric. She'd stolen the bunch in the Forest of Tears, secretly eating a clove a day. It was said to make the taste of one's blood unappetizing to the Vampire palate. Carefully, she chewed it.

Mary ate her piece in a single grimacing gulp; Nancy sucked on hers meditatively. Eric put his clove under his tongue, and soon forgot it was there.

Dicey brought the garlic to her lips, then dropped it in the dirt; then pretended to chew, as she covered the clove over with leaves and moss.

It was raining again, Jasmine made slow headway through the matted overgrowth, her companions just behind her. Gnarling tendrils caught their feet, scraped their faces. Roots twined over the ground like bloated fingers. Branches dangled, vines twisted. The jungle pressed.

Abruptly, a space seemed to open. Jasmine began to enter, caught a glint in the carmine glow, and stopped short; eight feet high, spanning the entrance to the clearing like a gauze door, a sticky spiderweb shimmered tautly, inches from the Neuroman's face. She took a step back. From the geometric center of its sheer woven lair, the hairy, melon-sized spider eyed its would-be feast.

"Back up," said Jasmine over her shoulder. "We'll have to walk around."

They veered right, chopping through the tangle

with their blades every few feet. They passed an area fragrant with rotting fruit. A well-fed snake undulated over Joshua's foot, then vanished once more into the brush. It stopped raining. Something flew overhead.

They came to a wall of hanging vines. "Here we are," Jasmine mumbled, and began hacking at them vigorously with her épée. The others sat back, resting, watching. Josh was tired. He'd never seen terrain like this, and he didn't know what to expect from it. The constant physical duress, the protracted tension, the unknown dangers—these things were beginning to take their toll on the young hunter. He was beginning to jump at noises.

Beauty was feeling less anxious, more purely distasteful. To him, the jungle smelled foul, decayed; self-strangulating. The creatures who thrived here seemed ill of spirit to him. Wryly, he realized he was not a creature of the Rain Forest—something else he was not; no closer yet to what he was.

After fifteen minutes of chopping, Jasmine had cleared an inroad four feet deep into the viny wall, when suddenly the last creeper fell away; and revealed before them, a path.

"My Word," said Josh. Beauty was silently impressed.

They entered the hidden trail. Its floor was white limestone, sanguine in the luminous algae. In width it measured ten feet, but felt more like a tunnel than a path, the jungle around it was so dense. Jasmine began to relax as soon as they started walking.

"Don't mind telling you now, I was a little afraid I'd lost my bearings there for a while. Right on track, now, though. We used to call this the Yellow Brick Road." She laughed.

Josh looked confused. "Why?" he said, since it was obviously neither yellow nor brick.

They walked with long, easy strides, releasing most of a night of thickening tension. Beauty even galloped a few paces down the gently curving footpath. "Why, indeed?" mumbled Jasmine. "A good question. Oh, I remember. In fact, that was how I met Lon, when we first started running together." Her memory ran back to those days, poured over them like honey down a throat. "Now, wasn't that a time," she recalled.

Josh waited a minute, but when Jasmine continued to remain silent, he finally prodded, "Yes?"

"Ah," she jumped back to the present. "Well. I had just come to the Terrarium. This was probably . . . oh a hundred years ago, give or take. Well after the Great Quake, though. I'd been lured here by rumors of a Lost City, a magical place, cached with riches. Stories like that brought a lot of prospectors down here. Most just got eaten by the jungle."

A determined column of blackish Ants cut across the pathway before them.

"Step over them carefully," Jasmine warned. "They're missionary Ants." Josh and Beauty did as they were told, jumping gingerly over the Insect procession, and continuing on down the lime trail.

Jasmine went on with her story. "Anyway, I checked it out by myself here for a couple of years. Got to be a regular jungle-junkie, had a few close calls, discovered some nifty hideaways. Became a brigand. It was pretty easy pickin's, all in all—there were a lot of dodos running around down here, most of 'em ripe for harvest. And I was the reaper. Always left 'em enough so they could make it back to the coast with their skin still on if they were smart and careful, though. Thought of myself as a sort of self-appointed evolutionary force— only the fittest survived after I lightened their load." She laughed joyously at the recollection, then became quieter. "It was my adolescence, down here, mine and the world's, what the world had become. We were a rowdy lot, and never a thought about consequences."

Josh and Beauty let her walk in silence a while, to follow her thoughts. Finally her smile returned and she continued.

"There were some tough nuts too, of course. This kind of place always attracts the hard case. Ovenhead Daley used to hunt these parts; Snake Alder, too. And of course, old Dundee himself. But that's another story.

"Anyway, I was walking down this very path one

day, when what do I see in the distance but a big gorgeous Vampire dragging a wooden box out of the jungle, across the width of the trail, and into the jungle on the other side. Well, I just hopped right up, put my blade to his chest, and advised him that I'd be taking ownership of the box. He put his index finger on the tip of my sword, pushed it to the side slowly, and said with the utmost disdain, 'You've made your point.' Those were the first words Lon ever spoke to me."

"Lon? The Lon we met?" Josh asked.

"The very same. I backed him off a few steps and opened the box with my blade. And what do you think was in there? Ninety pounds of raw flake cocaine. I knew immediately what it was for, of course—the Howlers. They were a tribe of insane commandos, had a little village on the Big Sticks, and they were always amassing an army for their next war. They just loved to kill and die. And they all snorted coke, especially before and during big battles, because it gave them so much strength and energy for the hand-to-hand combat. They howled when they fought, too, just to be scary. Had a lot of *chi*, those Howlers.

"Anyway, Lon was a smuggler, I'd seen him around the ports once or twice, and he was obviously moving this shipment from the *coca* regions in the east, down to Howler-town. A big score, no question. Enough for both of us, I told him, but he wasn't interested. So I turned him around and tied the box to his back so it bound both his arms and his wings down flat. 'Start walkin',' I said. 'Where?' he said. 'This trail goes right into Howler-town,' I said, and pointed him south. Well, I tell you, he wasn't too happy about the idea of walking down an open path with his hands tied. It's always safer to stick to the brush. The path was faster, though, and my thought was the faster we unloaded these goods the better. Lon was pretty reluctant about the whole situation, so I had to prod him a bit with the talkin' end of my saber. 'Just follow the yellow brick road,' I told him, 'and the Wizard will reward you.' So off we went, him in front, me behind."

Josh was astounded at this new picture of Jasmine

as rogue and scoundrel. He stole a glance at Beauty, who was too engrossed in the story to notice.

"Well," Jasmine lowered her voice, "we'd walked about a day like this, and we were both pretty tired. I was about to look for a tree to camp in, when suddenly a huge trapdoor opened in the walk, and we both dropped in. I was grabbed and spun 'round by these horrible hairy legs, wrapped tighter and tighter in this sticky suffocating silky thread. By the time I got my bearings and looked around, I realized we were done for. Spiders, the size of cats, dozens of them. When I looked over at Lon, he was practically a cocoon, all wound up in webbing, spiders crawling all over him. It made me cold to watch, I tell you. Just before they wrapped his head up, he looked over at me and said with a smile, 'Well, Toto, I don't think we're in Kansas anymore.' Then they covered him over.

"Several of them bit us—on the belly, on the face— and injected their poison. Painful it was, and paralyzing, though it didn't affect me nearly so much as it did poor old Lon, since my plastic skin is so thick. Then they hung us upside down in netting, so they could snack off us at their leisure. Spiders never kill you outright, they just paralyze you and slowly eat you alive. Then when you're about half dead, they eat little holes in your belly and lay their eggs in there, and then when the baby spiders hatch they live off you until you die. I tell you, my thoughts weren't very pretty right about then."

She shivered at the memory. A snake hissed from somewhere out of sight, and they all jumped. The Forest glowed.

"Something funny happened then," she picked up. "The cocaine strapped to Lon's back started leaking out, making a pile of flaky white powder on the ground at his feet. Some of the spiders circled around it, touched it, tasted it, tasted it some more, called over their friends—and before you know it, every spider in the cave was wired. And I mean righteously. They were zinging back and forth, spinning webs, fighting, chattering, really frenzied. Some of them started to run out of the cave, and suddenly, they were all running out of the cave, off to who knows what. With me and Lon left hanging.

"Well, like I said, I'd only gotten a mild dose, so I was in pain but I could still move some. I finally pulled an arm free and tore myself down. Tore as much web as I could off my legs, grabbed Lon just as he was, slung him over my shoulder, and dragged us both out of there. I could hardly move, but I'd never been so scared, and that goes a long way to motivate you. I pulled us through the jungle for a whole day before I finally got to one of my own hiding places, in a cave behind a waterfall I know. I collapsed there. We both slept fitfully for about two days until the poison wore off. I nursed Lon for another week and we got to be pretty close in that cave, behind that waterfall." The feeling was strong in her voice and her eye. "Anyway, ever since then, we called this the Yellow Brick Road."

Josh looked mystified. "I still don't get it," he said. "Yellow? Brick Road?" He'd been thoroughly engrossed in the story as it was being told, but now at the punch line he had the feeling he'd missed something essential.

Jasmine just smiled, shrugged. "You had to be there, I guess."

"Did you ever see Lon again?" asked Beauty, keen on the postscript.

"See him? We went into business together. Gunrunning, bounty-hunting. Five, six years we gamed. Lon made his fortune and retired."

"And you?"

"I made the best friend I ever had." She smiled, remembering Lon in his younger day, her boisterous, strapping Vampire lover, brother scoundrel, mentor, and friend. She had a momentary flash that she was somehow maybe becoming some of these things to the two seekers who followed her now. It gave her a warm feeling, the specifics of which she could not exactly trace, though it had to do with kinship and the passing of torches and secret knowledge and a sense that life goes on. In the midst of these thoughts, she recognized a landmark and stopped.

"Ah, we're here," she said, and stepping off the limestone path, plunged back into the twining jungle. The others followed.

Isis was queasy. She'd eaten a beetle of some kind, and it hadn't agreed with her. Her head ached, her eyes burned, her stomach twisted. She lapped at some water from an algae-filled pool; but it, too, tasted queer.

This was no time to let things slide. She'd followed her quarry through the Forest of Tears, across the hard, trackless Thenar Plains, over the Saddlebacks, and into this vile flowering jungle. Sometimes she'd remember it was for Joshua, and she'd double her resolve. Bandits had almost snared her once, for food; and once she'd lost the scent of her prey, but found it again. Now she could no longer see her Vampire pack, but the smell of their trail was still strong. She forced herself to plod on, one step at a time.

Suddenly, another smell. Not a track, but only the faintest waft of an odor, from far away. As subtle as if the rain had fallen on the smell, and then evaporated, and now the fragrant vapor had condensed and fallen on Isis. Subtle, but distinct. It was Joshua's smell.

She was torn now by which way to go. She didn't want to lose track of the Vampires; but Josh was somewhere about. Momentarily it sent her into a frenzy of indecision; she chased her tail in a circle four times, paused, spun twice more, and finally sat panting on a mossy rock.

What to do? She could continue being exceedingly trailwise, following the Vampires and the Human with the blood-smell. But without Joshua, there would be no one around to see how clever and pretty she was. She gloated over herself a few moments, preening the fur that was beginning to grow back after the Dragon accident.

Or she could go find Josh right now, show him what he'd been missing. But then he wouldn't be very proud of her, if she'd lost the trail of the blood-ones.
What to do? What to do?

Suddenly a small rat-monkey skittered across the pool and into the thicket beside Isis. She reflexively swatted at its tail, then plunged in after it. It darted: under vines, around trunks, through leafy shadow. Isis gave chase. They tore up trees, leaping branch to branch, scattering birds and small critters in a cacophony of shrieks. Isis caught the rat-monkey by the hind foot briefly, but in the end the miserable beast escaped into a lizard burrow that Isis had the good sense not to enter.

Disgusting worm-food, she thought, licking her paw. *Lizard fare now and good riddance.*

She felt suddenly puzzled. She looked around at the layers of rotting mangoes, flowering vines, proliferating ferns: *What place is this?* she wondered. *What am I doing here?*

An odor caught her nose, then—she turned her head instantly to the left, sniffed the heavy air; stood poised, motionless. She knew this odor. It was Vampire, and Accident—unmistakably Accident—and the Human with the blood-smell. That's right, now she remembered—she was following them for Joshua. At the thought of Joshua, she paraded back and forth beside a still pond, viewing the reflection of the sultry Cat she saw there. Joshua's Cat. Haughtily, she approved of herself, and closed her eyes to an invisible adulating audience. Indelicately, the smell returned, stronger than before.

Isis crouched, squinted. She had them now, they would not elude so easily. With particularly audacious cunning, she set off in pursuit of the smell. Yes, Joshua would be pleased.

She stopped a minute to retch the half-digested beetle out of her stomach, then dizzily moved on.

Rose heard Nancy whimpering behind her. "What's the matter?" she whispered over her shoulder. They were walking with difficulty through a rough-hewn half-path. Steam was rising everywhere. The night's evil glow was beginning to fade as the sun shed its first light on the topmost leaves.

"He's dead," Nancy moaned. "My Billy's dead." She began sobbing uncontrollably.

Rose turned to look: the small baby sagged limply in Nancy's arms, its blue, still lips open at her breast. Rose spoke softly but forcefully: "Keep quiet."

Nancy shocked into silence, stared blankly at Rose.

"Don't tell anyone," Rose went on. "Pretend he's sleeping. If they find out he's dead, the Accidents will eat him."

A cry fell from Nancy's mouth like a crippled dream. Rose took the baby from Nancy's grip and held it to her own breast. Was this to be the extent of her motherhood? she wondered: nursing a dead baby. Under these circumstances, it was a revolutionary act.

She wondered about Beauty and Josh. Would they find her? Were they still alive? She loved them both, and the thought that they'd die in search of her made her lip quiver, her eye moisten. She wanted badly to have a child with Beauty. She wanted badly to ride him once more, now, to feel the wind in her hair and his back between her knees. She wanted to braid his mane, she wanted . . . but these were idle thoughts, she knew.

Suddenly, before she'd even really made a coherent plan about the infant in her arms, opportunity presented itself rudely and without sentiment: she found herself walking beside a boiling sulphur pit that filled the air with acid stench. The edge of the pit ran along their path for about fifteen feet, then curved off into the jungle. At the last moment, without letting Nancy see, vowing not to think about it again, she dropped the lifeless child into the elemental pool, where it quickly sank in the currents.

Ena, the hungry Vampire, heard the splash. "What was that?" she demanded, striding over to Rose.

"A log by the path," said Rose tiredly. "I kicked it in."

Ena leered. "Strong, aren't you?" Rose remained silent. Ena felt Rose's neck. "Good strong pulse, too. I like a person with spirit." She fondled Rose, handled her. "I could make things easier for you, bitch," the Vampire growled. Rose shrank into herself as far as she could. Ena bared her fangs, hissed, put her mouth to Rose's, bit the Human's lip, licked the drop of blood that formed there. "I could make things harder, too."

It was in a particularly dense matrix of creepers and runners that Beauty caught his hind hoof, tripped; fell.

He didn't say anything at first, thinking to get up immediately without bothering anyone. By the time he did call for help, Jasmine and Josh were fifteen, twenty paces up, so it was another ten seconds or so before they got back to him. By that time, he was up to his haunches in quicksand. The look of white terror filled his face. He was sinking fast.

Josh began to hold out his hand, but Jasmine pulled him back. "Cut long vines," she ordered.

Immediately both of them were hacking off thirty-foot lengths of one-inch-thick tendrils. When they had five such ropes, Jasmine sat down and began braiding them.

Beauty was fast up to his man-belly. "Hurry. Please," he spoke in a perfectly even tone. He knew that now more than ever it was essential that he maintain his sense of balance, internally as well as externally. Any thrashing or groping—any disequilibrium of any kind—would only pull him down.

"Good God, we haven't got time for that!" Josh snapped at Jasmine, grabbing one of the vines and throwing it out to Beauty.

Jasmine snatched it back furiously. "How much weight do you think these little stalks can pull?" she seethed, and continued braiding. "A thousand pounds? You know what Beauty weighs in that much quicksand?"

Josh writhed in impotence. He felt suffocated, watching his sinking friend, unable to help, unable even to know how to help.

Beauty's ears twitched. He was up to his nipples, now.

Jasmine finished braiding, then tied one end of the bulky cord into a large loop. Beauty was up to his neck, his eyes open wide, his arms over his head.

Jasmine threw the loop end to Beauty, then tossed the other end up around the high crotch of a massive tree, using it as a pulley wheel; and she and Josh pulled.

As in an evenly matched arm-wrestling bout, neither side gave at first. There Beauty stood, his chin in the ooze, his outstretched hands grabbing the loop. Finally, slowly, the bog began to lose. The Neuroman and the Human exerted their last ounces of strength, spurred on to continue by every inch the Centaur rose from the mire.

It took an hour of pulling.

When at last he was fully out on hard ground, his legs trembled and he fell. The other two collapsed shortly thereafter, of exhaustion. They all lay where they dropped, oblivious to the world, in each other's arms. But just before she fell asleep, Jasmine raised her head, to see Beauty's face beside her. His eyes were open, and they shared a long moment locked in visual embrace. They both closed their eyes; and slept.

Dicey wore only her thin cotton shirt as she walked, hot and wet in the steaming rain. Beside her walked Bal. His wing unfurled slightly around her, protecting her from the eyes of the company behind them. She gazed raptly on his face. He was speaking quietly; passionately.

"... Thus, though we cannot make our sun stand still, yet we will make him run."

He stopped speaking. She continued staring at him, waiting for more words, magic words, book words; but none came. He was silent. She felt his power when he spoke these words to her from the poetry books; but she felt it tenfold when he stopped the flow of words, kept the words from her. It made her neck tingle, the way it tingled just before his lips touched it. She thought she must be going mad.

"How old were those words?" she asked him.

He smiled distantly. "Six hundred years. And still potent."

The warm flush around her throat spread down to her breast; lower. She could feel her breath quickening. She brought up her hands, circled his powerful biceps with her fingers. Involuntarily, he flexed. She continued hanging on. They continued walking.

Josh dreamed he was choking and woke up. The noon sun cut brightly through the forest, making it almost too hot to breathe. The young man roused the others, and they resumed their journey.

Soon a partial clearing emerged, gravid with orchids. Hothouse vapor made respiration difficult. The sweet aroma seemed to make time thick.

A delicate green filament, hanging from above, brushed Joshua's arm; coiled around it. He cut it free with his knife. It bled.

Beauty snagged a fingernail on a shred of bark. He swore—something he never did—and angrily pared all his nails to the quick with the buck-knife from his quiver.

A small violet bird flew out of the trees. Jasmine fell to the ground, shaking.

Looking over their shoulders, they left the strange place.

"Haunted," whispered Jasmine.

"One of the Accidents has fever, Bal-Sire." Uli spoke nervously. A delirious Accident was a dangerous beast.

Bal thought a moment. "Let Scree take care of him."

"But the other Accident . . ."

"Tell Scree to fly home after he's done. The other Accident will follow him. And bad blood on them all."

Uli nodded. "And the prisoners?"

Bal raised his eyebrows. "Surely we can take the prisoners the rest of the way ourselves. . . ."

"Of course, Sire Bal." Uli backed off.

Uli gave Scree the order. The Griffin opened its beak and let out a single crow. It flew up into the high branch, waited for an opportune moment; then dove full force at the sick Accident's belly, tearing it open from flank to flank. The Accident screamed, as Scree flew off toward the south.

"What was that?" asked Josh. The scream riveted them in midstep. For a long moment the entire jungle was silent, listening to the echoes of the wail.

"Somebody dying hard," said Jasmine. The forest resumed.

They walked alongside a small cool stream for a while, wary, but gaining confidence. Josh stooped to drink; the others followed. All along the bank wild flowers sprouted colorfully, interspersed with ferns, mushrooms, clover. The travelers lay in the flora for many minutes—unexpectedly tranquil—and quietly contemplated the humming stream, its lucent depth; its smoky curve into the trees. Josh flared his nostrils. He savored the flowers with them, for a moment at peace beside the crystalline water. Beauty dipped his head into the stream and kept it under, letting the refreshing currents play in his beard. And so immersing his senses in the soothing liquidity, he too was calmed.

When finally Josh stood up again, he paused, cocked his head. "Did you hear that?" he asked. It was something like a sound, but subtler than thought.

"What?" said Jasmine, rising.

"I'm not sure. It sounded like a song. Or something."

"There, I hear something now," Beauty claimed. His ears pointed. "It is music."

Finally Jasmine heard it. A voice: plaintive, keening, beckoning. She didn't like it. "Let's leave. This way. I think I'm on to Bal's sign. . . ."

But the other two didn't move.

"Come on," she shook them. She didn't believe in enchantments, but she had a bad feeling about this place; and she did believe in feelings.

Reluctantly, they followed her, off the course of the river.

Ena pinned Rose to a tree, drinking from her neck. Rose put herself into trance. "I will not die," she thought. "I will not die, I will . . ."

Ena backed off and spat. "You've been eating garlic, you foul-blooded—"

"Sire Ena!" Bal roared. Ena stopped. Rose gasped, put her fingers against her neck wound to halt the bleeding. Bal continued in a softer, sterner voice. "No more blood from these prisoners. We have lost too many as it is. Is that clear?"

Ena nodded sullenly. Uli smiled to himself. Bal turned back to join Dicey at the head of the troop.

"Thank you," whispered Dicey. She stood facing him, looking up to him from the depths of eyes that were black with hunger, bright with knowledge.

"No, you were correct. Your friend *was* looking pale. And Ena is a fool." He breathed through his mouth.

She cupped her right palm around his muscular left breast; and tilting her head, exposed her frail peaked neck to him.

Ena looked on from a distance, fuming.

"There it is again," said Josh. He stood listening by a banyan tree.

They all heard it clearly. Two voices, now: seductive, ancient. Pleading.

"I have . . . never heard such singing," whispered Beauty. He took two steps toward the melodious sounds.

"This way," said Josh, passing the Centaur and going five paces farther.

"Wait," said Jasmine. "The Vampires are this way," pointing away from the brook they'd left behind.

Hypnotic, runic. Sensual. Begging.

"Wait," Jasmine repeated; but now even she was beginning to forget what was so important about the direction they'd been following, was beginning to wonder what manner of Angel could be singing such compelling music; was beginning to walk, enraptured, toward the sound.

CHAPTER 11

In Which The Travelers Lose
Some Time

THEY followed the creek downhill until it became a river, as the singing voices swelled, then faded again into the afternoon steam. There was a dropoff suddenly, the running water cascading over the twenty-foot falls. The hunters scrambled down the embankment.

Here the singing was intense. Whimpering, teasing. The companions looked at each other. Multiple emotions played across their faces in quick succession: fear, excitement, bewilderment; despair, obsession. The song seemed to be coming from the waterfall itself. With a single motion, the three friends stepped into the river; plunged under, and then through the pouring falls.

When they emerged on the other side of the falls, they found themselves standing in a still, green pool. It was fed, at its darker end, by a small quiet stream that wound back into the descending caves. They waded through the water, which was quite shallow, as it twisted even deeper into the caves. Up, down, spiraling away. At every turn the music became clearer, until, at last, a new cave mouth opened, emptying Jasmine, Josh, and Beauty into a sunny, grassy clearing. And there, by the side of the crystal river, lounged the three laughing Sirens.

They were exquisite: frail, blushed faces; lithe woman-bodies, lusciously covered in fine down and dove feathers of raging color, covered everywhere except over their sensitive faces, delicate necks, pale-skinned breasts. Bird-women, softer than sleep.

The Sirens rose, speaking a strange musical language in voices like harps. They came forward, took the three wanderers in hand, and led them up a gentle

rise to a poppied knoll, from which they saw before
them a city: a garden city, cut out of—yet still laced
through with—the jungle. Verdant, sultry; fantastic.

Buildings were the first element that caught the
eye—ancient buildings, hundreds of years old, made
of brick, cement, steel, glass; crumbling with age and
weather. Every structure was partially or completely
engulfed in a mantle of foliage: crawling ivy, matted
iris. The windows were mostly broken, the iron rusted.
But for all their decay, they stood, some taller than
imaginable. Some even seemed to scrape the sky.

Connecting the buildings were discontinuous, pocked
cement walkways. Interspersed among the buildings
—roughly demarcated by the geometric shapes the
walkways enclosed—were the gardens of the city.
Fabulous gardens, like little transplanted sections of
jungle. An overgrowth of purple orchids beside this
building; a riot of exotic fruit trees over here: melons,
pomegranates, figs, passions. An avalanche of ferns, a
lake of poppies, a wall of shaggy moss. A thousand
varieties of palm proliferated, some taller than the tallest buildings. And spattered everywhere were flowers.
Cerulean, magenta, emerald-green, memory-violet,
colors from a different spectrum.

Joshua felt exhilarated, disoriented. Standing uncertainly on the rise with the Sirens' perfumed laughter in
his ear, and this strange vision before him—Josh felt
his mind begin to slowly, subtly distort. In what way
he could not say; but he was aware of some alteration
in his senses, some ongoing process, which came from
within and without. Pleasurable, but intricate.

As they stood there, each absorbed in confused
wonder at what was happening, the sun dipped below
its distant, mountainous horizon. And as was its habit,
the jungle night fell quickly. But the city did not stay
dark.

A large, central pond—filled not with red, but with
turquoise phosphorescent algae—cast a diffuse ethe-
real glow in the heart of the main grouping of buildings: blue-green walls, cobalt shadows. And studding
every tree that formed the perimeter of the mystical
city, every tree and plant within the city, every vine or

bush that climbed or grew, studding them all were millions and millions of fireflies. Spread thin in some areas, clustered elsewhere, they blinked on and off randomly, like stars in the black night sky. Sparkling, dazzling.

Truly, a jeweled city.

The Sirens laughed joyously at the transformation, and ran down the hill into the magical village, calling behind them in their lyrical, alien tongue. Neither Josh, nor Jasmine, nor Beauty knew the language; but somehow they all understood what the Sirens had said: "The city is yours."

Ena dragged Mary behind a rock, muffling the girl's cries with a handful of ferns. She slapped the Human roughly, once, twice; and savagely bit her throat. Blood flowed, the Vampire drank; other pleasures were crudely taken.

When she was done, Ena dropped the unconscious girl and walked back out into the camp. Everyone was watching her. There was a crescendo of whispers, which came to a dead halt as Bal stood up to face Ena. Even the jungle, night-red and steaming, seemed to watch.

"Sire Ena," said Bal quietly. "There is blood on your mouth."

She touched her finger to her lips, wiped a sticky drop off, put her finger to her tongue and sneered. "Tastes good, too. What of it?"

"Whose blood is it, Ena-Sire?" His voice remained modulated, nonaccusing; yet almost imperceptibly the corners of his mouth upturned in the mask of barely restrained anger.

Ena shrugged. "The blond slut with the long hard nipples." Uncontrollably, she leered at the memory.

Bal snapped his fingers. Dicey's head shot up, but the call was not for her. Uli jumped up, walked behind Ena's hiding rock, walked out again. "The Human is dead," he said gravely to Bal.

"Dead," Ena mocked. "The thin-blooded tramp, she—"

"You were given orders," Bal declared, his voice a whisper.

"Orders," she spat, "you dare give me orders not to take my pleasure on this fodder whenever I please, while you suck that little bitch dry in—"

He flew at her with such speed, the movement was a blur. With his right hand he pulled back her head. She was quick too, though, and jerked to the side, so his fangs landed in her shoulder. At the same moment, she slashed her claws down his neck. They broke apart, both drawing first blood.

They circled each other slowly, as the astounded, terrified Humans watched the deadly dance. Uli stood behind the prisoners, to make certain no one took this opportunity to escape.

Both Vampires had their wings half spread, for balance and quick flight. Bal was bleeding from the neck, Ena from the shoulder. Their eyes were electric. Suddenly Bal flew straight up twenty feet, Ena backed to a tree. Bal pulled in his wings with one huge beat, and nose-dived his braced opponent. She bared her fangs, struck out with her talon-nails as he closed— when suddenly he opened his wings, stopping short, and her claws missed him by inches. Before she finished her follow-through, he was on her.

With his left-arm he pinned one of her wings; his right hand pulled up on her chin from behind, forcing her jaw shut, exposing her throat. Viciously he plunged his razor teeth into her jugular vein. She snarled like a rabid wolf. They fell to the ground, his jaw still clamped to her neck. She reached around behind her and dug her knife-claws into his face, through his cheek.

Dicey stared on in shock. Who would win? She turned to Uli. "Help him," she pleaded.

On the perimeter of the camp, Rose sorted her own mixed emotions. Should she run? No, Uli was vigilant. If Bal died, could they escape? Bal was probably their only protection at this point, at least until they got to their final destination. But if Ena won, maybe she and Uli would fight. Maybe . . .

With a sudden twist, Ena got her wing free and

flapped skyward, Bal still gnashing at her throat. As she wrenched free momentarily, he spread his wings as well, and maneuvered to get a new tooth-hold in her chest, over her heart, while he pinned her arms behind her with his own. The wounds in her neck were gushing blood.

Wings beating rapidly, the two locked Vampires tumbled and spun erratically near the treetops. Their piercing, inaudible radiowave screams drove icily into the brains of the terrified Human prisoners, causing many of them to wail or writhe. Ena managed to get one arm free, tearing a hole in Bal's wing near the shoulder. She pulled up on his head just enough to sink her fangs deeply through his scalp, and they plummeted and crashed down into the nearby brush.

All was silent.

Uli and the others ran over to view the wreckage of the death struggle. The two figures lay still in the undergrowth, clutching, bleeding, wings askew, fangs in flesh. A heavy hush.

Slowly, Bal extricated himself from the ruins and stood. His shoulder, wing, face, and head were all badly gashed. Ena did not get up.

Bal stepped forward. "Put the prisoners to bed, Uli-Sire, and you take the first watch. I will rest; and take, perhaps, some nourishment."

Dicey's pupils dilated; her teeth chattered; her neck tingled. She went with Bal.

They wandered through the ancient streets as in a dream, half-focused in the shimmering light, the primal shadows. They moved together at first, then separated, straying alone down side alleys, up cul-de-sacs, sometimes running into each other again, sometimes accompanying each other for a while, finally separating to explore alone once more. At first they thought they were alone here. Presently, they found they were not.

Jasmine ambled down a brick path between two low buildings. One had no roof, and the firefly glow from inside puffed above the ragged walls like a halo.

The other was glass and steel, and still bore a faded, falling sign over its front window: LESTER'S LAUNDRO-MAT. Inside, rows of cuboid rusting shells lined the floor. Lightning bugs flashed amid the sleeping shapes.

Jasmine shook her head. "A lost civilization," she pondered. How long ago had she seen such structures as these? Under what peculiar circumstances? It could have been three hundred years or three thousand. And who could possibly describe the circumstances defining the points in space and time she had occupied when these buildings were new? It overwhelmed her, this thought. She cried.

Suddenly, she thought: "But Neuromans can't cry." And this scared her. She felt her sense of self being undermined, starting to dissolve. "No," she thought, and ran into the roofless building.

She found herself in one large room, furniture strewn around the floor. Torn upholstery, rusty springs, rotting tables, all twinkling with fireflies. And sitting on a broken vinyl couch in the corner was a naked woman—no, not a woman: a beautiful female creature, almost Human, but with black hair that strayed down all over the floor, and a face hollow with lust, and eyes dark with madness: a Maenad. At her breast she suckled a small furtive monkey with antlers sprouting from its head.

Jasmine stepped back, aghast. Something about this scene gripped her, took her breath. The shadowy sexuality, the shattered windows, the animal abandon, the human despair; a memory without substance, rich in feeling; something to conjure with.

She backed out the door. She headed toward a flickering garden.

Joshua saw one of the Sirens scamper into a two-story brick house. As he approached it, he saw one entire wall was gone. Beyond it, inside, stood shelf after shelf of books. He entered.

He walked slowly down the aisles, gazing at the ti-tles: *Robinson Crusoe, The Hound of the Baskervilles, Murder in the Cathedral, Spartacus.* His heart filled with emotion: so many souls alive here in the glimmering firefly light, waiting to be reawakened by the brush of his eye across the page. With trembling hand he reached for *The Lost World,* and pulled it from the rack. Surely this book was left here for centuries for Joshua to find now; left for him alone, to tell him where he was, what this mysterious place was all about. Momentously, he opened the covers—and the book crumbled in his hands.

Into moldy dust. Into nothing. He stared through his fingers at all the souls disintegrating into timelessness. All those years, all those lives. Dead in his hands. His sense of loss was stupefying.

He steadied himself on the stacks, breathed deeply, pulled down another tome. It broke into flakes before he opened it. He thrust his hand rudely across an entire shelf—not an ounce of resistance; nothing left but a scattering of mildewed powder.

He staggered. The meaning of this was unimaginable, earth-quaking: the written words had lost their power. The power to create, the power to preserve eternally—crushed into ash. So, was Scribery a false path and Scribes false prophets? Lies, then, all of it? If he wrote Dicey's name and story, would she not live on, after all? Would the words wither and blow away, just like her body, her soul lost forever? If so, Scripture was merely a poor ruse. Meaningless scribble.

Sick in heart, he braced himself on the wall. A small moan tumbled from his twisted lips. Fireflies floated like sparks in slow motion around the room. There was a sound behind Josh. He turned. It was the Siren.

She laughed. A sound like the ringing of rose-crystal bells floated from her mouth. Her lips closed, then, into a tenuous smile that said she understood the pain of loss. She held out her arms; caressed her bare, featherless breasts; held out her arms again.

He looked at her grimly. "What's the use?" he said.

She answered in birdsong.

"Nothing lasts," he bemoaned, "we're all sliding . . . into the abyss."

She fluttered, cooing.

"Even our words . . ." his voice broke.

She stroked her soft hand feathers down his cheek, absorbing his tears.

Josh felt the urgency of his grief melting into the urgency of passion. "But *you're* here," he said to her. "*You're* alive. And so am I."

Her lips parted, her tongue came out. He pulled her down, his hands in her feathery warmth.

Beauty stared into the deep blue-green pool for a long time, an infinite moment.

A glowing blue Man, cut off at the waist and jammed onto a Horse's body. A freak of some archaic religion called genetics. A lost member of an ancient tribe that wasn't ancient, from a continent that never existed. A myth, then. Possibly even a complete figment of someone's imagination. A passing whim. Possibly he did not exist at all, and would disappear when the whim passed.

His despondency grew deep as the blue people into which he lost himself. And lose himself he did; for as he watched his image reflected in the water, he saw it slowly disolve and vanish. "Truly, then. I am nothing."

A column of hooded monks walked in procession down the main street. They chanted an unknown hymn in a subterranean language. In their midst, they carried a great black box, obviously heavy. Upon reaching the edge of the forest, they set fire to the box with torches. When the flames died down, the monks retreated to the caves at the end of the village.

Jasmine stepped into the garden. It was thick but low to the ground with lilies, daffodils, snapdragons. Looking up, she saw the night sky actually clearing somewhat, the star-lights blinking down at the fly-lights winking up. There, a million miles just past the apex of the tallest building, she saw Venus, the spring evening star.

Who will love me? wondered Jasmine.

She meandered deeper into the shrubbery, directionless as a waif. Broken objects from another age were strewn about the flora—telephones, toasters, skulls. Nestled in a splash of tall reeds and galloping overgrowth was the rusted hull of an old car. Its hood was long gone, its windows empty sockets.

Probably cannibalized for parts, she thought. *Probably my parts,* she thought.

She looked inside. In the torn back seat, a light blue Goddess with at least four arms, draped with gold chains, was using all her hands to caress the tooled muscles of a blond sensual God. Shiva seducing Dionysus. Suddenly the young man's features began distorting, though, his body changing form. He was horrible now, now a loathsome crone; and now again changed to a mirror image of the many-armed Goddess. The two beautiful blue deities embraced, entwined, lost in each other. Shiva seducing Shiva. Until the final change, and the protean flesh of the one melted, leaving only a skeleton in the other's arms. Death seducing Shiva. The radiant blue Goddess tried vaguely to push his bone-fingers from her loosening thighs, but he teased her lips, her lips were moist, and finally, she pulled the skeleton fingers in.

Jasmine turned from the scent, her heart as hollow as the decomposing shell of the dead auto.

Who can love such a thing as me? she echoed. *Not even Death.*

A young bronzed man approached her. She could see at a glance his name was Priapus. It stirred her loins, but without feeling, without soul. Casually she fondled his namesake until it swelled, rose, grew hard and long as her arm. Jasmine felt empty as a rusty car in the jungle, though. She could feel Death's cold fingers prying at her knees, but she was dry as summer straw, and she knew he would soon lose interest. She felt parched by her unloveliness, a creature of a dead technology. Dead past, dead future. Only the final Event itself eluded her. The skeleton turned to Priapus. Jasmine walked away.

A bird flapped into the open. It screeched once, dove into the blue-green pond, went deeper, disappeared.

Rolling down a side street, a large steel ball rumbled ominously. It stopped for a moment before a partly crumbled wall, then rattled on, into the dark at the end of the city. A long moan bubbled up out of the central pool, collapsing to a whisper before it died.

Josh lay on his back, staring at the stars. How deeply they swam. Time played tricks on him. It stopped; froze the constellations in inkwell space. It raced, spinning like a skyrocket. Stop-time, rush-time. Dream-time. Space-time. Space. Time.

A Maenad lay down beside him. Her eyes were mirrors, so as she looked up, they went deep as space. "Words are written there you will never see," she said, in the glass-language he understood but did not know.

"Perhaps my child will read them . . ." he began.

She shook her head. "The words were lost in Time."

"In time for what?" he asked, confused.

"In Time, forever."

"Forever is a long time." He couldn't grasp the conversation they were having. He kept almost getting it, and then it would slip from his ken once more.

"Forever is No-Time. Time-less." A short laugh broke shrilly from her. "We have No-Time."

"No time for what?" he asked. What was he supposed to do?

A resounding thump filled the air, like the beat of a heart, as if the whole city were a heart. The trees vibrated, the buildings shook. It happened once again, some time later, but no more.

Creatures walked past Beauty, but did not see him. He moved from empty fear to empty insight. Invisibility cleared his vision, so he saw things as they really were.

A cluster of Satyrs turned into swine. A preening cat became a languorous woman. Birds were flowers, skin took on wrinkles, limbs were deformed. Hearts showed through, some red, some black. He saw them all but himself: to himself, he remained invisible.

A ball of flame appeared, hovered above a garden, changed color, floated down, sank into the earth. Somewhere, a giant bell tolled: gong, gong, gong.

Josh walked up to a mysterious box, muddy glass on one side, wood on the others. Jasmine appeared. "It's a television set," she said.

"What does it do?"

"It made moving pictures of people. It made them look like real little people, running around inside."

"Real people?"

"No. Well, yes."

Three Devils with cloven hooves, horned rams' heads, and serpent tails burst in, reeking of debauchery and decay. They pushed Josh into Jasmine, held him against her, taunted and poked at the two, jabbed them, tormented them. They pushed Jasmine to the ground, pushed Josh on top of her. Every time Josh tried to rise, they pushed him down again. They squatted, rubbed themselves on the two cowering figures, handled each other, made wild, foul ejaculations, ran away.

Josh and Jasmine fell apart, limp, without will. Longing, unsettled. Sick at heart.

Wraiths floated across the pool like uncertain thoughts. In the western trees, a stale wind.

Beauty stood at the edge of the Forest, staring out. Only blackness beyond. The moving blackness of his life.

Josh walked up, stood beside him. He saw the same blackness.

They stood like this, before the blackness, sharing their lonely losses, their separateness. They did not touch; but they felt the sharing.

A fetid smell accumulated. Musky, overripe. Not of death, but of death's wake. It blew away, into the trees.

A sustained note, monotonal, deep: mmmmmmm-mmmmmm . . . . It caught the resonance of the Forest, of earth, the stone, the brain. It opened eyes.

Jasmine sat in the garden facing the feathered snake.

"What is this place?" she asked.

"It is you," said the snake.

She shook her head. "Only my losses. Only my fears."

"The night is yet young. There is still much time for triumphs."

Her face wilted. "I've lost so much time."

"Time is never lost," hissed the serpent. "It ends, it begins again. The past is part of the future. They are one." The snake took his tail in his mouth.

"Other things, I've lost. Loves, I've lost forever. They are dead now, or I'm dead to them. Worlds, I've lost, they will never come back, and opportunities lost, and moments, and feelings, and innocence . . . and my humanness. Something left me when I made the change to . . . what I am now. But what am I?"

"A woman of many parts."

"Many spare parts," Jasmine whispered hoarsely.

"Parts make a whole."

"A whole what?"

"Only you can know."

"I know nothing," she shook her head.

"Ask the stars," rasped the feathery snake.

She looked at the sky. Past the tip of the skyscraper, she looked for Venus, the love-star, once more. It wasn't there. In its place brooded Sirius, the dog-star.

"I don't understand," Jasmine complained. "Sirius shouldn't be there yet. What happened to the evening star?"

"It's been a long night," nodded the serpent.

But Jasmine didn't understand. She held her head, tried to keep it from getting any bigger. She felt locked in a time lapse, and no way out but in.

The air congealed. Motion ceased. Time was the distance between matters. Matter was revealed as energy; no more. No matter: matter was no more. And no more time for the matter.

A pure, low, demented cry tore the fabric of the night. A blind, inhuman sound, terrible and brief. A windowpane broke. In the turquoise pool, the water froze over for a moment, then melted again. From the topmost branches, leaves fell.

Riders in black leather masks galloped up, dismounted. Joshua backstepped, but was stopped by the wall.

"This is the Scribe," growled a masked man. He hit Josh across the face. The second one wrote Joshua's name on a piece of paper, then set fire to it. The paper turned brown, then black around the letters. The words became lost in flame. The mask-men rode off.

Joshua lay, dazed, on the ground. Slowly he found himself getting sleepy. His eyes blurred, he lay still. Fireflies began to settle on him, another inanimate life form to illuminate. He closed his eyes.

The blackening void, the soft sucking wind, the distant light, magnetic light. Only not so distant now. Much closer now, a brilliant pulsing ball, pulling him, pulling him in, like a great white hoe, pulling, pulling.

The pressure dropped, a wind came up. Autumn weather. The sky turned pale.

Beauty approached Jasmine in the garden. She turned to face him. Long slow communion. They fastened gazes, connected raw ends; and somehow bled into each other. Miraculously, as the Centaur looked into the Neuroman's eye, he saw his image reappear there: he was no longer invisible.

In the shadow of his golden beard, she saw her lost soul: nestled, hiding. Tenderly, she touched it, recaptured it; held it. She felt a great, woeful joy.

A tear welled in her lower lid, and he saw his re-

flection shimmer. She held out her hand: their hands
fused. Their spirits melded, they became one spirit.

They made love.

Josh awoke by the turquoise pool. Jasmine and
Beauty sat before him.

"Are you all right?" asked Jasmine. "You were
screaming and running. We were worried."

Something about them was different, Josh felt it immediately. Something they exuded. Solace.

"My spells," he said groggily. "The blackness, and
then the light . . ."

A tall man suddenly appeared before them. He had
two faces, one staring out either side of his head, eyes
that glowed green, a voice like an echo. "I am Janus,"
he bowed. "I am the Priest of Time." Both mouths
spoke at once.

Jasmine's head felt clear for the first time that night.
"Where are we?" she asked the Priest.

"You are in the time-less place," he smiled. "There
is no motion here, no forward and backward. Only the
Time-less center." He raised a hand-mirror to the face
directed away from the travelers, and they saw it was
a skull.

Jasmine felt some kinship with this strange being.
There was recognition. "You're a Neuroman, aren't
you?"

His two mouths smiled inscrutably. "In this life, it
is my pleasure to manifest that particular energy."

"Then tell me, fellow Neuroman, is there a way to
leave this place?"

"You are already on your way," he assured her.
"You and your four-footed friend. You have become
grounded, and you will once again flow down the
river."

"What river, what are you talking about?" She suddenly found herself cross. She didn't like the Priest's
implication-by-exclusion that Josh was not free to
leave; she didn't like the way he talked in metaphors;
she didn't like realizing she hadn't been in full control
of her faculties all night.

The mysterious Neuroman closed his four eyes.

"Time, do you see, is a river, flowing from the mountains down to the sea. It twists and turns, it goes faster and slower, it backtracks on itself, it even goes uphill now and then. It has undercurrents and undertows. It finds natural dams, where it sits still and deep, and then overflows, and rushes down in gushes and waterfalls. It has eddies, and whirlpools and backwaters, and shallows and fathoms. There are tidepools, tributaries, watersheds, dropoffs.

"Sometimes it even freezes over.

"There's a source, and a delta, and there's the sea. And all along the course of the river, the water is evaporating, and that's part of time, too. The vapor of time, it rises and floats, and finally condenses and rains down into the mountains, into the river again, and starts its flow all over. Only this time the flow is just a little different. It's the same river, do you see, but now perhaps it changes course a bit here from the spring rains, or here it overflows its banks, or there a fallen tree has made a new dam." He smiled enigmatically.

Jasmine suddenly knew she'd been drugged. The mushrooms by the stream, probably; hallucinogenic. She was coming down; but feeling shaky.

"So if we're already on our way, as you put it, what are we still doing here?" She strained to keep the edge off her voice.

"Here abide the vapors of time. The river crashes, and sprays a million droplets. Some float here forever. You two, you and the Centaur, have coalesced, and the gravity of your union has pulled you back into the river. Grounded you. If you check closely, I think you'll find yourself already bobbing right along again in your time-directed current."

She felt something, all right—crashing after a very strange magic mushroom trip. She could see Beauty was aware of the change, as well—self-aware—and briefly they made eye contact, reassuring, validating.

Janus went on. "Your Human friend here, on the other hand, is still lost in the vapors. He may rain down one day, back to the river; but here in the vapor, there is no time, and when he finally does find ground, you may well be out to sea. Still, there is no cause for concern: the river is One."

"I dislike enigmas."

"Enigma is inner beauty," smiled Janus, "and like surface beauty, resides solely in the eye of its beholder."

"Stop being so coy," Jasmine snapped. "We're leaving now. With Joshua."

"Coyness is our prerogative in this universe—here there is world enough, and time, for all things."

He bowed slightly. He walked away.

Jasmine helped Josh to stand. "Can you walk?" she asked.

He held his head. "I'm getting so sleepy again . . ." he mumbled. "And my head . . ." He pulled at his hair. When Jasmine tried to comfort him, he pushed her away. She looked at Beauty fearfully.

"Joshua . . ." began the Centaur, but got no further. Josh suddenly broke free and started running, wild-eyed, toward the cave that had first led them into the city.

Jasmine and Beauty set off in pursuit. Into the cave mouth, up the dark stream, around winding caverns; finally through the waterfall that curtained the original portal, out into the jungle, just as the sun began its morning blaze.

Josh leapt from the river and was quickly lost in the trees.

Jasmine and Beauty stayed close on his trail, deliberate, urgent. Beauty noted the look in the Neuroman's face. "This worries you," he said, continuing to follow the leaf-torn path.

"Yes," she said simply.

"What are your thoughts?" he prodded. He, too, was concerned—with his friend's bizarre behavior, with memories of the previous night, with an increasingly cold Vampire trail.

"I think we were drugged last night—probably those mushrooms where we drank at the river bank. Maybe the poppies, too. I'm not certain anything we saw in there was real. I think maybe Josh is having what we used to call a bad trip. If not . . ." she paused, tearing a branch out of her way, "he may have something wrong in his brain."

"His brain . . ."

"It's possible," she postulated. "He was having some of these symptoms before last night—grogginess, blackout spells, strange lights. Now he's holding his head and acting berserk. Yes, it worries me deeply. It could be a tumor, a blood clot, a—"

"We cannot let this happen to him!" Beauty clapped a hand on Jasmine's shoulder, stopping her. "He—I—love him." He focused hard on her face, trying to make her understand.

She understood fully. She put her hand on his, answered his gaze. "And I, you."

His heart jumped. He'd been trying to ignore this particular segment of the previous night, bury it soundly under the morass of *Shoulds* and *Shouldn'ts* in his life. This confrontation now with the intentionally dim memory made him sweat in the morning drizzle. "I—I—" he stuttered, "we—all did some—felt some strange things last night. You say yourself it may have been drugs. I think we—"

"You once told me," she stopped him, "I could not convince you with words of something which you knew to be false by feeling or experience. I could say the same now. Some things don't change when the morning rises, Centaur."

He squeezed her hand, but was too confused to answer. She turned, and they resumed the hunt.

The jungle was getting thicker, and since Josh was the one cutting the path, his progress was slower than the others'. Before too long, they were able to hear his breathing in the near distance. This went on for ten more minutes, when suddenly, the crashing and panting from up ahead ceased entirely. With a surge, Beauty and Jasmine forged on, until they broke, falling into a wide open space.

Josh sat on the ground before them, looking dazed. "Where am I?" he beseeched them.

They sat either side of him. "You're all right now. You're with us. Tell us what happened."

He knitted his brows. "One of my spells again." He

strained to recapture it. "They're coming more often, aren't they? I got so sleepy, I couldn't keep my eyes open, and then it was all black. And then the light. But bigger this time. It was huge this time, and strange, like a magnetic star. It pulled me so hard, it just dragged me off my feet, like it was sucking me through the air, right into it. Only I didn't quite get to it. And then I woke up." He looked up. "Hello."

Beauty's forehead finally relaxed its knot. "Hello," he said emphatically.

They helped Josh to his feet. "Any headaches?" Jasmine asked.

"Only a loud sort of wind inside my head, a kind of energy or something . . ."

They all paused momentarily, looked each to each, breathed a collective sigh: another crisis weathered. They felt stronger, closer. Older.

Jasmine smiled. "We're becoming survivors with each other."

They walked westward slowly for a short while, after that, each lost in thoughts of the previous night. It was in a lichen-filled glen that Beauty stopped them all with a shout, and pointed sternly ahead. The others followed his finger to the brush at the edge of the clearing. Lying there was a dead Vampire.

The remains of one, anyway. Almost entirely decomposed, there was not much left besides a contorted skeleton, bits of skin, skewed claws. Its jaw was fixed in a hideous grin.

"Odd," mused Jasmine.

"Why odd?" asked Josh.

"Well, the way it's lying, there was obviously a fight. Not many things besides an Accident can kill a Vampire, their skin's too tough. And an Accident would've torn it apart more than this."

"No weapons around, either," commented Josh. "Wonder when it happened."

"Few months ago, I'd guess, by the state of the decay. The skin takes forever to go. . . ."

They were alerted once again by a sound from Beauty; and walked over to the rock he was standing behind. There, on the ground, were the bones of a dead Human. Skin and flesh were completely eaten away by jungle, but a few tattered clothes still remained draping the skeleton.

"That jacket," Beauty spoke haltingly. "It is Rose's."

"Are you sure?" asked Josh, but he was certain Beauty was right. He remembered Rose wearing the tunic the last time he'd seen her, on the farm in Monterey. A tightness filled his throat, a darkness his mind. Was this to be the end, then? Shriveled remains, halfway to nowhere?

"It's not possible," Jasmine shook her head. "Yesterday we were no more than a day behind them. This body's been here at least three months, probably more. Maybe Rose left her jacket on this skeleton, to warn us of something."

They considered this. Beauty said, "But even the jacket appears so worn . . ."

"Did Rose have any bone wounds?" Jasmine pursued. "Any bullets, or . . ."

"Her left arm was broken three months ago," Beauty answered.

"Well, here then, see? This arm is fresh as a baby's, hasn't ever been a fracture in it. And this hair lying around the skull, it's blond. Didn't you tell me Rose had dark hair? See? It's not Rose at all."

Beauty was reassured, but still confused. He brought his hand up to stroke his beard, and stopped short. "Look at this," he said somberly.

They all looked at his hand. The nails were an inch long. "I cut these nails yesterday, when they were getting caught in the vines." The others acknowledged the recollection. Josh held up his hands: the fingernails were equally lengthy.

And then suddenly Jasmine flashed on something that had happened the night before, one of the million insane episodes. She'd been looking at Venus high in the sky, right where it belonged on a clear spring night; and then when she looked again later, Venus was gone, and Sirius was in its place: a late summer star. Spring to summer in half a night.

"It wasn't just one night," she whispered in amazement.

"What?" Josh tried to understand.

"Last night. It was months long. That's why your fingernails are grown out. And these corpses, they *were* part of the group we were tracking. Rose probably gave her coat to this dead Human. As for the Vampire . . . who knows?" The jungle.

"But how . . ." Josh began, incredulous.

She shook her head. "I don't know how. I don't know how."

Beauty squinted. "Then the trail is months cold."

Jasmine began walking down an overgrown path leading southwest. "Then we'd better get started," she said.

They walked a day and a night and most of the next day, stopping only to eat, following barely discernible paths. They slept the following night, watching by turns. Josh had ample opportunity to set the record, but lacked the heart for it; and in any case, couldn't fathom how to translate his latest adventure onto paper.

On the third day they were aware of a gradual upgrade to the jungle floor, accompanied by some thinning of trees and shrub. By noon they smelled salt air.

There was a rise, a series of dips, a higher rise. With a sense of mounting exhilaration, they climbed the final crest: below them in the middle distance sat the bustling pirate city of Ma'gas', its evening lights sparkling luminously onto the dark waters of the great Pacific.

CHAPTER 12

On The Waterfront

It was a jangling city. The streets were alive with the spasms of dancers, jugglers, beggars, fire-eaters. Wild creatures ran free—thinking this just one more strange part of the jungle—and free creatures ran wild.

Ma'gas' was an open port, situated on the rising edge of the Terrarium, on a natural cove that commanded a view of the sea—and any possible attack. No one ever attacked, though: there was nothing to be gained. The city's value lay in its accessibility to every earthly creature with an angle, with something to sell or to buy. Consequently, there was no law—only personal settlement.

Pirates lived here. Smugglers, mercenaries, slavers, prospectors: thieves and knaves of every shape walked these alleys, looking for action in den or bar. They were the heart and blood of the city. And the skin of the place was gaudily tattooed with minstrels, whores, actors, street musicians, and clowns. A thoroughly degenerate sort of habitat.

As the three travelers entered the city from the jungle, night came on full. Their senses were assaulted by a cacophony composed of laughter, shattering glass, arguments, and lights. Brightly colored paper lanterns hung along all the main streets; candles and alcohol lamps flickered in the windows. The buildings were a conglomerate of materials scavenged from the Rain Forest—palm logs, daub and wattle, bamboo, pieces of tin siding. Raucous voices mixed with the sounds of breaking waves: and sometimes, breaking heads. Nights here were rowdy. The three hunters walked slowly toward the docks. Josh and Beauty had never seen anything like this. Jasmine cautioned them to keep eyes open and mouths closed. They marveled to watch her: she dipped into this milieu like fingers in a worn kid glove.

She fended off the initial rush of beggars and urchins with a jibe here, there a gesture; so that quickly they were left alone, much to Beauty's relief. Beauty did not like cities.

Josh, on the other hand, was mesmerized by the lights, the activity, the interplay. He had a constant urge to get it all down in scripture before it disappeared: it seemed that unreal, and he was that caught up.

A furtive Human without a face sidled up and asked them if they were interested.

"Interested in what?" Josh asked naively.

Girls. Boys. Nymphs. Clones. The faceless man became more descriptive. Josh was dumbfounded. He'd never known anything but absolute freedom, and here was someone actually selling creatures. Beauty's response was more single-track; one of this scum's properties might be Rose. He grabbed the pimp by the neck with a controlled righteous fury.

Jasmine stopped him, though, her ears alert. "What's that?" she demanded of the purveyor. "What's that about Clones?"

He didn't reply, however; only skittered off into the night, leaving the remnant of a bad smell. Beauty was raging, Josh astonished, Jasmine curious. "Odd," she mused. "There haven't been any Clones in over a hundred years." She was silent a moment, then went on to the others. "In any case, this was not the way to go about things. We've got to be very careful in a place like this. The wrong gesture at the wrong time . . . anyway, what we do is, we scout things out first. This is a city, and there are nuances and crosscurrents that have to be sensed before you can make your move. Before you even know what move to make. Now I know this city—I hung around here on and off for fifty years. But that was fifty years ago. Things can change. So we'll go down to some of the bars on the docks, I'll see if anyone I used to know is still around, and we'll feel things out. Okay?"

She was obviously in her element, so without further delay, they resumed their walk to the waterfront.

City of shadows. Back streets entered cul-de-sacs. Furtive transactions between receding silhouettes seemed to fill the alleys: some sexual, some violent; all unsettling, like half-remembered nightmares. There, panthers attacked a drunken sailor urinating against a door—tore out his throat and dragged him, gurgling, back into the jungle for their evening meal. Behind a darkened wall, two young boys took turns giving oral favors to a Chimera. In a recessed doorway, some shapeless creature groaned: in passion, or in death? The colored paper lanterns over the street jumped in the light sea wind, making the shadows dance.

They reached the dockyard without incident. In the harbor, two dozen ships gently rocked. Some were tethered to one of the long wooden piers that serviced the port. Others were anchored to the sandy floor, farther out in the bay. All were sail ships, though a few had auxiliary steam engines as well. One vessel was being unloaded, its cargo dumped roughly onto the wharf from the gangplank: Humans.

Beauty's nostrils flared, and he almost galloped across the promenade to see if Rose was among the goods. Jasmine stopped him, though. "Remember what I said," she cautioned. "It's different in a city."

He let himself be restrained. Slowly, the three comrades walked up the wharf, past a series of sleazy waterfront bars. They looked in each one, but each time continued walking. At the fifth tavern, Jasmine stopped. It had no windows. The white flaking sign on the old oak door said CASA BLANCA. She smiled and went in, followed closely by her mystified cohorts.

It was a big place. Twenty round, candlelit tables were scattered over the main floor. Side rooms and bead-curtained alcoves abounded off at the edges. The back wall was one long bar. Beside the bar, a set of stairs led to a sizable loft, but it wasn't well lit, so not much could be seen.

Tending bar was a Cyclops. Large, mean, suspicious. He eyed their entrance, made a quick appraisal; then went on with his other business, though he never lost sight of them. They sat at a corner table.

The café wasn't crowded yet. Two Harpies, woman-headed, vulture-bodied, stood at one end of the bar. Around a large table near the door, five creatures sat playing cards—a Gargoyle, a Devil, two Furies and a Human. None of them looked very happy. Over by the stairs sat a Troll, drinking alone.

The three hunters took it all in: Jasmine, easily; Josh, excitedly; Beauty, guardedly. A Sphinx walked through the front door. It had the head and breasts of a woman, the body of a dog, the tail of a serpent, the wings of a bird, the paws of a lion; and it was drunk. It looked around, then made straight for the corner table.

"Leave this to me," whispered Jasmine. "Could be trouble."

The Sphinx approached them. "My friends," it said, grinning, "I have a riddle for you. If you answer it, I buy you all drink. If not, you buy me all drink. Yes?"

"We don't—" began Jasmine.

Josh interrupted her. "That's okay, I like riddles," he said. Then, to the Sphinx: "Go ahead."

The animal grinned again, spittle running down its chin. "Okay, amigo. Why did the chicken cross the road?"

Beauty tapped his fingers nervously on the table; Jasmine raised her eyes to Heaven; Josh looked consternated. "What's a chicken?" he demanded.

The Sphinx smirked, but before it could speak, Jasmine said, "To drink on the other side. Now here, amigo—" she pulled a sou from her cape and stuck it in the creature's paw—"take this and drink up on the other side of the dock."

The Sphinx snarled, smiled, and staggered out the door. Jasmine sighed relief. "Lucky she was drunk as she was."

Josh still looked baffled. "What *is* a chicken?"

Jasmine laughed. "An extinct animal. Wiped out by a famine and then a virus. Here's the bar-tart, now, you two order first."

A sassy Hermaphrodite walked up to their table.

S/he was naked, save for thick leather thigh-boots
—an essential accessory for anyone who made love to
things with claws—and s/he looked the hunters over
with wanton zeal. Her arousal was obvious—in fact,
frankly tumescent—but such was the nature of these
creatures.

S/he leaned gamely against the table, and said in a
voice that suggested even her vocal cords were engorged, "Well, what'll it be, sweets? See anything you
like?"

Beauty would not look at the bar-tart, and Josh
could not look away. Neither spoke. Jasmine smiled
and ordered for them.

"Apple wine for my friends," she told the Hermaphrodite; paused; then said, "And I'd like to see
Sum-Thin."

The man-woman took two steps and sat down hotly
in Jasmine's lap. "You'd like to *see* somethin'?" s/he
said from the throat. "Sweet, you're looking at everything I got right now."

"That's not the Sum-Thin I want," suggested Jasmine, fondling the outrageous creature all the same.

"Well, then. Somethin' like what, then?" S/he
moved her hips, sliding into Jasmine's casual caress.

"Sum-Thin Seaufein," Jasmine whispered against
the bar-tart's ear.

"Who's asking?"

"Tell her Jazz has floated up here from downriver
just to watch her move." With which she patted the
man-woman's bottom and pushed the gorgeous creature back to a standing position.

The Hermaphrodite pouted. "Well. This is a fine
state to leave me in." She turned to go, then stopped,
and added with a sultry glower, "By the way. My
name's Cork." At this, s/he turned for good, swaggered over to the Cyclops bartender, and began whispering rapidly, pointing back at the three friends
around the corner table.

Josh was agape; Beauty aghast.

Jasmine read the Centaur's dismay and tried to
quell it. "That was just a little ritual dance, we were
just feeling each other out, you know? We both know

some things, now. I know, now, for example, that Cork keeps a knife inside the top of her left boot. That's something we should all be aware of. She, on the other hand, now knows I'm a Neuroman. There were subtler things going on as well of course, but you get the idea. Anyway, the barman is going into the back room, now, so I assume he'll be telling Sum-Thin we're here."

Cork returned to deposit their drinks on the table, but didn't stay: it might be impolitic.

A few more customers rolled in. A couple of Vampires, a Gargoyle, a female Centaur. The card game started getting louder. Cork drifted around, made some conversation, and got handled with care by the Troll. Some more Humans came in, a couple of upright Lizards; Satyrs, Lupines, Demons, Chimeras; and suddenly the place was packed, the air dense with perfumed smoke and electricity. Jasmine hung her cape on the back of the chair.

The Cyclops was back behind the bar. Cork was getting low-down with a black-robed sorcerer in a dark corner, under the loft. Suddenly the door to the back room opened.

Out walked a tall, thin, exotically beautiful woman with Eurasian features and the grace of a cat. She was statuesque, nearly seven feet. Her hair was black, her cheeks flushed. Draping her frame was a red-and-black-flowered silk kimono that barely touched the floor as she approached the corner table.

"You wished to see me?" she addressed the group.

"Privately," Jasmine specified.

The Oriental bowed slightly and extended her arm toward a paisley curtain hanging in a doorway to a small side room. The searchers rose and passed through the partition, followed by the mysterious figure.

The room was small. Pillows were scattered all around the dirty floor, in the middle of which stood an ornate hookah. Candlelight leapt.

When they were all inside, Jasmine and the woman broke huge, intemperate smiles, embraced, and exchanged a long, passionate kiss.

"Sum-Thin," breathed Jasmine.

"Dear Jazz," exclaimed the woman.

Beauty and Josh, of course, were speechless. The city was, indeed, a strange place.

Finally they all sat down on the cushions. Introductions were made.

"Joshua, Beauty—my ancient friend Sum-Thin. She's owned this place a hundred years, and we go back together two hundred."

Only then did Josh detect the pale, pearly skin of a Neuroman under Sum-Thin's rouged blush.

"Please excuse my cautious behavior out there," she nodded past the hanging curtain, "but a gram of care is worth a black hole of regret." Then, lowering her eyes apologetically: "I am always watched."

"But seldom seen," added Jasmine with an affectionate smile.

Sum-Thin laughed softly, from the heart. She turned to Josh, touched the back of his hand with her delicate fingertips. "This is a private joke she refers to; it was hopelessly tactless of her to make such an allusion, so I will let my vanity apologize *for* her, at the expense of boring you: when I chose this body— this life—after leaving my Human form two hundred years ago, Jazz wrote me this poem:

> "Long and lean,
>   Dragon Queen,
>   kind of hungry and kind of mean,
>   and so far out
>   you are seldom seen,
>   Dragon Queen."

She opened her eyes wide, placed two long, black-nailed fingers tentatively to her lips, turned back to Jasmine. "There, that's what you get for telling secrets in front of people."

Jasmine stared tenderly at her friend. "Poem or no poem. You always wrapped yourself in a cloud."

"The reason the lining of every cloud is silvered, is to allow for deep reflections." She smiled enigmatically. "But enough about me. What brings such honored guests to my enclave?" She looked to each face.

"Hunting," said Josh. He was feeling recharged after all the jungle torpidity. The hunt was taking longer than he wanted, and he sensed that Sum-Thin could get them back on track.

Beauty was still too confused to speak—at odds with himself, uncertain about Jasmine, overwhelmed by the city ways.

Jasmine interrupted, "Before we get to that, tell me —what month is it?"

Sum-Thin shrugged. "I no longer count. Autumn, by the weather."

Jasmine shook her head. She told Sum-Thin about their loss of time in the strange jungle city, and of some of the surreal encounters that took place there— some, but not all, to Beauty's silent, shamed relief: he had still not resolved the strong and constant love he felt for his lost Rose with the jangling emotions Jasmine aroused in him, particularly with the intense memory of their lovemaking in the city of lost time.

Sum-Thin listened to Jasmine's story and nodded. "I have heard of the place. The old man is a Wizard. He uses psychotropic pharmacologics and hypnosis and what else I can only guess. He is a Deiton. You were fortunate to have escaped—few ever leave. Those who have come out say it was by virtue of a powerful emotional shock or transcendence that the spell was broken. Perhaps someday you will tell me your experience." She looked directly at Beauty as she said this, and he had the distinct feeling she was looking through him, into him. He shifted his eyes down. Jasmine wisely kept silent. Sum-Thin concluded, "Another time. In any event, I have no doubt it was an awesome place. It has been compared to Heaven and Hell."

"What's a Deiton?" asked Josh. He was fascinated by this tall, gaunt woman who intimated so much, specified so little.

"The Deitons were one of the Fourfold," Sum-Thin squinted, remembering. "Deitons, Cidons, Hedons, and Cognons. Neuromans, all. But Neuromans who entered the Fourfold path committed themselves to a single-mindedness you and I can barely appreciate."

Josh beamed internally, that Sum-Thin had included him in her own poor understanding. He listened even more intently as she continued. "The Fourfold were Neuromans who underwent cerebral microsurgery—they had microelectrodes implanted in various loci in their brains, connected to self-stimulating devices, powered by their plutonium battery packs.

"There were four well-delineated cerebral locus clusters at the time the operation was popular: the pleasure center, the aggression center, the cognitive integration center, and what for want of a more complete understanding we called the PINEAL—an anagram that stood for Passion, Intuition, Nothingness, Energy, Altruism, Libration." She smiled, eyes closed.

"I don't understand," Josh pressed, floundering in Sum-Thin's terminology. "What do you mean by . . ."

She stopped him with upraised hand. "A thoughtful patience is the hunter's friend."

Josh dropped his mouth closed. With a feeling almost of *déjà vu,* he remembered speaking uncannily similar words to Beauty at the very beginning of their quest. He stared at Sum-Thin in wonder. Could she know his mind so well? Was she mocking him?

She continued narrating. "Neuromans who had the electrode implanted in their pleasure centers were known as Hedons. Most did not long last. They were wont to push their self-stimulating buttons continuously sustaining peak internal sensual experiences for days, often until they starved to death—at least until they fainted. Then they would awaken, eat a little, and begin the process again. Few, I think, remain.

"Those with electrodes in their aggression centers were called Cidons. They loved to kill—which of course, put them in so many violent circumstances, most of them are by now also dead. They were like the Howlers, they took a special glee in death. Some even lived in Howler-town, I believe. They had a certain purity, like all in the Fourfold; but I did not like them.

"Cognons were exclusively thinkers. They parted ways with emotion, sense, body. They became obsessed with their own cognitive processes. The more they discharged their electrodes, the more they turned their thoughts in on themselves, analyzed each thought, then each analysis. Some of the most highly developed logicians I ever met. They were not really able to communicate their knowledge to anyone but each other, alas. I've not seen one for many years.

"But the Deitons were the most interesting, to my mind. Their electrodes were placed in the PINEAL center—a clearly localized area of the brain structurally, but one whose functional characteristics could be described only by approximation. People whose pineals were stimulated exhibited first, passion—not the passion of sensuality, but passion in its deeper sense: the agony and power of receiving; the ardent intensity of all emotion—hate, love, grief, fear, joy, the compulsion of zeal. Next, they were highly intuitive—they had a sense for the way things were, for instantaneous comprehensions, for understanding things *without* cognition. They had, further, a deep-rooted conviction—a perception, it was said—that nothing in the universe actually existed as matter, that all was energy, that you and I were merely shades of the same energy, melting into each other, that nothing had identity in and of itself, that there were *no things,* that what truly characterized the cosmos was its very nothingness. It was perhaps this insight which made them so altruistic; but whatever the reason, they were known for their selfless giving to others, their true egolessness. And finally, libration: the slow, hovering oscillation around a central point, as a beam about to poise in eternal balance on the fulcrum over which it has been rocking.

"So, these were the manifestations of the Deitons: Passion, Intuition, No-thingness, Energy, Altruism, Libration. They were, truly, Godlike creatures. The pineal center was more or less developed in ordinary Humans; but these Deitons electro-stimulated the nucleus at will. Truly, they knew something the rest of us did not."

She stopped talking; stared into the past. Jasmine nodded agreement. "You're right, of course. It hadn't occurred to me, but the Wizard in the City of Time must have been a Deiton—along with whatever else he was."

Josh and Beauty both were entranced with the picture Sum-Thin had painted—Joshua particularly with the unimaginable intellect of the Cognons; Beauty more with the attributes of the Deitons, especially the concept of libration.

Jasmine went on. "The Wizard's passion wasn't evident, but it was there, without a doubt. Heaven and Hell is just what the place was. Every moment was intense. And yet, somehow, moment to moment, the time just disappeared."

Sum-Thin wagged her finger in thought. She pulled an opium pipe out of her kimono and fired it before speaking. "You know, time has not been quite the same anywhere since the Coming of Ice. Have you found that? It may be just because there are so few Humans left, and it was always the Humans who kept the time. They tried to keep it so structured and invariant. Of course, it is not. The animals always knew that, it's as subtle and textural as any dimension. So perhaps merely the Human misperception is vanishing, along with the race."

Josh looked askance. "My race isn't vanishing. What do you mean?"

"You are the last of your breed, I'm afraid. There were few enough of you left in the time the Ice Age began, after the Clone Wars, and now . . . well. You're at a dead end, I'm afraid. Between the Scylla of glacial Ice that creeps ever closer and the Charybdis of all the ingenious, diabolical predators you genetically engineered. We're all quite fortunate, in a way, to be witnessing the demise—a remarkable piece of evolutionary history is concluding right—"

"Stop!" Josh quietly commanded, holding her arm, fear and disbelief on his face.

She stopped, fastened her gaze to his for a long moment, reflected from inside her cloud. "I'm sorry," she said quietly. She drew on her opium pipe. "We were talking about time, a stitch in which, et cetera. Time was, it seemed very constant to me. Now it is thick and thin, like the weather."

"It's just our longevity," Jasmine mused. "It's changed our perspective. I know what you mean, though."

"Perhaps. As if the subtleties of time's changes in speed and depth can be appreciated only if seen in the long view . . ." She passed the pipe to Jasmine.

Jasmine toked, smiled. "It was at the speed of light when we were running guns through your back room here. . . ."

Sum-Thin joined the memory at the speed of thought. "When hepatitis was sweeping the Vampire colonies. Not many guns left anymore, though . . ."

"No," Jasmine agreed, "they were pretty much all destroyed during that spasm of animal self-righteousness in the Clone Wars. . . ."

"Along with all the Clones," Sum-Thin laughed.

Jasmine paused.

Josh found all this banter rather distressing. He was still brooding over Sum-Thin's cavalier comment about the end of the Human race. He remembered Jasmine once talking about the way Humans had *almost* destroyed themselves, but he took it for granted they would repopulate, grow strong again: their time would come.

But perhaps it would not.

These Neuromans knew more than most animals; they'd seen more. Sum-Thin's offhand remark chilled him deeper than December rain.

Jasmine broke her pause. "About the Clones," she said. "We were offered one tonight. Is it possible?"

Josh and Beauty both refused the pipe, so it went back to Sum-Thin, who drew long on the sweet resin before answering. "They were being made once more, for a time, some few years ago—practice runs. There is a nucleus of Neuroman bioengineers, in a castle at the mouth of the Sticks River. They have been dabbling again. There have been experiments. . . ."

"Truly," Jasmine nodded slowly. "Then the rumors of the New Animal have some basis. . . ."

"Not rumors." Sum-Thin lay back on a pillow. "There is a New Animal. The Neuromans have engi-

neered it and made it Ruler of their city." Her eyelids
dropped halfway down.

"What's it like, the New Animal?"

"No one knows. No one but a small cadre of
Neuroman engineers has ever seen it. Reputedly, it
has great powers."

"So it was said of many Accidents," Jasmine grimly
intoned.

"Accident or Grand Design. Only one thing this
says to me: those who will not learn from history
are condemned to repeat it."

Jasmine's lips thinned. "What more is known of this
Animal?"

Sum-Thin lowered her lids even farther. "Only
speculation and surmise. It may demand Human sac-
rifice." Josh and Beauty tensed. The Neuroman continued. "Or perhaps all the Humans are being taken
there merely for the purpose of experimentation." She
stared cannily at Josh, as if to say: *Eat this truth;
your days are numbered.*

Josh spoke in anger muffled by despair. "That's
why we've come. To save them."

Sum-Thin smiled, some thin opium smile. "Bravo.
The Human spirit."

Josh made a fist. Beauty seethed. Jasmine saw the
situation souring badly, unexpectedly. They didn't understand each other, Josh and Sum-Thin, they were on
different wavelengths. Josh saw only Dicey, while
Sum-Thin had seen it all. Jasmine stood to defuse the
situation.

"It's time to split up, I think," she said to the other
two hunters. "I'll stay here with Sum-Thin a bit longer,
gather more intelligence. Why don't you two head out
by the docks, nose around. Make some discreet in-
quiries." She put her powerful hands around Beauty's
waist and pulled him—with his subsequent surprised
assistance—to his feet, facing her. "Discreet," she repeated, holding her eyes firmly on his.

Beauty had the distinct impression that everything in
his life was taking on double meanings. He walked out
of the small den with Josh, two dismal spirits in search
of a vanishing memory.

When they'd gone, Jasmine lay down with Sum-Thin and kissed her affectionately on the cheek. "Do you *always* have to play the Dragon Lady?"

Sum-Thin closed her eyes, smiled; picked up her pipe.

Josh and Beauty left the Casa Blanca in silence, walking slowly along the old wooden docks. The sound of waves gently sloshing against the pilings had a calming effect; and so, lulled by the ocean's unhurried respirations, the two friends meandered.

"What's the point?" Josh wondered. "What's the point of Scribery if there are to be no Scribes to read in a hundred years?"

"She did not mention Scribes," Beauty corrected. "She said only that Humans would disappear."

"Either way. This quest, my writings, all our trials: it's all without meaning. Empty as wind."

"Your life may yet be long and full," Beauty soothed. He tried to sound consoling, yet his heart was heavy as his comrade's.

Joshua's face was wry, bitter. "I was smug when we found your people had no past; how hollow it is, now that mine have no future."

"We seem ever destined to share our losses," said the Centaur. His feeling for the Human was great.

"Ah, Beauty, it was triumphs we used to share. What's happened to the world?"

A great gull flew over the harbor, studied the lights on the water, flew back into the darkness.

"I will become a Scribe," Beauty said quietly. The idea had come to him only that moment, as great inspirations sometimes will, without considerations or intent. And once he said it, it seemed immediately and certainly right.

Josh was shocked. "But you've told me a hundred times how you mistrust Scribery. What could ever possess you to—"

"To diminish our losses. Your pain will be less if your religion lives on after your race has died. And as your pain is less, so is mine."

Josh was moved to silence. Beauty went on. "It is a

small enough thing, to learn these scribbles . . ." his voice trailed off, minimizing.

Josh put his hand on his friend's back, his eyes moist with love. "Friend, we'll triumph still. . . ."

Beauty felt twisted with unanswerable grief, though, at the complexities life had brought them; and soon the words overflowed his lips, like a pot that finally boils. "Clone Wars, Race Wars, kidnaping, vendetta. Is there no end? No end at all to what our peoples must suffer before the world is through with us?"

Josh stopped, looked up at the mighty Centaur. "Here is our solace, Beauty. Leave behind the emptiness in your history and my destiny. Here and now, we are what we are. You've been searching, since Jasmine's story, to know who and what that may be. Well, you're yourself and nothing else. As am I."

Beauty stared into the truth in Joshua's face, and it was a long moment before a weary smile crested over the surging of his doubts. "Old friend, it is good to be me, beside you."

They were quiet with each other for a while, walking once more along the wharf. Glowfish shone softly in the shallow waters below, eating the insects that floated on the surface. Above them the moon beamed as proudly as the sun's only child. Momentarily, at least, all the world seemed at peace to the two travelers.

Josh kicked a stone into the harbor. "What do you think of Sum-Thin?" he asked.

"She knows much," Beauty said, considering. "But I think she has been un-Human too long. She lacks the quality of empathy."

Josh nodded, heading away from the water. "Maybe she just lacks someone to empathize with," he replied charitably.

They passed a cooper's shop, a few taverns. Suddenly Josh halted in midstep. "Look," he whispered.

Beauty looked at the storefront Josh was staring at, but nothing struck him. "What is it?" he whispered back, feeling Joshua's tension.

"The Sign of the Scribe," said the young man. It was only at this coaxing that Beauty saw then, carved into the wooden scrollwork surrounding the old door, the symbol he'd seen Josh draw so often before, the snake in the circle:

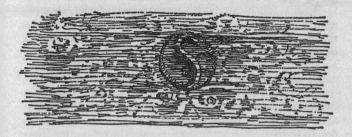

"I'm going in," Josh continued with contained excitement. "You go into the bar next door. Scout around, see if there are any back entrances or communicating halls."

Beauty nodded and went into the adjoining café. Josh entered the doorway under the Sign.

Inside, various creatures sat around tables, smoking opium, drinking yucca whiskey, casting bones. It seemed to be a bar. Dim candles flickered here and there like half-remembered thoughts. Perhaps half the patrons were Human. Josh walked slowly up to the bar at the back of the room, sat on the only empty stool—between a Ghoul and a Werewolf, and drummed his fingers on the liquor-rotted surface.

The bartender strode over in two long, slow steps. He was Human, but scary as any creature Josh had ever met: nearly seven feet tall, thick as a Bear, his lower lip chewed off in some ancient fight, his gnarled left hand bound with wire mesh to resemble some medieval weapon. "What'll it be?" he queried Josh without friendship—only the grim artificial scowl sculpted by his absent lip.

"Tequila," said Josh. The Werewolf to his left drooled onto the bar, glowering at nothing in particular. To his right, the Ghoul—an ugly creature whom Joshua did not care to observe too closely, but whom he assumed to be a Ghoul because of this quality which made other animals wish to look away—darted sidelong glances of a distinctly unsavory nature in Joshua's direction.

The bartender returned, set down a full shot glass and a quartered lime. Josh withdrew a gold piece from his belt and handed it over. The barman pocketed the coin and left Josh the bottle; but not before Josh saw the candles on the bar glint off the gold out of the eyes of every animal there. He sipped his drink, as his eyes opened to the shadows.

At one of the tables, a disagreement briefly flurried over a cast of the bones, then settled down. A small Dog gnawed a table leg. In the corner, two Humans whispered to an upright Lizard. Josh dipped his finger in the shot glass and traced lines on the bar. The Ghoul eyed him disconcertingly.

Joshua felt eyes on him from all over, in fact. He wasn't certain if he was just being paranoid, but decided that in any case he had to make a move—either leave, to see who followed; or something more daring.

Nonchalantly he extracted a small, blank slip of paper from his pocket—as if he'd been looking for a cigarette or a coca leaf, and come up with this disappointingly worthless piece of refuse; half a rolling paper, no more. He dropped it on the bar, too insignificant to bother with; and aware of eyes still on him, left it there as he continued to nurse his drink, continued to trace lines on the bar. Only now, some of the lines he traced on the bar managed to track over the paper as well; and every so often his finger would rub over the cut faces of the quartered lime, as if it were a touchstone.

Until, at the right moment, he glanced down, as if noticing the discarded paper for the first time. He picked up the paper, examined it disinterestedly, pulled a candle over, examined the paper in the light, to demonstrate to himself—and anyone else watching —that the paper was blank. And then Joshua held the paper over the flame. Toying with fire.

Slowly, the faint brown letters began to emerge out of the invisible citrus ink. They were clear only a brief moment before the paper burst into flame—long enough, perhaps, for the passing bartender to notice what was written, if he noticed, if he knew what writing looked like, if he could read: HELP! Long enough to get Joshua killed if the barman wasn't a friend; if the wrong person saw the script.

Josh dropped the burned-out ash onto the bar top as the last of the cool flame licked at his calloused fingertips. Nothing else happened. The barman continued serving drinks, the Werewolf drooled; intoxicated beasts traded words and fortunes. The Ghoul seemed to be edging closer. Josh finished his drink and made to leave.

"Just a minute," snarled the bartender. "You didn't pay."

"No. Yes. Yes, I did." stammered the young hunter. "I gave you—"

The brute clapped a massive right hand on Joshua's shoulder, and slammed his head down onto the wood, knocking him dizzy; then pulled him like a rag doll across the bar to the other side. "Stiffs don't drink, they get drank," he growled; whereupon he opened a trapdoor in the floor and dropped Josh through it into the waiting harbor water below. There was a loud splash. A few customers laughed, as the bartender closed the trapdoor. "Country trash," he muttered.

Josh revived immediately upon hitting the water, but not before inhaling a lungful. The next thing he knew, though, there were hands all over him, hauling him up some rickety, slime-covered steps. By the time he stopped sputtering and coughing he found himself lying on a bare floor, in a quiet, well-lit room—surrounded by a dozen grim, waiting figures. Quickly, he ran his eyes over their faces: all were Human.

"Welcome, brother," said a thin man near the door.

Josh sat up shakily. "What place is this?" he asked.

They all smiled to see that he was well. Several left immediately by the door the thin one seemed to be guarding. One went to cooking something on a small coal stove, two returned to sorting knives in a box. One sat at the table, picked up a pen, and to Joshua's heart-stopping joy, began to write. The three nearest to Josh sat down on the floor beside him.

"We call ourselves the Bookery," began the fellow

who sat closest to Josh. He was a serious young man, with red hair and rimless glasses. "We're all Scribes here, but our society is secret, even from other Scribes. My name is David." He held out his hand.

Josh took it. "Joshua," he answered, feeling totally safe for the first time in a long while.

The two others said Hello. One was an intense, wiry girl named Paula, her hair bobbed short, her face freckled. The other was a lad of no more than eighteen years, though in weight he nearly equaled the other three together. His name was Lewis. He seemed rather shy, and Josh liked him immediately.

"How did you find me?" asked Josh.

David laughed. "Percy threw you down to us. He's the bartender. He signaled us you'd be arriving soon, and we were waiting for you to . . . drop in. We're in a hidden room under the docks at the moment."

"You can help me?" Josh pressed. He was certain they would. They had the feel of good fortune.

"We can help each other," Paula said. "What is it you need?"

"My bride, my brother, and a dear friend have been stolen, my family murdered. They've been taken—"

"They've been taken south, to feed the new animal," David said stonily. Two older people who'd been reading to each other in the corner stopped when these words were spoken.

Josh remained speechless a moment. "Then you know of . . ." he began.

"We know there's a fiend afoot in the land. We know we will kill this new animal or turn into scripture trying."

"Will you join us?" asked Lewis.

"I . . . I must find my people first," Josh declared. The sleep-feeling was suddenly starting to come over him; a spell in the offing, without question.

"But our fight is the same fight," Paula insisted.

"My . . . my . . ." Joshua tried to speak, but his mind was clouding rapidly, as the darkness welled in him like a flood of night.

The void. He floated, weightless, in a dimension

without space, time, sense. Nothingness. No-thingness. Where had he heard that before? *Déjà vu.* So perhaps there was time. Back time, like the river twisting around on itself, old undercurrents pulling against the tide. Pulling, there, the light now, pulling him in, sucking him down, reeling him in on a line of pure energy, throbbing, pulsing, brighter, brighter . . .

He woke up shaking, on the floor, David and Paula holding him down. Beside him, Lewis lay unconscious, twitching, held by four others. Through his quickly vanishing grogginess, Josh felt somehow ashamed and afraid.

"I . . . I'm sorry . . ." he began.

"Don't talk, you're all right now," Paula soothed him, stroked his forehead.

"So you're one of the Touched," David murmured.

"These spells . . ." Joshua tried to explain.

"We know of them," David nodded. "Lewis, here, gets them, too."

Josh looked over to see Lewis just beginning to arouse. "Lewis, too?" he gasped incredulously. "Others have these trances? But what do they mean, what are they?"

"No one knows," Paula shook her head. "I've seen several people possessed by them. They all describe the spells in the same way—a blackness, and a magnetic light . . ."

"Yes, yes, that's it!" Josh sat erect, desperate for someone to understand his affliction.

"No one knows," Paula only shook her head again.

Lewis sat up. He and Josh stared at each other for a long second, looking for the answer to their common mystery. They found an ambiguous empathy: some measure of shared circumstance, pain, and confusion. Briefly, they held hands.

"Whatever it is," David interjected, "those who are Touched seem to be gathering in the south, though none can say why."

"We all gather in the south," said the old woman writing at the table. "Here we fight our future."

"Scribery is the only future," said another.

"*The Word, the written Word,*" they all chimed in.

David put his hand on Joshua's shoulder. "Join us," he said quietly.

There were two quick knocks on the door, and suddenly everyone was up and running in all directions.

"What is it?" whispered Josh, on David's heels out the side door.

"They've discovered us. Run for it!" David rasped.

"Who?" Josh asked as they raced down a long dark hall.

"JEGS, BASS, Vampires. Who knows? It's all the same. We've only enemies in all the world. Trust no one but your own, lad."

They emerged at water level, under the wharf; ran along a slippery catwalk and up a flight of splintered stairs to the dock. No sooner had they reached the upper level than shouts and shuffles echoed from down the promenade. Someone cried out. Joshua crouched to get a better look, and in that moment an arrow zinged by, creasing David's scalp.

The Scribe leader stumbled, fell, and got up again, blood oozing from his wound. "Split up," he whispered, and disappeared down an alley.

Josh circled around behind a blacksmith shop, cut across two back streets, and came out near the bar he'd originally entered. He slowed to a casual walk, quieted his breathing, forced himself to stroll toward the pier. A moment later he sensed the presence of animal behind him, though, and turned in a flash, hand on knife. It was Beauty.

"You appear to be in need of a good animal alibi," said the Centaur. "May I join you?"

They walked the waterfront without haste, letting Joshua's adrenaline dissipate as he told his story to Beauty. Occasionally Josh would jump—at the sound of a distant yell, or the swoop of a sea bird—but he finally settled down. Beauty told his end of the interlude, though there was little to tell. He'd found a back entrance, waited, heard a ruckus, came back out front —and found Josh wandering calm as a tide pool.

They decided to go back to the Casa Blanca, to give this new information to Jasmine and formulate a plan. There were still many loose ends, but among them, now, Josh felt the thrill of glimpsing the end in sight. Unconsciously, they picked up their pace back toward Sum-Thin's bar.

Out of the black night leapt an animal: small, dark, sinewy. It wrapped itself around Joshua's face before he even registered its attack. First he was aware of the creature's black, warm fur, then two piercing blue eyes staring point blank into his own; then a hot growly voice: "Where *werrrrre* you?"

It was Isis.

She licked his face madly, until he finally tossed her to the ground. Laughing, he knelt down and scratched her roughly between the ears, his hand vibrant with her purrs. She was leaning so far into his massage that when he stopped she fell over sideways. On her back, legs in the air, still purring, she looked at them fondly. "You're alive," she said.

"No less than you, Fur-face. We were prisoners of time for a time, but now we are free. And what use have you made of yourself since our separation?"

"Saw your girrrl," she purred smugly.

Josh started. "What! Here?"

Isis nodded. "Gone nowww," she mentioned in disinterested afterthought.

"Gone where?" Josh demanded. "What happened?"

"South," pouted Isis. She was annoyed that Joshua's interest and affections had transferred so quickly to the girl with the blood-smell. "With Vampires," she added in a tone of disapproval. This did not have the desired effect, though, for rather than make Joshua renew his focus on Isis, it just made him more distraught. She gave him a consolation prize: "Scree here, though. Mrow." She sidled up to Joshua's ego. She suspected she could get Joshua's attention off the lost girl-Human by mentioning the broken-beak; and she was right.

"Scree? The Griffin?" Joshua's face relit.

"Where?" came in Beauty, fists clenched.

She saw immediately she could endear herself with this information. "Herrrre," she purred coyly, and began slinking up the wharf with an occasional flip of her tail. The others followed.

They quickly came to a scummy bar called The Pit Fall. A sign in the window said NO HUMANS ALLOWED and beside it the mummified skeleton of a man hung by the neck from the rafters. Various creatures did various revolting things among the shadows inside. A small Accident bit off and ate its own fingers at the bar; two Vampires molested a young Equiman; a frothing Satyr fondled a corpse. And perched in a corner, sharpening its talons on the skull of a newly dead reptile, was the green-and-gold, broken-beaked Griffin.

"Scree," whispered Josh. He started to enter, but Beauty held him back.

Isis put up her paw. "You stay herrre. Bird will commme." With which she strutted straight into the bar.

Josh and Beauty watched through the window as the small Cat sauntered over to the Griffin, squatted, and urinated on the creature's claw.

With a screech, the Griffin spread wing and tore around the room in circles after the crazy Cat, who jumped over the bar, under tables, between chairs, and finally out the front door. A second later when Scree emerged from the tavern hot on Isis' tail, Beauty was there. He grabbed the Griffin's extended wings from behind, at the base, and twisting down with all his force, broke the animal's shoulders. Scree gasped in pain and surprise.

Josh and Beauty immediately dragged the crippled beast around the corner and into a lightless alley. Beauty held it down, squirming. When it got its first good look at Joshua, it spat. " 'Uman stink," it cawed.

"Keep talking," whispered Josh, coming close, his knife out. "The right words may ease your suffering." He stared at the gnashing creature through the memory of his family's gored remains. He raised his blade and tickled the Griffin's throat. "Keep talking," he repeated solemnly.

"You remember when you took your name?" Jasmine reminisced nostalgically. They sat along cushions on the smoky floor, near enough to touch without touching.

"Do I not. You walked into my room the day I woke up from the surgery. I felt like Frankenstein's monster. I said I must look hideous—different face, different gender . . . different being. And you said I looked like 'somethin' so fine.' That was all you said. I swore to myself I'd keep those words with me forever, and took them for my name on the spot."

"Do you know what I promised myself on that day? That we should never be apart." Her eyes twinkled at her adolescent naïveté.

"Well, I am glad one of us knows how to keep a promise," Sum-Thin warmly scolded.

"Ah, but it was grand while it was," Jasmine pursued. "The better part of a century, I make it."

"The best part, by far, Jazz. The very best."

They studied one another with that peculiar love it is possible to feel for an earlier time of life, when—in retrospect—things seemed more simple, more pure.

"We had this town by the tail a hundred years ago," Jasmine let her memories wander to and fro. "Right after the Ice Change, remember? Nobody knew *which* way was up, except us. . . ."

"I remember. Refugees were flooding in. Running from the Ice up north, and from the mosquitoes in the south . . ."

"And everyone looking to get right or get out. What a time that was. Running drugs, smuggling émigrés out to the islands, selling everything from bearskins to bug repellent . . ."

"It was a time, was it not," Sum-Thin began replaying the same movie. "We have seen many changes, you and I. The bacteriological warfare just after I became Neuroman strikes me now—I'd have certainly died if you hadn't persuaded me in time to have the operation; my health, even for a Human, was never good. . . ."

"The Germ War, yes. Not many people left after that one. They had to abandon the space colonies, I remember, because—"

"The space colonies, God, I'd forgotten about those. . . ."

"How could you forget, they made such a big deal about them in the last half of the twenty-first century, all those orbiting stations, and moon colonies, and space probes—they were going to save us, it was going to be a new era. . . ."

"It was a new era, all right . . ."

"Wonder whatever happened to them?"

"The colonies starved, the orbits degenerated, reentered, and crashed, the probes are on eternal probation," Sum-Thin smiled.

"Then there was the Limited Nuclear War . . ." Jasmine was becoming almost gleeful at this resurrection of historical catastrophes.

"Ah, yes, July 4th, 2117. Limited to major cities . . ."

"And then the Clone Wars . . ."

"Now *there* was a war. Human ingenuity at its quintessence. Thousands of Human Clones created to restock the race, and then all the *other* creatures we created take it as the final insult and destroy them all . . ."

"Ah, the Age of Beasts . . ."

"Literacy becoming a religion . . ."

"And the Coming of Ice. My favorite natural disaster." The reverie was off-tilting, taking a slightly hysterical tone, like a gyroscope starting to lose speed.

"Yes, the Ice Age. We really peaked with that one, you and I. The ruling queens of Ma'gas', we were . . ."

"We have to write this all down, it's too good to lose . . ."

"And then you left me." Sum-Thin's words froze the patter. The gyroscope stopped.

"A hundred years is a long time," Jasmine said quietly. "It was time to leave."

"I know, it was the right thing for you. I remember, old Dundee used to come into town for supplies, and tell all his wild stories about the Terrarium, about the Howlers, and the Vampire colonies, and the lost cities and strange sorcerers—and your eyes would turn glassy, and your breath quicken."

"I stayed down there fifty years. It was a grand old time I had, but you know, I always missed you not being there to share it with me. Ten times a day I wanted to be able to nudge you and say 'Look at *that!* Look at that!' "

Sum-Thin smiled again, her lids heavy with what they'd lost, what they still had. "You found others, I was told."

"Lon, for a while," Jasmine nodded. "The noblest Vampire I know." Briefly, she let herself think of Lon. "I've been alone for sixty, seventy years, now, though."

"And I, since the day you left."

Jasmine touched her old friend's cheek delicately, traced its outline down the perfect hollow, along the fine lips. "So you haven't left the bar in all that time," she said with tender regard.

"No need," Sum-Thin shrugged. "All come to me. See—even you are here again."

"Maybe. You certainly seem to've found your niche. Me, I'm still searching for mine."

"Rolling bones gather no flesh," Sum-Thin advised.

Jasmine sensed her dear companion of so many years was becoming reserved once again, retreating into her cloud of philosophy. "I'm not sure anymore of flesh really has much value," she retorted.

"What, then? The 'Great Spirit'?" Sum-Thin gently sneered.

"Energy, maybe. You mean you've never had an intimation of some singularity to the universe in all your three centuries?"

"Yes, I've had such feelings, but I always lie down until they pass over." She laughed, and this seemed to thaw the momentary chill that had congealed their space. When she went on, it was as if some undefinable tension had resolved between them, left them at peace. "Energy without substance, without flesh—it is nil, Jazz. Matter is what matters in the universe. Energy flow, Oneness, underlying Singularities—meaningless abstractions, luxuries of meditation. Matter is the Without Which Not: without which not space, nor time, nor thing nor thought. *This*, then, is the *All*." She reached over, lay a considered hand on Jasmine's breast; measured, weighed, contemplated, and palpated the matter; then fell back finally to her pillow, her eyes closed, mouth askew.

Jasmine smiled at her old friend. "Philosopher-stoned again."

"Blarney-stoned, you mean. But ah, the opium billows my cloud."

Jasmine rose. "It's been good to see you again, Sum-Thin, but these bones of mine have got to get rolling."

"Having a tilt at the new animal, are you?"

"I might. When I finish helping my new friends find their people."

"Well, luck to you all. To be honest, it would make my Teflon heart glad to see the new animal fall. I don't like what I hear of the beast."

"Such as?"

"Oh, nothing specific. I am afraid they're making a cult of it, though. The inner circle even calls itself LOS ANGELES—Associated Neuroman Genetic Engineers, Lords, et Sages."

"Well, it's pretentious enough to be a cult. What's the power base, though?"

"The animal." She stood, and the two Neuromans faced each other, joined by all they'd seen together, separated by all they'd seen alone; connected by waves of darkness and light.

They touched hands.

"Perhaps," said Jasmine, "it's time to spend some time here again; after this hunt."

The curtain parted at that moment, admitting Joshua, Beauty, and Isis. The Cat walked directly to a corner pillow, where she sat mutely licking her paw. Josh and Beauty stood tautly at the entranceway.

Jasmine looked from one to the other. "What," she said.

"We found the Griffin," Josh replied. "Bal took our people to the new animal's castle. The Vampire lives there. He kept some of the captives for his own, he gave the rest to the animal."

"The Griffin?" asked Jasmine.

"The Griffin is dead," Beauty spoke with a quiet finality. Josh kept his gaze fastened to the floor.

Sum-Thin stared deeply into Joshua's desolation. "Nothing is sweeter than the pursuit of revenge," she said, "and nothing more hollow than success."

Josh turned his anger outward. "The world's a better place with that monster dead." Silence surrounded him.

Sum-Thin's eyes were fine slits. "What was the Griffin's name?"

"Scree," answered Josh.

Sum-Thin's eyebrows raised a notch. "In that case," she said, "please have one last drink on the house before you go." She bowed at the waist and ushered them out to the bar. "Eyeball," she said to the Cyclops bartender, "one drink for my guests, for the road." With which she bowed once more, and disappeared into her back room.

The barroom was swirling with crosscurrents. Vampires, Satyrs, Humans, Harpies, Furies, Devils, Gargoyles, and mixed breeds of every genotype drank, gamed, and conspired from floor to loft. Jasmine, Josh, and Beauty stood at the bar and took three coffees, while Isis sat warily by the exit. Josh told Jasmine briefly about his meeting with the book-people; then about Isis' tale, which—insofar as Josh had been able to determine from the marginally articulate little Cat —was that she'd abandoned the hunt here, when it had seemed likely that Josh was dead, and thenceforth had eked out a fairly "borrrring" existence as an alley cat, keeping close tabs on the Griffin she knew to be somehow responsible for Joshua's disappearance; until suddenly she'd become aware that Josh was in the city, and tracked down his smell as soon as she could.

Finally, Josh told Jasmine about the information Scree had given them.

"So it's the castle we want, at the mouth of the Sticks," Jasmine said softly.

"How far is the Sticks?" asked Beauty.

"Not far," Jasmine answered, "but it's through more jungle from here. The easiest thing would be to hire a boat, take it down the coast and get put ashore a bit south of the river. I've no idea how we'll get inside the castle once we're there."

"We'll figure something out," Josh spoke moodily. He was feeling surly after the encounter with Scree. It had gone badly: the lust of vengeance had wilted in the face of the broken, snapping Griffin. He'd been urged on by Venge-right so long, and finally the moment came, and he was impotent. It was Beauty who had to do the deed. Now Josh found himself confused and seething.

"Maybe," said Jasmine, "but you can't just storm a castle with rocks and wishes. You need a plan. We don't even know—"

"We know they're there, we know we're going to get them."

"Yes, yes, but Neptune's Middle Fin, Joshua, you can't—"

A hand slammed down on the bar with such force as to startle everyone in the room into silence.

"Blasphemy," rasped a voice. A figure stood back, facing Jasmine: it was the tense form of a naked woman, a black hood over her head, an upright trident branded into her right shoulder. Through two slits cut in her hood, green eyes stared out furiously. She gripped a saber.

"The hooded woman," whispered Josh.

"Be careful," Beauty spoke softly to Jasmine's ear, "she's Born-Again."

The hooded woman stood away from the bar. Behind her, the man with no arms and the head of a bird stood like her shadow, making clicking sounds from its open beak. "You profane the Lord's name," said the hooded woman.

"I meant no disrespect," Jasmine said gingerly. "I'm sorry if I've offended you."

"You have not offended me, wretch. You have offended my Lord." The hooded woman slammed her blade on the bar to punctuate the accusation. All eyes were fixed on Jasmine, awaiting her response.

"Please," said Jasmine, pausing to point the request with a measure of menace. "Accept my apology."

The hooded woman may have been drinking. "I demand satisfaction," she hissed. "A duel."

The Bird-man clacked like a ratchet. The crowd murmured. Eyeball, the bartender, knocked quietly thrice on Sum-Thin's door, and the Oriental Neuroman immediately came out, stood beside the bar, watched.

Josh stepped forward. "You know me," he said to the hooded woman. "I have the water-power."

She squinted at him, her green eyes flaming.

He went on. "My friend here is helping me on my journey. I apologize for her."

The hooded woman shook her head once. "The challenge is not to you." Then, to Jasmine again: "Here and now. Choose your weapon."

The room came alive. In an excited hush, tables and chairs were moved to the walls, leaving a huge clear space in the center of the floor.

Jasmine looked questioningly at Sum-Thin. "It's the fashion here, over a quarter of a century now," Sum-Thin said quietly. "There's nothing for it but to fight."

Jasmine stood back from the bar and faced the hooded woman. "Epée," she said, drawing her sword. The woman in the hood lay her saber on the bar, walked over to a group of BASS near the stairs, conferred briefly, and began weighing the épées gathered among her assembled cohorts.

Sum-Thin stepped around the bar, moved over to Jasmine, spoke more loudly, more officially. "Will you keep your sleeve down, or wear it rolled, or cut it off?"

Jasmine looked a bit surprised. "Well. I don't know. What do you think, what's best?"

"I am not allowed to say," Sum-Thin declined tactfully.

"Well. Cut it, I suppose," Jasmine said after brief consideration.

"That is preferable," Sum-Thin nodded. "That is correct." She held out her hand, the Cyclops put a knife in it, and in a flash she cut the right sleeve off Jasmine's blouse, at the shoulder.

Josh looked worried. "Must it be to the death?" he asked. "Isn't first blood sufficient?"

Sum-Thin only smiled without humor.

"I do not like it," said Beauty to Jasmine. "Death is sport with these people. Be wary." He felt himself in a grip of nervous tension for the Neuroman; found himself wishing he were about to fight rather than about to watch her fight.

The duelists walked to the center of the room, tested the flex of their blades, made practice lunges in the air, feinted with shadows. Presently, they stopped. Sum-Thin came out to where they stood, facing, and took her post between them, out off to the side. They saluted each other with sword, bringing handle to chin, then swishing the blade through a wide arc to point finally down and out. At last, both turned to salute Sum-Thin in a similar fashion.

"Fencers, *en garde* . . ." said Sum-Thin.

They faced off, assumed the *en garde* position, crossed blades.

"Prêt . . ." said Sum-Thin.

"Prêt," said the hooded woman.

"Ready," said Jasmine.

A long pause. The stillness of a photograph.

"Allez," said Sum-Thin, jumping back.

In a fury, the blades clanged three times: feint, parry, *riposte,* parry, *riposte,* parry. Then silence once more, and the fencers circled.

They each had a sense, now, of the other's speed, but little of timing. So it was to each to initiate a series of simple and composed attacks, to see how the other would parry, to gauge reaction time, to glimpse patterns of response. Jasmine advanced with a *dou-blé,* the hooded woman answered with a counter-parry. Jasmine declined the counterparry, proceeded to *triplé,* went to a *coupé-dégagé desous,* going over opponent's blade, then under it again in the low line. The hooded woman lateral-parried, but Jasmine dropped down almost to her knees—extending her épée out, and inches below the hiss of the hooded woman's steel, which sliced horizontally through the air: the Neuroman's point struck the hooded woman in the right side, below the liver, penetrating a full inch before the woman leapt back in surprise: the triangular blade left an open black hole in her belly, almost immediately oozing thick and red. First blood.

The crowd gasped. The hooded woman glanced down at her wound, and her green eyes jumped in the candlelight. Again the adversaries circled.

Whispers rose and fell among the surrounding onlookers. Bets were taken, odds given, deities invoked, course of action urged. The hooded woman seemed to be the local favorite, but the Neuroman's tough plastic skin and her well-timed touch were weighty factors.

There was another flurry of swordplay, stopping all conversation. It was a lengthy exchange, a complex array of feints, deceptions, and attacks that ended with the duelists' *corps-à,corps* swords crossed at the hilt, panting heavily and staring only inches away into each other's eyes. Jasmine pushed off, slamming her foot down for distraction, and swung the blade forward. The hooded woman jumped back swiftly but could not avoid the tip of Jasmine's blade entirely—it carved a thin red line across her chest from shoulder to shoulder. It was a wild stroke, though, and it left Jasmine somewhat exposed: the hooded woman ignored her own injury and made a lightning thrust—in and out—piercing Jasmine's upper arm, through and through. Once more, they backed apart.

Jasmine had scored twice, now; the BASS woman only once. But Jasmine's wound was a dangerous thing: Neuromans had no hemostatic mechanisms, so even the smallest cut would keep bleeding until the wound was repaired. Jasmine could bleed to death from a small tear in her fabric. As she circled the floor, she managed to plug one hole with cloth from her shirt, while dodging and parrying a few noisy thrusts. She couldn't reach the exit wound at the back of her arm, though, so it continued to bleed.

Josh and Beauty stood tensely at the bar, alert to every move, every nuance. Only with great difficulty could they keep themselves from entering the match. Blood lust in the room was high, the air crackling with dark energy. Joshua's senses were torn by the strange setting, the uncertain stakes, the crossing currents. Beauty, too, was thick with worry; black demons filled his chest: he did not want this special Neuroman to die. The fencers stalked. The room held its breath. Suddenly, with almost theatrical precision, several things happened, virtually simultaneously.

Jasmine circled cautiously, her back to the ring of spectators. Briefly, she paused, near the far side of the room. Behind her, Cork, the bar-tart, stood whispering to a cluster of BASS. Beauty watched from across the bar as the Hermaphrodite reached surreptitiously into the top of her boot. The Centaur had his bow drawn as the Hermaphrodite's knife came out; and at the same moment that Cork pushed the knife into Jasmine's back, Beauty loosed his arrow through the bar-tart's neck.

Cork fell, gurgling. The sound distracted the hooded woman, momentarily—the same instant Jasmine, propelled by the force of the knife in her back, thrust her blade forward, running the hooded woman through, above the right breast. Both fencers fell, eyes wide, to their knees. The hooded woman twisted. Jasmine's blade broke, still lodged deeply in her opponent's chest.

All this in a second. Tension in the room was at a critical mass. Josh, acting as if in a dream, seized a nearby whale-oil lantern and threw it against the wall. With a tremendous crash the entire wall burst into flame. This in the second second. The third second was bedlam.

Creatures ran in every direction, screeching, trying to get out, trying to douse the fire, clawing each other, flapping into walls. The conflagration quickly spread to the ceiling and jumped from lantern to lantern along the bar. Gargoyles tried to bite off their own burning parts; Vampires beat their wings to gain the altitude of the high windows over the loft, but this only fanned the flames; Harpies wailed, Lizards scratched at corners, animals hissed and swore. Beasts in a nightmare. Visions of Hell.

Sum-Thin slipped, unnoticed, through a secret trapdoor in the floor behind the bar. Josh raced to where Jasmine was kneeling, back-stabbed in the middle of the room. He picked her up and headed for the doorway, but in the chaotic swirls of smoke and noise, he faltered, and fell.

Beauty charged over to the front door. It opened inward, normally, but was jammed shut with bodies and desperate crawling animals now, so it didn't open at all. He battered it with his hooves a few times, but caught a lungful of smoke and doubled over coughing. A flaming beam fell from the rafters.

Cries could be heard outside, as animals on the dock tried to quench the fire with buckets of sea-water, before the flames spread to adjacent buildings.

Inside, the cries were diminishing.

CHAPTER 13

In Which The Travelers Reach
The City Of Light

IT was Isis who saved them. She bit Beauty's hindside hard, bringing him instantly to his feet. Next, she took his tail in her mouth and guided him, pulled him, stumbling, backward to where Josh slumped with Jasmine. She transferred the bushy tail to Joshua's free hand, saying "Hold onnnn!" Josh gripped the Centaur's hind hairs with the ferocious spasm of a final act.

Isis then jumped on Beauty's shoulder. "Behind the barrrr!" she shouted. His eyes were blinded, watering: he lost his direction. She climbed into his mane, pulled his flowing hair right to make him go right: left to go left. Josh and Jasmine were dragged along the floor behind them. A few seconds later they all stood in back of the bar, over the open trapdoor. Fire rimmed the lips of the hole: beyond was blackness.

Without a thought, Beauty leapt through the gaping flaming maw, taking the others with him.

Through the void they fell. Warm, black air whistled by, tumbling until—*whhhp*—they were sucked with a shock, into a soundless, lightless, weightless, airless cold. Here they floated, dreamlike, until buoyancy prevailed; and they broke the sputtering surface. They were in the water, fifty feet below the dock.

Above them the fire roared.

They all thrashed about for a time, exhausted, half suffocated. Josh, Jasmine, and Isis clung to the Centaur's back as he flailed toward what he thought was the shore. It wasn't.

It was sheer cliff. Beauty clung to one of the pilings for a minute, catching his breath, when suddenly flaming debris began to fall from the docks overhead. He had to get them out from under the pyre. With grueling strokes, he began to swim.

His strength was at an ebb, though, and he was not aided by the three friends tugging him down. The night was bearing heavily on him; the water, increasingly, a source of rest: after thirty or forty yards paddling into the harbor, he began to sink. As if in a vision, he saw a craft floating slowly toward them in the silence. A ghost ship. He couldn't see it clearly until it was almost upon them; then suddenly it was clear: a small junk, without running lights; Sum-Thin at the helm. With powerful Neuroman arms she helped pull them all aboard.

And so they lay, in puddles, half-conscious, as the Oriental Neuroman guided the old junk among the myriad anchored vessels into the quiet breezy bay.

Throughout the night the little ship bobbed serenely in the cove among its fellows. Below decks the seekers slept fitfully, running from dream to dream. Ashore in the distance, buildings burned, smoldered, flared.

When things had quieted a bit, Sum-Thin took a fat, burning joss stick and melted closed the holes in Jasmine's arm and back, to stop the slow, steady bleeding. The damage done was relatively minor: the arm wound had severed connections to the hand, so now her two middle fingers were completely dysfunctional. As for the back wound, little was harmed. Neuromans had, in their chest cavities, a nuclear power cell, jacketed in lead, then cased in steel, consequently impervious; and a glucose storage reserve, less well protected, but also less consequential if damaged. It was Jasmine's glucose pack that had been pierced by Cork's knife in the back, and all the Neuroman had suffered was a slow trickle of sugar mixed with Hemolube. Sum-Thin replaced the lost fluid with one of the spare cans of Hemolube she kept stored in the junk's hold.

Of course, they'd all suffered from smoke inhalation. It wasn't until next morning that they began to

rouse and cough. Beauty ached everywhere. Isis hated
being wet. Josh threw up over the side, and Jasmine
just kept sleeping. Sum-Thin brooded.

"I'm sorry," Josh apologized for the third time. "I
didn't really want to burn your place down, I just
wasn't thinking, I—"

Sum-Thin held up her hand. "It is done, we'll not
discuss it further." The event clearly pained her. "We
are all alive. Our only thoughts must be to staying
so."

"Howwww," muttered Isis into her matted fur.
Rarely had an animal looked so miserable.

"We cannot go back, that much is clear," Sum-
Thin cautioned. "You'll be hunted now by friends of
Scree and of the BASS woman."

"They will think us dead in the fire," Beauty suggested.

"Perhaps," said Sum-Thin.

"But what about you?" asked Josh. He felt deeply
troubled for having burned down Sum-Thin's life.

"I am, for better or worse, allied to you. We were
seen talking and smoking. It would not go well for me
here now. At best I would be tortured on the off
chance I knew your whereabouts. No, best for me to
vanish for a generation. Perhaps in time, I can rise
from the ashes. When the smoke clears, when the
embers cool."

Joshua did not understand Sum-Thin. He found
her mysterious and obscure and powerful, and he
didn't trust his conclusions about her motives. He suspected she was a sorceress. "How was it you happened to find us under the burning dock last night?"
he asked her.

She laughed a short, dry laugh. "I did not 'happen' to find you. It was the only way out, and I was
waiting for you. My junk is anchored there at all
times, for just such urgencies."

"But how did you know we'd make it out?"

"I did not," she spoke softly, in a tone meant to
end conversation.

Josh let it pass. There was much, he knew, he
would never understand.

Beauty rested against the port hull. He was glad just to be free of the city. Like Josh, he found Sum-Thin's ways difficult to grasp; but this was of no consequence to him. She was herself, and he was himself: there was nothing in that to cause either discomfort. Still, he did feel sorry for her that her life had been burned into smoke—it was a state to which he felt some closeness, and this moved him to speak to the otherwise distant Neuroman. "I, too, apologize for the upheaval in your life. I know what it means to lose your home to fire. Yet I cannot regret the destruction of so many evil beasts. And our search has been furthered. Surely, there is good in that."

Sum-Thin smiled wryly, pointedly. "As I said, we will speak no more of it. Let me only quote Long-Chen Pa, an ancestor of mine upon whose wisdom I've often called during my sojourn in this city: 'Since everything is but an apparition perfect in being what it is, having nothing to do with good or bad, one may well burst out in laughter.'"

She smiled, let out a single throaty chuckle, hoisted in the anchor; and the little ship set off to the west, full in the breath of an autumn wind.

Once out of the bay, the junk blew southwest over the pacific waters. It was a seaworthy craft despite its small size, and followed the currents without mishap under the dazzlingly sunny sky.

The voyagers rested on the deck, gathering strength. Each took a turn at the tiller, and, under Sum-Thin's direction, at the sail. They caught fish, traded stories, nursed burns, lolled—recuperated. For the most part, they were contemplative, preferring to reflect on the green crystal jewel of the ocean as it sparkled to the thin horizon. And all the while the wind took them effortlessly south.

Sea birds called greetings to them along the way. Dolphins kept pace, then found other amusement. Twice, ships could be seen in the distance; twice, they disappeared over the distance's gentle curve. Slow was the day, and peaceful.

Around dusk, when the water was violet under the

setting twilight, Josh quietly dissolved into the abyss of another mysterious spell.

Fearful, empty blackness. A hollow electric wind blew from inside, out. From the depths, a light: pinpoint at first, then swelling, pulsing, pulling. Until soon the star—heavy brightness filled all but the farthest reaches of the void—a massive white-hot magnet, sucking Josh into its center, and now he saw the center for the first time: buried in the blinding radiance, the outline of a face.

Josh jumped awake.

Around him, his friends stood, their faces scared, their hands holding his body down to the deck.

"You were having convulsions," whispered Jasmine. "You were hurting yourself. You're okay now."

He closed his eyes again. What was happening to him? He could not falter, with his quest so close to its finish. Sleep frightened him now. He must not sleep. Yet these ordeals tired him so.

Nor was he alone. Lewis, of the Bookery, had these spells. And others, too, they'd said. But why? All moving south, they'd said; even as he, now, was drifting. He thought of the face he'd seen in his last trance, the face in the light. A strange face, there and not there, horrible and compelling. An inner face.

He felt himself fading again, into sleep. And who were these Bookery people? David, Paula, Lewis, and the others. After the new animal, they'd said. A secret society within a secret society. Trust no one, they'd said. But that wasn't right, he trusted Beauty, and he trusted Jasmine, and Rose and Dicey. Only your own, they'd said. But who were they? Why did some of them have spells like his? What was the meaning of it all? Where was the sense?

He let himself fade; he could no longer resist.

Cool breeze over the night waves. Round moon, lonely clouds. The companions sat or stood at the rails, watching flying-fish break the silvery water, like discrete thoughts springing from the primordial subconscious of the earth. The watchers hoped for sign; but the fish immediately resubmerged, leaving unmarked the face of the endless sea.

Once, in the middle of all the silent night, there was a sound. A wail, or a moan: a long, low plaintive sound that rose from the water and implored the stars. It quickened the blood of the sailors on the junk; made them look briskly to the sixteen points of the compass and scan the ocean with hard night eyes. Nothing about.

The sun rose behind a murmuring of gray thunderclouds.

Jasmine felt strong as ever now, physically. Her two fingers continued to work only intermittently, but she was otherwise fully recuperated. Except that suddenly she was feeling mortal. She'd almost died. Died. Bled to death. To death. She dwelled on the word, tried to consider what it meant. Around her was empty sea all the way to the sky, then empty sky all the way to the sea again. Was this what death was like? An empty, drifting undulation. It was something she hadn't thought about much in over two hundred years; but now, in four months, she'd almost bled to death twice. To death.

Was it a sign to be more cautious? More restrained, perhaps. No, such was unthinkable. A life of caution could hardly be worth living.

The clouds that had brought on the day vanished to the east. The sun and rocking water soothed her spirit, in time. She closed her eyes, let all considerations float out of her mind.

Beauty watched for the shore. Land meant Rose, the end of the journey. It invigorated him to be so near. He was glad to be rid of the city, glad to be in balance with nature again, glad to be forging on in good company. The sea was not his most favorite place to be, but for Beauty, for the moment, all was right with the world.

He loosed arrow at a tuna swimming too near the surface, and when it bobbed up wriggling, Beauty pulled it out of the water, the shaft through its head. He cut it into morsels; and the crew feasted.

Isis had never felt so sick. She was sun-dried, now, at least; but too nauseous even to think about anything as once-wonderful as tuna. She hoped they would land soon. Even alley food was better than this. She watched her beautiful Joshua, peacefully asleep at the bow. How good to be with him again, in spite of this watery hell.

She watched Jasmine sleeping too; the Neuroman did not sleep restfully, but tossed and grunted, as if wrestling with the sleep-creatures. Isis felt sad for the troubled Neuroman, whom she liked greatly without knowing why. She walked queasily across the boat, sat beside Jasmine's head; and quietly, methodically, unhurriedly, began to lick the Neuroman's face.

Sum-Thin stood by the sail. Life was strange, was it not. Jasmine had brought her to Ma'gas', left her there, returned a century later to take her away. She felt herself to be riding life on a slow, ineffable tide, just as she rode this little ship. Winds, currents, swells. Ma'gas' had become a doldrum, from which she'd been snatched by a flashflood. What was to come? she wondered. Undercurrents, typhoons, maelstroms, becalmings. How little one could do with sail and tiller against the whims of the deep.

They had done with eating; all were awake. The day was strong, the sea unfathomable. The little ship bobbed tiny as a lost thought.

Yet they were together. All of them felt this, acknowledged it tacitly, to themselves, to each other. For a time they felt buoyed on the impenetrable calm of their unity, and it was of no consequence that they were but an infinitesimal speck in the belly of the raging universe. They were an organism. They were huge in their togetherness.

The thunderclouds returned. The sea rolled the shaky boat over swollen waves that never quite broke.

Sum-Thin tried to steer them toward the shore, but made little headway in the tricky wind. They began shipping water.

Josh and Beauty bailed. Sum-Thin hauled sail, while Jasmine sat tiller. Isis stared cold and awful into the waiting deep. For the better part of an hour, they coped with the angry sea, second-guessing wind changes, constantly reorienting the prow into the waves; bracing against imminent destruction. They were all so absorbed, in fact, not a single one noticed the massive ship until it was almost upon them.

And a strange ship it was.

Hundreds of palm logs, lashed side to side and end to end, stretched out eighty yards in the long plane, fifty yards wide. It was a raft the size of a field.

A solitary mainsail rose from the center of the raft. Dozens of small accessory sails sprouted up every ten feet along her perimeter; dozens of sailors ran frantically from one canvas to another, raising some, lowering some—all at the direction of an insane-looking dwarf who stood on an elevated platform beside the tall central mast.

As the great vessel drew near, its crew members threw lines across Sum-Thin's junk, and rapidly pulled the small craft to; then kept pulling until the junk was hauled up onto the giant raft. Josh, Jasmine, Beauty, Isis, and Sum-Thin were immediately seized, their weapons confiscated. They were tied together and bound to the single mainsail near the raised platform upon which the dwarf captain stood.

The capsized junk lay askew on the raft, and Josh watched in wonder as a group of sailors began pulling excitely on a long vine that dangled from the back of the junk into the sea. For at the end of fifty yards of vine was the hooded woman: bedraggled, water-logged, Jasmine's blade still in her chest—hanging on in tow since the night of the fire.

She was apparently still alive, and all the crew seemed quite overjoyed to see her. Some of them rushed her to a small cabin at the opposite side of the mainsail from where Josh was bound. The others pushed the junk back into the ocean, where it quickly floundered and sank.

Finally the strange captain began shouting orders again, and the crew ran around taking down and putting up sail, until slowly the lumbering raft began to turn in the wind, and head back over the high seas whence it had come.

They reached Venice the next morning. It was an opulent city, shimmering with glass structures and statuary that glinted in the reflected light of a thousand canals. The city was, in fact, composed of hundreds of small islands, separated by canals ranging in width from several feet to several hundred. The sun illuminated all the buildings not only from above, but indirectly as well, its rays bouncing off the water. Venice had long been known as the City of Light.

The prisoners were taken off the great raft and marched to the Ducal Palace. Hundreds of citizens paused in their activities to gawk at the little procession—Josh and his fellows, bound in rope, surrounded by guards, led by the frightening dwarf with the goatlike face. The inhabitants of the place seemed not much different from the creatures of any city, though they tended to be perhaps a bit more humanoid. Children played with balls, creatures milled and tinkered, old men swept the streets. It seemed a cheerful place to Joshua, particularly after the ordeal behind them.

The streets themselves twisted and wound along the canals and over them; between buildings, under bridges, and spiraling down to the water that lapped at the very skirts of the city. Finally the small entourage came to a great enclosed square, located near the middle of the largest of the many islands. They stopped at the entry gates while a guard unbolted the locks. The doors swung majestically open: and there stood the glimmering palace.

It was a work of love and vision. Occupying virtually half the entire island upon which it rested, it rose hundreds of feet, like a single raw gem thrust out of the ocean. It was built of specially fired, impervious, rose-colored glass bricks. Some were lucent, some opaque. Real jewels studded the façade—diamonds, pearls, garnets—and the dome was gold-leafed lapis lazuli, with a huge crystal trident atop it, pointing to the sky. Its sheer radiance made it difficult to see. Josh shaded his eyes, staring in awe.

The captives were ushered into the main anteroom and made to stand, shivering from their wet journey, at the center of the chilly quartz floor. They were left without guide or guard, but there was quite obviously no place for them to go. No one spoke. Lack of food, sleep, and warmth over the past days had robbed them of vigor. Now they waited, suspicious and tired.

After some time a page brought them soup in a large pot, from which they all drank. Sunlight flowed through the glass walls, warming the room with morning glow. Clatter and noise resounded through the building from within and without. Beauty lay down to nap. Jasmine assumed the lotus posture and went into a trance. Josh stared above them, through the glass ceiling, to the shadows of people moving in the rooms overhead. A waterclock at the end of the room poured the minutes away. Noon approached.

With a small flurry, a small courtier emerged from the far door, stood at attention, and made a loud announcement: "What it is! What it is! All rejoice to the face of the Doge!" Whereupon he bowed and exited.

Immediately thereafter, another figure came through the door and advanced toward the prisoners. He was a wide man, wearing a red and gold gown, a jeweled pointed hat, and a harried expression.

"I am the Doge of Venice," he said. "You've come at a most inopportune time. Today is a celebration day, I'm afraid—the Marriage of Venice to the Sea. I'm performing the ceremony, of course, so I won't be able to spend much time converting you." He stopped short, looked stern, then added: "Are you heathens or pagans?"

Jasmine, who was now standing behind Sum-Thin, muttered under her breath into the other's ear: "Lord spare me from pompous monks."

The Doge looked up sharply. "Your remark is in

poor taste—but it is not possible to mock me: I'm a believer. But no matter. Your conversion will be short and ecstatic or short and painful. In any event, you will all convert. Come with me." He turned on his heels and walked to the far door; and after a moment's hesitation, the others followed.

They followed him up flight after flight of winding quartz staircase. At the top they passed finally through a crystal door, into a room without ceiling, with floor of clearest glass. Placed carefully around the room were instruments of torture.

"This is the Conversion Room," said the Doge without malice. "Open above and below, for the Sun and Neptune himself to assist with the conversion."

Jasmine was about to grab the Doge—take him hostage on the spot and effect an escape—when suddenly several armed guards entered, each one holding a weapon on the prisoners. The captain of guards strode forward and whispered into the Doge's ear.

"Oh, I see," said the Doge. His look became more stern. "In Ma'gas' you attacked one of our priests and I am told she died a few minutes ago." Before anyone could answer the charge, he went on. "Here all men are sailors. She is dead, now—our disciple, the Priest of Hoods. She is with the water now."

Joshua's eyes darted around the room, seeking escape. Beauty pawed the floor. Jasmine wondered if she could possibly throttle this meddlesome priest just to rid the world of him before she was tortured to death. Sum-Thin hoped she would be given the opportunity to give some mild resistance and then convert with fervor. Isis scratched a flea out of her ear.

The Doge hung his head a silent moment. "You must not further delay the ceremony, however. You will spend the night in the tombs close to the water. You shall drown at dawn, to join your ancestors in the sea. The Priest of Hoods will convert you on the other side." Saying which, he turned and whisked out of the room.

Immediately, the guards collared the captives and took them back outside, then down several more flights of winding stone steps, beneath the castle, within the substance of the island. They were waded, ankle-deep, through a series of murky grottoes, coming finally to a large damp cave. A two-foot hole in the high ceiling let in light from the outside. Here the prisoners were left, cuffed, and chained to steel rings in the cave wall; here they sat, contemplating the events which had led them to this abrupt and unsatisfactory conclusion.

"I can't believe she was hanging on that rope in the water all that time, with your blade still in her chest. It's unbelievable," Josh shook his head.

"The water nourishes these people," Jasmine answered. "She did better being dragged by our boat than she would've on the shore."

Sum-Thin agreed. "They are possessed, these waterpeople. The cry we heard on the water the second night—it was the hooded one signaling her legions. That's how they knew to find us."

"This is leisure talk," snapped Beauty. "You would all do better to chatter us out of this foul cave." He pulled at his chain. It held fast to the rock. He feared the BASS, and held little hope for their chances of escape.

"He's right," agreed Joshua. "We've got to get out of here. . . ."

"What? You've no interest in joining your ancestors beneath the sea?" jibed Jasmine. "In being converted by the late, wet Priest of Hoods?"

"It is better, perhaps, than conversion in the glass room with Neptune watching," Sum-Thin commented.

They spent the next ten minutes pulling at their chains, testing the fastenings, smashing the clasps against the floor—all to no avail. Beauty reared and battered the links repeatedly, but only succeeded in cracking his hoof. Disconsolately they sat, trying to ponder a way out. Their frustration was made ever worse by the fact that their weapons lay only fifty feet away—well out of reach, but well within eye-shot; for the BASS believed in burying their enemies as heroes, fully armed and ready to battle the demons of the sea.

After long and grim consideration, Josh found a piece of chalkstone on the floor and began writing on the cave wall: his name, his story, his date of birth, his date of— Sum-Thin stayed his hand. He stared into her eyes. "I'm sorry," he said. "This wasn't your fight. And now we've made it your end."

She only smiled. "One thing have I learned in these many years. Everything that happens in one's life is a part of one's life. When I learned this, my life became a tiara and every day a jewel."

Josh put down his chalk and everyone went back to quiet puttering. Sum-Thin studied the veins in the rocks. Jasmine tried lubricating her hand with algae, to slip it out of the iron cuff. Beauty pulled at the chain in the rock face, pulled steadily, did not cease. Josh chipped away at the wall fastening with a piece of hard stone he'd found, without much effect. Isis took it upon herself to get what food she could find for everyone—this amounted to a small pile of snails, barnacles, and crayfish who'd unhappily wandered into the area.

An hour later they were no further along in their efforts; but something even more disturbing was becoming distinctly clear: the water in the cave was several inches higher.

Josh noticed it first. Coldly he recalled Rose's prophecy, from months before: he would drown and live again. Live again with his ancestors in the sea? he wondered now. "We're going to drown at high tide," he predicted.

"Most probably," Sum-Thin answered, her fingers playing lightly over the rock veins.

Sullenly, Josh thrust his hands in his pockets. Something there. He withdrew his right hand curiously and examined the unexpected contents: Dragon's teeth. Eight of them sat in his palm; flat, triangular, sparkly, flinty gray. "Hey, look at this," he said. "Can we use these?"

They all looked. "Where on earth did those come from?" Sum-Thin demanded.

"We killed a Dragon," Jasmine whispered excitedly. "Months ago. Sum-Thin, your Hemolube is one of the more volatile mixtures, isn't it? You were in the QZ/700 series?"

"Yes, it was a standard aeromatic hydrocarbon base with—"

"Never mind that. Joshua, give me one of the Scribe-tubes."

Josh pulled one of his two Scribe-tubes out of his boot and handed it to the Neuroman. She unscrewed the cap, took out the rolled-up sheets of black paper, wrapped the Dragon's teeth in all the papers save one, set the bundle on a moist, flat rock, and laid another moist, flat rock on top of it. "As gently as you can, Beauty," she said, "crush them into powder."

Firmly but gingerly, Beauty began repeatedly tapping on the top rock with his forefoot. Every few taps they could hear a tooth crack or crunch. While he was doing that, Jasmine had Sum-Thin tilt her head back as far as it would go. When it was parallel with the ground, Jasmine opened Sum-Thin's head-valve, and allowed a slow trickle of Hemolube to flow into the Scribe-tube. When the tube was a little over half full, Jasmine resealed Sum-Thin's head valve, then re-capped the Scribe-tube.

"This is done," Beauty urged. There was an air of excitement in the cave.

Jasmine lifted off the top rock, to reveal a pile of shredded paper, blackish powder, and irregular chips of all sizes. Carefully she scraped the mixture all onto the last clean sheet of paper, which she'd kept separate. "This is all wet, now. It's useless to us as it is, we'll have to dry it as fast as possible." Gently but constantly, she began to blow on the little pile of crushed Dragon's teeth; the others quickly followed suit. The water in the cave was now up to their knees. Isis sat on the highest rock permitted by the chain around her neck, and watched with wild eyes the sea only inches below her.

Jasmine spoke between breaths. "I'm not certain what all is in these. Magnesium, for sure. Some iron, some calcium. Coated with flintstone. Dragons chew the stuff like candy. Anyway, here's my plan. We'll make the bomb and blow one of us free."

"The guards at the cave mouth will hear . . ."

"I'm counting on it," Jasmine continued. "One of us will lie face down in the water, as if injured. When the guards come in to examine the situation, whoever's free will have to overpower them and get the key." She tried to sound much more cocky than she actually felt, to give them hope. In fact, she wasn't even certain the bomb would work and if it did, whether it was strong enough to blow the chain out of the wall.

"What if the guards have left?"

"Then one of us has until high tide to save the others."

They kept blowing. Gradually the black powder looked more and more light gray, as the moisture slowly evaporated. After an hour it had stopped changing color. The waterline was marking the hairs on Isis' neck, as she strained against her iron collar. Her eyes were desperate; trapped.

Delicately, Jasmine folded a V in the middle of the paper, and poured the ground-up teeth into the Scribe-tube. The Hemolube overflowed the lip of the tube, dripped down the side. Jasmine recapped it, punctured the thin top with a sliver of jutting rock, and stuck a long strip of paper into the dripping hole. The paper was soon saturated with gritty Hemolube.

She held the cocktail high. "Who'll it be?"

Sum-Thin bowed low. "You, my dear, and only you."

The others concurred immediately. Jasmine wedged the device into the link that was hammered into the rock, then ran the paper wick along the chain. "Everybody down," she whispered. When they were all submerged as well as possible, she began striking the iron chain with the last bit of Dragon tooth, directly over the wick. Each time she struck, sparks jumped from the flinty tooth. On the fifth knock, the wick flamed. The fire jumped instantly down and engulfed the tindered casing. Jasmine just had time to plunge under the water as the inside of the tube ignited and the bomb went off.

The explosion wasn't particularly big, but the acoustics of the cave made it echo for many seconds.

Jasmine hurriedly stood up and, with almost over-whelming relief, saw she was free. In a matter of sec-onds she loosely hooked the last link of the chain back in place, so it appeared as if she were still shackled.

None of her fellows moved. They'd forgotten to ap-point anyone to be the apparent victim; and so rather than ruin the plan, they'd all independently decided to float face down in the rising tide. Only Isis remained afoot, her head up, chin barely above water level.

Almost immediately, Jasmine heard the guards sloshing up the half-flooded grotto to investigate the noise. She decided to play along with her pals, and lay spread-eagled on a boulder, her eyes slits, her cuffed right arm tense.

There were two of them. They clearly didn't know what to make of the scene, but were suspicious enough to stop short of the dead-floating bodies.

"A clap of thunder, and now they be dead," said one. "We'd best take the bodies back out for proper inspection. . . ."

"Best do nothing of the kind," rasped the other. "It were Poseidon's own yell we heard, callin' this scum down to their eternal judgment, and I ain't about to—"

Josh, finally out of air, chose this moment to stick his head up.

"Hey, look there!" yelled the first guard, and waded over to the Scribe. As he bent down to grab Joshua's hair, Jasmine jumped up, took two long, clumsy steps, and whipped her chain around the neck of the other guard. At the same moment, Josh pulled the first guard down into the water and beat his head against the stone, knocking him senseless. Jasmine snapped her chain with a powerful jerk: the second guard hit the wall and lay still.

Quickly, Jasmine searched both bodies until she found the key to the shackles. She went directly to free Isis, whose nose alone could be seen above the water. The poor Cat crawled forlornly to the highest place she could find, where she sat shivering and retch-ing.

Jasmine rapidly unlatched all the padlocks, liberating the hunters. They collected their assortment of knives, bows, and sabers, and waded swiftly up the cave tunnel to the mouth of the catacomb. Here they paused a moment: to breathe the fresh sea air, the smell of freedom and hope; to weigh the fraternity of the moment, before anything else had time to go awry. Then, once again, the hunt was on.

Cautiously, the little band made its way out into the sunlight. The ocean spread away to the west, vast and thoughtful. To the east, broken steps led back up the main island.

"I know these islands some," Jasmine intoned. "This used to be part of the mainland before the Great Quake and the Ice Change. L.A., Malibu, Santa Monica, Venice. It's all veined with canals and deltas now, and rebuilt, of course, but the basic layout of the city is unchanged, I think. If we can just get oriented, I might be able to get us to—"

"Wait a minute," said Josh, squinting back in time. "I know this place too—if it's the same place as old maps I used to read in the Scribrary back home . . . Yes, look, it is, I know that street!" He ran, crouching, up the turning stone steps, from the outlet of the tombs where the others stood, to the edge of a crumbling brick street that angled down and off into the city. At the point where the street disintegrated entirely—falling away onto the rubble and steps that led back to the catacombs—stood a sign. A street sign. Joshua read the black marks on the thin white-painted metal: SUNSET BOULEVARD.

Jasmine ran up the steps to join him. "South of here," she whispered, "should be a large pier. We're likely to find whatever size ship we need, to pirate."

Josh nodded. "Or we could parallel this street directly east. There must be docks on the other side of the island, as well, facing homeward."

It was a deserted area, and Jasmine motioned the others to join them. Soon they were all gathered at the end of the street. After a brief discussion, they decided to head south, toward what Jasmine called the "Santa Monica Pier": they'd have to sail around the islands to get finally back home, but it avoided having to sneak through the busy afternoon city. So off they went.

Their plan went sour almost immediately. Over the next rise, not two hundred yards distant, a collection of fishermen sat congesting the beach, blocking access as they repaired their nets. Josh and the others were forced to turn east—into the island.

The city streets were labyrinthine here—turning, twisting, narrow—so that try as they might, the escapees could not turn back toward the western pier. Instead they kept heading deeper into the city.

The religiosity of the city was evident at every step. Trident patterns were glazed into most doorways. Icons of the great sea bass—the holy fish—adorned every windowsill and filled the tiny altars that stood on every street corner. The God of Venice was everywhere, here; in every thing; and it gave the escaping hunters the eerie sense that they were being watched by the very stones of the city.

Citizens were starting to notice them now, too. Centaurs were uncommon sights on these islands. News of these villains who'd murdered the Priest of Hoods was everywhere, as well—so at every cross street people stopped to stare at this ragged, motley bunch.

Then the ruckus behind them started. Apparently one of the unconscious guards had awakened, and called the alarm. Creatures began following the renegades. They stopped trying to look nonchalant and began to run. Citizens gave chase, joined by soldiers, dogs, children, birds. Down alleys, around buildings, through squares and over bridges. Josh and friends ran faster; the town closed in.

They came to the end of a street that emptied into a large square thick with celebrants. There were no side streets, and they couldn't turn around—their pursuers were too close. So into the piazza they strode.

A great cheer went up. The square faced on the Grand Canal, and the Doge was just floating by in the royal gondola, preparing to throw the city's ring into the sea.

Josh and the others stepped quickly into the pressing crowd, to lose themselves in the crush. It was a reasonable thing to do, and would have succeeded, but for Beauty's great height. He was clearly visible over the heads of all the other onlookers. When the vigilante band finally burst into the square, they moved immediately in on Beauty, and began shouting: "There he is! The Centaur who murdered the Priest of Hoods! Stop him!"

People all around began to look at Beauty. The jubilant holiday hilarity turned to angry grumblings, pointed fingers, hushed glares. Someone threw a stone; it hit Beauty in the shoulder. "Let him breathe water," someone shouted. "Kiss waterbottom," yelled another.

Instantly, the helpless Centaur was being borne on a wave of frenzied hands and fists over the sea of people, toward the deep Grand Canal. As he was carried along, metal chains and jewelry of all kinds were thrown around his neck, over his body; to weigh him down, tangle him up. Josh and Jasmine tried frantically to get to the Horse-man, to help him somehow; but like sticks in the ocean, they were soon separated from Beauty and from each other, by the swells and crosscurrents in which they were trying to float. Isis had all she could handle just not getting crushed under the tide of feet; and Sum-Thin steadfastly watched, alert, ready.

Beauty was scared. He writhed and bucked, but the mob heaved him powerfully, inexorably to the water's edge. Hating fingers dug into his flesh; spit and curses stung his face. His struggles were futile. As he was brought finally to the rim of the canal, a somber thought, like a shadow, passed his mind. "I am an object of vengeance."

Over the edge they threw him, and into the profound gray waters, where, jewelry-heavy, he sank like a statue.

A great cheer went up. Almost immediately, the sky darkened, as if the sun were eclipsed, or the air a blanket of smoke. The crowd gasped as a single organism and silently looked to Heaven.

What they saw was the most strange and terrifying scene anyone had ever witnessed. Across the sky, blotting out the day like a cataract, flew silent legions of Vampires wing to wing. Hundreds of them soared in tight formation, a diaphanous black apparition about to settle over the city; night's dark victory.

In the hush that ensued on the banks of the Grand Canal, the first distant rumbling of a thousand flapping leather wings began to stir the air. Someone screamed; and the next moment was total chaos.

People in the square started running, in all directions at once. Children were trampled, carts overturned. Some of the soldiers fired arrows skyward, but the Vampire battalions were much too high, and the arrows fell back into the crowd. Some of the citizens brandished tridents at the advancing creatures; some hurled curses. Nothing helped.

A heart-stopping scream—almost a siren—rang down from the head of the Vampire fleet. Then the foremost Vampires began a wide slow spiral dive toward the city. All the succeeding ranks followed, until the entire formation was flying headlong into the islands, looking like nothing so much as a black, swirling cape.

In the square, frenzy was at a peak. Isis, Josh, Jasmine, and Sum-Thin climbed statues, hid behind stairs and flattened against walls to avoid being crushed in the melee. As soon as enough people were gone from the square—either fled to their homes, or dead in the street—Josh leapt from beneath the bridge he'd crouched under, and ran to the edge of the canal into which Beauty had been thrown. Jasmine joined him in a second.

The first wave of Vampires began swooping down out of the last leg of their descent, wrenching terrified Humans off the ground, gnashing their necks, then dropping them once more to the earth. Soldiers and sailors were emerging in force now, as well, killing some of the Vampires with arrow and spear, grappling hand to hand with others. The streets were sticky with blood.

Josh and Jasmine dove into the canal simultaneously. Joshua swam straight down, and in the clear water quickly saw his beloved Beauty, snagged and still at the bottom. The Centaur had managed to pull off all but one of the heavy chains around his neck, but that one had caught in a tangle of seaweed near the canal floor; and there he lay.

Josh reached his motionless friend in an instant and tore the golden harness free. Jasmine was soon beside them, lending assistance. A minute later, the Human and the Neuroman were pulling the cold Centaur up on the bank. His color was blue, his eyes waxy. Lifeless. Jasmine began mouth-to-mouth resuscitation.

All around them the fighting continued. Sum-Thin ran up, crouching, to Beauty's side, and started cardiac massage over the great Horse-chest. Josh did the same to the man-chest. A Vampire fell screaming from the sky, spinning out of control like a broken kite, into the water fifteen feet away. Black smoke could be seen rising on the other side of the city. Bedlam was everywhere.

Suddenly Beauty coughed, vomited, moved; breathed. The others sat back in grave relief—none yet allowed the luxury of joy to intrude: the air was still heavy with death and insanity.

Before anyone could utter a sound, there was a great rushing of wind, and into their midst—from nowhere, it seemed—dropped a dark winged figure, terrible and grand and ready to strike. Jasmine, Josh, and Sum-Thin crouched in a line before the prostrate Centaur, facing their towering attacker with the desperate strength that comes near the end of a long struggle.

No one moved. Slowly, Jasmine stood, her legs weak, her mouth open. "Lon?" she whispered.

The great Vampire smiled. "None other, Yasmeen."

Jasmine shook her head in confusion. "But . . ."

He held up his hand. "No time for questions now, please. We must hurry. Is this all of you?"

Isis skittered across the square, ran between Lon's legs, and jumped up on Joshua's shoulder.

Josh took a quick look around the ragtag bunch and smiled. "This is all of us," he nodded.

Lon turned his head up and opened his mouth to yell. They heard no sound, but in a few moments, three more Vampires flew down and stood there with wings unfurled.

"Three more friends," Lon spoke softly. "Lev, Ula, and Aba. They've come to help me take you away. Come." He held out his hands.

Jasmine walked over to him, and he wrapped his powerful right arm tenderly around her waist. Then he took two long steps to Joshua's side, gripping the Human in a similar fashion. Then he spread his wings and flew.

Josh held his breath, in pure wonder as the earth receded below him. He held Isis tightly, just as Lon was holding *him,* and watched the figures on the ground shrink to the size of rodents and insects. Two of Lon's Vampire friends picked up Beauty in a hammock-contraption and began flying in Lon's trail; the last Vampire followed, carrying Sum-Thin.

The wind raced across Joshua's face as Lon's slowly beating wings lifted them higher, finally leveling off somewhere over the sea. The Venetian Islands were far gone, no more than stones in the glittering ocean. Josh was mesmerized: such depths to such heights, in such a short time. His mind reeled.

They headed south and east. A big hawk paced them for a time, then veered off for more interesting companionship. Occasionally, they went through clouds—cold, wet, white-bright. Sometimes they'd catch an updraft, at which Lon would simply spread his wings straight, and sail. Josh felt giddy.

Some time later—Josh could not say how long—they saw land. Lon set his course on a gradual descent, and in a few minutes they touched down on a high cliff overlooking a black-sand beach. The others landed within minutes, carrying Beauty and Sum-Thin.

The Vampires spoke to each other briefly—silent mouth movements, with an occasionally audible *beep* —and flew off in the direction of the setting sun. Lon remained behind with Josh and friends. Beauty was awake now, if a bit unsteady on his feet. The others stood facing Lon.

"That was quite a rescue, Lone Ranger," said Jasmine. "How'd you do it?"

"This gentle creature showed me where to look," said Lon, pointing to a small cluster of elms behind them. From out of the trees flew Humbelly, the long-lost Flutterby. When she saw Joshua in the clearing, she fluttered madly all around his head, humming like current down a wire. Josh gasped happily. Isis assumed a reserved, if suspicious, crouch. Humbelly lighted, grinning, on Joshua's shoulder.

Lon continued. "Our search for you is a long story. But first, before we trade adventures—look north."

They did. Some miles distant, on somewhat lower cliffs over the coast, stood a massive black castle, surrounded by what looked like walls and a city.

"Behold, the City With No Name."

Gleaming red in the sunset, a river could be seen as well, flowing past the castle and emptying into the ocean.

"The castle on the Sticks River," Lon went on. "There resides the New Animal, and there will your people be."

With clarity, Joshua stared at the gothic structure. It was the end of his quest. Dicey was being held there, and Rose, and Ollie. Like a lens, the castle focused all the events of the recent past—the struggles, escapes, bonds, losses, lessons, and hopes—into a crystal point; almost a physical manifestation.

Without warning, and quite without meaning to, Joshua began to cry.

CHAPTER 14

The City With No Name

THEY sat around a small campfire in the clear black night, obscured from view of the distant castle by a tiering of brushy knolls. To the east and south stretched the uncharted expanse of the Ansa Blanca —the great empty desert that no animal had ever crossed. To the north was the waiting fortress, and to the west, the ageless ocean. But here and now was a pause: friends telling stories, sharing secrets with the campfire.

"The Flutterby came for me some week or two after you'd left," Lon began. "It was very upset. It carried in its feet the locket I gave you," he said to Josh, and handed the young man the pendant that looked like a golden blood-drop.

Joshua checked his belt and ascertained that the locket was, indeed, missing. "When could I have lost it?" he pondered, taking the memento once more from the vampire, affixing it again to his belt. It felt somehow like an action in a recurring dream.

"So I wondered myself," continued Lon. "So I followed the little Flutter, who was in a frantic state and clearly quite keen for me to come along.

"It brought back memories, I tell you, seeing the Terrarium again—it almost felt as if I hadn't ever been away. In any case, I followed the beastie down, and we soon picked up your trail—though the jungle had erased most of it. We came eventually to a small stream that poured over a waterfall, and here the Flutterby nearly flew itself senseless. I examined the area closely. Only hints of sign remained, but they all seemed to point into the falls. I told Humbelly to remain right there until I returned—and I went under the waterfall.

"I followed the stream through a series of dark caves to an opening—where I encountered the strangest jungle city I'd ever seen."

"We were there . . ." began Josh excitedly. "It was . . ."

"I know you were there, I saw you," Lon went on. "Later that afternoon. At first, though, I saw nothing but the marvels of the city! Beautiful Muses beckoned me, sang to me. I avoided them at first, to search for you—but their music was insistent; and finally, irresistible. I drank from their necks; they drank from my excesses. We passed half a day thus, when suddenly they transmogrified into Dragon-snakes and entwined me nearly to death. Only narrowly did I escape.

"With jolting clarity I remembered my mission here, and set off once again in search of you. Many strange and unsettling things did I encounter. Old dreams and fears come to life, mythic creatures, temptations and torments of every variety. And then you, Jasmine, I saw you. In a garden, speaking to a feathered serpent."

"It *was* me," Jasmine declared. "The serpent was speaking to me of Time."

"So he was," nodded Lon. "I called out but you did not hear me. I walked toward you, but could not reach you—first a ravine separated us, then I could not fly. I tried to cross on a plank, but fell in. I crawled out with great difficulty, but now I could not calculate how best to reach you. I approached from this way, but as fast as I walked, I got no closer. I tried coming around from the other side, but lost direction. Finally, I stumbled into the garden—almost by accident, trying to avoid a falling tree—and you were gone.

"I searched for one more hour, during which time I glimpsed each of you. A moment, here; in the distance, there.

"Night was coming, though, and I wanted to let the Flutterby know not to worry—that it might be a while before I found you, but that you were here, and all was well. I went into the caves again, along the stream

and out through the waterfall. When I re-emerged into the evening jungle, two things were apparent, one
unsettling, the other blood-chilling.

"First, Humbelly was gone. This surprised me, since
I'd told her to wait. As I looked around I became
further aware that the jungle looked different somehow from the way it had looked a few hours earlier:
a wild cluster of orchids beside the river where there
had been none; a new bend in the course of the
stream; a hill of giant Ants. I brought my hand up to
scratch my chin, and I got my second start: I had a
beard!

"And no ordinary beard. Now I must tell you, I
once let my beard grow, uninterrupted, for fifty years,
and its growth was unhurried but steady. Four centi-
meters a year, like a clock. Well, when I looked down
at the growth I had beside that jungle river, I can tell
you, for just a moment my heart stopped. That beard
was two feet long: over ten years! I looked for other
explanations, but there simply were none. Ten years.
It was preposterous, but inescapable.

"There was nothing to do but go back in."

The others listened with rapt attention. Jasmine
rhythmically stroked Beauty's flank, as he lay, still
weak, beside the dying fire. Josh quietly honed his
blade on a flat rock. Isis lay motionless as a Sphinx.
Sum-Thin's eyes were lightly closed. But each, in the
night wind, listened.

"So back I went," Lon continued. "And wandered
for a year."

"A year!" Josh exclaimed.

Lon lowered his eyes in assent. "I saw many things
in that time. The changing of seasons, the drama of
many lives. I explored the limits of the city, delved
into its recesses. In the still waters of its many pools,
my soul was mirrored. I saw you, at times, too; but
could never reach you. You, Joshua, trying to read
ashes in a library. You, Jasmine, making love to
Beauty." They all lowered their eyelids. "I met a two-
faced Neuroman called Janus, who told me the entire
city was in a maelstrom whirling at the speed of light,
that it contained All-time and No-time, that I would

never leave, that I would never die. I met devils, and angels. I rode photons, and battled monsters. I asphyxiated. I met myself.

"And all at once, after a year of this—it felt like a thousand—I saw you again—all three of you—running toward the caves, Josh in the lead. I gave chase. You weren't far ahead, I could see you burst through the waterfall only thirty yards or so ahead of me. Yet when I jumped through, you were gone, nowhere to be seen. I searched the area quickly, and found your track, though—it was at most one or two days old. And when I felt my face, my beard was only half an inch long: three or four months from when the Flutterby brought me here. Suddenly, Humbelly *did* fly up—and led me into the jungle again, right in the direction your prints led.

"I tell you, I didn't know what happened then, and I don't pretend to now. But that's how I found your trail."

"Hypnosis," Sum-Thin conjectured through closed eyes.

"Perhaps," Lon acquiesced. Josh was wide-eyed. Jasmine squinted. "Howsoever," said Lon, hands to the fire, "I followed you down to Ma'gas'. Unfortunately, I arrived the day after the fire. I snooped around. I contacted some old friends I hadn't seen in many years. Many years. It was popularly believed that you'd escaped the blaze—no Neuroman parts could be found in the ashes, and no Human bones. And I had no reason to doubt it—you'd come through worse than fire.

"And I knew where you were headed, to the city on the Sticks. So I began flying back and forth, between here and there, over the sea for two days. And that's how I found you. Tied to the mainsail of a BASS raft headed for Venice. I knew you wouldn't last long there, but I couldn't imagine single-handedly charging into that enclave of cultists to save you. So I arrived at an ingenious plan."

"You engaged a thousand Vampires to attack the island?" Jasmine asked incredulously.

"I flew home at top speed, got the three friends you met, and brought back a film from my library."

"A film?"

"A sunlight-activated holographic movie—from my museum collection. A fabulous movie, depicting a Vampire invasion and battle. A classic, probably a hundred and fifty years old. Aba and his brother, Lev, hovered with the projection equipment between the sun and the island—hand-turned the reels—and it looked to everyone below as if Vampires were swarming down in droves, as if people were fighting and dying. It caused pandemonium, of course—the Venetians were running around everywhere, shooting at illusions. Meanwhile, I scoured the town for you. And brought you here." He laughed, a hearty bellow. "When they find no one is dead in the morning, they'll swear it was a collective vision, a message from God."

"A hologram," Jasmine marveled.

"What's a hologram?" Josh was supremely confused.

And so the hours passed, with attempted explanations of three-dimensional holography, attempted explanations of the Lost City through which they'd passed ("Maybe all Time is locked in there. Maybe we're still in there." "Maybe it was just what the old priest said . . ."); reminiscences of times past, speculations on times future, until at last they all drifted off to sleep, nestled into each other's warmth under the vague shadow of the morrow.

In the morrow it was decided that Jasmine and Lon would go spend the day scouting the sinister city, while the others remained behind. Beauty was still too weak for much adventure, and Humans (according to rumor) were not allowed past the main gates. Sum-Thin stayed with Josh to help tend Beauty. Isis and Humbelly just stayed close to Josh.

Josh took out his quill, intending to set the record for the first time in many days. He stared first, at the falcon feather, for a long time. Torn, water-spoiled, and filthy, it was a sorry-looking pen indeed. Yet still it let the words flow. Joshua wrote with it: *Dicey. Ollie. Rose.* The quill had weathered much, as had they all. Josh wondered if the falcon Rose had set free so long ago was still flying. He wrote Rose's name again. He appealed to the word that he might return her wing feather to her and set her free. "The Word is great, the Word is One . . ." he solemnly intoned.

Sum-Thin left briefly and returned with a breakfast of scavenged nuts and crow's eggs; but by the time she was back, Lon had already taken Jasmine under his wing to fly the several miles north to the gates of the City With No Name.

It was a walled city. The outer walls were stone, one hundred feet high. There was but one entrance, across a moat formed by two large tributaries of the Sticks River. Guarding the entrance was a pack of Cerberi—vicious creatures with the bodies of Humans, each with three Dogs' heads, trained to sniff out and attack any animal that wasn't a Neuroman or Vampire. Lon and Jasmine got past this first station without problem.

Once inside the Outer City, these restrictions were obvious: Vampires and Neuromans were the only creatures to be seen, with few exceptions. The exceptions were Human, and fit into two categories. There were Humans leashed at the neck, led usually in groups of two or three by their Vampire Pashas. And there were Humans in carts—usually five to ten per tumbril—being pulled by Neuromans in official uniform toward a large gate that led into the Inner City. And in the center of the Inner City, looming dark and blind as a *pavor nocturnis,* stood the castle.

At first Lon and Jasmine simply walked up and down streets, monitoring the feel of the place, noting exits, hideaways, bars. A minor branch of the river flowed under the eastern face of the outer wall and cut through the city neatly, dividing it roughly in twain. A series of bridges crossed over the tributary, connecting the northern half of the enclave to the southern. Jasmine and Lon memorized the location of every bridge. For a while, they loitered near the main entrance to the Inner City, watching movements in and out, looking for hand signs, listening for passwords. There was a fifteen-foot brick wall precluding a view into the city, but it appeared that only Neuromans—and their Human prisoners—ever entered or exited. Vampires stayed entirely outside this inner wall. Lon was tempted to fly up and look in, but no one else was airborne, so he decided there was probably a rule against it.

They decided to part company here. Lon would remain in the Outer City, to snoop around for Bal, and whatever else he could find. Jasmine would enter the Inner City, gather information, penetrate the castle itself, if possible. They would meet outside the front gate at dusk.

They looked fondly once into each other and hugged.

"Almost like old times," whispered Jasmine.

"I could almost wish we were running contraband again."

"We may yet," she smiled. "In Humans."

"Until then."

They parted.

"Eurydice, come here."

Dicey stood and walked over to the pillow Bal was reclining on. "Yes, my Blood," she replied.

"Do my nails," he commanded.

"What color, my Blood?" she queried.

"The apricot, I think." He didn't look up from the book he was reading.

She bowed. "Yes, Redness." She glided over to the vanity to get the apricot nail polish, and as she did so, the tiny bells on her golden ankle bracelets tinkled playfully.

Bal admired her discreetly over the top of his book —the pale, lithe body; the classic beauty of sunken eyes, pallid lips, flushed cheeks; the elegant jewelry adorning her neck, wrists, and ankles. A thousand sheer silk threads were sewn into her skin all around the base of the neck, from which point of attachment they hung loosely, flowing to the floor. Bal was pleased.

She came back, sat at his feet; carefully began to

paint the nails on each of his eight toes. "What are you reading?" she asked him.

"*The New World*. It's the Queen's manifesto."

"May I read it when you're finished?"

"It's not a book for you, Eurydice. It would only upset you."

She brought the heel of his foot up firmly between her legs as she continued to paint the nails.

He rang a small glass bell on the table beside him. A young boy—naked save for the beautifully mounted jewels sewn into his skin, adorning his chest and face—entered quickly, carrying a rose liqueur on a silver platter. Bal took the drink from the tray. "Thank you, Ollie, you may go. Oh, wait, bring one for your sister, too." Ollie bowed, ran out, and returned immediately with a goblet for Dicey.

"Thank you, Ollie," she said. His only answer was a glassy stare. He left again.

Dicey sipped the brew, closed her eyes, pressed Bal's heel in harder between her whispering thighs. "Take me," she breathed.

Bal kept reading. "I drained you almost dry yesterday," he monotoned. "You need at least another week to renew your hemoglobin, you know that by now. I'll have Angie tonight, or Michael."

She rubbed his thigh, imploringly. "I love it best, though, when—when I—when you almost take me to —when it's almost too much—after I swoon, when I'm out and you're still drinking, when I'm right at the edge, looking down into the eternal blackness, and your lips are the only thing holding me at the brink— I love it then, please, Bal—" she moved her hand higher up his thigh—"Take me to the edge."

He relented. "It won't take much tonight, my little nymphet, a cupful, perhaps . . ." He pulled her into his lap and put two fingers on her carotid pulse. "Why, your heart is already racing at a hundred twenty . . ."

"Only my excitement, Blood-sire . . ."

"I shan't take much tonight, missy. When your pulse reaches a hundred fifty, I stop, no matter—"

"I beg you . . ." She put her hand down between her legs to grip his hardness as he laughed lasciviously, buried his fangs into her neck at the angle of the jaw, and drank her insensate.

Jasmine tried to look interested in a street vendor's wares—a Neuroman, selling transistorized parts, probably pirated from dead Neuromans—while keeping her eye on the gate to the Inner City. Most of the comings and goings were Neuromans in official dress; even those out of uniform showed a badge to the Cerberus guarding the portal, though—and Jasmine had no badge. She wondered how to get through. Bluff? Over the wall? The solution came unexpectedly.

From the top of the inner wall, fifteen feet up, came a great crackling and hissing. All eyes looked up. There on the battlements lay a twitching Human, mortally tangled in a wide grid of fine electrified wires that Jasmine could now see formed a crosshatching over the entire city, running from the outer wall to the inner wall to the castle spires. The Human, trying to escape over the wall, was instantly electrocuted.

This was most important information for Jasmine. First, it demonstrated the existence of the screen covering the city—fine wires crisscrossing at two-foot intervals, effectively preventing all ingress and egress except through the one main gate. It was no wonder she hadn't seen any of the Vampires flying; she thanked their good sense for keeping Lon from winging up to look over the wall. Second, there was electricity—a massive power source, probably driven by the river.

The dead Human continued sparking, his clothes now aflame. It caused a commotion on both sides of the wall, and all the creatures in the area—including the guards at the gate—flocked to the scene to try to pull the carcass down. Jasmine took the diversion for what it was, and used the opportunity to slip past the gate, into the Inner City, unnoticed.

The Inner City was smaller in size than the Outer, but no less crowded. The populace here consisted almost entirely of Neuromans, some in uniform. No Vampires were to be seen at all. Occasional Humans, on leashes or in cages, were apparent; and a number of Clones—usually in packs of three or four—ran briskly here and there, along a myriad of streets, all of which seemed to lead to the castle.

Jasmine wandered, ears alert, her peripheral vision never removed from the fortress. She stayed generally astern of groups of chattering Neuromans or Clones, and in this way learned several essential facts relating to the castle and the functioning of the city. The castle was the home of the Queen and her council. This Jasmine understood to mean the New Animal and the genetic engineers who'd created it. Also in the castle were the Neuroman technicians and organizers responsible for the general operation of the city— hence, the official uniforms. The laboratories were housed in the castle as well: secret rooms in the keep, where Human experimentation went on. Finally—and most important—it became evident to Jasmine that only official Neuromans on official business were allowed into the castle proper. If she was going to get in, she would need papers.

This wasn't quite as difficult as it might have been, for one simple reason: Neuromans came in models. Jasmine's model number, for example, was AR/83075. Walking along the street were dozens of Neuromans from the same line who bore at least a family resemblance to her; numbers from the same year with whom she shared arguably sibling features; and randomly, a Neuroman who could have—and probably did—come from the same mold. It was one of these that Jasmine chose to follow closely.

As luck would have it, her doppelganger turned into a small tavern, called The Oligodendroglial Cell— a pun, Jasmine noted, that could be appreciated only by a Neuroman. She entered, sat at the bar, and ordered a sugared rum. Her uniformed look-alike took a table near the window, and was immediately joined by a later-model male with a loud voice and a glad hand. Jasmine stared into her glass as she listened to their conversation.

"Elektra, where have you been?" demanded the male Neuroman. "You were supposed to come over last night, you know."

"I'm sorry, Balis," Jasmine's double replied, "I've been working so much lately. I spent all night at the lab. Good news for the Queen, too."

"Really? What?" asked Balis with some interest.

"Can't say yet. Nothing earth-shattering. It'll depend on what Zubin's results show."

"Well, let's celebrate anyway. Tonight, at my place."

"Can't tonight, gotta go stand by with Zubin's group."

"But that means hours of waiting with nothing to—"

"I know, I just gotta be there, that's all, in case anything—"

"Wait, wait, I've got an idea. You on your way home now?"

"Just to get some papers, then I got to get right back . . ."

"Okay, okay. Listen. Drago is up in Ma'gas' for the week, picking up a shipment of bauxite. So his lab is completely empty. Meet me there for an hour at 2200—if you can break away," he added sarcastically.

"Okay, maybe. Where's Drago's lab?"

"B-347, just two doors down from Zubin's. It's perfect, if anything happens at Zubin's while you're gone, you can be back over there in thirty seconds."

"Well," Elektra said coyly, "it might take me a *little* longer to get back there."

Balis leered with foreknowledge. He leaned over, licked her behind the ear, and stood to go. "See you tonight," he said in a suggestive growl, emphasizing the spaces between the words.

She surreptitiously squeezed her own nipple and winked at him. He left. She looked vaguely annoyed, finished her drink quickly and ordered another. She read over some papers she pulled out of her briefcase, making occasional notes. She ordered and drank a third drink. She left the bar. Jasmine got up and discreetly followed her.

Elektra walked down one block, turned left, up another side street. Jasmine stayed twenty paces behind. At the next turning, Elektra went over a small walkway and entered what appeared to be a housing complex facing directly on the street. Jasmine retarded her pace, waited a minute, then knocked on the door Elektra had gone through.

There were footsteps, and Elektra opened the door. "Yes?" she said. She was still in uniform, but her tunic was unbuttoned now.

"Is this Elektra's residence?" Jasmine asked in a ponderous tone.

"Yes, I'm Elektra, what is it?"

"I have a message from Zubin," said Jasmine.

Elektra's eyes opened a bit. "Yes, go on," she coached.

Jasmine feigned uncertainty. "You have some . . . identification, perhaps?"

Elektra was impatient. "Just tell me the message, of course I'm Elektra, who else would—"

"I'm sorry, I just have to see—"

"Okay, okay, I'll get my card, wait a minute . . ." She turned in exasperation and walked back into the small room behind her. Jasmine entered, shut the door, and followed.

"Here," Elektra fumed, pulling an I.D. card out of the briefcase on the low table in the center of the room.

Jasmine took the card, examined it, studied Elektra's face. "It says here your nose is from the 1200 series, but you—"

"Here, let me see that!" Elektra stormed over and took the card out of Jasmine's hand with uncontrolled scorn.

Standing beside the Neuroman scientist, Jasmine reached up—quickly, cannily—and broke open the hidden valve at the back of Elektra's head.

Elektra wheeled, alarms going off in her body instantly as the vital Hemolube began pouring out. "What did you *do?!*" she gulped, fearful, disbelieving. She put her hand to the back of her head, then brought it before her eyes: it was covered with the viscous fluid. She looked starkly at Jasmine. "Wait a minute, you're not in uniform," she breathed. "And you're from my series, aren't you? You . . ." But she didn't get to finish.

Jasmine was on her in a second, tumbling her to the floor, pinning her to the carpet, holding a pillow over her oozing head to muffle the cries. Being virtually identical models, their strengths were the same, but Jasmine, with surprise on her side, had gotten leverage. So she had simply to hold her position while Elektra struggled and strained uselessly, her resources ebbing, as her life's blood flowed into the rug. It took fifteen minutes for her to die.

Jasmine didn't move for twenty, just to make certain. When she was sure Elektra was lifeless, she rose and examined the apartment.

One room. Bed, table, two chairs, two lamps. Sink, bookshelves, cabinets. A telephone. She went through all the cabinets: cans of Hemolube, polysaccharide foodstuffs, household tools, soaps, a box of petri dishes, a sexual device, some spare light bulbs, two bottles of perfume, a broken slide rule, and an empty picture frame. Next, the books: almost all antique genetic texts, including an atlas of Human mapping.

There was a small electric oven in the corner, containing incubating cultures; and at the other end of the room, what appeared to be a rather large refuse bin. Jasmine lifted the lid to look inside, but to her surprise, it was bottomless. Or not quite. She shined down a flashlight she'd found in a drawer, and saw that the bin was actually the top of a tube that went straight down, perhaps fifty feet. There was a glint of reflection from the bottom, and Jasmine thought she could make out the sound of running water. Her luck was running, too: she looked for, and found, a thin ladder of rungs going down the inside of the tube, apparently all the way to the bottom. She stuck the flashlight in her belt, climbed into the bin, and slowly lowered herself down on the rungs.

It was farther down than it looked. Estimating by the distance between rungs and counting a rung for every step, it was probably closer to one hundred feet before she dipped her left foot into the rushing water. She pulled back and turned on the light.

What it was, was a tunnel, maybe fifteen feet wide, cut out of the rock, with about two feet of water flowing briskly along its bottom, carrying all manner of debris: soggy papers, dead animals, Vampire feces, machine parts, broken bottles, organic matter. It wasn't the best smell, ever, either.

So it was what Jasmine had hoped: the sewage system. Probably tributaries—artificial or otherwise—of the river; probably emptying out into the sea. She climbed back up to Elektra's apartment in a hurry.

She took off all her clothes and threw them down the bin. Next, she stripped Elektra, putting those clothes on the bed. She found a reel of copper wiring in a drawer, unwound about thirty feet, cut it off, and wrapped the corpse up with the last ten feet, twisting the end into a good strong knot. Finally, she hoisted the body up on her shoulder and climbed back down the tube into the sewer with it. When she reached the bottom, she dumped the cadaver into the moving water, where it bounced slowly in the current along the stony ground. The other end of the copper wire Jasmine tied around the bottom rung, so it kept the lifeless body on a twenty-foot tether down the dark bend of the sewer. That done, she climbed, once again, up into the apartment, rinsed herself off in the sink, and put on Elektra's clothes.

She went through the papers in the briefcase, but most of it was technically above her. She put the I.D. card in her pocket. She meditated for five minutes. She knew that if she simply acted as if she belonged wherever she went, she was unlikely to be challenged too strenuously. She was encouraged by how smoothly everything had gone thus far. She breathed deeply. She got up, walked out the door, turned right: up, toward the castle.

She crossed over the bridge nearest the castle, spanning the river just before it plunged below ground, seemingly to run under the building itself. When she got to the western gate leading into the main body of the fortress, she flashed her I.D. card disinterestedly at the guard; and he let her pass.

There was a knock on the door. Renfield opened it with a decorum suitable to his place of seniority among the servants. On the doorstep stood a noble Vampire.

"Your pleasure, Sire?" said Renfield.

"Your master is Sire Bal?" asked Lon of the servant.

"Yes, Sire," Renfield replied.

"Is he at home?" Lon went on.

"He is." The servant was polite, but protective.

"Announce me, then. I am Sire Lon," he said, and entered the foyer.

Renfield left the room to make the announcement, and a few moments later Bal appeared.

"Lon-Sire," said Bal.

"It's been a long time," nodded Lon. They bared necks to each other.

"Come join me in my study," Bal intoned, "and tell me how it is I am so honored."

They walked through a bedroom into a book-lined den. Servants and concubines lounged everywhere, but cleared out of the room at a sign from Bal as he entered. Only Dicey remained, unconscious, pale as a white rose petal. Bal and Lon sat facing, the frail quiet body on the floor behind them.

"We parted in bad blood," Bal began. "It is something I have always regretted."

"There is an ebb and flow to these things," Lon mused philosophically. "You seem to have prospered."

"I abide," Bal conceded. "I am well cared for. By my Queen."

"Ah, the New Animal. Yes? It is word of this new creature that brings me here. I am curious. Possibly interested."

Bal eyed his old companion with the barest hint of suspicion. When last they'd parted, some sixty years earlier, it was without malice; but without much fondness. "You are sincere?" Bal inquired.

"Quite," said Lon "My harem has been thinned to nothing by disease, and I understand this New Animal may be able to help. I come to you first because I . . . trust your judgment."

Lon knew his mark well. The incidental flattery tipped the scales.

"The 'New Animal,' as you call her, is Queen here," Bal began. "But much more"

"What does she look like?" Lon wondered.

"I wouldn't know. Few have ever seen her, except for a small circle of ANGELS—Associate Neuroman Genetic Engineers, Lords, Sages. It is said she's rather horrible to gaze upon, though, almost deathlike in some way. And yet her voice is sweet, like a young girl's. She is an aficionado of the musical classics, as well, I understand—another interest you share with her, if I recall your tastes correctly."

Lon bowed his head graciously. Bal went on in a more serious tone. "It's not what she looks like, though, of what her dispositions are—it's what she says and does that keeps me here. She's creating a new world order."

"Oh?" suggested Lon.

"Yes. Humans are the mortar. She is beginning by eliminating the Human race except in its capacity to supply specially bred animals for experimentation—and of course to breed for Sire-harems and stables."

"Of course."

"Your own misfortune is immediately soluble here. Just join our ranks and the Queen will stock your home with as many Humans as you need—more, if you merit."

"This begins to sound enticing. Tell me, though. What's the nature of this new world of which your Queen speaks?"

"It is all spelled out in her statement here—" he held up the book lying open on the table—"*The New World*. Please, take my copy and read it."

"Thank you, Bal-Sire, I will." He took the tract, thumbed through it. Dicey stirred on the floor. Lon looked at her. "You won't have that one much longer," he said to Bal. "She has the waxen glow."

Bal smiled fondly at the still body on the floor. "You may be right, Lon-Sire. She loves too much the tooth. One day she will goad me too far. After all . . ." he held out supplicant hands, "I'm only Vampire."

Jasmine walked briskly down the narrow stone corridor. Window slits looked out one wall onto the courtyard below; the other wall was marked periodically by doors. She noted the numbers until she found—in the basement, after a fifteen-minute search through the most deserted halls she could find—the one she sought: B-347. Drago's empty lab.

She tried the handle. Locked. She extracted a piece of twisted copper wire from her pocket—designed specifically for the occasion—and quickly picked the lock on the door. Catlike, she let herself in.

It was a small lab. Beakers, burners, flasks, and tubes sat patiently on the slate tables, awaiting Drago's return from Ma'gas'. It suited Jasmine's needs perfectly, being an empty, isolated base inside the enemy camp, in which she could pause and plot; from which she could venture forth; to which she could repair.

She began by searching the place. Fortune continued to walk with her here, and several potentially useful items were yielded in the process. First, a simple schematic map of the castle grounds turned up in a bottom drawer, labeling the main animal labs, the power plants, various administrative offices, conference rooms, cafeterias, central supply, even the Throne Room. On a desk beside the telephone was—not surprisingly—a thin phone book, listing the phone and room number of everyone in the castle. And from an instrument drawer near the sink, Jasmine helped herself to some scalpels, syringes, and other implements that she put in her pockets. Finally, she ascertained that the waste bin was, as before, a direct conduit down to the sewer system.

When she'd done all this, she sat down and studied the map for a half-hour. When she was confident she had it memorized, she put it in her tunic along with the phone book, and set out.

She walked back down the corridor by which she'd entered, found a stairway, and ascended one floor to the main level. Here she found herself jostled along one of the main thoroughfares of the castle. She moved with the flow until she saw some room numbers and signs that oriented her. Once she had her bearings she moved quickly, up one more flight and down two corridors—to the Human quarters.

Thus far, no one had challenged her: she looked, in dress and demeanor, like she belonged. Furthermore, no one had ever tried to infiltrate or otherwise sabotage the castle, she imagined; so she had aiding her her opponent's hubris and lethargy. And so armed, she brazenly entered.

It appeared to be a prison. Barred cell after cell lined the walls, floor to high ceiling. Four Humans filled each cell. Some sat vacantly in corners, some stared through the bars in despair. They all looked near starvation. Beside the entrance two Neuromans sat playing cards. Three microcephalic Clones walked here and there, sweeping the floor, carrying food trays to the cages, emptying garbage into the large waste bin by the door.

Jasmine strode up to the front desk where the Neuromans sat. "Hello, maybe you can help me," she said.

"I bet I can," the first one leered slowly.

Jasmine decided to play to the oaf's come-on. "I bet you can," she replied, leaving much to the imagination. The Neuroman guards exchanged a look. Jasmine continued: "Listen, I'm new here, and I just started working for Drago, who's in Ma'gas' now, but he told me that when he got back he wanted the names of five or six Humans from up in the Monterey area. Something about testing their livers for acetylase because of certain soil conditions up there. So how do I go about finding Humans from Monterey?" She smiled hopefully at the Neuroman with the leer.

"Shouldn't be too hard," he winked. "Follow me." He stood and walked into an adjacent room, with Jasmine close behind him.

The room was filled with large file drawers along three walls, and a huge card catalog against the fourth.

The Neuroman opened a long card drawer and began sifting through it rapidly. "Monterey, Monterey, Monterey . . . here we are. Monterey. All the Humans from Monterey, followed by age, date of arrival and disposition. Have a look."

She had a look. It amounted to eighty-five names during the past four months. Dicey and Ollie were not to be found. There were two Roses. One was sixty-two years old. The other had the right statistics, but the word DECON was stamped on the card in red.

"What's DECON mean?" Jasmine asked.

"Final decontamination. That's the last step before Nirvana. Only the Humans chosen for the Queen's Experiment get shunted that way. This one here, let's see . . ." he peered at Rose's index card, "she got sent up days ago, so she won't do you any good. Of course, no one really knows how long decontamination lasts. . . ." Slyly, he put his hand on her bottom.

She slammed the card drawer closed, turned to face him. "You've been very helpful," she said sweetly, "but there are just too many names here. I'll have to ask Drago when he gets back. . . ."

The guard fondled her without subtlety. She let herself be kissed. Then, as if reluctantly, she pushed him away. "Meet me tonight at 2200 hours. In Drago's lab." She ran out the door, a smirk briefly lighting her face as she thought of the mismatched rendezvous at 2200 hours.

She recalled the location of the Decontamination Lab from the map: third floor, center. Up she went, but at the door to the third floor corridors a sign was posted, stating NO ADMITTANCE WITHOUT AUTHORIZATION. She tried the door anyway. It was locked. People were constantly going up and down the stairwell, so neither could she stoop to pick the lock. She walked back downstairs.

She wandered around for an hour, looking for nothing in particular, learning nothing of use; until she came upon a small door in the west wing labeled DEPARTMENT OF SANITATION. She paused, thought a moment, and entered.

It was a small office, with what seemed to be another small office adjoining it, an open door between them. An officious clerk looked up immediately from behind his desk. "May I help you?" he offered without interest.

She caught his tone and returned it neatly. "I'd like

to speak with your supervisor," she replied. She was imperious.

It clearly took him off guard. "I—that is, he is out to lunch at the moment. On a job—that is, won't be back until tomorrow. Perhaps I can . . ."

She shook her head. "I need to see the blueprints for the sewer system. For the whole city. There has been an accident in Drago's lab." She allowed a note of fear to shade her voice.

"An accident?" His ears pricked up.

"A spill," Jasmine admitted. "Down the waste tube. Nothing . . . serious. But we need to know what structures are distal to the flow from Drago's lab. Quickly."

The clerk stood up. "But shouldn't we notify—"

"We don't want any panic, do you understand? If we can be rapid and discreet . . ."

He hesitated. Then: "Yes, yes, of course, I can show you the plans, they're right here . . ." he said in some confusion, walking into the next room. Jasmine followed him. He pulled several pages of rolled-up documents from an open safe and spread them out on the table.

She scanned the prints briefly over his shoulder. It was even better than she'd hoped.

"Now," the clerk went on, "your room number, work number, and city number . . ."

He was looking down at the desk. In one long, intricate second, Jasmine broke open the valve at the back of his head, pulled a big syringe out of her pocket, and rapidly pushed fifty cc's of air into the dripping hole. He instantly slumped forward. He was dead.

She picked him up and threw him down the waste bin. There were several seconds of silence, followed by a distant splash. Next, she rolled up the blueprints and stuffed them into her tunic. She closed the safe, wrote a note claiming illness and left it on the chief's desk. That's when the chief walked in.

He knew immediately something was wrong. "Who are you? Where's Trout?"

Jasmine was cool. "He took ill, sir. He just asked me to—"

"Here, what are you doing in my office? What've you got there?"

"Just a note from Trout, sir . . ."

"Let me see that. The Devil. This isn't Trout's writing." He picked up the phone. "Give me Security . . ."

Jasmine tore the cord from the wall and jumped him. They rolled on the floor, neither able to get an advantage, knocking over bric-a-brac as they struggled. She pulled up on his head from behind, but he broke the grip easily, since two of the fingers on that hand were still inoperative from her duel wound in Ma'gas'. Suddenly, somehow, he rolled over and got behind her, pinning her to the floor. He had the leverage: she couldn't break free. With a wave of chill terror, she felt the Neuroman bureaucrat bring his mouth to the back of her head; felt his teeth crack open her valve; felt the warm, thick fluid run down the back of her neck.

She twisted and jerked and managed to wriggle one arm free, but he held tight. Minute by minute, her strength flowed out of the open spigot in her scalp. Reflexively, her nuclear heart pumped faster.

The supervisor began to yell for assistance. "Guard! Somebody!"

The image of his open mouth beside her suggested an idea. With her free arm, she reached into her tunic and withdrew one of the long-handled scalpels she'd found in Drago's lab.

There was one significantly vulnerable part of a Neuroman's anatomy: the soft palate. Its plastic malleability, so essential to ingestion and phonation, was necessarily less impervious to trauma than the rest of the Neuroman polymer covering. Furthermore, it was separated from the point at which the brain joined the spinal cord by a thin centimeter.

The next time the supervisor opened his mouth wide to yell, Jasmine plunged her blade back through his posterior pharynx as far as she could, severing his spine.

He fell back with a gurgle, the handle of the knife sticking straight out of his still open mouth. His eyes were wide, his nostrils flared. He lay on his back, unable to move anything below the neck.

Jasmine got up slowly, examined herself for damage. Nothing serious, except for a profound weakness. She locked the front door. She rolled the quadriplegic Neuroman onto his side, opened the valve at the back of his head, applied her syringe to it, and withdrew fifty cc's of his Hemolube. Then she uncoupled the syringe, fitted it onto her own valve, and injected the oily liquid into herself. She repeated the process until she felt strong and full, then recapped her valve and put the syringe away.

"Sorry, Chief," she said to the pale, oozing Neuroman on the floor, pulling the scalpel from his mouth and putting it back in her pocket. She carried his motionless body to the waste bin, and avoiding his staring eyes, threw it down the tube. *Splash.*

She righted the furniture, the signs of the struggle; cleaned herself up. Finally, she hoisted herself into the waste bin, closed the lid over her head, and began climbing down the rungs of the shaft.

Two hundred feet later, she reached bottom. The water was only about a foot deep, but the flow here was very fast, making it hard to stand without holding onto a wall. Slowly, Jasmine walked in the direction of the flow.

It was dark, but not entirely lightless. Approximately every fifty yards, a weak electric bulb hung from the ceiling to illuminate a few yards of tunnel in all directions. Jasmine waded to the nearest light and stopped to take her bearings.

It was like a maze. Tunnels crossed in and out from every direction, some straight, others curved; some running with water, others dry as stone; some fed by vertical shafts; some fifteen feet wide; some barely big enough to crawl through; some shadowy as bad dreams. Some black as death.

Near the light bulb she stood under, a shaft angled up. Beside its bottom rung, a number was etched in the rock: P-116. She checked her map briefly, but under these conditions at least, was unable to find any corresponding designations. She refolded the prints and started to walk in the direction of the flow.

There were dozens of forks, side channels, offshoots, bends; and the flow of the rapid water followed them all. In general, Jasmine followed what she sensed to be the larger divisions, the deeper water. She stumbled once, and fell—over the dead body of one of the Neuromans she'd killed. Its time-frozen face bobbed above and below the surface, peering at her through the rushing water, its dense shadows thick with life's other side. Jasmine returned the stare, momentarily arrested. She looked up beside the rung the body was snagged on: P-116. After an hour of walking, she'd only come full circle.

She refused to let herself panic. Once again, she walked with the flow.

She made different choices this time; in any case, she thought she did. A left turn where, before, a right. An ascending fork instead of a descending.

She came, after what time she could not say, to a rising turn in the maze that left the water to flow down an alternate path. She went up this dry stone walk a short distance, until it dead-ended at a vertical tube. The cul-de-sac glowed in the orange rays of a carbon filament bulb. And painted on the rock, just beside the entry to the shaft, were the words HEART STREET. Jasmine rolled down her pant legs, which she'd had up to keep dry, and began climbing the rung-ladder.

She reached the top in fifty steps, gingerly pushed up the lid, and looked around. It was a deserted street corner. She jumped out.

It seemed to be late afternoon. The container she'd just left was a public trash bin, located at the corner of HEART STREET and 7TH AVENUE. A Vampire turned the corner, leading several Humans on a leash, walked past Jasmine, and went into a nearby house. Two Neuromans came out of a bar across the street, laughing.

Jasmine laughed, too.

She walked down Heart Street to First Avenue, which was much more crowded with Neuromans and Vampires; then up First away from the castle until she reached the outer wall. She left the city by the main gate. A mile down the road, in the afternoon shade of a grandfather elm, she found Lon waiting for her. He was reading a book.

"Quite the Vampire of leisure," she observed.

"I trust your talent for espionage bore fruitful results this afternoon?" he smiled at her, closing the copy of *The New World*.

"It was just like the good old days," she beamed. Then, diminishing her smile somewhat: "We've got a long night ahead of us."

He handed her the book, put his arm around her shoulder, and started walking toward the distant grove where their friends were waiting. "Indeed, we have," he agreed. "Indeed we have."

CHAPTER 15

In Which The Hunt For The Lost Children Concludes

". . . AND last but not least," Jasmine concluded, "there's a two-foot-square electrified wire grid blanketing the entire city, making it impervious to attack or escape." The others listened in rapt silence as she finished recounting all her impressions of the fortress town. The moon was on the rise. "Frankly, I think the only thing to be said for our position is that they feel so safe in there—so haughty—their security inside is a bit lax. They think they're invulnerable."

"They may be right," Sum-Thin shrugged.

"Merely challenging," smiled Lon. "In my reconnaissance flight over the area I found the mouth of the sewage drain you discovered. It is large, and empties directly out of the cliff face, perhaps fifty meters below the promontory on which the castle stands, perhaps two hundred meters above the sea, into which it pours. I believe it is an admirable portal through which to infiltrate this camp."

Jasmine grinned. "You sound hungry," she said in undertone.

"Starved," he admitted. He looked at his hands: "I'm starting to atrophy. . . ."

"But the blood-lust surges back fast . . ." Sum-Thin interjected.

Lon looked at her sternly. "I am here to help my dear friend Yasmeen, who is here repaying a debt. I am enjoying my little adventure. And what keeps you here, philosopher?"

Josh clenched his fist with impatience. "We're here for one reason, to find our people. If any here be at odds with that—"

"Tell them, Joshua," rasped Beauty. He was yet quite weak, and had developed a cough, but refused to falter with the journey's end so near. There were still too many hunters to suit him.

"Please, please," Jasmine calmed them all, "let's not fall out now, we've almost won. . . ."

Sum-Thin raised her hand. "I am here that I am here," she spoke to Lon. "I meant no offense by remarking your obvious glee in this pursuit. Indeed, I envy you for it. Jasmine is a friend of mine, as well, and I am honored to accompany her. I am, in addition, curious as to the nature of this New Animal about whom the whole world is whispering, and I think an animal's true nature is revealed best when it is threatened—another reason for joining in this enterprise. Ultimately, I am content to follow this adventure wherever it may lead me, since it seems to be the direction my life has taken." She smiled obscurely.

A moment passed in silence before they all burst out laughing. "I never had such a comrade-in-arms," coughed Beauty.

Lon relaxed again. "Truth be told," he conceded, "I've developed a passing interest in this New Animal myself. I like her not." He held out the book Bal had given him. "She is the Queen of this city, and she would be Queen of the world. This is her manifesto."

Josh took the text, looked at the cover. *"The New World,"* he read.

"And new it would be, if she had her way," Lon continued. "No more Humans, except in harem. Vampires, the high priests of a new religion—of which she is the high priestess. Aside from that, no natural animals of any kind. All engineered to her specifications, by her ANGELS, to repopulate the earth. Engineered without disease, without degeneration, without—"

"I care little for this Queen," said Beauty quietly. "Neither do I care *about* her. Let us save our people, and later discuss the future of the Universe."

There was a quiet pause. The moon hid behind a cloud, the stars blinked. There was a hot wind off the Ansa Blanca. Humbelly sat sleeping on the grass; Isis sat without movement in Joshua's lap, staring thought-fully at the Flutterby.

"Here are the plans," said Jasmine, unrolling the blueprints on the ground. Everyone gathered closely around to look. Three large pages, spread edge to edge in the dirt, illustrated the whole layout of inter-connecting tunnels, like an underground delta of the Sticks River, draining the waste of the city. And every point in the city at which a conduit shaft joined the surface to the tunnels was marked on the blueprint by a number—every waste bin, from the castle to the outer wall, showed up as a number on a diagram.

The fourth page was a list of these numbers; and next to each number was a city address, or a castle room number.

"Combining this diagram with the map of the cas-tle here," Jasmine went on, "I've been able to come to some conclusions." The others followed her intently. "Number 212 . . . here—" she circled the number on the tunnel blueprint with a piece of charcoal—"should be right at the shaft leading up to the Final Decontamination Lab, whatever that may be. That's where Rose is." She looked at Beauty, then went on deliberately: "If she's anywhere." She paused to let this obvious truth reiterate itself yet again. "By the way, if you look here, it appears to be directly next to the Throne Room and Queen's Chamber, numbers 213–18."

"And Bal's house," Lon nodded, "which was 18 Street of Wings, should be right . . . here." He circled numbers 47–91 on the diagram. "I couldn't find out if Dicey was there or not, Joshua. But he *did* have a young boy called Ollie."

Joshua's teeth clenched.

Beauty sat up. "Joshua, you feel well? Here, be careful."

The others looked from Josh to Beauty, concern and question in their eyes.

Josh looked down. "I had another spell while you were gone," he admitted. "The most powerful one yet. It gripped me for two hours . . . while this damned son of a mule held me down." He smiled weakly and touched Beauty's hand.

"Perhaps," suggested Sum-Thin, "you should not go on this mission. Perhaps that is the meaning of these spells."

Josh looked up. "No. That is not the meaning of these spells."

No one replied.

Jasmine pulled scalpels, syringes, and needles out of her pockets, passed them around; demonstrated on herself how to position a syringe in order to inject air into a Neuroman head-valve. She produced two flashlights; one she kept, one she gave to Sum-Thin. "Now," she said, "I have a plan.

"Lon will fly three of us into the tunnel exit in the cliff. Two of us—Sum-Thin and I—will make our way through to the power station . . . here—" she circled the area on the diagram. "We'll be able to surface there more easily without notice, since we're Neuromans. The city is not so big or complex, so neither will the power center be. We're both familiar with electronics. We'll analyze the situation once we're there, and plan to cut all power to the city—or as much as possible—at 0400." She took a stolen watch from her pocket, set it, and gave it to Lon. "This should cause general confusion and diversion, and if you haven't been able to make your move up to that point, you should be able then, under cover of darkness and alarm, to effect whatever rescue you're going to. Our sabotage should also cut electricity to the grid covering the city, so if for any reason the tunnels are blocked for our escape, Lon can fly us over the wall. If that *should* be the case, we'll rendezvous in room B-347 in the castle. Failing that, we fall back at the main gate to the Outer City."

They all listened attentively. Lon noted the time on the quietly ticking watch: 1900 hours. Jasmine continued. "Meanwhile, Lon and Josh will be on the rescue end of things. They will surface at Bal's, at the Decon Lab, and wherever else they may have to, to locate the lost family. They will escape back down the tunnels, if possible. Beauty . . ." she hesitated, "you must remain on the outside. . . ."

"Absolutely not!" he whispered harshly, then broke into a paroxysm of coughing.

Jasmine waited until he'd quieted down again before continuing. "I understand your feelings completely, but it's the only logical way to go. You're too weak to be of use in a fight the way you are. Your cough would give us away. You couldn't climb up the shafts into the city in any case." She spoke compassionately, to soften the blow. "Besides, we need someone on the outside to prepare our retreat. When they finally discover what's happened, they'll surely try to follow us. What you must do tonight is ready our hideaway. I want you to go—"

"What I will do tonight is storm the front gate, if I must, to deliver my people," he whispered fiercely.

"To be killed instantly, and give us all away," Sum-Thin understated. Then, more acerbically: "I didn't realize you were so keen on being a dead martyr. How Human."

Josh stood up, enraged. "How *dare* you . . ."

"Please," Jasmine tried interceding. "We have to remain . . ."

"I was merely making a point," Sum-Thin commented calmly.

"Maybe if you spent more time on feeling and less on points . . ." Josh muttered.

"All of you. Cease!" Lon boomed. Quiet fell, like a sulking child. "We are all of us tense anticipating tonight's campaign," he went on, "but let us not release the tension on each other. We must remain cohesive and single-minded, else we are lost. Now, I have a role for Beauty—it may or may not prove to be crucial. Will you listen?"

The others sat silently, feeling chastised but calmer from the small release of pent-up energy. Lon continued. "Good. Now the river breaks into several tributaries just to the east of the castle. One has been dammed, to feed into the power generator. Two more branch at the castle, and surround it to form a natural moat before pouring over the cliff's edge in waterfalls into the sea. A third seems to run directly under the castle—this is the one that undoubtedly forms the subterranean tunnels, emptying in its own waterfall out the cliff face beneath the castle's western wall. It is this last tributary that Beauty must enter.

"If we look at the map here . . ." he went on, drawing their attention to the blueprint of the sewage system, "we can see that the shaft to the Decontamination Room is quite near the point where the tunnels begin, at the entrance of the river beneath the city's eastern wall. Beauty—as I see it—will enter the river east of the city, float downstream along this tributary, dive briefly underwater—under the outer wall —float as invisibly as possible down the river as it turns through the city, then once the inner river enters the castle sewage system proceed past what appears here to be two short turnings in the tunnels, to the shaft below the Decontamination Room. There he must wait. There we will all meet—with Rose, if we can find her. If it happens that, for unpredictable reasons we cannot exit the cliff face as planned, it may be that our only escape will be upriver out the tunnel source, back out the way Beauty will have come."

They considered this plan. Jasmine spoke first. "Why don't we all enter this way, with Beauty? It does seem considerably more direct."

"Mainly because Beauty is the strongest swimmer amongst us—even in his weakened condition, I think. He is the natural choice for this approach. As for me," Lon raised his hands apologetically, "I fear and detest water. I cannot swim, nor can I hold my breath. You've already outlined my only feasible approach. As for the rest, I think we are less likely to be noticed entering from the west. One of us can surely float through the city's river without being noticed in the dark—but all of us? I think not."

Beauty nodded slowly. "And if all goes well? If escape back out the cliff with our people is successful?"

"Then your role will have been a superfluous precaution. You will go back upriver—swimming against the current where it runs too deep to walk—and leave the river some point east of the city. I suggest we all rendezvous where the river meets the Rain Forest, in the east."

"It is the hardest thing I have ever said," replied Beauty, "but I hope I am not needed."

They all smiled. On a keener note, Josh added, "There's another reason for your exit to be separate from ours. If all else fails, if we don't return, someone must be left to carry on."

There was a quiet minute during which everyone reflected. "I do foresee some problems," said Lon at last. "If we lose these maps, or if the lights in the tunnel go out, how will we find our way back in all that maze?"

Jasmine pulled four lumps of chalk out of her pocket, giving one each to Lon, Josh, and Sum-Thin. "We have one flashlight per group, if the lights go out. As we go in, every ten paces, we make arrows on the tunnel walls. If we lose our bearings we simply follow the arrows back to the exit in the cliff face. For Beauty, a similar solution occurs to me. Let him string together a hundred yards or so of vine, collected from the forest east of the city. He can tie one end to the eastern wall, and unravel the rest as he goes, into the tunnels. When it's time to leave, he can just follow the vine back out."

Lon nodded in agreement.

"Howww 'bout me?" Isis meowed.

Josh scratched her head affectionately. "I want you to hide in the shadows of the eastern wall, and make certain Beauty's not seen entering. If anyone wanders too close at the wrong moment, it'll be up to you to cause a diversion, to let Beauty slip in unnoticed. It's a very important task, Fur-face, and I'm counting on you."

She purred contentedly.

They all sat, comfortable with the plan, unable to find flaw save for the unknown. There ensued a moment of quiet contemplation.

"And if you cannot find your people?" Sum-Thin put the question to Josh.

"If they're alive, I'll stay until I've saved them. If they're dead . . . I'll go home." He looked at Beauty, spoke more softly: "I've done with Venge-right."

Beauty nodded sadly. "That suits me."

Sum-Thin shook her head. "I think this Queen may not be so agreeable."

Beauty stood. "A fruitless thought," he said, "and the night is aging. I'm off to the river. Fare thee well, good friends."

They all stood. Josh put Isis on Beauty's back, then placed the still-sleeping Humbelly on Isis' back. Isis was not pleased, but did not move.

Jasmine approached Beauty. "I feel I've grown in your company," she said quietly. "Thank you." They both knew they might not see each other again; or if they did, that it might all be changed. They hugged briefly, wanting more, but Beauty had no words for his feelings, and had to turn away in tender confusion.

He found himself facing Joshua. They also knew they might not see each other again; but even that being so, they knew they would abide with each other forever. They hugged long and richly, and their feelings were clear, without shadow.

"Until soon, good friend," Beauty murmured.

"Until soon," said Josh.

Then, without looking back, the graceful Centaur trotted over the hill to the north, the Cat and the Flutterby on his back.

"Go in good blood," whispered Lon.

Sum-Thin closed her eyes. "Joshua, Beauty, Jasmine, Sum-Thin, Humbelly, Isis, Lon. Go now we magnificent seven samurai into the breach," she proclaimed.

Lon gathered his remaining three comrades up in arms, and flew with them out over the sea.

Night flight was a scary, exhilarating experience for Josh. Like a real dream. The few minutes it took to reach their destination was quite enough to prime his adrenaline pump for the night ahead. They approached the cliff from the west, flying low over the water. Perhaps a quarter of the way down the sheer rock face, a black hole gaped, like a huge maw; and out of it water rushed, white in the moonlight, tumbling to the sea below in a great waterfall. Lon flew directly for the mouth of the cliff.

The opening was just a foot wider than his wingspan, so he had to judge his entry with detailed accuracy: even a slight error would have caught his wing tip on the rock, and probably sent them all crashing down to a watery death. Fortunately, he used his batlike sonar, and with a series of continuous high-frequency *beeps,* kept them right on course.

Once inside the main tunnel, he continued flying in the absolute blackness for twenty or thirty yards, the water rushing just beneath them. Josh was terrified, but at the same time, strangely, had a profound sense of safety in the Vampire's arms. At last Lon set down, waist deep in the turbulent stream. It almost knocked him over.

He waded quickly to the side of the tunnel, where the velocity of the flow was considerably less. Bracing himself against the wall, he put the others down. Joshua, a little vertiginous from the flight, immediately lost his footing and fell into the grip of the current. He was churned rapidly toward the falls into the sea. Only by great will was he able to cling to a jutting rock at the last moment, pull himself upright, and wade against the heavy flow back to his friends. They kept their flashlights trained on him—once they'd steadied themselves—helpless, at that point, to do anything but watch him as he made his way slowly back to them.

When he reached them, no one said a word. Jasmine drew a chalk arrow on the wall. Single file, they walked upstream, into blackness.

At the first major bend, progress became considerably easier: a light bulb glowed dimly from the ceiling, allowing them to pause, turn off their flashlights, check the map; the water level contracted precipitously to a manageable one foot, and the current was reduced to a fraction of its outflow strength. They collected themselves, breathed deeply; and exchanged broad, nervous smiles. The assault was begun.

Isis crouched in the shadow of the drawbridge on a
piece of the one-foot perimeter of land that ran all
around the outer wall, between the wall and—ten feet
lower—the flowing river. She'd jumped off Beauty's
back at the first sight of the river. When the Centaur
turned east to collect lengths of vine from the nearby
jungle, the Flutterby nestled in his mane, Isis ran
west. After much thought, she'd decided she didn't
want to miss the fun; nor did she trust Joshua to take
care of himself without the benefit of her watchful
eye.

At the base of the outer wall, she looked up: mor-
tared granite, straight to the sky: she could not see the
top. Near the gate, she heard a rustle—one of the
three-headed Cerberi had picked up her scent.

No point in thinking about the top until she was
there. And only one way to get there. She put her
claws out, jumped to the first obvious foothold and,
head up, began the vertical climb.

It didn't take her long to reach the hundred-foot
top. She looked for the wires Jasmine had spoken of,
to avoid them. They were immediately apparent, one
every two feet, stretching into space toward the castle.
The castle itself looked simultaneously foreboding
and warm. It was dark, gothic, impregnable; yet the
windows were all alight, inviting. The whole city, in
fact, twinkled with the incandescence of street lamps
and porch lights. Isis sat coolly on her haunches, ob-
serving with circumspection.

She dilated her nostrils, twitched her ears, scanned
with her eyes; sensed with her Cat-sense. She sat thus
for an hour. Then, deliberately, felinously, she descended the inner face of the outer wall.

The four figures moved slowly through the shadow
turnings. The water was only a few inches deep here,
barely trickling over the cold stone, so they sloshed as
they walked, each footstep a jumble of echoes.

Periodically they passed a dim light. Here they
would pause, examine the maps to ascertain position
and direction; mark the wall with an arrow; proceed
in silence.

Tunnels branched, stopped, doubled back. All was shadow. Josh felt a continuous strain on his eyes, his nerves, his ears. His ears. Focusing suddenly on his auditory powers, he thought he heard something.

"What's that?" he whispered.

"What's what?" said Sum-Thin.

"Footsteps," whispered Josh, "somewhere behind us."

They stood stone-still.

"I hear nothing," said Sum-Thin.

"No, he was right," whispered Lon. "I heard them too, but now they've stopped."

They all listened: silence, save for the water's low and omnipresent *shhh*.

Delicately, they began to walk again. This time they all heard it—the muffled clump and splash of footfalls in the impenetrably dark recesses behind them. Then, just as suddenly, the sounds faded and disappeared.

"Biped, I think," whispered Jasmine.

Sum-Thin and Jasmine drew their scalpels; Josh held his knife. Lon marked the place in chalk. They resumed walking.

It remained quiet for two more turns; then once again, the footsteps. Then a new sound: a soft, short scratching. The hunters—or were they now hunted—stopped. The sinister footsteps echoed in the distance once more, closer perhaps, then farther again. Then they ceased; then the scratching sound again; then the footsteps again; then silence yet once more.

"Come on, then," said Jasmine, looking all directions at once. She led the way to the next dim light, twenty yards up. They all stood under it to read the map.

It was a crossing of six major tunnels, some inches deep in fast water: and two smaller tunnels, both dry.

Jasmine drew an arrow on the wall pointing back down the way they'd come. "This is where we split up," she said, studying the map closely. Josh kept one eye on the diagram, one on the tunnels. "Sum-Thin and I go this way," Jasmine continued, pointing down to her right, "and you two go up this channel toward Bal's house." She pointed up a smaller, dry cavern.

Joshua's mouth felt parched with exhilaration. Unknown, imminent dangers awaited him. He licked his lips. "Good hunting," he whispered, pressing one of Jasmine's hands in his left, one of Sum-Thin's in his right.

Jasmine felt keyed, alert. She'd played this part so many times in her long life; but always the final moments were like opening night. Still, underneath it all resided a great calm within her. She returned the squeeze of Joshua's hand.

Sum-Thin said: "There is no luck but destiny. However: good luck to us all."

Lon regarded the blueprints one last time. Jasmine checked her flashlight. Suddenly Josh froze: he felt a presence somewhere near. The next moment, Lon, too, became motionless, staring into the darkness. A shadow moved across Jasmine's face. From the opposite tunnel: slowly emerged the Minotaur.

It stood upright—easily eight feet tall—with the body of a man, the head of a bull. A huge man, a fierce bull. It stood unmoving, smiling grimly in the shadows at the four who stood grimly unmoving beneath the light. Slowly, it raised its powerful hand to the wall, where it made a short, soft scratching. When it lowered its hand, the others could see it had drawn a chalk arrow on the wall, pointing up the tunnel it stood near.

Still facing them, still smiling, the beast moved sideways to the next tunnel, where with another scratching sound, it drew another arrow, pointing in a different direction. Then a third arrow, at the mouth of a third tunnel. The same scratching sound they'd heard following them, accompanying them, down how many turns in how many tunnels.

The Minotaur's mouth was open, and he drooled as he watched the dawning comprehension on the faces of his prey. He suddenly let out a brief, insane burst of laughter; then with a speed incomprehensible in a creature so large, he lowered his head, rushed at Sum-Thin, gored her almost in half with his massive horns, and returned to where he'd been standing.

The others stood mesmerized as Sum-Thin crumpled

and fell. Her belly was torn pole to pole, her red oily
fluids spilled on the water. Her eyes remained open,
but she was dead. The fast, shallow water bounced
and scraped her broken body down the tunnel and out
of sight. The Minotaur threw back his head: another
short, mad laugh.

In that instant, Josh threw his knife, Jasmine
knocked out the light, and all three of them separated.
There was a strangled hiss in the blackness, a shuffling
of feet, a growl, a tumble. A flashlight beam shot on,
flashed over a terrifying purple eye, flashed off again.
Josh heard a body thrown against the wall. Two lights

flashed. One beam fell over Lon, his side bloody; one shone upon the Minotaur's terrible face. Squinting, the creature charged the light. The light went out.

Josh rushed toward the source of the extinguished light, where the beast had lunged. He ran into a giant muscled form, the thing's fetid breath hot on his face. He brought his scalpel up into the twisting flesh, as a massive arm circled him, squeezed him, threw him to the ground.

There was a spastic scuffling, which stopped immediately, and suddenly all was silence.

Josh raised his head out of the water. More silence. He shook the water from his ears.

"Lon?" came Jasmine's voice, to Joshua's right.

"Yes," came the choked reply, immediately behind him.

"Is it over?" asked Josh.

Both flashlights came on. Lon played his over Josh, then over Jasmine, who was crouching at the mouth of a small recess. Jasmine shined hers on Lon. "You're hurt!" she gasped.

There was a two-inch wound in his right side, bleeding freely. "It is nothing. Where is the monster?"

They both scanned their lights around until they located the felled beast. He lay sprawled on his side, half in the water, half up a dry tunnel. Joshua's knife stuck angled into his throat; Lon's claws had gouged deep tracks across one eye and through the great black nose; his hand was impaled on Jasmine's scalpel, and Joshua's scalpel was buried in his shoulder. He was very dead.

"Looks like your first knife-throw did the trick, Joshua," Jasmine commented. "He kept fighting just out of sheer meanness."

Lon sat up against the wall. "We were lucky," he said quietly. He was shaken.

The others gathered around him, and they all assessed the damages. Lon's bleeding was slowing—the abdomen had been penetrated by the tip of the Minotaur's horn, but the severity of the wound wasn't immediately apparent. Jasmine was unscathed. Josh had several large bruises, and the skin over his left arm had somehow gotten scraped bare, but nothing major seemed to be wrong.

"Sum-Thin is dead," Jasmine spoke blankly. Her friend of two hundred years.

Lon lingered his light over the monster in the corner, still frightening even in death. "We were lucky," he repeated.

For some minutes, they pondered in silence. Neuroman bodies were unable to cry, but Jasmine wailed on the inside. She felt as if a large piece of her had been wrenched out, leaving her raw, empty, exposed. She tried filling up with determination, or anger; but the hole was large and didn't yet want filling. Sum-Thin was gone.

Josh stopped his shaking. It was close, but they'd won, and now they were one devil closer to Dicey. He breathed deeply. He felt ready for anything.

"Well, let us proceed," Lon finally halted contemplations. "Yasmeen, you go on to the power station alone. Joshua, if you think you can rescue your people from Bal by yourself, go do so. I need to collect my resources. I shall wait here, replenish myself on the monster, attend to my wound, and guard your rear in the event there are more such demons in this labyrinth. If you do not meet with success, come back to me here."

It was a less than satisfactory plan, but alternatives were scarce. Ultimately, they agreed. Josh and Jasmine retrieved their weapons, each took a map and a flashlight, and set off up their respective tunnels; to the power plant, and to Bal's house.

Josh looked back as he made his way up the dry tunnel. The last thing he saw in the diminishing light was Lon's winged shadow-form, its face buried thirstily in the neck of the dead Minotaur.

Isis crouched just inside the inner wall. A soft wind ruffled her fur: she made no other movement. Black on black, she was invisible.

Voices mingled with footsteps in the streets around her. She sniffed the air: no Joshua.

Like a fog she glided silently over the ground, paus-

ing once more in a lightless hollow. Towering in the
near distance was the resounding castle. Obviously,
the castle was the place to be.

She found herself at the castle wall with all the furtive speed of a small dark thought. Nicely done. She
sat up. Fitfully, she remembered she hadn't cleaned
herself lately, and quickly became totally absorbed in
the process of licking the fur of the inner side of her
right hind leg.

Beauty slid silently into the moon-shimmering river.
The current pulled him along effortlessly, as he
steered himself with an occasional stroke down the
central tributary, directly toward the body of the castle. On his back coiled many pounds of sinewy vein.

He registered his fatigue, then ignored it. It was not
helpful to dwell on liabilities. Especially so near the
end.

The critical branching approached, and passed,
veering Beauty to his dark destination. In the near
distance the wall loomed, soon obliterating all else.
Twenty yards; ten. With a muffled *thuk,* Beauty
floated gently into the towering stone. The river flowed
on past him beneath the wall, through an enormous
hole whose upper limit was just below the water line.
Beauty pulled himself along the wall, feeling the
upper lip of the tunnel mouth until it began to curve
downward into the river's depth. He estimated the
width of the subaquatic entrance to be about fifty
feet. Looking north and south, he could barely make
out the banks of the river, flowing ever faster around
the outer walls of the city before it tumbled into the
sea.

He waited until the moon hid behind a fat cloud,
then dove under the wall. He stayed underwater,
swimming with the current, until he could hold his
breath no longer; then let his face break the surface
gently, without a splash. He found himself floating up
a waterway perhaps twenty-five feet wide, the clatter
of activity ringing from both banks: microcephatic
Clones washed clothes, Neuromans sat talking, Vampires walked their Humans. Beauty looked ahead to

see the inner wall quickly approaching. He took a
deep breath and slipped underwater once again.

With a combination of fear and triumph he felt the
cool river carry him swiftly to the end of the hunt.
What the conclusion would be he refused to think
about. Jasmine he refused to think about. All he
thought of was Rose. He hoped she was well. He
hoped he could play a part in her rescue.

Once more he lifted his head—just in time to see
he was fast reaching the point at which this small
inner city tributary dove into the knoll on which the
castle stood, to branch into its subterranean maze of
tunnels. He caught the edge of the portal, stopped
himself from riding the current in, and deftly tied one
end of his coiled vine to a jutting rock. Then, with a
last look around to make sure he'd not been observed, he ducked his head under the stone arch, and
unraveling his length of vine, rode the flow into the
underground tunnels.

With long-practiced stealth, Josh climbed rung after
rung up the shaft to Bal's quarters. He was possessed
by the studied calm of the hunter closing in. Every
sense, every inkling told him this was the moment:
his prey run to ground; the beast so vulnerable in the
imagined safety of its own lair.

Josh reached the topmost rung. Lightly he held the
dagger between his teeth as he barely lifted the lid of
the shaft. What he saw was an empty, candlelit bedroom. In a single motion he raised the lid and jumped
out of the shaft. It took him only a few seconds longer
to lower the lid silently and crouch in tense readiness
beside the tube he'd just left.

All was quiet. He looked around the room. Candles,
mirrors, an enormous four-poster bed. He steadied his
hand around the hilt of his blade and crept to the
doorway.

A dim corridor, perforated at intervals by open
doors. With feline precision Joshua tiptoed along the
paneled wall; stopped; peered into the first room that
led off the hallway. It was a large kitchen, lit by electric bulbs. An older man—Human, by all appearances

—stood at the sink, washing dishes. Josh left him undisturbed and proceeded silently to the next door. Here he found what seemed to be a great dining room: there was a connecting door to the kitchen; a long wooden table surrounded by twenty or thirty chairs; windows floor to ceiling, overlooking the night. At one end of the table three more Humans sat chattering, playing cards. Josh left them to their game and continued his cat-walk down the corridor.

He paused a moment before peering into the next room. Many voices could be heard inside, conversing in a low register. Taut as a spring, he crouched; subtle as half-shadow, he peeked around the lintel into the murmuring chamber. There in the candlelight lounged twenty Humans: men, women, boys, girls, jeweled, perfumed, naked, veiled, sitting, reclining, smoking, laughing, teasing, dancing, sleeping, weeping, pale, thin, and generally purplish about the neck: the harem.

Joshua's hair stood on end. He seethed, but made no sound. Carefully, he studied every face. None were familiar. With increasing tension, he moved on.

He made to inspect the next room down the line, when something caught his ear: at the end of the hall, a soft-lit room; and somewhere inside to the right of the doorway, two voices. Clear, precise voices. One baritone, controlled; the other high, young: a voice Joshua knew. For a moment, he was paralyzed by this knowledge. Fear rode him wildly, alongside uncertainty, excitement, and rage. Finally, gripping his knife more tightly than was good, with every muscle ready, he walked toward the door at the end of the hall, toward the sound of the two voices.

"Bal-Sire," whispered Dicey, "something for your palate?" She parted her lips, tilted her head, exposed her neck.

"Begone," he mumbled. He was absorbed in his book.

"Please, Sire," she stroked his arm, "I'd like to—"

"Begone, I said." He pushed her off. "You have no judgment, you never know when you've had enough.

Besides, I'm reading." He paused, tried to read again, but his concentration was broken. He slammed the book shut with a scowl. "Besides which, your blood is so thin now, it tastes like beet broth."

She walked behind his chair, her breathing fast and shallow. With delicate fingers she rubbed his temples, cupped his cheeks, massaged his neck and shoulders. He drew away at first, then ignored her; then tolerated her; then began to respond. Her lips drew wider, her breath quickened. She guided her palms down his chest, caressed his bulging pectorals, played her fingertips over his nipples, lightly at first, then harder. His head lolled to the side. She brought her head behind his, then beside it, as her hands went farther down, over his belly, to spread his flexing thighs. She kept one hand there, and brought the other up to grasp a bush of hair at the back of the Vampire's head; turned his head forcefully until it faced hers; pushed his wet mouth against her hot, ecchymotic neck. "Bal," she whispered, "take me to the edge."

He bit deeply into the side of her throat. Her eyes shut, her grip tightened around his blood-thick phallus. He lapped and sucked at her flowing wound. He bit again. She purred; swooned.

With uncontained fury, Joshua leapt into the coupled lovers, knocking them to the floor, plunging his knife to the hilt into the Vampire's heart. Bal screeched and twisted, simultaneously throwing Josh and Dicey to opposite sides of the room.

Dicey lay there without moving, bleeding from the neck. Josh and Bal slowly stood, facing each other, twenty feet apart. Both were wide-eyed, panting, tense. The commotion had also aroused all the members of the harem, who now gathered around the doors to stare in confusion and horror at the confrontation.

Josh stood poised, scalpel in hand.

Bal loosely unfurled his wings in the attack position. He looked down to the knife sticking straight in his chest; then up at Josh in disbelieving rage. He pulled out the knife, then dropped it to the floor. Blood spurted, then poured from the slender hole it had left.

Bal hissed, and grinned the ritual grin. Josh

crouched. Bal flew at the invader with all his immense strength, knocked the scalpel away in a stroke, and set his angry fangs deep into Joshua's neck.

Josh had never known such pain. The Vampire's teeth were like electrified spikes, sending waves of agony from their point of entry, across his entire body. It paralyzed him, blinded him. Yet it left his mind perfectly clear as to the nature of the pain. Nerve pain. Death pain. Vampire pain.

They rolled over and over, Bal's teeth locked in Joshua's throat. Josh was dimly aware of people scattering around their struggle, or whimpering, or simply frozen in panic. He put them all from his mind. With every fragment of strength he had left, he brought his knee up into Bal's groin. Reflexively, from the pain, the Vampire's grip loosened.

In the same instant, Josh felt frail Human hands clawing at his back, trying to pull him apart from the bleeding Vampire. He threw the Human off against the wall with little effort, simultaneously pushing Bal's weakening jaw away from him. The Vampire dug four mean talons into Joshua's arm, but Josh no longer registered pain. He found a broken chair leg beside his hand, and hit Bal in the head, and hit him again, and again.

Then suddenly it was all over. Josh sat up. Beside him on the carpet, Bal lay dead. The knife wound in the Vampire's chest wasn't bleeding anymore: there was no blood left in him, it was all on the floor.

Joshua, on the other hand, was bleeding profusely from his neck bite. He applied pressure to the lacerations with a small pillow and crawled across the room to Dicey.

She lay, semiconscious, still bleeding slowly from her own neck wounds. He took her, held her in his arms, encircled her with his trembling arms there on the floor. She remained limp. He pressed his face to her face, his neck to her neck: wound to wound, they bled into each other.

He sat against the wall and laid her down in his lap. Her eyelids fluttered open. She gazed on his face as if it were an unexpected memory from a different life. Then she died.

Josh could not understand the meaning of this moment. After all these months of chase and hardship, to come so far simply to watch his love die in his hands, under the bewildered gaze of an audience of slaves, in the middle of a city of Vampires on the edge of a jungle, on the edge of an ocean, on the edge of a desert—where was the meaning? What the lesson? He took several deep, bottomless breaths, but could not find enough air to fill his hollow chest. His head was a frenzy of random, high-speed thoughts and visions he felt he could not contain: felt his head must burst. Yet he sat. Completely motionless, he stared vacantly into space. He made an attempt, but could not even cry.

He sat trying to compose himself as the terrified onlookers—Bal's harem—continued gawking from the doorways. No one spoke, no one moved. All seemed to be in a state of shock. After some long moments, a little boy pushed his way through and walked tentatively up to Joshua.

Josh looked up. His faced softened "Ollie?" he whispered. The little boy's lip trembled. "Ollie," Josh whispered again, and pulled the boy to him in a hug of desperation that all but crushed the child.

Finally, Josh held him back at arm's length. "Ollie, how are you?" he asked. "Are you all right? You're safe now." Josh was joyous. He had something to focus on. His brother was safe.

Ollie smiled so broadly it was a grimace. He hugged Josh again. He nodded his head rapidly that he was all right. But he didn't speak.

Josh didn't press it. He just kept hugging the boy, stroking the back of his head, saying, "There, there. You're safe now."

At last Josh stood up and looked around at the hushed group. "You're all safe now," he said to them. "I'm taking you all with me. We're getting out of here now."

They all looked to each other, uncertain what to

do. Their master lay dead on the floor. They were free. They all began talking at once.

Some were elated, some terrified, some indignant, many confused. Some had been born in Bal's harem, and didn't know what freedom meant. Some thought it meant they now belonged to this person who'd just killed Bal. A number had loved Bal, and wept over his body. Some had only been captured recently, and they immediately began scouring the house for possible weapons.

Renfield, the old head servant, was one who simply assumed this to be a change of tenure. He efficiently sat Josh down in a chair, washed his wounds off with alcohol and neatly bandaged them. Ollie, still mute, held on to Joshua's belt the entire time.

Finally Josh stood. "Okay, listen everybody," he raised his voice. The cacophony immediately ceased. "Now we're all going to leave this city. Secretly, through the sewers. After we've escaped, you're all free to do whatever you want. You can come with me if you like, or you can go your own way." Renfield whispered for a long time in Joshua's ear. When he was done, Josh nodded and spoke again to the assembled group. "If you feel you must be in someone's harem, we're going now to meet with an exceptionally kind Vampire, named Lon, who is helping us out of here, and who will be happy to take you on, I'm sure." Relief was obvious on many faces. Josh continued. "Now we're going to climb down the ladder inside the trash bin over here, down to the sewers. I'll go first, with Ollie here. You'll follow one at a time. Bring only what you can carry easily. You, with the knives, space yourselves out among the others to see that things are going along okay. Renfield, you bring up the rear. Close the lid over you."

A wave of excitement filled the room, and everyone began talking again, running here and there. Josh forced himself to sling Dicey's body over his shoulder, and with it made his descent back into the tunnels. Ollie was right behind him.

When Josh got to the bottom, he laid his love's lifeless form in the fast water of a crossing tunnel. It floated quickly out of sight. "To the sea," whispered Josh. He then went directly back to the shaft from Bal's house and stayed there until the entire group was reassembled. When he was satisfied they were all safe and sound, he had them all hold hands; and led them, single file, back toward the rendezvous point with Lon.

It was a frightened, reluctant string of escapees that made its way through the tortuous dark maze. If it hadn't been for Joshua's constant pulling and Renfield's patient, nudging encouragement, the group would certainly not have lasted fifty steps. There was a continuous drone of whimpers, *shshs*, and gasps along the way, and one young man even became briefly hysterical until Renfield put him right.

But they arrived without mishap.

Lon had replaced the light at the intersection with a bulb from another tunnel, so Josh—with great relief—saw him immediately. He looked much better; his color was back and his belly wound was clotted shut. They exchanged a look of shared triumph.

The dead Minotaur still commanded one tunnel. As people began to filter into the area, they had to pass the corpse. Some stared in fascination; others looked away.

The whole motley party was soon clustered expectantly around Lon and Josh. "I'm going to leave you now," Josh told the crowd softly. Ollie gripped his leg in wild fear. Josh picked the boy up, reassuring. "I'll be back," he continued. "I still have to get one more person out of there. Lon will take you all now. You'll be safe with him."

Josh gave Lon back the map to the cliff face, but kept the map to the castle. They agreed to meet here at the intersection as soon as they'd each completed their respective missions.

"Take care of Ollie," whispered Josh. "I mean, if anything happens . . ."

"Like my own son," answered the Vampire.

The group formed a single file once more, and Lon led them down the dark trail home.

Josh moved quickly in the opposite direction, toward the Final Decontamination Lab, and Rose.

Beauty stepped soberly up the left-hand fork. Once the river had entered the tunnels beneath the castle, the water had become shallow, easy to traverse. He felt safer, now, as well; rid of the city's ruthless eyes on his vulnerable back. Yet he was greatly worried.

The map had said that upon entering the tunnels from the east, there was a fork to the right, and then one to the left, and that marked the shaft leading to the Throne Room. But Beauty had come to two turnings before he found a right-hand fork; and three cross tunnels before any fork to the left. He stood tentatively now, at the vertical shaft that may or may not have been the Queen's, and wondered what to do.

He could wait. He could retrace his steps and begin again. He could explore further—he still had fifty yards of coiled vine to play with. He could call out to see if Joshua heard him.

In the dark, hostile tunnel, now, none of these alternatives seemed entirely satisfactory.

He silently cursed. Well. He'd taken the right and the left fork, and the unlabeled turnings be damned.

He waited.

Jasmine climbed the last rung up the shaft. She lifted the lid half a centimeter, and through the crack peered at the room beyond.

It was a large, high-ceilinged place. The two walls she could see had great consoles along them, filled with switches, lights, and knobs. Only two Neuromans were visible. One sat in a swivel chair in front of the left wall console, the other walked here and there, checking settings. In the background, the hum of turbines masked any noises that might have otherwise been evident, such as voices in other rooms. Perhaps it was simply a small night crew.

Jasmine could just barely read some of the nearer switches: SECOND FLOOR WEST; LUNARIUM; AUX LABS. This seemed to be the place. It was the forth shaft she'd come up. The first three were variously interesting, but not what she wanted. This was what she wanted. At least it bore further investigation.

She got as comfortable as possible and settled down to spy for an extended period.

Isis sat, Sphinxlike, on the outer ledge of a window-slit four stories up the castle's façade. She was content. She would know when it was time to move.

Below her, the lights of the city gradually winked out. It was getting late. The city was preparing for sleep. She brought her paw to her mouth and bit at an itch between two footpads.

So satisfying. She closed her eyes with the ecstasy of feeling her own slender corner tooth dig closer and closer to the recess where the itch crackled, trying to drive her mad—but it would not! because—ahhh—she had it now, there, she bit it again and again, annihilating the focus, destroying the itch in one long, divine, orgasmic—

Something happened. She didn't know what, but she knew it was something. Something to do with Joshua. Moreover: Joshua was in the castle.

Leisurely, she rose, walked through the thick stone window frame, jumped to the floor, and padded up the hall.

Lon turned left down a half-lit tunnel. There was an arrow on the wall here, and he couldn't be sure, but it looked like Sum-Thin's mark. He held on to Ollie's hand, who held on to the woman behind him, on and on down the line.

There was a cross tunnel here with a cold wind blowing through it, making a scary moaning sound, like an animal in misery. It frightened two young girls—sisters—about ten people back along the line. They broke rank and bolted up another cross tunnel.

"Stay! Don't run!" shouted Renfield, but the patter of their feet receded up the black hole.

Lon ran back. Renfield told him what had happened. "We must get them," said Renfield.

Lon shook his head sadly. "If I search for them, I'll never find my way back to you. They are lost.

Keep moving," he lowered his voice under the weight
of a great sadness, and went back to the head of the
line. "Join hands and keep moving," he repeated,
and resumed his steady pace.

Isis came to the end of a windowless corridor. Obviously a dead end. She sat, licking her paw, wonder-
ing why she'd come here, when there was clearly
nothing happening. In the middle of a lick she
stopped, though, and sat without moving, staring at
her paw for several seconds. Then she looked up.

Six feet above her, in the wall, was an air vent: a
one-foot-square hole in the wall, covered by a thin
wire screen. *Of course,* thought Isis: *the special halls
they've built for me to get around.*

In a single jump she made it up to the vent, hooked
her nails into the screen covering, and hung there by
her foreclaws, simultaneously battering the bottom of
the mesh with her hind legs. In a few moments the
screen, the flimsy brads holding it in place, and the
Cat all tumbled ignominiously to the floor. Isis picked
herself up immediately, leapt up into the now ac-
cessible vent, and began quickly walking down the
narrow, dark ventilation duct.

Now this is the correct size, she thought as she
padded her way easily down the invisibly black, foot-
square tunnel. The ducts twisted and turned, blind as
a maze; but somehow Isis never missed a step. She
seemed to know intuitively which tunnels to take,
which ones to avoid. The choices did not faze her.
She stopped, once, to kill a rat, but didn't even spend
much time playing with it. *I have better things to do,
Foultooth,* she said to the rat as it lay dying, and resumed her tunnel-walk.

Somehow, she knew, through smell or Cat-sense,
her beloved Joshua was waiting at the end of one of
the turnings.

Silently Josh raised the lid of his shaft: the room
above was empty, so up he went.

It was a big place, with dozens of tables and
benches. Long tubes of deep violet light ran the ceil-

ing from end to end, making Josh feel this to be yet once more a strange spell through which he was perambulating. Flasks of broth bubbled softly on several surfaces, heated by orange-red coils. A wire cage in one corner bore a sign: HIGH VOLTAGE: DANGER.

He examined everything, he understood little. There were two doors. One said OPERATING SUITE, the other was unmarked. He opened the labeled door and walked in. This room was smaller, but also void of life. Two great lamps hung down from the ceiling over two large steel tables. On a counter by one wall were rows of instruments: scalpels like those Jasmine had stolen, scissors, needles, strange things Joshua didn't recognize. A large glass vat stood in the corner. Josh peered into it in the dense blue light. It was filled with clear liquid. At various depths, Human bodies floated. Josh held his breath and walked away.

He breathed again. Two smaller vats stood beside the first, but these were empty. A green metal ball sat humming in the center of a table, which Joshua decided not to go near. There were no other doors in the room, so he went back out again.

In the first room he now noticed a box full of electrical devices. He sorted through them, but they were indecipherable. On the wall was a large diagram labeled HUMAN NERVOUS SYSTEM, depicting a brain and the root-system of nerves it trailed. Beneath it on a desk lay a giant book: *Atlas of the Human Brain.* Josh leafed through it, but it was beyond him. He went up to the unmarked door in the other wall and opened it.

Beyond was a short hall, and two more doors. He tried the first door; it was locked. The second bore a sign: CRYOGENIC HUMAN STORAGE. He opened the door.

On the other side was a small bare anteroom, suffused with purplish light like all the others. In its far wall were yet three more doors, each carrying its own lettered sign. One said LIMBO; the next said NIRVANA; the last, COMMUNION. Josh opened the left-hand door, the one marked LIMBO.

He stopped short, sucked air. Before him in a room

the size of a barn were hundreds of glass coffins, spread out row after row; and in each coffin lay a Human body. Slowly, Josh walked forward.

They looked morbid in the surreal light: bluish, frozen, still. There was scattered frosting on the inside of each glass covering; there were tubes connecting each container to conduits on the floor. Josh moved as if in a trance, up one row, down the next, staring deeply into each motionless face. Each appeared peacefully asleep, each was young. Josh studied them all. He recognized no one.

He went back out into the anteroom and approached the middle door: NIRVANA. He entered.

It was identical to the other, row upon row of iced Humans under glass. He began his deliberate funereal march down the first aisle, searching each face with increasing fear, diminishing hope.

He thought he recognized the sixth body down the line—it looked like Lewis, the fat boy from the Bookery in Ma'gas', the one who'd had spells just like his own.

Josh halted abruptly. The rim on the glass obscured the head somewhat, so he bent closer, stared intensely. It was Lewis. Blue-white, his entire body, and inflexibly smooth. Like a marble statue. Joshua's heart beat faster. He looked more closely still, and what he saw made his heart almost stop: the top of Lewis' head was gone, had been neatly sawed off at the forehead; and he was brainless. His brain was gone. Had been removed. Taken elsewhere. Stolen.

Joshua's eyes widened in speechless rage. He quickly ran to the next glass casing and the next and the next: every body here had the top of its head cleaved off, its brain removed. He ran back to Lewis, put his hands on the glass. He wanted to scream, but no sound came out. He beat on the glass until his fists were sore, but it didn't crack; he tried to tip it over, but it wouldn't budge. Lewis continued to lay there, eternally calm, unperturbed; without a brain.

Joshua went a bit mad.

He rushed back into the first large room on a rampage. He overturned tables, threw beakers against the wall, tore books, broke machinery; spun in circles until he fell in a pile on the floor. For a few minutes, he sat there, nearly catatonic.

Dicey was dead. Dicey was dead. Ollie would live the rest of his life in the shadow of a nightmare. Lewis was . . . Lewis was . . .

Rose. He must find Rose. He could not let these insane images and demented machinations stay him. He would find Rose, at least, and take her from this castle of horrors.

He re-entered Nirvana.

Thoroughly, he examined every glass coffin, breathing deeply through his mouth to avoid vomiting. He recognized no one else.

The door to the third room—labeled COMMUNION —was locked; but with two almost inhumanly strong blows, Josh kicked it open. It left a small bone in his foot broken, but he was beyond caring about such things. There were matters of greater moment to confront.

Bodies filled this room, too. But unlike the others, these were not under glass. They were laid out side by side on huge feather mattresses that stretched from one end of the room to the other. Most were motionless, though occasionally one would twitch, or shift a little. With trepidation, Josh walked forward into the dimly illuminated chamber.

He touched the first body he came to. Warm, dry. Good pulse. It was a naked man, bald-headed, seemingly asleep. The body beside this one was also naked, also bald; and then Josh realized that all the sleeping Humans had had their heads shaved. And then Josh realized that the next Human was Rose.

He felt her pulse. Strong. He lay down beside her —between Rose and the adjacent Human. He remained motionless for some minutes until he gradually grew calmer, drew strength from her warmth, from her serenity. He stroked the softness of her cheek. "Rose, dear Rose," he whispered.

Finally he sat up. "Time to leave this place," he said resolutely, and began lifting her off the mattress.

But something caught, and he couldn't pull her up. Something at the back of her head.

He crawled over the cloth to where her head rested, crawled with growing alarm. He cupped the back of her head in his hands, and felt his alarm turn liquid: emerging from the back of her shaved scalp was a cord. Gingerly he turned her head to look. There it was, evil, sickening: a black, thumb-thick cable, plugged snugly into a three-inch-long, thin rectangular box implanted solidly into the back of her skull. The surgery was recent, the wound not completely healed, stitches still in place.

Josh gasped in disbelief. No, that was the horror, he believed all too well. With a strangled cry, he tore the plug from her head. Briefly, she twitched in his arms, then lay still. He felt her pulse: still full.

He was aware, suddenly, of a red light blinking on and off above the door through which he'd entered, and in the room beyond. He picked up Rose, carried her lightly out the door into the anteroom, and pulled at the door that led back into the main lab he'd originally entered: the door was now locked. He found the doors to Limbo and Nirvana locked as well. He tried kicking all three, but his foot was hurting now, and in any case, doubts had attenuated his strength. He ran back into the Communion room.

There was one more door, he saw, at the back of the room.

It was beside a large opening in the wall through which all the cables from all the shaved heads exited in a great twining bundle. The red light was still flashing. He tried the door. It was open. With Rose slung over his back, he entered the next room.

Here the light was bright as day, making him squint. He dropped to his knees and set Rose down, trying to get his bearings, accommodate his eyes to the glare. All at once, the door behind him slammed shut. Josh swiveled to find a tall, cherubic man standing behind him. Not a man; a Neuroman.

"Welcome," said the strange figure. "I am Gabriel. You have come to the end of your journey."

CHAPTER 16

The New Animal

He stood eight feet tall, pink and plump and dressed in flowing white robes, and he smiled an exaggerated smile that was somehow more mean than happy.

Josh moved between Rose and the towering Neuroman, and crouched, knife in hand.

"No, no," laughed the tall one, "I'm only Gabriel, and there's no need to attack me. You've had a long journey, I'm sure, and could undoubtedly use some rest. As for me, I'm only the ANGEL on the night shift, here. In any event, I *never* resort to physical violence."

This banter put Josh off his guard. He stood a bit, and lowered his knife, as Gabriel turned his back to the young hunter and walked toward the wall.

Josh noticed the room for the first time now—it was empty except for a large iron box into which ran all the cables from the preceding room. On top of the box was a panel of some kind, covered with buttons. Gabriel began nimbly pushing various buttons, his back still to Josh.

"What have you done to them?" Josh demanded. "Make her wake up," he continued, pointing to the unconscious Rose.

"Oh, I've done nothing," Gabriel answered, still pushing buttons. "The Queen's done it all. There; now you *must* be feeling just a little sleepy from your long trip . . . what did you say your name was?"

"Joshua. Joshua," he replied. He *was* feeling sleepy all of a sudden; so sleepy, in fact, that he decided to sit on the floor right beside Rose.

"Well, Joshua," Gabriel said, turning around to face him now, "our Queen is a remarkable animal. She is brilliant, beautiful, and gracious. She's taken droves of insignificant, directionless creatures and molded them into a coherent, cogent organism. She's creating a new order on this planet. By the stars, it's a new world!"

Josh felt vaguely entranced by this inelegant patter; he couldn't say why. An ambiguous combination of revulsion and hope rolled around inside him, like wineskins full of quicksilver. He found himself hopelessly unable to move; and then, with a start, remembered the anger that had brought him to this spot. "But the suffering you've caused . . ." he began.

"Means versus ends," the Neuroman glibly returned. "An old and fictional argument. It is all means, it is all ends. You believe there is more death and suffering now than there was before our time? No, there is not. We have merely redirected it toward a purpose. That is the only difference. We have injected purpose into the eternal process.

"You know what the world is now? It is anarchy, Joshua. Another indistinguishable phase in the endless cycle, on this earth, of conflict, struggle, domination, and confusion. We are changing all that. We are reordering the biosphere. We are raising the level of integration of this world into the meaning of the Universe. . . ."

Josh was losing the thread. He knew why he was here. "Dicey is dead because of your schemes," he accused.

"There is no death," Gabriel assured him. "This Dicey—she was a loved one?—her energy will return to us all. Her body will decompose in the sea, she will help the coral grow, she will be eaten by sea birds who will die and decompose and nourish the yellow flowers that give off oxygen that you yourself will breathe—molecules of your own dear Dicey—some of which you will keep, and some breathe out again, to shower over the earth, some to be expelled into the reaches of the Universe. It is all one field of energy, like the field of yellow flowers that perfumes the air with the sweet scent of Dicey's electrons, and yours and mine. We are all forever."

Josh strained to see the relevance of this to the

mass slaughter of Human beings, but he was having difficulty organizing his thoughts—difficulty concentrating.

"As for the rest of these Humans," Gabriel continued, "they are all part of the Queen's Grand Experiment. She has collected that lot with care, selecting for the most unique—the essential—brains. We ANGELS, of course, have been her hands in the actual surgeries —the implanting of electrodes in the critical areas of cerebral cortex, then making the connections to the computer. But then it's the Queen, herself, naturally, who integrates all that information, through the computer, into her own brain, to complement and augment her own not insubstantial cognitive processes.

"There has never *been* such an experiment!" he went on, becoming visibly excited, his cheeks flushing, his fingers working the air. "Imagine it! By the stars, it is monumental! A thinking organism, a great intelligence at its center, directing its processes, utilizing the information in a thousand lesser brains—using it, integrating it, reprocessing, relaying, recombining—and all electronically, so there is no loss of information, no communication breakdowns, no language barriers—no language at all, except for the language of one DNA, the language of the neurotransmitters, the language of the electrons. Whole new levels of consciousness, by the stars! New leaps of . . ."

Josh had been only half-listening at best, his mind turning obliquely in its own internal, autonomous rhythm on nothing he could fathom. Now, suddenly, he saw Rose begin to stir, and it jolted him more fully awake than he'd been since entering this barren room.

"Where am I?" moaned Rose.

Josh lifted her up into his lap, held her to his chest. "You're safe now, Rose. Wake up, we have to leave."

Gabriel laughed unkindly. "No, Joshua, you cannot leave. You're here for a reason, most fortunate Human."

Josh stared dully at the Neuroman, unmoving. Not that he *couldn't* move, necessarily; but simply that in some mysterious, indefinable way, he had no desire to move, no will.

Rose sat up. Her face was alert, her demeanor comprehending. She felt scared and happy. "Oh, Joshua," she said, seeing him clearly for the first time. She hugged him powerfully: feeling great love, and also trying to transmit some of her poised energy to him.

Gabriel smiled at the scene, then went on speaking. "You cannot leave because you are needed by our Queen, both of you. Especially you, Joshua. You see, every thought process is accompanied by a certain pattern of electrical discharges—perhaps I should say *caused* by a certain pattern of discharges—which can be recorded as a brain wave on an oscilloscope. Every type of cerebral process is characterized by its own peculiar pattern of wave, which may differ in frequency, amplitude, shape, and a host of other variables. Now the Queen, in her unknowable wisdom, has discovered she is in need of certain *classes* of thoughts —that is, certain categories of electrical patterns— caused by certain configurations of nerve cells, firing in just certain ways—in order to mesh with other patterns she and her brains *do* possess, in order to reach certain kinds of new understanding of the Universe, understandings which you and I could never grasp. And these discharge patterns she is desirous of are, of course, necessarily accompanied by certain specific and characteristic brain wave patterns."

Josh was no longer attending, he was lost in a gray zone of consciousness that touched back to earth only periodically. Rose, on the other hand—to her own bewilderment—understood everything Gabriel was talking about, even though she was certain she'd never heard any of it before.

Gabriel was now making fine adjustments on the knobs and buttons that lined the panel on the great iron box. He continued his monologue happily, almost as if to himself. "Now some Humans, it seemed likely, had brains that manufactured the electrical patterns the Queen wanted. The problem was how to find these Humans. By the stars, it was no problem! We simply built a wave generator. Like an old radio transmitter, really, only we could send out any frequency and roughly any shape wave we wanted.

So the Queen wanted a seventy-four-cycle-per-second-low-amplitude-damped sinewave: so that's what we transmitted. And that, Joshua, is what pulled you here." Josh responded to the sound of his name. His eyes flickered, his attention focused on the Neuroman. Gabriel went on.

"We generated this wave in its purest form, and you synchronized with it. Like the sudden waves of a passing boat in a pond rippling with frogs and leaves and fish—all the ripples vanish, the water bends to the imprint of the waves. And then the boat passes and the waves dampen out, and the rippling crosscurrents return. It is what happens to an epileptic whose seizures take control when he is exposed to lights that flash at the frequency of the focus of his seizures. It is what happened to you, by the stars, every time you had one of your fits, or trances, or whatever you liked to call them."

"My spells!" exclaimed Josh.

"Precisely. Which became stronger and stronger the closer you came to the source. There were, in fact, several different frequencies we transmitted—it is several different configurations of brain cells that the Queen is interested in. I've just been fiddling with the wave generator here, now, and by the way you've been responding to the low wattage signals I've been sending, I'd say you had the seventy-four CPS locus—probably just behind your Sulcus of Muldaur near the Sylvian Fissure, which makes sense, behaviorally speaking; those with your wave pattern, I find, are the most tenacious and ingenious, and invariably the ones who somehow manage to worm their way into the castle—to the source—before being captured. No wonder it's a trait the Queen wants to cultivate," he laughed brightly.

Rose sat motionless, in horrible fascination, rapt by what Gabriel was saying. She didn't understand all of it, but much was clear to her—and this fact alone riveted her to the floor. Beyond this, she had thoughts of assaulting the Neuroman—she found him hateful and low, and she knew this was their only chance for escape. But angered though she was, she could

move no more than Josh. Whether it was her weakened condition, or Gabriel's hypnotic speech, or some
pulse of wave signals he was generating, or some im-
plant they'd sewn into her brain, or some combination of these, she could not tell. She only knew she
must leave this place, and she could not.

Gabriel pushed more buttons on the keyboard. Josh
felt his gray limbo fade into blackness, into the
black sucking void with which he was now so familiar. The black void and the exploding light, imploding
light, stronger now than ever before, brighter than the
core of the heaviest sun, pulling Josh in, pulling him
apart . . .

Isis sat in the dark cool of the air vent. Through the
thin wire screen she looked into the brightly lit room.
There sat Josh on the floor, dozing beside a woman—
the woman tied up in the Vampire camp, the friend
of the girl with the blood-smell. Beside them, a tall
man—one of the creatures-without-smell—was saying
some boring thing. Probably that's why Joshua was
sleeping. Maybe she should wait until Josh woke up.
She didn't like this creature, though, there was something fetid about his odorlessness. She stared at him
without blinking.

Suddenly the tall strange man walked to the big box
he stood near and began turning dials. Isis didn't like
it. She watched Josh, looking for a cue. Josh rolled
over, lay still on the floor, unconscious. In a matter
of moments, his arms began to twitch; then his entire
body started jumping, jerked around by some invisible
force. It had to do with the tall one, Isis was certain,
the creature-without-smell. Softly, she hissed.

Once more, she hooked her front claws into one side
of the thin grating that covered the portal to the duct
in which she'd been crouching. With her hind legs she
bashed at the screen, and after two good blows, sent
both screen and herself sprawling into the room.

She landed on her feet, somewhat akimbo. The noise
drew the attention of both Rose and Gabriel, but before anyone could act, Isis leapt. In a second, she was
on the Neuroman's face, her teeth sunk viciously into

one of his eyes, her claws making deep furrows in his artificial skin.

They rolled wildly on the floor, Isis clinging to Gabriel in frenzied attack. Josh continued intermittently convulsing in the corner. The interruption broke Rose's trance somewhat, but she still hadn't the strength or will to join in the attack on Gabriel. Instead, with great effort, she picked herself up and teetered over to the console Gabriel had been manipulating. She didn't know exactly what to do, but simply began pushing buttons randomly. Nothing happened. Josh remained unconscious on the floor, twitching periodically.

The Neuroman threw the little Cat against the wall and stumbled to his feet, his face dripping Hemolube. Isis was on him again immediately, though, madness personified. Rose watched the struggle with grim stupefaction, then watched Josh convulsing on the floor. She turned more dials. Nothing. She tried to hit the Neuroman: she could not move.

"I must help," she thought, "but something prevents me from harming Gabriel directly. And poor Joshua is at the mercy of this machine I cannot turn off. A puppet of the radio waves. If only I could cut the strings . . ." The image was clear to her, though the entire concept was confusing, almost overwhelming. She didn't know what electromagnetic waves were, had never even heard the words; yet, somehow, she did know. Words were bombarding her from deep inside her consciousness, strange words that disoriented, yet inspired: *static interference, dispersion, scintillation, flux.* Her head was spinning, tumbled by the noise of the fight, the noise of Joshua's seizures, the noise in her brain. Suddenly out of the screaming jumble of nonsense came epiphany: without calculation or comprehension, she ran over and picked up the wire grating Isis had knocked into the room; then ran back to Joshua and wrapped the fine mesh around his head, bent it into place until it loosely cradled his skull, an ill-fitting, cross-hatching of wire.

Almost instantly, Joshua's convulsions ceased. The fight between Isis and Gabriel continued. The Neuroman oozed Hemolube everywhere from deep scratches and cuts; but he had Isis by the neck, now, and was finally strangling the weakening kitty.

Josh woke up. He felt groggy, but the sight of Rose brought everything back to him in an instant. His thinking cleared as the trance vanished like smoke in a fast wind. "Rose . . ." he said.

"Joshua," she implored, pointing him toward the diminishing battle. "Help her, quickly."

With the full image of the little Cat being throttled, Joshua's rage returned in full. He dove into Gabriel furiously. Isis pulled free and renewed her own attack. Josh quickly took a syringe from his pocket, tore open the fading Neuroman's head valve, and clicked the empty syringe into place. Gabriel raised his hands in lost fear. "Wait, wait," he pleaded, "I beg you, by the stars, do not inject air. I am beaten, I am yours."

Isis bit him once more on the leg, then sat, hissing, a few feet away, ready to pounce, her fur puffed out. Josh panted, his hand on the syringe. As he stood there, composing himself, catching his breath, he brought his hand up to pull the annoying wire cap off his head. Rose stopped him in time.

"No, no, you must leave this place," she warned. "It's all that protects you from your spells. I . . . I don't know why, but it does."

He nodded, accepting without questioning her knowledge.

"Please," Gabriel spoke up again. "Go freely. Only take the syringe from my head."

Isis bit him in the foot once more, then backed off again at a motion from Josh. "Keep quiet until you're spoken to," Josh advised the bleeding Neuroman. To Rose, he said: "Go back into the room next door. Unplug everyone from the cables."

Without a word she hurried into the Communion room to complete this task. Josh turned his attention again to Gabriel. "Now," he urged with quiet fury, "tell me where is your vile Queen, that I may have words with her. . . ."

"I cannot . . ." began the Neuroman.

"Tell me where or I empty this into your head," he

whispered, putting light pressure on the plunger. The pressure made Gabriel's wounds ooze even faster.

"By the stars, I cannot," Gabriel pleaded. "By the stars, there is no Queen."

"What are you talking about? Stop this bartering, man, these are your final moments."

"I swear, I swear," Gabriel begged, "there is no such animal. It was an invention, a figment of our imagination, we of the Inner Circle. These experiments are *our* doing, no one else's. The 'new animal' is just and only the computer-integrated accumulation of all the Human brains we've appropriated—"

"Stolen!"

"Stolen, if you will. But I swear by my final moments on earth we are creating an intelligence with these linked brains that we can apply to the good of all—"

"Murdered," Josh rasped.

"—and I swear by the stars that those with the most to gain are those fortunate creatures whose brains are in the circuit."

Isis bit him again on the ankle. He winced, pulled his leg back: and in the same motion twisted, throwing Josh down. He brought his hands up to the back of his head, to dislodge the syringe, but Josh and Isis were on him in a second. He fell back: his head hit the wall, depressing the plunger on the syringe: and he was dead.

Josh hugged Isis quickly but warmly, then carried her into the next room and set her down. Rose had just finished unplugging the last Human.

"Well, that's done," said Rose. "They'll wake up in a few minutes, I think. And look, I found a drawer full of these." She held up a little oblong, black lid that she placed against the outlet at the back of her head and with a *snap* capped the plug-opening. "We'll have to leave quickly," she went on. "How did you get in?"

Josh showed her the trash tube and shaft to the sewage tunnels below. "What about them?" he indicated the rows of unconscious Humans, some of whom were lethargically starting to awaken.

"They'll know what to do," Rose assured. "But with all these brains disconnected, alarms have gone off. Guards will be here any minute. We can't wait."

Josh clenched. He ran over to a Human sitting up, a few feet away, who appeared fully awake. "The tubes," Josh said to the man, pointing. "Escape down the tubes." The man nodded understanding; Josh ran back to Rose and Isis. "Come on," he said, putting the little Cat on his shoulder. He lifted the lid on the upright tube, and they climbed down the shaft.

At the bottom the water ran fast and shallow. A dim bulb glowed at the junction of three tunnels. Josh could see his last chalk arrow, thirty feet downstream at the shaft he'd originally gone up. Otherwise, the tunnel was empty.

"Beauty," Josh called out in a loud whisper. No answer.

"Beauty is here?" Rose gripped his arm in fearful anticipation.

"He was supposed to be," Josh said, heartsick at the Centaur's absence. What could it mean? Had something else gone wrong? "Beauty!" he called louder.

More silence. Then: "Here!" echoed a voice in the darkness.

"Where? Where are you?" Josh yelled. They ran toward the sound.

"Here, I am here! I ran out of vine, I can go no farther. You must find my voice. Is Rose safe?" the Centaur called.

"I am here, my love, yes, I'm well, we're coming!"

They called back and forth for ten minutes, turning down blind cross tunnels, backtracking, rerouting. Finally, they found each other, probably more lucky than clever. Beauty and Rose hugged with a great passion.

"We've no time to lose," Josh whispered to Beauty. "Take Rose out with you, upstream. We'll meet where the river leaves the jungle, just before dawn."

"Come with us this way," urged Beauty. "It is shorter and safer."

Josh shook his head. "I can't, I promised Lon I'd

meet him in the tunnels. He's hurt, and he may need help."

They clasped hands. "Until soon, friend," said Beauty.

"Until soon."

Rose hopped on Beauty's back and he began following his trailing vine back up against the current. Josh walked swiftly in the opposite direction, closely following the arrows he'd drawn on the wall. Isis remained on Joshua's shoulder: she felt totally safe there; and she hated the water.

It didn't take long to get back to the rendezvous point. Lon was there waiting.

"No luck?" asked the Vampire.

"Rose is safe. She's with Beauty now, on their way out. And you?"

"I shuttled most of the orphans three at a time to the spot we agreed upon, where the river meets the jungle. We lost some, though."

"Ollie?" Josh didn't hide the fear in his voice.

"He is safe," Lon touched Joshua's shoulder. "Let us join them." He stood up, and almost immediately doubled over.

Josh came to his aid. "You're hurt. You're bleeding again." The wound in the Vampire's side had reopened; blood freely trickled.

"No, I'm fine. But we must hurry." Without pausing, he started down the tunnel. Josh followed, with Isis on her perch.

They walked in silence. Lon was already rather familiar with the route by now, and his night vision was good enough that they made steady progress.

Pausing to get their bearings in what must have been a peripheral cross tunnel, they first heard the rumbling.

"What's that?" Josh wanted to know.

Lon and Isis both twitched their ears. "I don't know," said Lon, "but it seems to be getting louder."

Indeed, the walls were beginning to shake, the air to vibrate and then blow with a low, ominous thunder. All at once, the water hit.

In an instant, the entire tunnel was flooded, floor to

ceiling, with a crush of wild rushing water. The three
friends were violently torn apart and carried like so
much flotsam down the raging tide. Josh saw Lon
catch the bottom rung of a vertical shaft and pull
himself up out of the deluge. Isis, who never coped
well with water, was rapidly carried, legs askew, down
a battering surge through the largest tunnel; and was
not seen again.

Josh was tumbled under the water for a time—in
the tunnels themselves there was no way to get above
the flow. He held his breath as best he could but in
the constant buffeting he kept losing air. Several times
he was slammed against jagged walls or protruding
corners; twice, he almost lost consciousness.

At the very nadir of his strength, his foot snagged
in a bar, and pulling himself to it, he found it was a
rung leading up a shaft. With his last energy he pulled
himself up, found another rung, and pulled again.
One more rung, and he was out of the water, coughing, sputtering, and lost. He hung for a long time on
the ladder in the shaft—the water rushing below him
—resting, recovering, retching.

He wondered briefly why the tunnels had suddenly
filled with churning water, but did not dwell on the
matter. Their luck had soured, it remained only to
survive. He silently wished his friends well, climbed
the shaft and slipped over the top.

Night in the Outer City. A lost breeze found its way
over the wall to cool Joshua's face, as he ran across
the street he'd emerged on to crouch in the shadow
of an empty wagon. Street lamps made concealment
difficult. In addition, jolly groups of Vampires and
Neuromans roamed everywhere in search of night
pleasure. As a Human, in dripping Human clothes,
Josh was thoroughly conspicuous.

He waited until the area cleared somewhat, then
surreptitiously inched his way toward the outer wall.
Through alleys, against buildings, under causeways he
darted. The moon was hardly more than an intimation
behind black autumn clouds, but the street light brazenly followed his progress, tagging him with his own

shadow wherever he turned. He was halfway across a wide street when the alarm came.

"Halt! You there!" yelled a voice from a doorway.

"Look! There! A Human!" shouted another.

And then another: "After him!"

This was followed immediately by the rattle of numerous feet over the cobbles, but Josh didn't stick around to see which feet belonged to which voice. He dove into a shadow, and ran.

"Auxiliary Power check complete," said Neuroman One.

"Auxiliary Power function normal," said Neuroman Two, returning the Auxiliary Power switch to the *Off* position. It was a test they ran at 0400 every night, to check for malfunction in the Auxiliary Power system —a substitute power source that diverted the major force of the river through the sewage tunnels to alternate turbines in a different part of the city. Tonight, as always, the standby engines clicked in on cue, then shut down again as the test was concluded.

"Back to Standard Power," said Neuroman One.

"Standard Power," echoed Neuroman Two, rechecking all the switch positions.

Jasmine stood silently behind a relay box, out of sight of the two technicians, measuring her moment. She'd hidden in the shaft for hours, then gone undetected from the shaft to the console to this box, waiting only for an opportunity to strike.

Opportunity knocked.

Neuroman One lit up a cigarette. Neuroman Two said, rather curtly, "Go out in the hall if you have to smoke that thing." Neuroman One replied in tone and went into the hall. Jasmine tiptoed up behind Neuroman Two, popped his head valve, and blew fifty cc's of air in before the creature knew anything was happening. He slumped forward at the desk, never to move again.

Jasmine repositioned herself. In a few minutes, Neuroman One re-entered. "Wake up," he growled to his immobile co-worker. When Two didn't stir, One walked over and shook him. Jasmine slipped out, popped One's valve and applied her deadly syringe. She then tipped over some furniture, twined the bodies arm in arm, their hands on each other's valves, and let them bleed onto the floor: set piece of a mock death struggle. Now the room was hers.

First she broke all the levers off the Auxiliary Power switches. Then she turned all the Main Power switches to the *Off* position. Then, in the blackened room, with her flashlight on, she broke or removed all the levers on the Main Power switches. Then she walked out the door of the defunct room, locking it behind her, as the sounds of frantic commotion began to well in the corridors all around.

The lights went out. All over the city. Josh was hiding under a bush when it happened, and with grave relief, heard his pursuers run on by in sudden and equilibrating blackness. From all directions he heard shouts of alarm, dismay, confusion. No streetlights, no searchlights. No longer afraid of exposure, Joshua became bold. He left his bush.

He walked quickly but assuredly down a main walkway toward the outer wall. Vampires and Neuromans ran in all directions around him, but none paid him any heed. He could taste his imminent escape, smell it on the wind.

At the same moment, another nose was raised to the air. Cerberus, the drawbridge guard dog, had wandered inside the compound when the lights went out, to see what the trouble was. He flared his nostrils hotly, now, and bared the teeth in all three of his heads. "I smell Human," he said to himself, and walked stealthily toward the smell.

Lon flew to the top of the outer wall when the lights went out. With his razor-nails he began cutting a large hole in the electrified net that covered the city. Large enough to fly through, even if the electricity came back on. He felt woozy from blood loss, but put the feeling out of his mind for the more important matters of the moment. Far below him, the city writhed in turmoil. Methodically, he continued cutting the wires.

Jasmine walked out of the castle's main gate and into the Inner City. Patrols swept the ground, each with an emergency station to defend. Some, with flashlights, examined every face they passed; but Jasmine, still in stolen uniform, was ignored. She walked calmly through the chaos, like a slow boat through fast waters.

Beauty and Rose held their breaths; Rose held tightly on to her champion's back. With all his strength he dove under and swam with long powerful strokes against the steady current. When she could hold her breath no longer, she tugged on his mane, and he surfaced.

They were in midstream, now, perhaps thirty yards from the castle, floating, slowly back toward it, back to where it emptied into the tunnels, out of which he'd just swum. He breathed deeply a few moments, then submerged again and redoubled his efforts swimming against the flow of the river, away from the castle.

When he came up again for air he found he'd hardly gone twenty more yards: he was tiring rapidly, and the river was too strong for him. All around them the city was dark, and creatures ran every direction in mounting hysteia

"We'll have to walk," Beauty whispered to Rose. She nodded, feeling both tremulous and safe. He let himself drift to the river's edge, and stood as soon as his feet touched bottom. The dropoff was fairly precipitous, and he found himself standing chin-high in the river only a few feet from shore. Slowly, constantly watchful of losing his footing, he began walking upriver, the water lapping around his neck and that of his love, holding on behind him.

Only their heads showed above water, as if they were bobbing slowly east. And in the lightless city, under the cloud-covered moon, they were almost impossible to see. But then, no one was really watching the river; they were all running to their battle stations, to their labs, to their homes.

Slowly, Beauty made his way toward the inner wall.

The Human smell was strong now to the Cerberus. He drooled as he stalked, the spittle running down his three long, canine chins. The wind shifted momentarily, confusing his sense of direction. He stopped, listened, sniffed again: there it was. Much stronger now, from just behind that corner building. The Human!

The gap in the mesh was complete, and Lon flew down again into the city. He paused to rest against a tree, for he was sweating, and beginning to chill. The sun would be nearly up in an hour. All about him the city spun like beetles around an open drain: he wanted to leave before he got sucked in. But he wanted to find Josh and Jasmine first.

He began walking toward the predetermined rendezvous point. He would have flown, but he wanted to save his strength for the flight out of the city. And his side was hurting again.

Jasmine stopped short. A crowd bearing torches ran past her, hounding some invisible saboteur. In the distance, back at the castle, a bell began to toll.

She breathed deeply, continued walking. Somewhere to the west, a bonfire sprang up. It made Jasmine jump; she was getting jumpy.

Two hundred yards up, the final, outer gate came into view. The sight of it made Jasmine quicken her step, quicken her breath. Three Vampires flew low across her path, toward the conflagration. Their wind lifted her hair like fire for several seconds. Faster, still, she walked.

She was almost to the gate. Suddenly the full moon came out from behind its cloudy refuge, washing the city in frigid, white light. Jasmine began to run. Thirty steps from the gate, twenty, ten. She ran through, raced over the bridge, out into the dusty night beyond. And she was gone.

Beauty dove under the inner wall, came up again in the Outer City, kept walking. Briefly, the moon came out, then hid again. In its crystal glare, there appeared to be two bodyless ghost heads floating somberly, effortlessly against the moving current.

Neither spoke, they were concentrating so hard on maintaining low profiles. Ten feet from the wall, though, they were spotted; and the alarm was raised.

"Ho there. Creatures in the water!" someone shouted.

"Look! You there, in the water! Come out!"

"Stop them! Over here!"

At the first yell, Beauty dove underwater and swam doggedly upstream toward the outer wall. Muffled shouts rang out above them. He reached the giant underwater hole in the wall through which the central tributary of the river poured—reached it just as a massive, rusted iron gate was beginning to fall closed over it. With all his might, he grabbed the descending lip of the gate and pulled himself past it to the other side of the wall. He let go of the iron grating just before it clamped down hard against the sandy bottom, and floated gently back up to the river's easy surface. They were outside the city.

Rose slipped off his back, lightening his load a little. "My strength is returning," she said, treading water. "I can swim myself, now."

From inside the wall came the sounds of shouts, orders, splashes. Beauty and Rose smiled at each other, pushed off the wall, and with unhurried, steady strokes began swimming east up the black river, under the cool black night.

Josh saw the Cerberus in the moonlight just as it started its final run for him. He hadn't the strength to fight anymore, so he tried to get away; but with his every step, the Dog-man gained. Josh reached for his knife, only to find it was gone. He felt the creature's breath on his neck; and then the creature's fingers, grabbing at his flowing hair, pulling his head back. He fell to the ground at a roll, just ahead of the Dog-man's snapping teeth.

With a *whoosh*, the shadow of a Vampire descended on them, separating the Cerberus from Josh in a single motion. It was Lon. There was a frenzy of

indistinguishable snarls, growls, and yelps, and then
all was still. Slowly, Lon stood. The Cerberus did not.

Lon wobbled and fell. Josh ran over to him. His
left arm was torn ragged, his face pale as moonlight.
He stood again immediately, though, dismissing Joshua's concerns. "We must hurry," he whispered.

He took Joshua in his right arm, spread his wings
and flew. His failing strength was evident in his flight,
however—he rose, he fell, he almost spun out of control. He barely made it to the top of the outer stone
wall, in fact—to the hole he'd cut earlier in the wire
mesh. There he stopped, panting badly, and set Joshua
down. Together they rested atop the heavy granite
barrier, a hundred feet up, surveying the scene.

"I need but a moment," the Vampire breathed. His
blood ran thick off his shredded arm, then slowly
down the stone wall.

"You need more than that," Joshua inspected his
friend's wounds fearfully.

Lon looked down at his arm, then nodded grim
agreement. "My strength is bled away. I need time to
rest, and there is no time."

They looked at each other for a long moment of
understanding: then Josh bared his neck to the Vampire. Lon tore away the dressings from Joshua's throat
wound; and with an expression that bore the agony
of both compassion and desperation, sank his ivory
teeth into the boy's neck and drank.

Josh had prepared himself for the excruciating pain
he'd experienced when Bal had bitten him. But it was
not so. Lon's bite was searing, yet exquisite. Josh felt
weakened as his blood was sucked by the other; but
somehow, transcendent at the same time. He felt
drained, and nourished; taken from, given to. In some
way the ambiguities frightened him more than the
simple pain could ever have done. He laid his trembling hand on the back of Lon's head. He pulled the
fangs in deeper.

Lon withdrew, with tortured ambivalence. Somewhat restored, he rewrapped the bandages around
Joshua's neck to stop the freshly bleeding laceration.

Joshua's legs wobbled, Lon steadied him. Their eyes met.

For a moment all the lights in the city flashed on again, flickered, then extinguished once more. Dangling wires sparked briefly, where Lon had cut them, all around. The two comrades stood stranded on the wall, leaning on each other for support. Twice more in the next minute the power came on, then went out again. In the glare of the last burst, Josh pointed across the city: what appeared to be a Vampire sentry was flying the tall perimeter, scouting for invaders.

"He'll be here in under a minute," said Lon wearily.

Without enthusiasm, Josh reached for his weapons. He knew neither he nor Lon had any stamina for a fight; he doubted if Lon could fly. Even more glumly, he discovered he had nothing left but the needle and syringe set. He searched his pockets and belt in vain —no knives, no scalpels. In his boot, however, he found he still had one Scribe-tube left. He pulled it out and feverishly began unscrewing the top. The city lights flashed on and off again. The sentry was flying closer.

Lon, meanwhile, had picked up a twenty-foot section of unattached wire that he'd earlier cut free and draped over the wall. He was becoming weaker by the moment; every effort seemed to tax him. He now tied one end of the wire around the phalangeal tip of his furled right wing; pulled the wire across the back of the wing, looped it around two bony struts that jutted up midway; then pulled the wire tightly across his back, wrapping it under his arm and around his chest: the wire acted as an external extensor tendon, pulling the wing out to its full fifteen-foot spread, locking it in that position as he secured the wire around his chest. The manipulations left him completely winded; yet he forced himself to continue, finding another length of loose wire, attaching it in the same way to his other wing.

The sentry turned the corner in the distance, began flying toward Josh and Lon. Suddenly, the city lights came on again; and stayed on. Once more, the free

ends of the cut wires began sparking all around. The
sentry saw the two figures on the wall, and began flying faster.

Josh saw the Vampire increase his air speed, and
knew they'd been spotted. Urgently, he unscrewed the
other end of the Scribe-tube, removed all the hand-
written documents he'd concealed, stuffed them into
his belt. Next, he pulled the needle off the syringe,
pulled out the plastic plunger, and pushed the needle
through the end of the plunger until it stuck forward
out the tip like a nasty steel dart. Finally, he put the
whole needle assemblage into the Scribe-tube—now
open at both ends—and brought the Scribe-tube to
his mouth.

The Vampire sentry was flying at high speed now,
almost on them. Josh blew with all his strength, sending the makeshift spike into the oncoming assailant's
face. It struck him just below the eye: he broke stride,
lost his balance, brought hand to face, and tipped his
wing; and in tipping, came in contact with the electrified wire mesh over the wall.

With a great crackle and screech, the Vampire fell
inextricably into the high-tension grid: smoking flesh,
white blinding sparks. From their perch on the stone
barely ten feet away, Lon and Josh watched the grisly
spectacle.

"They'll *all* know we're here in a moment," said
Lon. "We must go now."

Josh turned and looked at him now for the first
time: his wings were pulled straight out by wire rig-
ging, taut, to their full thirty-foot span; his black hair
blew wildly across the full moon that hung above and
far behind his shoulder; blood flowed black down his
torn arm and belly; his skin looked hard as stone, his
eyes dark as time. His knees began to buckle, but
wires propped them as well, it appeared. Josh ran up
to him.

"Do not tarry, I beseech you," whispered Lon with
maximum effort. "Climb upon my back. Pull the right
wire to go left, the left to go right." He fixed his eyes
on the distance.

Josh went immediately behind his sinking Vampire comrade. Off to the side, the sentry's body continued to burn and jump on the wires. Josh put his arms over Lon's broad shoulders, jumped on his back, and started to ask, "How do we . . ." But his weight was enough to tip Lon forward over the wall; and with an exhilarating shock, he realized they were gliding silently into the night.

They kept level for a long time, rising a bit on updrafts, settling again with distance. The noisy hubbub of the city receded quickly, leaving them soon to their own thoughts in the night's black beauty. Josh straddled Lon's back, full of love and fear, peering out over the land like a child-king carried by his tutor, and wondered, briefly, if this were what Dicey had felt with Bal. The world was too strange to understand.

The desert appeared below them after a while, for they'd been heading generally southeast.

"Don't we want to go back north, to follow the river into the jungle?" Josh yelled into Lon's ear over the drone of the rushing wind. No answer came. Josh yelled again, was again met with silence. With hollow fear, he pulled on the wire that criss-crossed the back on Lon's right wing: the wing elevated slightly, and together they banked slowly off to the left. When they were aimed northeast Josh let up on the wire, and they leveled off again. He put his face down into the back of Lon's head; and wept.

Gradually they lost altitude, over what period of time Josh could not say. At a totally unexpected moment, though, with a large jolt, they skidded, on Lon's belly, across a flat grassy expanse, coming, finally, to a crunching, bouncing stop. Josh was thrown free.

He got up immediately and ran back to his friend. Lon lay motionless, prone, wings and legs tied out with wire. Dead. Sometime during the flight, Josh hoped. For a silent time he knelt beside his fallen comrade.

In the distance, to the west, Josh could hear occasional fragments of shouting carried from the castle

on the rising wind blowing east off the ocean. He
knew he should go quickly; but his strength was spent,
along with much of his blood and most of his spirit.
Dicey dead, and now Lon. Life seemed very hollow.

With little heart he began walking northeast. After
less than a minute, he heard the gentle sigh of running water. Thirty seconds later he stood at the river's
edge. Like time, it made its stately flow, unperturbed
by the million fish that prowled its depths. A living
thing, this river. After all was said and done, life did
go on.

And so must his, Josh resolved. Rose was alive, and
Ollie, and Beauty and Jasmine. And Josh.

Far to the west, unseen flames lent the horizon a
dull orange glow. Josh turned east and began walking.
Exhausted as he was, though, he knew he wouldn't
likely last a mile. He stopped, considered. The west
wind blew his hair.

Resolutely he walked back to Lon's sprawled body.
With great care he pulled up on one wing, lifting it
high, stood underside Lon's belly and tipped the
spread-eagled corpse over on its back. Then in a series
of debilitating fits and starts, he dragged it by the hair
to the river bank. There he sat a few minutes, regaining his strength, fighting dizziness, trying to keep a
hold on consciousness.

When he felt he could move without fainting, he
dragged Lon's legs into the water. Next, he unwired
one wing, lifted it erect—perpendicular to Lon's body
—and rewired it in that position, sticking straight into
the air. Then with a powerful sadness, he brought his
mouth down on Lon's and blew into it as much breath
as he could, filling the dead Vampire's lungs with air.
Before any air could escape, Josh filled Lon's mouth
and nostrils with mud from the shore. Finally he sat
on Lon's great chest, and pushed off into the river.

Lon's undisturbed wing spread flat across the water
like a paper pontoon: his air-expanded chest buoyed
his body, and supported Joshua atop it.

The current ran west, but the strong wind to the east
caught the sail of Lon's upright wing, billowed it full,
and carried them, with sorrowful grace, up the river.

He reached the edge of Rain Forest as the sun was rising, and steered the proud dead body in to shore. Once there, he unwired the wings, folded them in, weighted the carcass with stones and set it adrift. It floated out to midstream, turning, slowly sinking in the westerly flow. Josh watched until he could see it no more, then set off into the jungle.

He was almost immediately greeted by Jasmine, who'd been lying patiently in wait. They exchanged hurried, affectionate greetings, and Josh was briefly tearful. Jasmine led him a mile farther in, to a secluded spot where the others fitfully slept or anxiously waited up. Beauty, Rose, Ollie, Humbelly, and all the orphans of the harem crowded around, but there was no time for reunion.

Jasmine led them all, in semi-forced march, through another half-day of jungle hardship, to a place she knew—a large, hidden den, which none of her enemies had ever discovered. It was a comfortable cave, stocked with canned and dry food stores many decades old, stocked for a long stay. Jasmine, Josh, and Beauty put the new brood of orphans to bed beside the gentle flow of an underground spring. It gave Josh much joy to see Ollie sleep so quietly at last; but deep melancholy would not abide with them both. So many souls lost, dear friends and true. The price of a young boy's peaceful dreaming? Josh wondered. The meaning was obscure; the price, too painful to contemplate.

He picked up Humbelly and placed the sleeping Flutterby beside Ollie's head, where it hummed softly into the boy's ear. Both little creatures smiled.

And finally, finally, safely ensconced within the jungle cave, the adventurers deeply slept, saving their stories of victory and loss for another day.

Epilogue

THEY slept all that night and all the next day and most of the next night. On the second morning the entire troop gathered around for a great communal breakfast of jungle fruits, lizard jerky, and cave-spring water.

"To those we found, and to those we lost," Joshua toasted.

All raised their cups.

"And to the love of our finders," answered Rose.

A great cheer went up, and the feast began. Food and stories were devoured with a vengeance.

Rose's ordeal was wailed over. Ollie was hugged almost into speaking; but not quite.

Everyone had something to say about the collection of stolen brains the ANGELS were molding into the collective consciousness known as the Queen. Rose spoke to that hue and cry.

"As dehumanizing as this whole experience has been, that particular episode was one I gained from. They used what knowledge I had; yet they gave me knowledge too. I know things I never knew."

"That could be said for all of us at the end of this quest," commented Beauty.

"Perhaps," nodded Rose. "Perhaps we've all found new knowledge, without understanding exactly how it came to us. Still . . . I feel I know *so much* more. And so much of what I now know remains yet a mystery to that in me that was." She could not begin to count the ways in which this was true—ranging from new knowledge of herself, to such strange bursts of understanding as had led her to wrap Joshua's head in wire to screen him from the effects of the wave generator.

And although she didn't say so out loud, she had the persistent feeling that perhaps there *was* a new animal, a superior guiding intelligence, in spite of what Gabriel had said. But then she knew she was only Human; and Humans always had a need to invent omnipotent characters in their lives, whether or not such characers existed. She smiled tenderly at Beauty: he'd been right again, in his simple Horse-sense way: *all* of them had gained new, special knowledge on this journey; and none could fully describe their own insights to the others.

Josh had a hole in his heart where Dicey had been, made even more ragged-raw around the edges by Lon's demise. He fingered the blood-drop pendant Lon had given him so long ago, and again so recently. "My grief is my mystery," he answered Rose. "Its depth is beyond my understanding. And I don't know what it's taught me. Lon saved my life three times— twice after his own death. How can I discharge the grief that I may never repay him, never thank him? Must I forever carry that burden?"

"Lon did what he did of free will," responded Jasmine from across the floor. "You have no debt to his actions. That weight is yours only if you want it."

The subject of free will was no less on Joshua's mind. He'd undertaken this journey ostensibly of his own free will, for his own purposes. Yet Gabriel had told him he was there at the pull of the wave machine. It was nonsense, of course, the ANGELS' claim —Josh knew he'd come for one purpose only: to save his people. Yet, what of that action was purely Joshua, and how much was dictated by conflicting outside pressures, such as Venge-right, and species elitism, and . . . Josh fingered the wire-mesh helmet he now kept hanging at his belt. He could not fathom.

Nonetheless, he looked warmly at Rose and Ollie, and was reassured somewhat. Two good reasons for having chosen the path he'd taken. If only the others could be with them now, to bathe the empty shadows in the light of their presence. "And poor, sweet Isis," he said aloud, giving voice to his last thought; "we may never learn if she died or escaped." He shook his head. "She was always so afraid of the water."

"I am confident the fur-face swam to safety," Beauty assured with a quiet smile. "Her aversion to water, I have no doubt, was purely aesthetic, and unrelated to her swimming abilities."

They all laughed, and toasted that thought; except Josh, who sadly smiled, saying softly, "But we'll never know."

Jasmine put her hand on his. "Life is like that, sometimes," she allowed. "You can't always know."

Beauty agreed, as if from special understanding. "Humbelly did not know, when I left her in the vine grove at the edge of the jungle, if any of us would return. Yet, she waited." He looked directly at Jasmine as he spoke, and their eyes met: they both knew that along with all the myriad subtle ambiguities their lives would bring them over the years, none would remain more ambiguous, or more ambivalent, than their brief union. They smiled with the collusion of uncertain sweet shared remembrance. It was yet one more thing they would never know.

Joshua's melancholy grew even deeper, now, under the weight of all the things he would never know. He would never know a child with Dicey; or the meaning of Time; or the powerful sorcerer's language of the genetic engineers; or the kind, overweight boy in the Bookery. "I'll never know Lewis," he said under his breath, and somehow this loss seemed the greatest of all.

Jasmine interrupted his brooding. "I have a present for you, Joshua. Lon made it when we first left his den; he brought it with him all the way to our campsite south of the castle. I picked it up there the night of our raid, after I escaped the City—in case Lon didn't come through. The last entry is mine." She held out a book.

Joshua took it gingerly in hand. Leather-bound, with strong leather stitching at the spine, its cover was embossed with the snake in the circle that was the sign of the Scribe: It was beautiful.

He opened it to the first page. There, in heavy bookhand script, was the title: HISTORY OF THE HUMAN RACE. And then, in small italics at the bottom: *for posterity*.

He delicately turned the page. At the top, it said *Prologue*. Below this, the page was filled. Joshua read.

1,000,000 B.C.–1960 A.D.—Generally progressive evolution of the Human species.

1961—Mutant virus leak during army experiments sweeps the world, causing the beginning of subtle changes in the Human personality.

1986—Nuclear plan meltdown at Oceanspring. Jasmine's birth.

2006—Culmination of world energy crisis with total blackout.
Development of alternate sources over the next thirty years.

2010—Cloned horses become widespread.
Mass immigration to orbiting or journeying space colonies.

2020—People begin dying of radiation-induced cancer.
General increase in mutant births.

2030—Jasmine becomes Neuroman.
Perfection and proliferation of Neuromans, Deitons, Cognons, Hedons, Cidons.

2070—Creation of all the genetically engineered species.
General decay of society, increasing collective obsession with sex, death, and dream.

2110—Sum-Thin becomes Neuroman—one of the last.

2112–14—Population overgrowth, famine.

2115—Bacteriological War kills all but the resistant Humans.

July 4, 2117—Nuclear War, most major cities destroyed, increase in ambient radiation.

2120–2140—Ascendance of new species, anti-Human riots, book burnings.

2140–2150—Neuroman genetic engineers make thousands of Human Clones to regenerate the race.

2150—Clone Wars: most Humans killed, children spared; reading is outlawed;
the age of Creatures, the rise of Vampires.

2160—Emergence of secret society of Scribes.

2162—Quakes of Fire and Rain; formation of the Terrarium.

2191—The Great Quake; Dundee descends into the Terrarium.

0—The Coming of Ice.

0–50—Age of Ice: re-ascendance of Humans.
Jasmine and Lon explore the Terrarium.

100 A.I.—The Race War: Humans and other species strike a new balance.

121 A.I.—Josh and Beauty begin their quest;
joined by Isis and Jasmine, Lon and Sum-Thin; the journey leads toward a New Animal on the Sticks River.

The journey ends with the rescue of Ollie and Rose, and the grievous deaths of the bride, Dicey; the hero, Lon; the philosopher, Sum-thin.

Josh finished reading the last entry and turned the page. It was blank. He turned the next page. Blank again. All the pages were equally virgin.

"It's meant for you to fill in," Jasmine spoke again. "Lon wrote that much the week we left his home in the Forest of Accidents. He meant to give you the rest to finish. He showed it to me the night we assaulted the castle, and asked me to give it to you if he died. He said when you finished the journal, he would take it back and keep it in his library, that it would share its thoughts with his books until the dusk of time. It was his gift to you, and to your people."

Josh looked at her, then looked around the assembled group. He was lifted by the power of the gift, lifted out of the abyss into which he'd been sliding, as if he'd been a feather on the wind. *"Our* people," he said, with a new strength.

"If I may inquire sir . . ." It was Renfield who spoke now, with deference to his new masters. "What will we do now?" The question was tinged with hope and fear.

"Lon had two close friends—Aba and Lev. Those of you who feel safer in Harem can go with them. We'll escort you—Lon told me where they live."

Beauty added, "The rest of you are free to go as you will. Joshua has told us of the underground book-people—you may wish to join them in their struggle. If not, you are free to accompany me so far as you wish. I am returning home, to Monterey."

Rose reached over and held his hand. She'd been somewhat ashamed of her appearance—her head showing barely a stubble of hair, yet; the slightly raised black-capped outlet sticking out the back—but she knew that in Beauty's eyes, she remained a beauty true. "I go with my Centaur," she said.

Jasmine scratched her chin. "I'm not sure *what* I'm going to do, now. Go back into the jungle, maybe—still a lot to learn about life down there." She smiled gleefully. "I know one thing I'm *not* going to do, though. I'll never say 'Neptune's Middle Fin' again as long as I live."

Beauty winced and laughed. "If that be truth, Neuroman, you may yet live a long life."

Ollie ran over to Josh and hugged his brother uncertainly.

"Yes, you'll be coming with me, Ollie. Wherever I decide to go." He set the boy gently aside, and stood, holding his book. He walked a few steps, then sat again, beside a great flat stone. The Flutterby lit upon his shoulder. Josh took the falcon feather out of his boot—Rose's ancient present to him—and stared deeply at it. It was tattered, but still proud; and could yet make words fly in the singing wind.

He opened the book to the first blank page.

"Life is big," he said quietly, and began to set the record.

ABOUT THE AUTHOR

Born and raised in Chicago, James Kahn attended the University of Chicago for both undergraduate and medical studies. During this time, he was encouraged to begin writing fantasy by the Byronic scholar, Jerome McGann. Shortly afterward, Kahn began publishing short stories in *Playboy, Gallery,* and elsewhere. Since then he's done postgraduate training at USC-L.A. County Hospital and UCLA, specializing in Emergency Medicine. Dr. Kahn is the author of another novel, *Diagnosis: Murder,* and coauthor of the poetry collection *Nerves in Patterns.* Currently, he is completing the trilogy of which this book is the first volume, and he is preparing a book of short stories. In addition to writing and practicing medicine, Dr. Kahn is a singer-songwriter with a local folk-rock group, *Silver City;* he is an unclassified foil fencer and a great lover of cats.

ABOUT THE ILLUSTRATOR

Born in 1949, Jill Alden Littlewood was raised on the south side of Chicago. At the University of Chicago, she studied with the artist/illustrator, Virgil Burnett; she then finished her studies at the School of the Art Institute of Chicago. Her credits include poster illustration for the 1975 Ravinia Festival; masks and props for the Free Street Theater; assemblages and collages, some of which are included in Donna Meilach's *Box Art: Assemblage and Construction;* illustration and design for the poetry book *Nerves in Patterns;* and fossil renderings for the L.A. County Natural History Museums. In addition to illustrating, Ms. Littlewood works in Los Angeles as a calligrapher, a graphic designer, and a fine-artist. She plans to open studios in L.A. as a base for drawing, printmaking, bookmaking, and related areas of printing art and craft. Her other interests include Chinese calligraphy, silhouettes, and gilding.